D1570873

SPIN THE SKY

Other books by Katy Stauber

Revolution World

AN ORBITAL ODYSSEY

SPIN THE SKY

KATY STAUBER

NIGHT SHADE BOOKS
SAN FRANCISCO

First Edition

ISBN: 978-1-59780-340-3

Night Shade Books
Please visit us on the web at
http://www.nightshadebooks.com

PROLOGUE:

TINKER SHIP CAPTAIN

Excerpt from Trevor Vaquero's "Tales of my Father" Archive

I don't remember my dad as anything more than a giant shadow with a rough beard, a ready smile, and a warm hug. He left before I turned two. My mom doesn't like talking about him so I collect these stories, mostly recordings from travelers and war veterans. Everyone seems to have a story about my dad even if they never met him. They all have a theory about how he died and why he did what he did. This story I got from Nomie, the colony engineer for New Siberia, over a big plate of enchiladas when she came to visit my mom.

—*Trevor Vaquero*

So Captain turns to us and he says, "Do we die slow or just take a walk out the airlock? My money's on the airlock."

Seriously.

That's what he says and he's totally calm about it. He fixes us with that steely look and drinks his coffee. Because Captain is just that cool and that's how life was on the tinker ships after the Spacer War, right?

In the history archives, they optimistically call them merchant ships and say we carried trade goods between the orbital colonies above Earth. But it's a tiny bucket of bolts held together by duct tape and prayer, so everybody calls them tinker ships. We were a bit like tinkers, sailing around swapping this and that for this and that, but really the name was a rip-off Tinker Toys.

You know those old wooden toys? The ones that were so popular with kids growing up in orbital colonies? I guess because they were one of the few default toys, the ones all the manuvats had plans for.

This time I'm thinking about was almost two years after the Spacer War. Our ship was cobbled together from war wrecks and crewed mostly by soldiers too broke to go home. Most didn't have homes to go to anymore.

Damn dirt-loving Earthers. The Spacer War was just so devastating. Not that the Earthers got out of it looking so pretty. It was a long time before they recovered too. But we got our independence so now we can enjoy all the poverty and anarchy that entails.

So we're all freaking out, of course, but trying to play it cool because the Captain just doesn't do freak-outs and we were all desperate to not disappoint the guy. Especially me, since we're in these dire straights because I totally jacked up the day before. Sleeping at the console when pirates attacked, if you can believe it.

Me! The best, brightest and, if I do say so myself, cutest pilot this side of the stars. Nomie the Tinker Treasure, they called me. Sometimes. When I saved them from certain death and got them into port two days early on half a working thruster. When we were sucking on carbon dioxide and praying for a miracle, they called me all sorts of names not fit to repeat.

Of course that was years ago. Nowadays I'm just slightly less cute and instead of piloting tinkers, I spend my days running the logistics of this orbital and raising my little ankle-biters. Sure never would have guessed things would turn out this way.

So anyway, pirates attack. Life was like that back then. Only two years after the Spacer War, there were plenty of not-so-funny ways to die. Don't get any ideas, kid. There is nothing romantic about these pirate guys. They were just a little more hungry and desperate than us and more willing to be jerks about it.

They blindsided us in a ship only slightly faster and less shoddy than our own. They'd never have gotten close to us except the portside sensors only worked some of the time and not at all that day. Also, I was taking a nap.

We escaped, mostly intact, but limping and slow. The ship was losing pressure and it was a long way to the main shipping lanes. Decompression is a nasty way to go.

So the Captain gives us a second to gulp like goldfish and then he says, "Or maybe you bright boys could come up with some other options?"

I forgave him for the two or three hundred times he called me a boy. It was his way of saying that even though I was the hottest girl pilot in the system, he wasn't gonna try gnawing on my bra strap any time soon. You appreciate that, after a while.

How to get out of this mess? It's not like we could call anybody for help. The Spacer Army was in shambles and a police force was just a dream to argue about over dinner, if you had any. These things hadn't been thought about in the heady days of revolution. Earth just hung in our faces like a big ball of suck, ignoring our last gasp for life.

Finally Mike pipes up, his voice cracking a little, "There's a Russian tether close enough."

Mike was our lone Earther but we didn't hold it against him. He said he'd been a Spacer soldier, but no one believed the kid. He looked about twelve years old and even the Spacer Army had standards.

The Captain winces, but the rest of us openly groan. Me, I flick on my comm and start plowing through the data like a salmon heading up river, looking for any solution that didn't involve us flinging ourselves across the sky with a Russian tether.

"The idea is to find a way to live, not a more interesting way to die," the tall Asian woman pointed out.

No one could pronounce her name and she never talked about her past. If we had to call her anything, we called her "Asia." Her specialty was electronics and information. Over rounds of beer, we speculated that she'd been a spy in at least one of the Worlder Wars, but we never could agree which side. I could never keep track of who was fighting who in all those wars the Earthers fought amongst themselves before they started in on killing us.

Mike flushes.

"Tethers can work," he insists. "They just don't like to. I've used 'em before. If you got a better idea, I'd love to hear it. Only no one seems interested in our distress beacon."

"Please? What is Russian tether?" asks Alex.

Alex had a thick Spanish accent but moved like a Spacer. I wondered where he came from, but the past just wasn't something you ask about on a tinker ship. Sure, if you were drunk and a guy started talking, that's one thing. But to just ask? Never.

Oh man, did I have a thing for Alex. Spanish accents are like catnip for this girl's ears. He was very easy on the eyes too. Think dark wavy locks and full sensual lips. I loved to watch him talk just as much as I loved listening to that accent.

So Captain clears his throat and starts lecturing. "A Russian tether is like a slingshot for ships. One end is attached to a weighted motor with solar panels to charge it. The other end is attached to us. It spins us around like a dead cat before pitching us. It's cheap energy, but if you don't let go at the right moment, it will pitch you into Earth or out into void space so far you can't get back. There's a bunch of them out here. They never break, but…"

Nobody says a word. Finally Captain sighs and says, "We can last maybe another twenty hours without docking for repairs. The repairs are easy, but we need new air. No one's answered our signal for three days. Tether's not a good choice, but it's our best one."

Captain pauses, rubbing his thumb thoughtfully. No one offers any criticism so he slaps his palm against a table and says resolutely, "We do it."

He doesn't wait for agreement. He just flips on his comm while we throw ourselves into action. I start the docking procedures for this little suicide run, while praying to whatever gods might listen to a bunch of tinkers.

The comms were your basic ear-bud computers with retinal projector screens that operated using your finger movements. The whole thing looked like a pair of glasses with matching earplugs and bracelets. These days everybody's got to have those cochlear implants jacked right their skulls, but I miss my old comm. It was nice to be able to unplug once in a while.

We only had three working comms on the tinker because even black market ships from Earth came practically never. So the others only get a turn when Captain, Asia and I aren't busy keeping us all alive.

"I always did like roller coasters," mutters Mike with a crazed gleam in his gray eyes. He straps in, rubbing the stubble on his shaved head.

We find the tether and lock in without incident. It takes a long time for the torque to spin up. We get a kick out of the brief feeling of gravity, even if it had us standing on the walls. We were cooped up for close to two weeks without grav on that run.

Ships all travel slow in the orbitals. Everything is a lot farther away than you would think. Especially after the War, fuel for speed was too expensive for Spacers. Even on Earth, everyone moved slower than they had in the past. We gave them as good as we got in the War.

Asia and me, we check and recheck the flight figures frantically. As if our lives depend on it. Because they do.

Tinkers tend to know a bit about almost everything. Knowing a million ways to jury-rig every system in the ship with a pair of boots and an old ration box will greatly extend your life span. And if you dock at a colony that doesn't need the goods you have to sell, knowing your way around a water filtration system or a solar generator is always good for a meal and a beer. We'd been doing pretty good before the attack, all things considered.

"Here we go!" announces Captain.

Of course, he sounds dead calm, but I catch the slight tremor in his hands. His face always remained blank, no matter how insane his curly red hair got or what kind of crap we were knee-deep in. We break loose from the tether and go hurtling through the void, powerless to stop.

I would vomit, but I'm too scared. Alex closes his eyes and begins a prayer under his breath in Spanish. Captain starts telling a very unlikely story about a distant wild night with a dazzling senorita. It is momentarily distracting and that's a blessing.

The minute the spinning stops and we are all able to gulp down a few relieved breaths, Mike practically crawls into my lap, trying to see my retinal screen. I push him away.

"Well? Nomie, where are we? Where?" they all start yelling.

"We are not exactly where we would like to be," I say, trying to break it to them easy.

Mike weeps.

Alex starts praying more loudly and more rapidly. I think I can make out a few very strong curses concerning God and his orifices mixed in with the litany, but my Spanish is not great.

I keep working the comm, trying to get us safe or at least safer, while

Asia calms them down. She doesn't stop working her comm though, because Asia can multitask her way to hell and back.

"We are very high up, very far out of the spheres," she tells them. There's some sort of long official name for the part of space around Earth that the orbitals colonized, but who can remember that? We always just call them the spheres.

Sounding surprised, Asia says, "There is an orbital up here we can reach. Perhaps there are others, but we are on a course outwards into void space. If we do not stop now, we may not be able to get back."

There is a collective sigh of relief. Just shows you how dismal our lives are. An unknown orbital, floating like a life buoy before certain death, and we actually think our luck is looking up. Alex crosses himself quickly and stops his prayer, if that's what it was. Asia begins hurriedly pulling her long glossy curtain of black hair back into a tight bun and that's how I know we are in trouble.

"This is not good. There is something wrong with this place," Asia says flatly, her black eyes flickering as she reads what the comm flashes onto her retina.

I don't want to hear that there is anything wrong. I want her to shut up and tell me everything was going to be peachy keen and they are serving ice cream in two hours, but it would never occur to Asia to sugarcoat the truth.

"This orbital is functional. It is small but there is air. There is power," she says slowly in that precise way she had about her. "We may be able to dock and repair our ship here. But it is not geosynchronous."

We give her a bunch of blank looks. Asia shuts her eyes and looks annoyed for a minute before explaining. "It does not revolve at a fixed point above Earth like normal orbitals with Earth standard days. This colony is heliosynchronous. It orbits the Earth at a fixed point in relation to the sun. They do not have light-dark cycles at all." She flips off the comm and shakes her head.

Mike snorts, "So they sleep with the lights on. Big deal."

"No, they do not. It is the opposite. They are parked on the night side of the world," she snaps, taking off her comm glasses and frowning. "They never see daylight. It worries me."

Mike shrugs and says, "Weirdos are still better than death by decompression. But how do they survive? The power cells, the manufacturing vats, their food foliage, even oxygen tanks—all of it needs sunlight, doesn't it?"

Asia pops an infrared scan of this weird orbital up on the vidscreen so everyone can have a good look at it. It is a squat, round spinning hunk of post-industrial metal with various globes and cubes attached to it. It doesn't have the solar sails or large solar panel wings normally seen on orbitals. I think it looks ugly without them.

The Captain sighs, rubbing his bright blue eyes, "Out of the frying pan and into the fire."

What can we do, but prep to dock?

The outer doors unlock and hiss open. We suck in greedy gulps of air on the docking bay platform. Customarily, there are officials at the door with a wide variety of questions to answer and tests to pass before you can enter an orbital. Here, we are alone on a platform bristling with sensors and cameras.

"It's just how I like my colony—dank, smelly and dark," says Alex sarcastically. At least, I hope he's being sarcastic.

"All colonies have their own smell. The Caribbean Coffee Conglomerate smells wonderful," Asia remarks. "I checked the air quality here before we entered. It's fine."

"Maybe they are all gone," Mike chirps hopefully.

Captain looks into the unblinking red eye of a large camera and shakes his head. "More likely they are just shy," he says firmly. "Let's get to work."

We move quickly, wanting to be gone as soon as possible. Captain sends the grunts we'd picked up a few weeks before, Mingo and Fishtrap, to go look for inhabitants. I never could figure out what language those two spoke so I don't know too much about them. Captain had some idea who they were and where they came from, though. At least, I think he did.

Anyway, recompressing the ship with air goes faster if the colony allows us to use the orbital's pumps and paying for air is smarter than just taking it. Stealing is a good way to get blown out of the sky.

"If you can't find people, make sure you find some food and water. Our supplies are low and we'll have a long trip back," Captain tells the grunts. But he says it quietly, away from the cameras.

Asia and me, we already have the breach fixed and we're looking at the damaged solar cells when the first colonist appears. He moves like a ghost, old and pale. Even his eyes seem colorless and strange, like a giant who shriveled up in the sun. The hair on my neck prickles, just looking at him.

He lisps slightly as he attempts what might be a smile, "Welcome. I am Dr. Voctoire, the lead scientist here." Dr. Voctoire has a decidedly thick Eastern European accent and he's well over six feet tall.

Mike is sitting next to me, pulling up schematics for the water pumps while keeping his eyes on this strange character and cussing under his breath. I lean over to Mike and whisper, "Is he being creepy on purpose or is he for real?"

"Can't tell and don't care," Mike whispers back without moving his lips.

Mike was pretty decent looking, if you liked them tall and stringy and young. Personally, I prefer big and beefy men like Captain. Not that he had an extra pound of fat on him. He is just a big guy.

Captain steps over and shakes the pale man's hand. In his booming Captain voice, he says "Sorry to barge in on you like this. We were limping along, looking to die if we hadn't docked here. Two of my men went in search for your people to ask properly for your help. We thank you for any hospitality you care to give us."

Dr. Voctoire smiles eerily. "Ah yes, I met your men. Please, we do not get many visitors. We would like to make a meal with you?"

We agree, because who turns down free food? Dr. Voctoire lets us use the orbital's pumps to repressurize the ship, saying we can haggle over the price after dinner. Captain tells Mike, Asia and me to continue with the repairs. Then he leaves with Alex, slipping a remote around his wrist so I can see and hear what goes on with them inside this place.

"Dr. Voctoire, we've been wondering how you guys manage in the dark like this," Captain asks with a cheerful lack of concern while his blue eyes dart around, taking it all in. The walls are covered with a slimy bioluminescent moss. If that isn't weird enough, the old man has two separate cochlear implant comms, one for each eye and both are activated.

I am used to cochlear implants now, the shiny metal disk with its red little light screwed right into a person's temple, but two is just beyond weird, you know? Have you ever seen that before? Because Voctoire's colony is the only place I ever did.

Dr. Voctoire says, "The dark? We have a series of mirrors that provide us with enough sunlight for survival. We find the dark preferable for our experiments."

Captain asks, "So you are a research station? Wonderful. Not too many of those left. What are you researching?"

I wonder if they were using fuel cells or nuclear for power, since they obviously don't use solar. I'm really glad I stayed behind. The tinker is a hunk of junk, but it has great radiation shielding and this guy didn't look like he cared overmuch about frying his gonads with badly shielded nukes.

The old man says dismissively, "Computers, we work with. Technology. Electronics. It is very technical, our work. I would not bore you with details."

Captain replies, "I see you have two comms. It's unusual. Do you run them at the same time? I didn't think that was possible."

"Yes, we must. There are few of us here and much work to do. All of us use dual independent processors. It is difficult, but achievable with the right, ah, modifications."

Captain gives one of his hearty captain laughs. "If it were me, I'd be tripping all over the place. Trying to walk and talk with just one on is bad enough and here you got two."

That's when I realize that Dr. Voctoire's eyes are moving independently, like a chameleon. So creepy! Through the video feed, I spy Captain shuddering so he sees it too.

Dr. Voctoire nods, taking the meaning of Captain's stare.

"Yes, Mr. Captain. It is unusual, what we have done, but necessary for our purposes. Our modified vision requires us to keep light to a minimum, but the computers allow us to see extremely well in the dark."

"Well, the skies are big enough for everyone and you certainly don't have much competition for this corner of the spheres, but you did startle me there, mister." Captain says frankly.

The old man stares at him with one eye as they walk. "Mr. Captain, you have introduced all your crew members, but not yourself. Please, what is your name?" Dr. Voctoire asks.

Captain just smiles, "Out in the dark on our tinker ship, I forget my own name more often than I care to admit."

That's the kind of thing Captain says if you ask about his name. We all learned pretty quick not to ask.

Back in the ship, I am freaking out again. Mingo and Fishtrap weren't responding on their remotes, which is bad enough.

Then Asia comes over and writes on a scrap of paper, "The colonists here can see everything on their colony, but they can't see in this ship. They can hear us. Very advanced security. Very secretive. Not much in the Ether about this place. Almost a hundred years old."

A hundred years make it one of the oldest orbitals still in use. That would make anybody nervous, especially after getting a look at that freak-show Voctoire.

I get on the comm and start squawking to Captain to come back. Since I know the people in the orbital are listening in, I use some of the code words we worked out beforehand. Sadly, this isn't the first bizarre situation we've been in.

Captain listens for a minute and then calmly says to Voctoire, "Sir, if you will excuse me, there is a minor problem with my ship that needs my attention before I join you."

Dr. Voctoire asks that Alex continue on with him. Captain agrees because he doesn't want to tip his hand. Alex is experienced enough to know he needs to be on alert because things are getting strange here.

We use the pencil and paper to explain things to Captain when he gets back. We make sure to speak out loud about general things like our food and air supplies.

"Gene mod?" Asia scribbles.

Genetic modification was a fairly routine thing in orbital space by that time. Colonies have very specific requirements for plants or animals and they have to balance the water, air, food, and whatnot in their biosphere or else they all die. Gene mods are usually the easiest way to do that. A good splicer can solve three life-threatening issues with one well-designed fungus. But gene mod is still never, ever used on humans.

That's because there were some very memorable, very horrific mistakes that no one dares repeat. While the black market thrives for all things under the sun, human mod is strictly off limits.

You'll never find a geneticist willing to risk professional suicide followed rapidly by fatal torture. That's the standard punishment for human gene mod. But Voctoire's orbital is obviously a very top-secret corporate research station so just about anything could be happening here.

Captain frowns and shrugs. Then he goes and rummages around in the supply room and comes back with a bottle of green liquid.

He says loudly, "Well, I see you have the repairs under control. I'll be back in a few hours." He takes the bottle and leaves with Mike in tow. Asia and I watch through the feed on Captain's wrist.

On the way, they meet another colonist. She is tall, frail and ghostly like the first. She also has the two implants jacked into her skull, glowing ominously. Both of her computers are engaged and she merely motions them to follow her as she slowly makes her way. When they reach the eating area, there are about twenty people in it, including Dr. Voctoire.

All are tall, gray and withered, like all the color has just washed out of them. When they enter the room, Mike's hand hovers over his weapon, but it drops away when he looks them over. I know what he is thinking.

How could this congregation of elderly be a threat?

Captain says in his big hearty voice, "Well now, I have here the finest old absinthe still circulating above the stratosphere that I'd like to share with you fine folk. But where are my three crewmen? Don't tell me they are off getting into trouble?"

Dr. Voctoire smiles formally and gestures for them sit.

"Your men are assisting us with a small problem. They are so kind to do so. We will join them shortly."

The table is heavy with bread, cheese, and some kind of thick stew. The shots I can see of it through the bracelet video make me drool. I hear Mike and Captain talking about how great everything tastes, but strangely spiced. I'm hoping they remember to bring some back.

"We had a special breed of sheep designed for us. They do not need light and live on our moss." Dr. Voctoire says.

He seems positively chatty now.

"So, your research isn't genetic, then?" Mike asks quickly, moping up stew with some bread.

"Oh no. We are more concerned with technical matters. Mediboxes, specifically. There are many very interesting applications of that technology. For example, there are certain surgeries that it can perform to greatly extend the human life span."

He sounds pretty reasonable and smart, but the thing is, you have to be a special kind of crazy to modify a medibox. You guys have a medibox on this colony, right? New Siberia does too.

They are a lot better than they used to be. Even back then a medibox could do the scans and tests necessary to diagnose almost any medical problem. They could perform surgeries too. They used a series of lasers that worked pretty well, although they left interesting scars. They also prescribed medicines, but most contained only basic antibiotics and pain-killers.

A rogue medibox is everyone's secret dread. Actually, it isn't that secret. Mediboxes are heavily featured in horror Ether flicks.

Captain expresses polite disbelief at their research success. I can see him squirming in his seat just a little before busying himself with pouring the absinthe and insisting they all try it.

Voctoire does not take a glass and will not be deterred in his enthusiasm for the insane subject.

He says proudly, "Yes, it's true. I myself am almost one hundred sixty years old. All of us here have had the surgery. No one here is under one hundred years old. There is no telling how long we will live. What do you think of that?"

Personally, long life as a wizened gray skeleton is something I'll pass on.

That's when Captain notices Mike snoring into his soup. He tries to leap to his feet, but staggers and falls instead. The food was drugged, you see.

Voctoire leaned towards him and says confidentially, "Mr. Captain, we have not had a shipment of experimental subjects in far too long and we have many new ideas to test. We are so pleased to have you here." Dr. Voctoire cackles while the Captain slides to the floor. The last thing I see through the remote is Voctoire switching it off.

Asia and me set a new speed record as we slam the ship's doors shut and pull away from the orbital. We don't stop for breath until we are well away from there. Then I start scanning and I see Captain's remote flick back on. So I pull the video feed onto the main vidscreen, hoping we can figure out what is going on in there. It's weirdly distorted but I can make out Captain sitting up in a medibox in a room that is full of them.

They look like normal mediboxes, except they have wires trailing out to large computer interfaces. There are several of the gray colonists hovering like harpies over a medibox on the far side of the room.

Captain spies Mike in the middle of them and utters a hoarse cry. Mike is yanking tubes out of his arm and throwing punches. Luckily, they both downed hypermet tablets on the ship against the odds that someone tried drugging the food. So they were only out for a few minutes instead of hours. We'd been around the block enough times to be paranoid like that. Voctoire's colonists certainly weren't expecting it.

Captain bursts out of the medibox with a cry of pain tearing through him before hurling himself into the colonists around Mike like a fury. I could tell by the angry red puckered lines crisscrossing his stomach and back that surgical lasers had been working on him.

I look him over later, but we never figure out exactly what they did to him in that medibox. Didn't seem to slow him down, whatever it was. The gray colonists scatter, bleeding and shrieking. Mike is also in working order, if covered in blood and raging, cussing up a storm.

Then they find Alex, Mingo, and Fishtrap. It's bad.

It's worse when they realize the poor bastards are still alive. Mike retches at the sight while Captain methodically puts his three men out of their misery, one shot to the temple apiece. Captain always had that old pistol with him. He kept it loaded with flechettes, the kind that don't pierce a ship's hull. I swear he slept with it strapped to his privates. There are many occasions for a reliable pistol on a tinker ship.

Then they run for the ship, Captain screaming orders into his comm and Mike just screaming. On the way, they find the dining hall from before. Captain snatches up the half empty absinthe bottle without breaking stride.

"What was in there, anyway? Some kind of toxin or drug to slow them down?" Mike gasps, taking stairs three at a time.

Captain laughs, "Just some damn fine absinthe. I figured it never hurts to be neighborly."

They almost make it.

When they reach the docking platform, Dr. Voctoire and a crew of heavily armed colonists are waiting for them. Mike and Captain have their guns at the ready.

"Your ship escaped, but you will not, clever Mr. Captain," laughs Voctoire cruelly.

I guess he's feeling pretty confident on account of Mike and Captain have at least four lasers apiece pointed at them. It's like high noon in an

Ether drama.

"I'd rather stay here and kill you monsters, anyway," Captain replies grimly.

"You will not damage any more of us." Dr. Voctoire chuckles. "But please, it will help our experiments to know who we are vivisecting. Tell us your name and we may at least send your ashes home."

Captain stands like stone. "My name is Cesar Vaquero."

The laughter and jeering stop suddenly. Even Mike gives him a startled glance, though his gun never wavers. I can hear Asia gasp next to me so I know she's listening too.

Dr. Voctoire begins to laugh again. This time, it has a more hysterical edge to it.

"Cesar the Scorcher? The Butcher of Mexico? You call me a monster for conducting important experiments on a few useless nothings? How many did you kill when you dropped that nuclear starship on Mexico City?"

It didn't occur to him that Captain gave him a false name. No one would pretend to be Cesar Vaquero.

Captain's face remains completely expressionless.

"Millions. I killed millions," he says flatly as he cocks his pistol. "I ended the war. Billions would have died if the fighting continued. How many of you do you think I can kill?"

That's when all the power goes out. Because Asia and me aren't just sitting out there, twiddling our thumbs. We have a plan. We smash an electromagnetic pulse bomb against their hull with the power cranked up as high as we can get it. If any of their fancy electronics work after that, I'd guess they don't work too well.

I can hear the sound of clicking triggers as the colonists fire their weapons reflexively, but it's too late. The lasers are just so much useless junk by then. Some of them scream and claw at their computers, without power for the first time in decades apparently.

Only Mike and Captain remain calm. I switch the video to night vision just in time to see the Captain smile. It's not a nice smile.

Captain knows immediately what Asia and I are up to. He cheerfully says to Voctoire, "I trust you ogres had the sense to run your vital systems off vacuum tubes like everyone else. No? Well isn't that terrible? Perhaps if you are quick, you won't lose the whole colony."

There is the sound of scrabbling in the dark.

Our captain, Cesar Vaquero, calls out, "I hope you will all notice that our guns are not electronic. And neither are the bullets we are about to fire at you."

It only takes a few minutes for the colonists to scatter, blind and toothless without their computers and lasers. Mike and Cesar fire a few rounds of flechettes to spur the exodus. And then I will be damned if Captain and Mike down race off into darkness after them. I thought for sure that's the last time I'd ever see those two, but they popped back onto the docking platform with what was left of Mingo, Fishtrap, and Alex. Those poor bastards.

We have the ship docked and the doors open in no time. Before we took off, we rigged the orbital's door to open manually. Sparing a minute to retrieve the bomb and store it for later use, we blaze away from that hellhole as fast as we can.

Only when we are sure they are not sending anything nasty after us do we stop to think about the man sitting next to us on the deck.

Cesar Vaquero, the Scorcher of Mexico, our Captain. Can you believe it? A war hero to Spacers, a genocidal maniac to the Earthers, a legend long thought dead and we'd been listening to his crazy stories and making him coffee for months. We watch him with horror and awe, but no one says a thing except for Asia. She only has one question.

"Are you sorry?" she asks.

Captain looks at his hands for a minute, and then slowly lifts his head to meet her eyes.

"The dirt-lovers were going to hit my home next. They had a bomb that could take out our whole colony with one hit. My parents, my wife, my son." His voice breaks over that last word. "I killed eighty million people to stop a war. Truth is, I would kill billions to keep my family safe."

He turns away from her and sets the coordinates for our next adventure.

No offense, kid, but your dad was... Well, he was your dad, wasn't he? The Scorcher of Mexico. Everybody's parents are crazy, but yours was always in a league of his own.

As if that weren't strange enough, when he turns away, I see a new shock of white in his vivid red hair. It'd never been there before. Over the next few weeks, his hair turns snow white and stays that way.

We wondered what had been done to him in that medibox. That is, until the next crisis drives it out of our mind. Maybe you think I made the whole story up, but I swear I'm not smart enough to think of something as weird as that insane little world. Stay away from heliosynchronous orbitals, kid. That's my advice.

I piloted that tinker for another few months for your dad. He was the best Captain I ever had, but then I met my man here on New Siberia and decided to settle down. Last I saw of him, your dad was headed for the Hathor Mining Colony with a ship full of drills to trade. I guess he never quite got there.

You tell your mom she's in all our prayers. I hope they find the bastards that are giving you people so much trouble lately.

CHAPTER ONE

Ironically, it was the most fanatic tree-hugging environmentalists who first went to live in space. They didn't go far. In the orbital colonies, they could preserve the sanctity of their enclosed piece of Earth while keeping a disapproving eye on those who stayed behind.

These little worlds offered a haven from the high tech, instant-access Earth. Many were there because of the lucrative opportunities space provided, but the sky was also the new frontier for all those who couldn't or wouldn't share with the billions of the Earth. Of course, that was before the Spacer War.

Fifteen years after the Spacer War started, the most expensive spaceship of the day still doesn't spin up to full gravity, but it docks like a dream. Cesar Vaquero stands tall on its docking deck. He is the very picture of weather-beaten cowboy straight from the American Wild West, though no Earther cowboy could ever afford Cesar's real leather pants or cotton shirt in this day and age.

Cesar's clothes are well worn and lovingly repaired. His boots are hand-stitched but cracked, with heels almost worn through. Time and fate have not been kind to him. The leather pants hold countless zippered pockets, each full of interesting treasures. His knapsack is made of good quality bioplastic, if torn and patched.

Standing still the way he is, you don't notice the hitch in his gait. His thick white beard almost covers the jagged scar that stretches from his right ear to his lip. There are crinkles around the eyes that speak of many tragedies and, in spite of them, a willingness to smile.

There is the telltale clicking of a ship docking on an orbital. Cesar shifts from foot to foot impatiently.

You are a right fool, he tells himself. *To wait fifteen years to come home and then feel like you're going to die if you have to wait another fifteen seconds.*

He shakes himself slightly, but still watches the door like a hawk. Earlier, Cesar tried watching on the observation deck as the ship approached the orbital, but gave up in disgust and came down to wait by the door when he realized that he didn't recognize Ithaca at all.

Cesar spent the first twenty years of his life inside that orbital, before he took off without a single backward glance, swearing he'd never come back. Sad to say, if his life depended on identifying his home from the outside, he'd have died long ago.

Ithaca seemed to be doing well without him. It wasn't as elegant as some of the other orbitals—the wheeling tori or globular colonies that stretch out across the sky like dew on a spider web. This one basically looks like a huge spinning beer can. It's a large cylinder, miles in diameter and length.

When he was standing on the observation deck earlier, Cesar listened to a man on the deck explain to his small son that Ithaca contains three levels with sectionals that seal off instantly if there is a problem, like most orbitals.

The outermost level spins at slightly higher than Earth gravity. That level contains a complicated interlocking ecosystem of plants and animals to support the inhabitants. Ithaca produces some of the best cheese and meat in the system.

The second level houses the ten thousand residents who call this orbital home. This level is also for the manufacturing plants that make almost everything the colonists need from bacterial cultures in huge vats. These bacterial manuvats are coaxed to produce anything from bac-wood for furniture to bioplastic for shoes.

The last, innermost level holds the docking station, storage bays, and freefall recreational facilities. Although Earthers always expect the orbital colonies to be dark and dank, the agriculture and habitation levels are engineered with ceilings higher than most Earth skyscrapers and a system of mirrors and windows that make the orbital more sunny and warm than most of the Earth below it gets.

Cesar listens to the man lecture his son while spotting new solar panels, large debris nets and window polarization that all seemed in good repair. Cesar didn't see the burns and dents on the outer hull that where from pirate attack, asteroid hit or some other calamity. He'd heard Ithaca was having mysterious problems lately. It's what finally made him get up the courage to come home.

He also saw that the communications dish was still smashed. Cesar smiled, remembering the day he did that. It didn't look like anybody had tried to repair it in the last sixteen years, but a small short wave antenna was installed next to it. That meant Ithacans only talked to their neighboring orbitals and got only Spacer Ether. They didn't communicate with the Earth directly.

Interesting.

Cesar is happy to see Ithaca looking so prosperous. He smiles at the merchant carriers tethered to the orbital, waiting for their turn to dock like whales on a leash. He also sees quite a few shiny personal transports docked. That he does not like at all. It means the rumors are true. The richer colonies are circling Ithaca like vultures.

Cesar is past speculating whether coming home was a mistake. He is worn out and beyond anything but the dull aching need to see his family. He tells himself that whatever he finds, he will at least have found it. At the very least, that will stop the nagging questions in his mind.

Will his ranch even be there at all?

"*The* ranch," he corrects himself. "Certainly isn't *my* ranch anymore."

And not like he had a right to it, since he hasn't laid eyes on the place in more than fifteen years. Cesar wonders, as he did thousands of times over the years, what he will find when he gets there.

Did his family leave the ranch to strangers and make their way in the spheres? Will he find it abandoned with sad little graves marking him as the last lonely member of his clan? Will he find it prosperous and happy? Run down and penniless?

Cesar curses the years he spent refusing to even look for news from home. At first, he told himself it was better not to know what his family was doing, but lately he'd realized that was just cowardice. He didn't ask for news about his family because it hurt too much to think of them. Right now, he'd happily listen to a rambling story about his old dad's bunions if that meant the rotten old bird is still alive.

Whatever he finds, Cesar resolves to be satisfied in the knowing of it and move on. Cesar is not a man given to deep thinking or conflicting philosophies so he comes spoiling for a fight, half dead on his feet.

The ship gives a final shudder as it locks into place against the floating little world and then a voice over the intercoms announces they just docked with Ithaca.

"Named *Ithaca* by my lunatic father," Cesar mutters.

He hears the final set of grinding clicks that indicate everything was locked into place. Space colonies, regardless of their design, always spin. Ships always dock on the part that doesn't spin, so that part never has much gravity. Which is why Cesar's hair seems even wilder, floating around his face.

Cesar steps toward the airlock, wobbling just slightly as his vision blurs. Fortunately, his grav boots hold him tightly to the floor. Cesar is extremely sick and he knows it. Weeks of battling some sort of bug have him fevered and weak. On the trip here, he did everything he could to appear healthy. Many orbitals refuse to allow a sick man entry. Others might quarantine him for weeks.

In some of the rougher colonies, quarantine means getting pushed out the nearest airlock since a bug-infested corpse can't be used even as fodder for the manuvats.

Cesar figures he is dying and he wants to do that at home, if he can. Fortunately, Ithaca is a medium-sized colony off the main shipping lanes but far from the well-populated Lagrange points. It doesn't have the most rigorous of security checks. Or at least it didn't when he left. If they've been having the kind of trouble he's heard about, that may have changed.

The airlock door finally swings open and he strides forward, trying not to look like he is hurrying. Cesar imagines that he can already smell his old home before he steps through the door, but he knows the pressure differentials keep that from happening.

The lone man at the gate is a frontier world's haphazard attempt at a doorkeeper. Cesar recognizes the oldster as one of his father's old drinking buddies, Mathis. Cesar smiles to himself and straightens up to begin the process of coming home.

Grizzled, cranky and suspicious of outsiders, Mathis lets returning locals pass through with a nod and pushes the leaving strangers out as fast as they will go. Mathis stops Cesar, squinting at him as though Cesar is some mangy dog trying to sneak past.

"What's your business here?" Mathis snaps, snatching Cesar's ident card but not really reading it.

On Earth, he'd have been DNA-printed and body-scanned and no one would care what his business was.

"I'm visiting some old friends," Cesar grins, waiting for Mathis to recognize him. It didn't happen.

"Old friends? Where?" Mathis gives him the kind of look you give a man when you are trying to decide if he matches any of the pictures from this week's *"Universe's Most Wanted"* posts.

"Vaquero Ranch. I'm an old friend of the family." Cesar tries to nudge the man towards recognition, but it is not to be.

"Vaquero? Listen, mister, those are good people out there and they don't need anyone else pestering them. You give them no trouble, you hear?" Mathis waves him on dismissively, grumbling about unwashed outworlders.

Cesar makes his way toward the elevators. He wanted to ask old Mathis about the rumors he's heard, about Ithaca in danger and under attack, but he can't risk old Mathis discovering how sick he is and detaining him.

Cesar is a little stunned that the old man completely failed to recognize him. How many times had he fetched his father home from Mathis' house after a few too many beers on a Saturday night? Has he really changed that much?

Cesar stormed off fifteen years ago to the Spacer War as a strapping young man with short red hair and an unmarked face. He knows he bears little resemblance to that young man now. Cesar feels his current long white beard and mane is rather dashing when his hair isn't matted and his beard isn't so long he might keep mice in it. He smiles at his own vanity. At least the beard covers some of the scars.

"And Lord knows, I've got little enough to be vain about these days," Cesar muses.

His days fighting in the Spacer War gave him a mild but definite limp. One of his later adventures earned him the jagged scar running down his right cheek. A narrow escape from a fire left him with a scarred and twisted left ear that his long hair helps to cover. For all the wear he's seen, he moves with vitality and the odd sort of grace that a man used to trusting himself in space carries.

Down the elevators, Cesar steps off and sucks down a deep breath. He bends down and flips the small switch in each of his boots to turn off the electromagnet. Most Spacers have grav boots with strong electromagnets in the heels needed in low gravity to keep them from floating away. Earthers who want to pretend buy the cheaper biosteel boots, but they aren't strong attractors like the pure stuff.

"Ah yes. That's it. That smells like home. I can die happy now," Cesar mutters to himself as people walk past him, looking askance.

Time to see the ranch.

The population of Ithaca is small, so they have plenty of room. Thus the space between habitations is large enough for privacy. Although the crops and livestock are on the level below, the habitation level is made to look as much like a small Earther city as possible. Gardens and small plots of well-tended grass separate the houses. The Vaquero Ranch is set far away from the shops, factories, moving sidewalks and the public elevators. Cesar plods along slowly, hoping he doesn't die before he reaches his goal.

After what seems like hours, Cesar spots a ranch in the distance. His breath catches and he shakes his head desperately to clear his vision. Then his heart sinks. This can't be his home. Cesar remembered well his simple one-story ranch with the wide porch. This house is twice as big.

It has two stories with biostone and other expensive trimmings. A lush garden surrounds the sides where there had only been dust and dirt. There is even a pen of mini-pigs. They must be fantastically rich to afford the water that supports all this.

When he left, Cesar's family was the most prosperous in this orbital. "These people must be ten times as wealthy as we ever were," he thinks to himself. With all the insanity after the War, many things changed and people moved on. His family must have gone.

"Probably did. Only to be expected. Well, maybe these folks will know where my people went," Cesar grunts, telling himself that this will be enough.

The sickness he kept a secret suddenly overwhelms him. Cesar staggers, flushed and weak, but he continues plodding forward, sure in the knowledge that when he stops, it will be for good. Cesar bends his head to keep from looking at the painful sight of this ranch and also to make sure his feet find steady ground.

The unmistakable sound of a shotgun cocking startles him from his private dreams and jerks his feet to a halt. Somehow he has managed to get within a stone's throw of the front door. Cesar's eyebrows shoot up with surprise.

The empty porch of the ranch in front of him now holds a person. He sees a shadowy figure in grubby pants and mud-caked boots, wearing a hat pulled too low to make out a face.

Must be some kid home while his folks are out, Cesar decides.

However, the kid is handling the gun with an ease born of much practice. Cesar raises both hands up in the air and hopes the youth isn't trigger-happy. He waits cautiously, but the figure seems content to stand motionless and silent.

"Son, I'm unarmed and feeling poorly. You got no cause to be worried about me. I'm just passing through," Cesar rasps in what he hopes is a friendly voice.

An abrupt wave of dizziness causes him to lurch forward suddenly. The shotgun roars in response, kicking up puffs of dirt not two feet in front of him.

"Come on, now!" he cries, stumbling back. "Don't kill an old fool when he's this close to death. I'm just looking for directions to the Vaquero ranch!"

He bends over, wheezing light-headedly with his hands on his knees.

"*Gringo*, you a friend of Vaquero?" the figure asks, not taking the gun off him for a second.

The voice has a soft Spanish burr and is unmistakably female. Cesar jerks his head up in surprise. She is still shadowed by the doorway, but now that he knows what to look for, he can make out the suggestion of gentle curves beneath the bulky clothes.

"Yes! You know Vaquero?" Cesar replies, his heart leaping as he fights to keep his balance. "You might say I am an old family friend."

She makes a very unladylike snort of derision.

"Mister, an old family friend would know he's standing in the front yard of the Vaquero ranch," she snaps, taking a step forward into the sunlight so he can finally see her face. Suddenly, the world seems to tilt on its side and slip away from him. His heart stops and his breath sticks in his chest.

Cesar knows her.

He knows the proud curve of that chin and that shining black hair, caught back in a thick braid. He's spent a hundred nights admiring her smooth Spanish skin. He knows those laughing black eyes, sparkling now with suspicion.

Even after fifteen years, a man knows his own wife.

Cesar falls to his knees there in the dirt. His strength is well and truly played out. He feels himself lurch and topple over with fever, overwhelmed. He hears his wife, Penelope Vaquero, run from the porch to stand over him.

"Hey, mister, you alright?" She shakes him roughly, but he is sliding from consciousness. Cesar fights to open his eyes as the landscape spins like a child's toy.

"Come on, *gringo*, wake up!" she insists as he closes his eyes again. He feels her small, cool palm sting sharply as she slaps him hard across the face.

"Yep," he thinks, "That's my wife."

He has one final reflection before the darkness swallows him. "If she knew I was her husband, she'd shoot me for sure."

CHAPTER TWO

Even after all these years away from the Earth, Penelope Vaquero still prays in Spanish. Muttering a rapid prayer for patience under her breath, she calls for Lupe and Argos to come help her.

"*Madre de Dios*, do I not have enough to do today?"

Penelope looks with disgust at the man collapsed in the dirt of her front yard. He is smelly and obviously sick. He looks like an old wild cat, still sharp in tooth and claw.

"This old man is probably going to die right here and make me bury him," she says ruefully to Lupe and Argos as they approach.

She feels a strong temptation to spit or curse, but decides to hang on to the tattered remains of her ladylike upbringing. Penelope sighs and mentally adds this stranger to her long list of tasks for the day.

Argos helps Penelope run the ranch that he grew up on, just as his father before him helped old Larry Vaquero. He's the lead ranch hand, gray but spry. Argos walks up in his perennially unhurried way. His dusty jeans and carefully mended cowboy shirt are the uniform of all well-fed ranch hands.

His leathery skin speaks of years in Ithaca's strong light and his laughing blue eyes say he's ready for plenty more. Standing beside her, looking down at the man in the dirt, Argos whistles as Lupe hurries behind.

Lupe, on the other hand, always looks rushed. Her short, round Mexican body speeds from one activity to the next even though her thick gray braid says she must have been getting close to seventy. Spacers rarely had the money for the expensive treatments from Earth that keep a body young and pretty, but Lupe wouldn't have bothered anyway. She's been on

Ithaca for over forty years, keeping house for the Vaqueros. She smells of spices and she keeps sweets and dishtowels hidden in the pockets of her voluminous skirts.

"*Híjole!* What did you do to this one, *mija*?" Lupe looks at Penelope accusingly, panting for breath. "Did you shoot him? Why are you always shooting people?"

"Nothing! I didn't do anything!" Penelope mumbles defensively, nudging the old man with the toe of her boot. He didn't react at all.

Penelope exhales noisily and says, "This old bugger just showed up to die on our front porch. Said he was an old family friend and then asked me directions to where he already was and passed out. I think he's crazy."

Lupe grunts and crosses herself. "Of course he is. Only crazy people come here. He probably took one look at you in those man clothes you are wearing and died of shock."

Penelope knows Lupe's favorite lecture is about to follow. The woman was obsessed with skirts. Sure enough, Lupe says, "Your *pobre madre,* rest her soul, would die all over again to see you in those pants. You are practically the queen of this place and you dress like the worst trash. Go inside and change before you scare the whole neighborhood."

"The nearest neighbor is kilometers away, Lupe. Would you rather I train mules in my skirts or tend sick cows in a party dress, *abuela*?" Penelope smiles sweetly at the older woman who immediately swats her in exasperation.

Pushing Penelope towards the house, Lupe hisses, "And you with a son practically a man! Training mules! Get one of your so-called cowhands to do it! Now out of my way, I'm busy."

The short woman bustles past Penelope and bends over to grab the unconscious man on the ground.

Shrugging, Penelope turns towards the house. Lupe struggles to drag the man by one arm towards the bunkhouse, the communal cabin for cowhands, muttering, *"Me estás tomando el pelo."*

Argos says nothing, but he smiles in good-natured exasperation as he takes the man away from Lupe and slings the limp stranger over one shoulder. Dependable to a fault, Argos isn't one of the world's deep thinkers. He is best pleased with someone telling him exactly what he needs to do.

The unconscious man drools and smiles vaguely, but doesn't wake. Lupe herds Argos and his passenger like a terrier nipping at the heels of a lumbering bull towards the bunkhouse, a long, low structure away from the main house. There is a small room in the back for sick ranch hands and that's where they take Cesar. Lupe lives in the main house with Penelope and her son, while Argos has his own snug cabin as far from everyone else as he can possibly get.

Penelope watches them go. She wonders who the man is without really caring. She knows Lupe will fuss and cluck over him like a mother hen. Penelope fervently hopes the man will not die because then Lupe will make the whole house mourn for forty days, wailing and tearing her hair over the death of a stranger.

"I need that like I need to swallow a shotgun blast, even if I do only load it with rock salt," she groans under her breath.

Penelope takes a minute to look with pride at the ranch. She even looks gladly at the little tequila still towards the back of the ranch where her father-in-law insists on living.

"Mine," Penelope says fiercely. "And no man will take it from me."

She just wishes she knew what was going on lately. There were those weird offers from strange men to "buy" the entire herd at exorbitant prices. As if she'd ever sell what she's worked so hard to make. Then followed the veiled threats from other strangers who looked like pirates and showed up in flashy ships. After her refusal they disappeared with promises to come back and "persuade" her. There was an attempt to kidnap her foiled by her ranch hands, followed by an attempt to kidnap her son, foiled by her shotgun.

The latest incident really had her worried. A dozen armed men with a map of the colony and Vaquero ranch circled in red were turned back before they could get off their ship. If Mathis hadn't been a chronically suspicious old coot and uncharacteristically sober that day, it would have been a very bad day for everyone at Vaquero ranch.

Penelope tries not to think about all that as she stares at her home. Usually when Penelope looks over the ranch, her mind's eye looks to the improvements she will make, but just now Penelope remembers the first day she arrived on Ithaca. Her first sight of the Vaquero ranch brought to mind the saying Germans had for Texas: "It's heaven for men and dogs, but hell on women and oxen."

She'd been tired, bruised and bilious, riding from San Antonio on that sorry excuse of a shuttle. To her adult eyes, the ranch looks like success, safety and home. But Penelope came here as an over-privileged eighteen year old with a husband she barely knew, fleeing from a life of privilege. On that day, the Vaquero ranch was a muddy and desolate confirmation that she had made a very bad mistake.

Penelope shakes her memories from her mind, wondering what set her thinking about the past today. Maybe it was that mysterious old man? But the tasks of the day won't wait, so she turns to meet them.

CHAPTER THREE

Cesar sleeps soundly, lulled by the unfamiliar scent of clean sheets and Lupe's gentle humming as she enters the room with a big bowl of warm broth. Then he hears a sound he hoped never to hear again. War whoops and gunshots make a kind of music to chill a man's soul. Cesar springs into a low crouch, ready for battle before he is even really awake.

Lupe erupts in a stream of virulent Mexican curses as the warm broth sloshes out of the bowl he upset with his flailing. Cesar gropes for his boot knife, only to find it missing. Quickly, he throws the bed over and hauls Lupe behind it.

"You idiot *gringo*, what are you doing?" Lupe sputters, smacking him with a spoon. "It's just Mr. Trevor, back from town. Little hooligan."

That makes Cesar sit down. Hard.

Trevor. My son. My son is out there.

His hands tremble as he slowly gets to his feet so he curls them into fists. Lupe heaves herself to her feet with great flourish and smacks Cesar with the spoon a few more times. This mercifully takes his mind off the boy in the yard. While Lupe sets about righting the room, he staggers to the door and peers out.

He watches a teenage boy clamber off a cart pulled by a little mule. The boy is wiry and tall and he moves with that awkward teenage vitality, yanking things off the cart and stumbling to the house with them.

Cesar hasn't seen Trevor since he was an infant, nothing but bright brown eyes and drool. The boy pauses to push his unruly hair out of his eyes. It's the same flaming red that Cesar's was at that age.

"Mom! Got this month's order from the manuvats. Looks right except this tub over here."

Cesar smoothes his clothes and beard ineffectually as he steps forward, following the boy's voice. The boy hands things to his mother on the porch while she lectures him about shooting off his gun.

"I don't care if it can't hurt anybody," Penelope says sharply. "Gunshots make people nervous. Don't shoot your gun unless you are in trouble or practicing with targets."

"Aw, Mom, come on," Trevor grouses cheerfully. "You're always firing off that rock salt in your shotgun. What's so wrong about a few potshots out of my pistol when there's nobody around?"

"Well," Penelope huffs indignantly. She looks like she's trying to come up with a snappy comeback and not finding one.

Finally she says, "It's wasteful."

Cesar must have made a sound because Penelope looks up at him, shading her eyes. The orbital's mile-high ceilings are covered with shiny reflective paint to capture as much sunlight as possible. At high noon, it is every bit as bright as the hot Texas sun Trevor has never seen.

"Well, old man, not planning to die on us after all?" she calls to Cesar.

"Not today, ma'am." Cesar ducks his head self-consciously. He almost wants to hide. He is sure his face gives him away.

How do I tell them?

Trevor abandons his project to stare at the man, fascinated by his scars and clothes.

"Who are you, anyway?" Penelope asks as she bends down to stack some bowls.

Cesar bows his head and watches her through his long, bedraggled hair.

She doesn't recognize me.

"I guess I don't look familiar," he mumbles, overwhelmed.

I can't do this.

Cesar has no plan for this. His original plan involved showing up and dying in his wife's arms right after he told his son that he loved him. It was a good plan except he continued to live. This significantly alters the original plan into what can only be described now as a bad plan. Cesar would smack himself in the head but that would only make him look even dumber than he already feels.

Penelope sighs, giving him a hard look. "No, you don't look familiar. I've never seen you before in my life. So if you are trying to play like an old friend of the family, forget it."

She really doesn't remember me, Cesar thinks with a sinking feeling.

As he looks into Trevor's eager gaze, he knows he just can't tell them today. Not like this. Not a beaten old wreck standing in their yard like a beggar.

"I'm a friend of Cesar's," he stammers. "We were close during the War. And after. I'd heard… I'd heard he was coming home."

He can't bring himself to look at them after this lie.

Trevor eyes get round as the Moon when he hears the name of his famous father. "You knew my dad? Wow! Where have you been? When did you see him last? What happened to him?"

Penelope scowls and looks away.

Cesar gives his son a long steady look. "I knew your father very well. Nothing happened to him. Everything happened to him. You look just like him." Cesar reaches out and claps the boy on the shoulder. He tries smiling at the boy, but fails halfway through.

Trevor's face takes on that aloof, cool expression that teen boys get in front of strangers. "People tell me that," he replies, stiffening under Cesar's hand. "I guess it's the hair."

Penelope hustles out to stand next to her child, as though to reclaim her son from stories of his father.

"Well, Cesar's not home. He hasn't been home since before the War. So whatever promises he made you are gone," she says flatly, with a slight hint of bitterness.

Cesar sits down on the porch and looks at his hands. He says, "Ma'am, I know that. But I also know how much he wanted to come home. How much he loved this place and how he missed his family. I just wanted to see it. I'm a traveler myself with nothing to call home and nothing of mine but what's in that bag I brought. I just wanted to see it. I'm sorry for bringing sickness with me and for being a broken old man."

He blinks back his sorrow. He has failed them. He has failed her. He isn't fit to sit on this porch with them.

Small cool hands on his shoulder bring him out of his despair. Penelope helps him up and guides him back to the little room in the bunkhouse.

She speaks low and soothing, as though calming a horse. "It's alright, mister. It's going to be fine. You are a friend of Cesar's and a guest in our home. You get better now and we'll talk about the rest later."

"And tell me about my dad!" Trevor calls after them, turning back to the mule.

Oh son, my son, your dad was a coward, Cesar almost cries.

His strength drains away and he collapses into the bed to obediently drink Lupe's broth. Then Cesar closes his eyes and wishes himself to sleep while Penelope watches him from the doorway.

"I'll help with dinner tonight," Penelope says to Lupe. "The girls are taking turns on guard duty at the main generator."

"And how long will they keep that up?" Lupe says, clearly disgruntled.

Penelope returns dryly, "Until they figure out who sabotaged it last month and make sure they don't do it again, I guess."

"Hmph."

Cesar doesn't need to open his eyes to know that Lupe is making the sign against the Evil Eye. Penelope just snorts, standing in the doorway, letting the quiet stretch out.

"Are they coming tonight?" Lupe breaks the silence as she gathers up her things.

"They always do." Penelope replies, but she does not elaborate.

Lupe purses her lips. "The boy should have stayed in town," she says.

"Why?" Penelope asks, even though the tone of her voice said she knows why.

"These men of yours are bad. They will hurt us. I can see it. You know I have The Sight," Lupe crosses herself and mutters something in Spanish having to do with devils and the need to cast them out. "I bet some of them are behind the sabotage attempts," she adds ominously.

Penelope laughs, "If you have The Sight, then I'm a dancing pig. I'm more worried he'll pick up bad habits. But I agree. Trevor should have stayed in town. What can I say? He's too good a boy to dawdle in town as we'd planned."

Lupe grins fondly, for she loves the boy as if he were her own grandson. "A very good boy. Just like his father. Well, except his father was a very naughty boy."

Penelope snorts, repeating Lupe's curse about devils and driving them out. He hears her footsteps disappearing out the door.

Cesar just smiles to himself and falls asleep.

CHAPTER FOUR

C esar awakens later to darkness and distant laughter. Many orbitals synchronize their rotation with Earth so that they have the same light-dark cycles as wherever they are originally from. He knows Ithaca is parked above the Gulf of Mexico.

Cesar also knows that from the Earth below, Ithaca twinkles like a star. A belligerent star that made it clear long ago that it wants nothing to do with the Earth.

He lies in bed listening for a few minutes. Soft music and conversation drift in from the main house. Cesar estimates a large party, maybe fifty or sixty people. He decides to investigate and looks for his pants and boots. He finds them cleaned and piled neatly next to the bed. After a few wobbly steps, he's happy to find some of his strength returning.

Cesar keeps to the shadows, wishing only to observe.

There are a few women but it is mostly men. The women are dressed well, for a party, but not extravagantly. He sees Argos making his way through the crowd with a mop and a bucket and can't help but smile. He should have known.

If there is one rotten board of Ithaca ranch still standing, Argos will still be here. Argos is a few years older than Cesar himself. The man started working on the ranch as a teenager when Cesar was barely big enough to sit on a donkey. They had some wild times before Cesar left.

Argos was loyal to a fault, but not exactly genius material. If Cesar wants to keep his identity a secret, he needn't fear of Argos catching him out.

Then Cesar catches sight of Penelope, shining like a jewel. He admires her from afar. She is still the most beautiful woman he has ever seen. Well, maybe not the most beautiful, but definitely the one he likes looking at the most. She is on the arm of a very elegant man, a man without gray in his hair or a hitch in his step, Cesar notes jealously.

Of course she remarried, he thinks.

Such a woman would not be left alone, especially up here, out in the dark. Women are still scarce, particularly rich and beautiful women who know their way around a shotgun.

Penelope laughs graciously at something the elegant man tells her, then excuses herself to enter the house. Cesar has strategically positioned himself behind a very large rosemary bush. He is far from the crowd, but now he spots two men walking towards him from the back of the house. They stop on the other side of the bush.

They discuss who they think will win the upcoming Nullball tournament, oblivious to Cesar's presence.

This year's tournament will be held on Ithaca for the first time. Nullball is basically an adaptation of American football or rugby except it is played in freefall wearing spacesuits with tethers.

Nullball started out as a training exercise played in the null gravity cargo holds of the orbitals. It was designed to help people become comfortable moving in spacesuits and using tethers so they would make fewer mistakes when they were in void space where every misstep can be deadly.

It evolved into a fast-paced high-impact game that both Spacers and Earthers follow enthusiastically. One of the men on the other side of the bush favors Ithaca, but the second says it will be one of the larger colonies clustered in the Lagrange points or else the Hathor Miners. After that conversation dries up, they switch to a subject that Cesar finds much more interesting.

"So all of these men are here to court the famous widow?" the first man asks with amusement. He sounds young but with a gravely voice. Cesar can see neither of them clearly from his side of the bush.

"In a way," the second voice replies ponderously. "But they have been going on for over six years, these 'courting' parties. Every week. There are even more people here since the sabotage attempts. Have you heard about that? Yes? Well, even with that, the widow seems in no great hurry to choose. Some say she still waits for her 'war hero' husband to return, though he must be long dead."

This second voice sounds older and has a trace of an accent Cesar can't place. He smells cigarette smoke. Smoking is very uncommon in the orbitals. It was impractical and dangerous in the first tiny colonies with their unreliable air scrubbers. Even now, on a large colony like Ithaca, too many respected the importance of clean air or at least respected that fact that most of their neighbors found smoking extremely offensive. Which is probably why these two snuck out of the party to indulge.

The first voice comments, "She is a beauty, but beauty alone cannot account for so many men here. Most of them are not from this colony, either. What other charms does she possess to inspire so many to make the voyage here?"

"The most charming thing of all—money." The older man laughs. "That little woman in there is one of the richest Spacers you will ever meet. Definitely one of the most powerful."

The younger man objects, "But I keep up with Orbie politics. She is not part of them. She is hardly mentioned."

The young voice must be an Earther. Cesar is surprised. Few Earthers came up, even ten years after the War ended. He must have arrived on the same transport ship Cesar did, though he didn't look familiar. Not surprising as Cesar was surly and sick for the trip so he kept to himself.

"You need to remember that Spacers don't like being called Orbies any more than you like being called a dirt-humping bastard, son," the older man says sharply.

Then more gently, "No, the lady does not actively play politics, but you can bet all the politicians jump when she sends an Ether wave. She's a separatist, one of the powerful ones. Many on Ithaca are interested in getting hooked back into the world Ether, but she fights it every time it is proposed. They only get short wave from the Spacer Ether here. Daily news downloads, if you can imagine anything so provincial. But she has large quantities of the one thing every orbital needs eventually and since we refuse to get it from Earth, she gets to do want she wants, even live on this absurd ranch."

"Really? But she doesn't even own this colony."

The second man laughs, "She doesn't have to. She owns the only herd of cows in space. Even for Earth, her herd would be large. This colony is the only one really designed or equipped to handle a large herd. So we all seek to either buy her out or marry her. So far, she's choosing neither."

Cesar can hear the older man carefully grinding his cigarette out.

The younger man says, "Well, we had the steaks for dinner. They do taste fantastic, but I had no idea you Spacers were such carnivores."

The he moves towards the house enough for Cesar to see him. He is tall and thin, dressed in the height of Earther fashion with a complicated scarf wrapped around his throat and long flowing locks.

The older man puts a hand on the younger man's shoulder to stop him. With his other hand, he pulls a flask out of a pocket and offers it to the younger man who enthusiastically agrees.

Wincing from the bite of the liquor, the older man rasps, "Son, it's not just meat. It's the milk and cheese. Practically half of this colony is devoted to making cheese. Fully a quarter of Ithaca's core is devoted to curing leather. She can ask any price she wants for a hamburger or a block of cheese and we all line up to pay. That bowl of cheese dip on the kitchen table in there would cost a year's salary in some of the outer colonies."

The younger man laughs, "Of course. He who controls the tasty tidbits controls the world. It's a concept that kept my family alive through the Worlder Wars. People might cry for their lost art, but they'll fling themselves on a live grenade for the man who can make chocolate so divine it makes you believe in God again."

The Worlder Wars, that time when it seemed the Earthers would kill themselves off trying to kill their neighbors, came just before the Spacer War.

Now the older man moves into view. Cesar takes in the leather boots and the hint of a belly that the man's well-cut jacket almost hides. The man must be from some prosperous colony to flaunt his wealth this way. After the Spacer War, there were enough rumors of cannibalism on the more desperate colonies to keep most people from looking like they had fat to spare.

The older man shakes his head. "That may be true, but her true power is manure. Not to put to fine a point on it, but most colonies are so poor, they have to import shit."

"Oh, please," protests the younger man, looking mildly offended at the topic.

The older man seems unfazed as he takes another swig. "Manure is the best way to replenish the soil's nutrients and keep the biosphere running smooth. If you are too broke to sustain herbivores, you got to get manure from somewhere and this right here is it. The widow Vaquero is the finest purveyor of crap in the spheres."

The older man stomps the dirt for emphasis.

The younger man looks shocked. He runs a hand through his hair and shrugs. "Well, I can see it. The whole Orbie nation is crap, so why shouldn't Madam Vaquero be the Queen of Crap? You would think she'd change her name, though. After what her husband did."

Cesar winces. He wondered that himself. Truth be told, he allowed a tiny flame of hope to flicker in his heart when he heard they still used his name. If she didn't reject his name, maybe some day she'd forgive him? Probably not, but it still gave him hope.

The old man laughs as he stows his flask in a jacket pocket. "Ah, you don't know her. That woman would find more ways to fling her husband's atrocities in your face if she could, just to see you squirm. She's a hard one, God love her."

Cesar remembers his pet name for Penelope when they first married. He'd called her "kitten." How could his kitten be the woman these men knew?

"Perhaps I myself can charm her in to hurrying her decision," the younger voice laughs as they return to the house.

"I wouldn't wish that fate on you, but don't let that stop your trying," returns the older man.

"Maybe with all the trouble this colony has had lately, she'll actually think about selling out."

Cesar catches no more of their conversation.

She's not married.

He is ridiculously pleased by that fact.

"But there's no way she stays single pining for my sorry self," Cesar tells himself, trying to shake the optimistic little daydream of reconciliation out of his head.

He remembers their parting and the angry words she'd said. Perhaps after marrying a worthless specimen like himself, she decided that getting another man in her life just wasn't worth the hassle? He can certainly understand that.

Cesar quietly returns to his room in the bunkhouse to try sleeping. He tells himself that he will leave this place as soon as he is better. Obviously, Penelope and Trevor are doing just fine without him. Telling the boy that his father has been alive all this time will only cause them pain.

On the other hand, there is something not quite right about that party, something a little ominous. And what was all this about sabotage attempts and trouble in the colony?

Perhaps he better stick around a little while to make sure Penelope and Trevor are all right? Cesar knows that what he really wants to do is stay right here and watch his wife and son greedily, like a housewife obsessed with her favorite Ether reality show. He is glad for any excuse to indulge that desire.

Much later in the night, Cesar hears doors shutting and the bustle of people going to bed after the party. He hears whispering voices, mostly women but a few men. He works so hard to keep himself from wondering if some man is spending the night with Penelope that he doesn't sleep a wink.

CHAPTER FIVE

For the next two days, Cesar does nothing but sleep fitfully and drink the never-ending stream of soup Lupe pours into him. Although Lupe practically raised him from infancy, she shows no sign of recognizing him. This depresses him even more. Cesar feels like a ghost, haunting his old life.

Finally, his fever breaks. On the third morning, he watches the reflected glow of the sun light up this little world. He finally feels human again, or at least human enough to desperately want to get out of bed and get clean. He hears footsteps approaching.

"No more nonsense. Today we put him in the medibox, Lupe," he hears Penelope say resolutely as she approaches. He can hear her determined stride, matched by the rushing steps of Lupe.

"Ach, *mija*. Those mediboxes are just coffins. You can't trust them. Lasers and scans and computers poking you. They are no match for rest and good food." Lupe is vehement in her dislike of the orbital solution to the lack of medical personnel and equipment.

Mediboxes were so reliable that every Spacer and Earther who could afford one had them, even if they were a bit claustrophobic. Although most of the time, a Spacer medibox would recommend diet and exercise modifications in keeping with Spacer's rabid dislike of "unnatural" remedies.

"Besides, my soup will cure him. My soup can cure anything," Lupe declares righteously. "If he doesn't die first."

The door opens and both women peer in at him. Cesar has never seen Lupe in anything but the colorful skirts and ornately embroidered blouses she loved. Today is no different.

When he was little, Lupe told him that her skirts reminded her of who she was and where she came from. That was something he could stand to remember now and then, she would inevitably add.

Penelope is wearing a pair of the multi-pocketed pants much favored by Spacer women. The legs are cut to fall in folds like a skirt. They have drawstrings to gather them tight to the ankle for the lower gravities where a skirt is an unfortunate fashion choice.

Lupe flatly refuses to wear them. But then, she has not left Ithaca in decades. She even refuses to visit the storage level. Weightlessness is her worst nightmare. Cesar could never understand what convinced her to leave the Earth in the first place.

"You look pretty bright-eyed today, *gringo*," Penelope comments as she inspects him.

Cesar gives her a wan smile.

"You see? My soup," Lupe pronounces triumphantly, poking Cesar like a steak of questionable tenderness.

She beams at him approvingly until she sees he has not finished the cup of soup she left him the night before. Her face takes on a look of steely disapproval. He drinks it cold.

"I am definitely on the mend, ma'am," Cesar agrees quietly, glancing quickly at Penelope. "I would surely love to get cleaned up. I know I must smell like death on a cracker. My last stop before I came here was the Satsuma Silk Colony and two billion tons of silkworms leave a stench that takes days to get out."

"Well, good. We have a medibox if you'd like to get checked out, just to be sure?" Penelope offers.

"If it's all the same to you, I'll skip it unless I'm still feeling poorly in a day or two," Cesar answers as he gets up and stretches. Cesar will die before getting in a medibox again, but he doesn't see the need to mention that right now.

Penelope shrugs. "Fine by me. I will be gone most of the day, but Lupe will point you towards clean clothes and a shower." And with that Penelope leaves without a backwards glance. Cesar frankly admires her retreating figure.

When he left all those years ago, she was his fluffy little kitten. He knew the only reason he'd ever gotten her aboard the ship from Earth was by appealing to that insatiable dream of travel. A dream that apparently died on the shuttle up.

Argos stopped by earlier to chat with Cesar and see if the new stranger would live or die. Argos had not recognized Cesar at all, but he did say that Penelope had not left Ithaca once since setting foot inside the orbital all those years ago.

Cesar could not get over the difference in her. His little kitten may have hissed and shown her claws on occasion, but that Penelope was too gentle and sweet to ever cause harm. The woman he saw now was a panther— sleek, strong and ready to devour those that got in her way.

What a woman, Cesar thinks appreciatively.

He smiles to think that if she'd been this confident and unassailable when they'd met, he'd probably have run in fear. He is deeply uncomfortable with the man he used to be, a man who had all this and walked away without a second thought.

Lupe helps him up, calling on various saints for strength.

"A shower is not going to cut it. I am filling up the water trough. You get a bath, mister."

Cesar thinks this is a grand idea, but he protests the decadence of it. You don't get a lot of baths in space. Water is at a premium. Most orbitals are designed with enough plants and culture vats to make air an easy commodity. They tend to err on the side of too much oxygen, building photosynthesis panels into the roofs of every building. Food is usually not a problem as the bacterial vats can supply enough to live on, even if bacfood tends to be mostly unappetizing. Yeast cakes smell like yeast cakes no matter how you culture them.

Which is why the majority of colonies devote the largest amount of room for raising food. But water was a real issue until they perfected large-scale asteroid mining.

Even now, nearly all orbitals try to clean their populace with the barest minimum of water. A bath is the ultimate luxury, even if it is in the trough used to water the mules. It was the greatest testament to how well Ithaca and this ranch were doing, that Lupe would offer a bath to a stranger. He thanks her profusely.

"Well, a bath will at least take a few layers of the funk off of you. The trough needed cleaning anyway," she says, brushing aside his thanks. "And don't think I won't make you scrub a mess of laundry while you're in there."

He follows her slowly, still unsteady and weak.

Lupe gives Cesar a cake of coarse homemade soap that he scours himself with. He washes his hair at least three times and then sits in the tub combing it. It is longer and more matted than he realized. Lupe brings out some scissors and does the best she can to hack his hair and beard into a more presentable shape.

But she refuses to touch a single hair until he parts ways with his filthy undershirt so she can give it a good scrub. Cesar doesn't want to get practically naked in anybody's front yard, especially this one.

He is careful to keep Lupe from seeing the large scar on his thigh. He'd gotten it as a youngster, the day he learned that cows may look stupid, but they bite pretty hard when you poke them with a stick. Lupe had been the one to stitch it up.

He remembers the lectures she gave him and all the soup she made him drink after that. If she sees the scar, she'll recognize him for sure.

Lupe grunts, "Cleaned up you don't look half-bad, mister. Especially now that you got a little color back in your cheeks. Thought you was a ghost that first day, staggering around half-dead like you were."

Caesar laughs his thanks. He is getting dressed when four women round the corner of the main house. They are all wearing the traditional roughneck uniform of boots, jeans and bandannas. They stop to stare when they see him. Three or four burst out laughing.

"*Abuela*, there's a naked old man in the yard," a freckle-faced girl drawls.

Even though he's got on underpants and an undershirt, Cesar curls up in a very embarrassed ball, quickly yanking on pants and a shirt.

"Not that old," a blond with pigtails giggles as she eyes the wiry body he scrambles to cover up.

"You girls are wicked," Lupe says, threatening to hose them down if they come any closer. "A good shower will clean out your dirty minds."

"You are so right, Mama Lupe. I'll take one right now if this nice man will wash my back," the dark-skinned blond winks at him as they all saunter inside, giggling and swishing their hips. He throws on the rest of his clothes quickly, but Lupe just laughs.

"Like they can see anything through all that hair," she clucks. But when Lupe surveys her handiwork with respect to his hair and beard, she is satisfied.

"Where did they come from anyway?" Cesar asks, retreating into the bunkhouse.

"Just now, they come from the Ag level, tending the herd. We've got a private elevator," Lupe can't help bragging.

Looking after the women, she snorts, "They call themselves cowgirls, if you can believe such a thing. They eat like cows, that's for sure."

Lupe starts towards the main house, her mind on cooking. Cesar knows this because she tells him so. He wonders if the woman has been talking nonstop these last fifteen years.

"No other cowboys here on the ranch?" asks Cesar, pausing in the doorway of his little room.

Lupe shakes her head. "No. The lady won't have them. Except for Argos. Those are his old clothes I'm giving you. All of these girls showed up like driftwood with nasty stories from other orbitals. She takes 'em in, puts them to work until they are strong enough to do for themselves. They keep her gentlemen callers on their toes too. She likes to take in strays, that one." Lupe plainly does not approve.

"Lucky for you," she adds. Then she turns and fixes him with a piercing gaze. "Mister, I need to start calling you by a name, don't you think?"

"Ulixes. Call me Jonas Ulixes," he lies smoothly. He's used the name before but never on this side of the stars. He runs a hand through his cropped hair, testing the feel of it.

Lupe snorts, but Cesar isn't sure what that means. "Well, Mr. Ulixes. You sure look like you been run over by a tractor and then maybe someone backed up to finish the job. Where'd you get all those scars?"

"That's a lot of stories. A lot of long stories. Mostly from the War. Some after." He closes his eyes remembering.

She turns back to the big house. "So tuck your shirt in and you can tell me one while you help me with lunch," Lupe calls over her shoulder.

CHAPTER SIX

They are sitting down to eat on long bac-wood tables, listening to Argos spin tales in the large dining room, warmed by midday light and the heat of the kitchen next to it. Cesar insisted he needed some time to think of one suitable for mixed company and Argos was happy to oblige with a tale of his own while Cesar thought it over. Penelope finished her work early and is happy to join Cesar, Trevor and the cowgirls for lunch.

Argos drawls, "No one ever thought our war, the Spacer War they call it now in the history archives, would last as long as it did."

The cowgirls glance at the older man occasionally, but they are more interested in shoveling down their food as fast as they can. Although the table is heavy with hot dishes, the women work hard, play harder, and always fight over the last of Lupe's homemade tortillas. Cesar has picked a seat where he can watch Penelope daintily sip coffee and Trevor inhale lunch while occasionally snatching second helpings of beans or whatever else was closest.

He reached for the *queso* earlier and almost got stabbed by a cowgirl's sharp fork. There is one girl sitting at the end cutting her enchiladas with a Bowie knife. Cesar notices the way there is plenty of space between her and the girl sitting next to her.

Argos takes a sip of his coffee and clears his throat before going on, "Five years is a long time to wonder whether you'll die in the morning from a missile or in the evening from lack of water because the supply ships don't run anymore. Ithaca was always a prosperous orbital and we were far enough out of Earth's missile range. The effects on us were less severe, in the way that a tornado is less severe than a hurricane."

Cesar turns to look at the others sitting at the table. Trevor's mouth is open and his burrito is dangling in one hand, forgotten halfway to his mouth. Beans drip out onto his plate unnoticed, even though he's heard this story many times.

Argos continues, "Spacers were lucky that the Earth had plumb tuckered itself out fighting wars down there. Pakistan fighting with India. The Muslim nations calling jihad against the European Union. South Africa warring with North Africa. Russia lobbing missiles at China. The USA was fighting everybody, seemed like."

He pauses while those old enough dimly remember the ever more bizarre and bloody news waves from that era. "Seems so strange now, but at the time, it was like the whole world was just so angry. That's what made so many people want to move out here, away from all that, I guess."

Penelope gives a quick laugh, "You remember that colony of hippies that built a free-love orbital with all those exotic animals right before our war started?" She looks at Cesar but he shakes his head.

Lupe wrinkles her nose and crosses herself as she bustles around the table, refilling bowls and swatting Trevor when he puts his elbows on the table. "Those poor kids. They called it The Ark. They were gonna protect all the endangered animals in their little commune in the sky. I wanted to call their mamas and tell them to teach their babies about reality. And baths."

Penelope catches Cesar's eye across the table and smiles at him.

"Lupe believes God hates dirt more than he hates sin," she explains. "We'd have those kids over for dinner whenever they could cobble together the fuel. For all their ideals, they sure liked steak as much as anybody else."

Cesar grins back at her. His eyes linger over her just a second too long. Penelope looks away quickly, stuffing a bite of food in her mouth.

"Those hippies and their condors and whatnot were only barely making it with regular supply ships," Argos says. "When all the wars down on the planet interrupted the supply ships, they had some rough times."

Penelope nods as she swallows the last of her burrito. Then she adds, "They didn't think to bring anybody with any actual knowledge of how to rig air processors or repair solar cells. And I don't know how they thought they'd feed all those animals, much less themselves."

Cesar frowns, pushing his fork around his plate, chasing beans and bits of salsa slowly. Unsure of whether he wants to break in to Argos's story, he says, "I saw some bad things in my travels. Empty orbitals filled with the wreckage of some story we never knew the beginning of. This sounds like the start of one of those ghost stories we never liked to tell. Did any of them survive to the end of the War?"

He takes a swallow of beer and smiles with pure pleasure. Ithacans brewed their own beer and he's never forgotten the taste. Plus, the cold liquid feels good against his dry throat as the bottle cools his hand, sweaty from the heat of the day.

"Some of them did. More than we thought," allows Argos. "A few of their carnivores got loose and wiped out a lot of the crew and their live-stock. Big shock, right? But those hippy kids turned out tougher than we gave them credit for."

Penelope clears her throat. "We tried to help where we could. Took in some of their people and their stock, but there's only so much room."

"I was wearing my knees out praying for those *loco bobos*," Lupe an-nounces. "But I wouldn't give a spit for their chances, until that little splicer boy showed up. Without him, they'd just be dust rolling around in a dead orbital, like lint in a clothes dryer."

"Oh?" Cesar asks, looking between them.

Argos and Penelope both nod.

"Yes," says Penelope. "That boy showed up on some hunk of junk tinker ship one day with a box of equipment under his arm like their own personal Jesus Christ. Took over the colony and turned it into one of the most valued exporters of small herbivores above the world and down on it."

Gene splicers are rare and treated like gods in the orbitals because they have, time and again, saved whole colonies from certain extinction. They can whip up a shrubbery that will conserve water and cure a disease that's crippling your colony at the same time. On Earth, splicers are still scorned and, in some areas, imprisoned and killed for practicing their genetic arts. But in the Spacer colonies, to cause the death of a good splicer would bring down the wrath of the sky.

Trevor blurts out, "They sell cashmere gerbils and milk koalas. They've got attack chinchillas too, but Mom won't let me get one." He cast a sul-len look at his mother.

She wrinkles her nose, "They give me the creeps. They've got those huge yellow eyes and teeth the size of my hand."

Cesar laughs quietly.

Lupe starts clearing away the dishes while the others still pick at the remains of their lunch. Penelope bends forward to explain to Cesar, "He came because of all the endangered species. He said it was like a treasure chest of genetic material just sitting up there, waiting for him. For the first year, he was like a kid in a candy factory, turning out all kinds of strange critters. Very interesting boy. A man now, I guess. He'll be here this Saturday, I think?"

She looks at Lupe as she asks this. Lupe nods with a smile. Cesar finds himself grinding his teeth, watching them smiling over this brilliant young man.

"Can I get some more beans and *queso*?" he asks. "Hadn't had anything that good in years. I never tasted TexMex this good and I been down to the Earth a time or two."

Lupe puffs up with pride and dishes him up an enormous third helping of everything. Cesar wolfs it down enthusiastically.

Penelope laughs, "Well, *gringo*, it's not like there's a whole lot places in the heavens or the Earth to get real guacamole these days, is there? Now that Mexico is just one big smoking hole in the ground. When I first got here, I remember Lupe telling me that there was no point in living in the stars if the food sucks."

Argos chuckles at that and then asks, "Lupe, have you ever cooked anything that didn't involve beans, tortillas, or jalapenos?"

Lupe sniffs, "I could, but what's the point?"

"You were telling us how the War started," Trevor prompts impatiently, licking beans off his hand.

"So I was," Argos says, remembering the thread of his story. "So what with all the wars down there, the supply ships got real unreliable. Some of them were delayed for months or stopped altogether. You can understand how a country struggling to survive wouldn't put a big priority on shipping water and food to some guys up in space. But for us, it was death. Corporations sponsored some of the colonies and governments put up most of the rest. Only a few, like Ithaca, were paid for by individuals."

The blond cowgirl breaks in, "Really? I thought the orbitals were all paid for by rich old guys looking for a pleasure planet of their very own."

Penelope shakes her head. "Nope. Old Larry raised money from individual investors who thought space burgers would sell like hell down there. But for the rest, if a corporation went bankrupt, the orbital was often just left to die. And if a government went to war, their orbital was the last thing on their minds."

Argos's face goes gray. "It was bad times," he says quietly. "The colonies started working together just to survive. It seemed natural that if you were starving to death and the next colony over was about to lose power that you'd work together so you could both live. By the time the Earth started settling down, most of the colonies up here were already wondering what we needed them for. They abandoned us when we needed them most. Why should they tell us what to do now?"

Penelope interjects, "Can you imagine? Surviving by your own wits for years and then some government a thousand miles away tries to tell you they are going to dump a bunch of lead-footed dirt-loving settlers, mostly criminals and malcontents, on you in the name of public policy? Or a corporation fires you from a job that hasn't paid you in years and now you have to pack up and leave the home that you fought with blood and tears to defend?"

The younger cowgirls and Trevor mutter revolution.

Argos says, "We already thought they were crazy down there, committing suicide by war. We thought we had a bird's eye view of the end of the Earthers. We felt like we were the only people left in the galaxy. Then one day they start lecturing us, throwing their weight around like we were kids playing while Daddy was at work? Of course we were thinking revolution from the start."

"Some were," Penelope says sharply. "Most of us were just trying to get by. There are plenty of ways to die out here and some of us didn't think picking a fight with the Earthers was a good way to go."

She picks up some dishes and takes them to the sink.

Trevor protests, "Aw, Mom. Of course we had to fight the Earthers."

Penelope snaps, "I had a baby to raise. Getting you to the age you are now was all I was thinking about in those days." But she ruffles his hair.

Cesar looks away, the sight stings his heart.

"I want to hear the rest," Trevor says mutinously as she pushes him towards the sink to help Lupe clean the dishes.

"Argos will tell that same tired story about Helen and Manny again tonight," says Penelope sternly, pointing him back to work. "And he'll ham it up and make them out to be comic-book superheroes even though he knows Helen is short and pudgy now and Manny has that gimp leg. Honestly, Argos, it might be better to let the kid watch Ether dramas."

"Those things will rot his brain," says Argos, though he never had enough brains himself to worry about, one way or the other. "Better he learn by talking to actual people about real things than all that make-believe muck. Oral histories were the best way to learn for thousands of years before they came up with the Ether."

"But I want to know how it ends," says Trevor, sticking out his lower lip.

Penelope sighs and rolls her eyes. "You know what happened. It was all over in the blink of an eye. Just at the end, when we thought the best we could hope for was to be shot out of the sky, Cesar the Scorcher obliterated Mexico. Then the Earthers were begging us to declare peace. Not only did they not want us back after that, they'd have pushed us out farther if they could. I heard tales of Earthers who wouldn't even look at the sky for years after. They didn't want to see the stars if we were up in them."

For the first time, Cesar wonders if he didn't get the better part of the deal. Sure everyone hated him for dropping the nuclear starship on Mexico, but how much harder has it been on the Ithacans? To live every day knowing that the millions of Mexicans had died to save them? To have to feel guilt for an act they had no part in?

Some of the cowgirls titter nervously as they file out of the room and head back to work. Trevor looks like he wants to argue about the ending of the story regardless of whether it was true or not.

Penelope sees that look and holds up her hands with exasperation, "Well, who could blame them? Eighty million people gone in the blink of an eye and with all the radiation, it will be hundreds of years before that land in Mexico is livable again. You know how this story ends, Trevor. It ends with you here about to get your bottom smacked if you don't go help Lupe with the dishes right now, young man."

The remaining cowgirls snicker and that alone is enough to send Trevor back to work. He is just old enough to be both fascinated and terrified by the cowgirls. Unable to decide which, whenever they notice him the boy usually flushes bright red and bolts like he does now.

Cesar gulps hard. He has spent years perfecting a blank look whenever people talk about Cesar the Scorcher, but this is literally too close to home.

"Feeling poorly," he mumbles as he staggers out the door.

He sits on the porch and stares out at the land. After a minute, Penelope comes out and sits next to him. "Need to go lay down again, Mister Ulixes?" she asks calmly.

It takes him half a second to respond to his assumed name, but Cesar shakes his head.

She gives him a charming grin. "Then maybe you can help me out in the vegetable garden this afternoon?"

This time, Cesar nods with a smile.

Penelope laughs. "You won't be smiling for long. I got weeds like a water filter has algae. We got work to do."

•

The therapeutic effects of hard work in the hot light of the reflected sun work their cure on Cesar. He labors alongside Penelope in an easy silence. She works just as hard as he does, pulling weeds, hoeing, and transplanting tomatoes from the hydroponics.

"You got to love a controllable environment," Cesar comments when they pause for a glass of iced tea. "I visited Earth a few times. Never could get used to rain falling whenever it felt like it. And the whole idea of seasons is bizarre. Sometimes it's hot and sometimes it's cold, but you never know what you're gonna get? Not for me. They can keep it."

Penelope chuckles. "So I guess you grew up in the orbitals? I was born on Earth, but I haven't been back in almost twenty years. Sometimes I miss the unpredictability of it all. But only sometimes."

"We got plenty of unpredictability up here," Cesar replies companionably.

Penelope smiles. "Plenty of work to do as well. We need to get some compost for the tomatoes now, if you're up to it."

He was, so they grab a large cart and push it to the elevator. They talk about weather algorithms and soil chemistry and all the other things space farmers talk about.

Finally, Cesar gets up the nerve to ask about Trevor.

"So that boy of yours looks almost grown," he says gruffly. Cesar knows perfectly well that Trevor is sixteen years, seven months and four days old. "He going to take over the ranch soon?"

It's a legitimate question. Earth might have rules about adulthood or child labor, but that means next to nothing in the orbitals. The Caribbean Coffee Conglomerate has been running smoothly for the last eight years under the leadership of a boy who inherited it at the age of thirteen.

Penelope shrugs. "We'll see. He wants to travel, you know? See the rest of the sky and maybe even visit Earth. Trevor is still young enough to think he wants adventure. He talks about piloting a merchant ship."

She doesn't sound enthusiastic about it.

Cesar isn't anxious for the boy to go flinging himself across the void either. Particularly since Cesar knows exactly what kind of trouble a young boy with wanderlust can find out there.

"Adventure," scoffs Cesar. "I guess all young men are foolish that way. I hope he survives to learn the value of a boring life."

Penelope sighs, "Me too. I think he's keyed up to go because of his dad being… not around."

Cesar scowls. "Maybe Trevor thinks he can find out what happened to him? Or maybe Trevor thinks he can right the wrongs his father committed?"

Penelope laughs, "Oh, he's just a kid. I doubt Trevor thinks about much of anything. He's got too many hormones running around in his body. There aren't enough pretty girls his age to distract him here so he's hot for space."

"Cowgirls aren't good enough for him?"

"They are all older than he is or too scary for my tender young boy," she laughs.

The elevator doors open onto the agricultural level. It's like a doorway to the Garden of Eden. Pastures, fields of crops, and other pastoral delights stretch as far as the eye can see. Of course, they stretch up and away, following the curve of the orbital's outer wall.

Until they solved the problem of how to shield plants and people from the deadly radiation in space, long-term colonies of people outside of the Earth hadn't been possible. The key to solving this complicated technological dilemma turned out to be dirt. Packing dirt several feet deep along the outer walls stopped the radiation. With tons of dirt lining the outer walls, it made that level of the orbitals primed for agricultural purposes.

As Cesar's father, Larry, said on more than one occasion, "If you got a pile of dirt, you might as well stick a bean in it."

The only down side is that complementary plants and animals must be genetically engineered to thrive at a higher gravity than Earth normal since the habitation levels were invariably above the agricultural levels. Spacers learned to spin their orbitals so the habitation level has Earth normal gravity. It's easier to sleep when your head weighs what it should.

Penelope turns and grins at Cesar. The sight of the herd always makes her smile. "You remember being Trevor's age? Doing insane things because you are too stupid to know better?"

Cesar vividly remembers the feel of Penelope in his arms the night she promised to fly to the stars with him. He also remembers a very steamy ride in the drone cab before they boarded the shuttle away from the planet. Cesar convinced Penelope to run away to Ithaca with him when she was only two years older than Trevor was now.

"Nope," coughs Cesar, turning away from her. "I'm too old to be remembering kid stuff."

Penelope looks disappointed, but not really upset. "Let's get this stuff over to the composter."

Every home on Ithaca has a small composting unit, but for a large garden on the upper level like Penelope's, it is easier to bring it straight down to the main composter for the herd.

As they unload the vegetable refuse, the herd moves toward them on the off chance that there might be tomatoes or sugar cane or something else that cows consider the height of sophistication in cud flavoring.

When Cesar sees the herd, he can't help but whistle in appreciation. "That's a fine looking head of beef," he tells Penelope. He inspects their hooves, checks their teeth and slaps their meaty flanks with frank approval.

They are too. Genetically engineered to have the tenderest, most delicious meat in the solar system. Larry Vaquero was scrupulously honest with the original investors in the mad scheme that was Ithaca. He insisted they spin the colony at just the right gravity and got the oxygen levels just so. The man was fanatical about setting up the perfect conditions for the penultimate steak, down to electronically monitoring the pH of their water three times a day.

Penelope basks in the reflected glow of Cesar's admiration. They pass the time discussing herd genetics and the troubles of trace mineral deficiency and whether supplementing bovine food with fungal protein was really beneficial or just the latest fad.

They are both pleasantly surprised to find another soul who knows and cares about these things. Obviously, Penelope takes her job as ranch woman seriously.

"How is it you know so much about cows?" she asks.

"Oh, I worked on a ranch and my old dad was crazy for cows," he mutters, hoping she'll assume he'd been an Earther ranch hand. She does.

Cesar knows much from his father and also because his bouts of homesickness over the years tended to manifest in the compulsive reading of literature on space ranching. Fortunately, there wasn't that much on the subject for him to read.

Cesar watches two cowgirls round up the herd and move them through the gate to the next field for grazing while Penelope brags that they have so many now that they had to split the herd in two or else the combined weight of several thousand tons of beef on the hoof will interfere with the orbital's rotation.

"Well, we better get going," sighs Penelope with regret. She's just as happy talking steers and calves all day. "I'm meeting with a man from Earth in a little bit. He wants to start importing our leather again."

"They want to buy your leather and transport it down to the planet? That seems like a lot of work for something they could do themselves," he remarks.

"Yeah, I was surprised too," replies Penelope.

Cesar laughs, "Well, who can blame them? Everything is better up here. Unless they've recovered a whole lot from the last time I was down there, they don't have anything to compare to Ithaca beef."

"When you've got a controlled environment and fine gene stock, it's hard to go wrong," Penelope allows.

"I would still think the cost of transportation would make it too expensive," muses Cesar.

Penelope shakes her head. "Well, we'd process the beef here so the weight would be much less of an issue than sending down the whole cow. Also, they've come up with some new designs for ships that function like space blimps. They basically just float down to the planet, using almost no energy. Then they shoot them back up here again with that laser umbrella launcher thingy."

"Still not a ride I'd like to take," says Cesar.

Penelope agrees, "I know they say it's safe, but I'd rather not find out in person."

Penelope tells him that the cowgirls move the herd each day to prevent overgrazing any of the fields that stretch around the orbital. The gates are set up to open automatically each day so they can move both herds at about the same time. Once they have all the cows through, they trigger the lock on the gate behind them.

Penelope asks the girl with blond pigtails, "Shani, any progress at the mating pens?"

"Nothing to report. And we already checked on the bulls, boss," says the blond, shaking her head. "We're going to go work on the gate locks in Section C. They've been slipping loose lately."

Shani leaves with a wink at Cesar. Cesar chuckles and Penelope rolls her eyes.

"That girl is the biggest flirt alive," she tells him.

"No need to apologize," replies Cesar with a self-deprecating grin. "I'm too old to read much into a girl's wink. You need me to take anything up to the house?"

She did.

Penelope shows him the mulch she wants to haul up to spread in her herb garden and Cesar begins shoveling it into the bin they brought the compost down in. Penelope watches his muscles ripple over his wiry arms as he works.

"He's not that old after all," she murmurs to herself. He was sickly, pale and filthy when he showed up, but now he looks like a strong, competent man who just needs a little feeding up.

Before she realizes what she is doing, Penelope lightly touches his arm. Her impulse was to feel his bicep like a piece of meat, checking its tenderness. When Ulixes turns to look at her, though, Penelope sees something in his eyes that makes her breath catch even though she isn't sure why. She snatches her hand away and shoves it in a pocket.

"Well, I've got to go," she blurts out. As Penelope hurries away, she turns back to look at this stranger she invited into her home.

The man is standing tall, watching her go. He looks straight into her eyes and the strength of his gaze causes something to twist free and flutter around in her chest, but she doesn't want to think too deeply about what it might be. On the way to meet the representative from Earth, she spends far more time thinking about the stranger in her bunkhouse than she does about the business meeting ahead.

MANNY'S WAR

Excerpt from Trevor Vaquero's "Tales of my Father" Archive

Manny's accountant, Castor, told me this story when he came to visit my mom. This was about eight years after the Spacer War and about two hours after Castor drank a whole pitcher of Lupe's special margaritas that she made when Mom wanted to get a good price on something. He'd been lying on the lawn, staring at nothing when I asked him how our War started. I'm not totally sure he understood that I recorded him.

—*Trevor Vaquero*

The Spacer War started on a Wednesday, kid. It began, like most wars I guess, with a fight over money complicated by a fight over a woman. Relations between Spacers and Earthers had been strained, to say the least. The Spacers were whispering revolution, sure, but only whispering.

Manny the Maker, though, was pissed off.

You have to understand something, boy. Old Manny didn't get rich by inheriting his fat piles of loot. He made every dime he had by selling things. That man could sell icemakers to Eskimos. He could sell sandpaper in the Sahara Desert. He had a silver tongue and he loved nothing better than new gold in his pocket.

Which was good, because Manny sure wasn't going to get by on his looks. Even when he was in his prime, he looked like a bulldog on a bender.

Old Manny was the second richest man on Earth when he decided to leave it. He convinced the Americans to sell him their military orbital. It was the biggest orbital out there at the time, plated to the gills with armor and weapons and enough security features to fight off a whole fleet of aliens if they ever showed up. The time before the Worlder Wars were paranoid days indeed.

But the big stupid thing had been mostly useless during the Worlder Wars because they never could get the missile guidance systems working or something and then the US was strapped for cash and Manny always made it sound like you were getting such a bargain.

If he told me once, old Manny told me a thousand times, "The meek are going to inherit the Earth? They can have it. The rest of us are going into space."

He'd growl, chomping on a cigar like a pit bull on a mailman's shoe. We used to have these guys called mailmen, kid, and they... Oh, forget it.

I've heard that he had the American military convinced he wanted the orbital for scrap parts or to hang on the wall in his mansion or maybe even to fly off to Jupiter and never come back.

With the money he paid for it, they could have built themselves two more even bigger and more lethal military bases in the orbitals, but they never did because Manny greased enough palms in the American government to make sure any plans for more military bases in the sky were abandoned. Manny never missed a trick, except the one your old man played on him, kid.

Whatever those military types thought he was planning to do with it, they sure had plenty of time later to regret letting him have it. Before the ink was even wet on the deal, Manny moved himself and his entire empire up into that floating tank in the sky.

"You can have anything in this universe you want, Castor old buddy," Manny told me. "You just have to commit to it. You have to believe in it. And you have to spend way too much time explaining to every other jerkwad out there that if they get between you and what you want, you are going to wear their guts for garters."

Before elastic, they used to have these things called garters to hold up your socks, kid. Did you know that? The Ether is supposed to have every scrap of human knowledge right there just waiting to get absorbed into your synaptic processes, but no one seems to know anything any more, do they?

Anyway, Manny was a big believer in the power of belief. That's why I followed him up here. To live the good life and keep an eye on Manny's money.

Of course, Manny's gorgeous wife Helen insisted on going with us. There's a woman I never got tired of looking at, that's for sure. Back then anyway. The old girl has let herself go a little.

Helen was a big star back in the day, the darling of the Ether dramas and twenty years younger than Manny. At the time, I thought what everybody thought. That old frog-faced Manny had got himself a trophy wife and she thought that his money was pretty enough to make up for his face.

But later... let me get to that part in a minute.

Manny and Helen set up their castle in the sky and they let the Ether stations document every minute of it. Manny would look into the vid-screen with that million-dollar smile and tell everyone on Earth, "The place to be is up here in the heavens."

Within five years, there was a waiting list for the orbital colonies with over a hundred thousand names on it. And that was before they started airing tether tantrum games on the Ether and forming the Nullball League.

They couldn't build orbitals fast enough. Everyone wanted to live in the stars like Manny and his megababe. Of course, I moved up with Manny and Helen and had a front row seat to the whole carnival.

There were tech millionaires who telecommuted and leper colonies and religious fanatics and that crazy Ark hippy colony and all the miners and even a fat farm that specialized in low gravity weight loss, if you can believe it. All of them trying to get away from the ugliness of Earth and hoping for someplace new to start over.

"And all them are crazy," Manny would laugh. "Well, that's all right with me. There comes a point in life when you realize that the fight for sanity is a losing battle. My own energies are better spent enjoying the benefits of megalomania."

If anyone was better adjusted to a wicked case of megalomania than Manny, I never met them.

Then the Worlder Wars started and the orbitals were left to fend for themselves as best they could. A lot of them didn't.

So many people died.

Those of us that were left were understandably less than enthusiastic about the Earthers who abandoned us.

Eventually the Earth ran out of oil and after a while they figured out that if there was no more oil, there was no point in fighting over it. It took them longer than you might think. They are still down there bickering over who actually won, if you can believe it, kid. Fortunately they are still too broke to do anything more than throw dirt at each other. Damned Earthers.

As soon as they got regular transport ships running again, Helen went down to her old Earth hometown to visit her parents for the first time in six years. The Ether news was overjoyed to be able to again cover every breath taken by their favorite golden girl. They documented her bumpy trip to America and her tearful reunion with her family. They also documented the American police throwing her in jail.

It seems America still considered Manny a citizen, a citizen who owed them a fat pile of tax money that he hadn't paid in the last five years.

They sent him a bill.

Manny sent them a video clip of himself using the bill to do something very rude.

So they arrested Helen.

The history archives typically refer to this as a "diplomatically poor choice," because Manny totally flipped out. I mean, bug nuts, kid. He raged on every electron of the Ether against the government that kidnapped his wife.

Manny swore, "I will not rest! I will not stop until my wife is returned! I will use every last cent of my mountains of money, every last person in my army of employees and every missile on my huge frickin' flying armored arsenal to see my wife home where she belongs! And God help her kidnappers if one hair on her head is harmed."

Meanwhile, some enterprising Ether journalist got herself arrested just so she could smuggle out a video of the lovely Helen looking stunningly tragic in a jail cell, tearfully looking into the hidden camera and saying, "Oh, I just hope nothing bad happens to my dear husband and my sweet cockapoodle before I can get home to them. Manny's health is delicate and CooCoo's digestion is fragile. They need me."

Not that anything about Manny was ever delicate and that stupid cockapoodle is still alive. It gnaws on my ankle every chance it gets. I'm sure the Americans spent plenty of time wishing Manny was anything other than the big healthy ox that he is to this day.

But with that drippy interview played back-to-back every fifteen minutes against Manny's frothing rants about the tyranny of Earthers, how could it not be a call-to-arms for every able body in the colonies? They were all still in love with the Helen they'd followed into space.

Now, kid, I know your mom was not a supporter of the Spacer War. There were plenty that weren't at the start, although most threw in eventually. I remember she was pretty dead set against your dad going off to fight. He told me once that she had some pretty strong words to say on the subject. He seemed fairly certain she didn't want him back afterwards. Maybe that's why he never came home? None of my business, I know.

Even with the sky spinning like it is right now on account of those margaritas I drank, I know she wouldn't want me telling you all this, so for the sake of my hide, please keep this story to yourself. I came here to negotiate with her for fertilizer and steaks and Manny will have my head if I don't deliver.

At first, it seemed like a fight between Manny and America would get settled pretty quickly. How could America, sucked dry by the Worlder Wars, as they now call them, compete with Manny and his flying battle station in the sky?

"We declare ourselves to be free colonies, a nation of anarchists, a law unto ourselves," Manny shouted into the Ether. "We will be beholden to no country or corporation, only to our own free will and our ability to carve a life out of hard vacuum."

Those were heady days.

You wouldn't mind fetching me a glass of water, would you, kid? That's fantastic. Thanks, boy.

Of course, the rest of the Earthers were willing to tear the planet apart in the Worlder Wars and they were willing to sit back and laugh at America's troubles with Manny. When it came to an orbital uprising, though, all those countries were quick to agree that our bid for freedom must be stopped.

They weren't quick enough.

The Spacers spent years thinking about how to stay out of the Earthers' way when they were on the warpath. One of the Russian research bases came up with a way for the colonists to disrupt all the satellites so the

Earthers couldn't even report the weather down there, much less have a look into the skies.

About five minutes after they declared independence, every orbital that could moved itself out of missile range, just in case the Earthers figured out how to launch a missile without using their satellites. Which they did eventually.

Almost got us with that. They would have creamed your little world if your dad hadn't done his thing, that's for sure.

Honestly?

We thought the Earthers wouldn't care what we did. We thought we'd declare independence, there'd be a month or two of fussing from down below and then they'd give up and decide we weren't worth the effort.

We just weren't prepared for the ferocity of their response. We also thought they didn't have the attention span to keep up a blockade for two months, much less five years.

We weren't totally wrong. The Earthers lobbed nukes and missiles and even a few neutrino guns at us before they gave up and just decided on a blockade. They figured that we'd eventually get hungry enough to mind our manners.

Over the five years of Spacer War, America sent up a few troop ships and what happened with them, you wouldn't believe. I'd tell you but I'll probably throw up if I start on that bloody saga and then your mother will definitely yell at me.

Anyway, we Spacers were all starting to get a little worried, you know? Down to eating our shoelaces because we'd already gobbled up the rats. Then the Americans started making noises, like they invented a longer-range nuke that could pick off the bigger colonies no matter how far out we parked them.

That's why we were so thrilled when that deep space mining expedition returned. It took them years but those insane Hathor miners went out and found huge chunks of rock and water. Water! There was rejoicing all over the sky about the water. They saved our bacon with that one.

Of course, Manny only had eyes for the huge chunk of plutonium ore they hauled back. They filled an entire mining ship full of it, one of the biggest starships ever built. That thing was the size of New York. No, that doesn't mean anything to you, does it, kid? It was bigger than this whole Ithaca colony. And after we found out how much plutonium that sucker had it in, there was no shutting Manny up about that rock.

I got so sick of hearing him go on and on about all the weapons we were gonna make and how Manny was gonna serve those Earthers up some of their own medicine.

And then I will be damned if your dad doesn't go and lob the entire ship full of plutonium rock right at the planet!

Not only does he kill all Manny's war machine dreams, but he ends the War doing it!

If Manny could have turned green with envy, he would have, kid. It's probably a good thing your dad disappeared right after the War, because I'm pretty sure Manny hired out a hit squad to find the runty little upstart that hijacked his war and stole all the glory.

Not that old Manny wasn't right on the Ether afterwards telling the Earthers that he never would have condoned such an atrocity, even if they did sort of ask for it by saying they were going to make an example of your dad's home colony. Oh, Manny wept for poor flattened Mexico on the vidscreen, but what really chapped his hide was that he didn't think of it first.

I guess you saw the touching drama that was Helen's homecoming right? The Queen of the Skies is released from her prison and flies back to her warty king and they have a wonderful romantic reunion?

No one ever gives Helen credit for her acting abilities, but that was pure fiction from the first close-up to the last elegant tearful smooch, kid. She was totally pissed off at Manny and for the first time in his life, the poor guy didn't deserve it!

Helen never would believe that he had nothing to do with lobbing the spaceship down at Mexico while she was in prison in Louisiana. She's just smart enough to know that it's not like you can aim a rock the size of New York and that nuclear bomb of a ship could just have easily landed on her. No, Helen has never forgiven poor old Manny for almost squashing her to death and she's been giving him merry hell ever since.

Now, if you'll excuse me, I need to go sit down and put my head in a toilet. I wish we still had proper toilets, not these uncomfortable gizmos they got to conserve water, but a nice cool, white toilet.

Someday, kid, when you're older, you come visit Manny and me. I will show you a toilet the way God intended toilets to be and if you leave your mom at home, I'll make sure you drink enough liquor to truly appreciate a real toilet.

Please don't tell your mom I talked to you at all, actually.

CHAPTER SEVEN

A few weeks later, Cesar and Trevor walk back from town alongside the little mule as it pulls its cart. They have walked in silence for a whole five minutes, but Cesar knows it's too good to last.

The boy is itching to ask him about his dad. Every chance Trevor gets, he asks for stories about his dad. At first, this was fine by Cesar, as he dearly loved to tell tales, especially daring adventures where the hero says something clever after foiling the bad guy and then he manfully folds a damsel under his bulging bicep. With so many years drifting in space and so little access to the Ether or other entertainments, he's told plenty of tales.

True stories, however, are an entirely different matter he's discovered. True stories about himself are not part of his normal repertoire. Cesar wants his son to know more about him and he's thrilled to find Trevor so interested. He thought it would be easy to spin yarns of his actual adventures, just from the point of view of someone else.

He was wrong.

Cesar found it deeply unsettling to talk about himself in the third person.

Worse, Cesar didn't know how to describe himself. He doesn't want Trevor to think he's a villain or an idiot, but he also doesn't want the boy going out and trying any of the fool things he did. It is equally bizarre to talk about himself as a hero or glorify his actions. Most of the time, Cesar ends up telling the story baldly, stating the facts and trying to leave the whys and wherefores out of it.

And then there are the stories themselves—gory, ugly, depressing, bawdy, gross. None of his adventures in the past fifteen years seem like good topics for a teenage boy and Cesar can't yet think of Trevor as a young man.

It's just too much.

He's almost been avoiding the boy for the last few days, but he couldn't refuse Trevor's request for company into town today to pick up supplies.

Hoping to avoid the inevitable for a few more minutes, Cesar asks, "Who won the Spacerbase game last night?"

Spacerbase is a game much played by kids growing up in orbitals. It's basically full-contact capture-the-flag in high gravity. Cesar knows Trevor went to play with some other kids down in the Ag Level. Technically, the Ag Level on Ithaca isn't really high gravity enough to count, but having played down there at least a thousand times himself, Cesar knows it is still fun.

"My team lost," Trevor tells him. "The other guys had three cousins visiting from New Siberia and that's a really high-grav colony. They creamed us. It was a bloodbath."

Kids from high-gravity colonies love beating the pants off their contemporaries in less harsh environments. Trevor has been through this before and is unfazed.

The boy enthusiastically describes how one of the off-worlder cousins scored a point by grabbing Trevor's head and using it as a springboard to the base. Cesar chuckles until Trevor returned to his favorite topic.

"Did my dad ever play Spacerbase?" asks Trevor, but Cesar is ready for this one.

"Of course he did," Cesar says. "Everybody plays Spacerbase."

"What about tether tantrum?" asks Trevor.

Tether tantrum is played in the null or low gravity parts of the colony. In Ithaca, this is one of the huge cargo bays in the large central tube that the rest of the colony rotates around.

It took the first orbital colonists very little time before they realized they needed to improve their spacesuits with tethers with magnetized latches that they could use to cast out and secure themselves and then unlatch when they needed. It took the kids in the colonies even less time to come up with fast and dangerous games to play with those tethers.

Tether tantrum is like dodgeball in null gravity with tethers. So once the balls are thrown, they keep ricocheting throughout the cargo bay until they hit someone or are caught up in a net. When there are twenty or thirty balls flying around with an equal number of players spinning themselves through the room on tethers, it can't be anything but perilous and a whole lot of fun.

Cesar broke three fingers playing tether tantrum once and he tells Trevor so, rubbing them at the memory.

"What about Nullball?" asks Trevor.

Cesar exhales slowly. "Well kid, he wasn't exactly a Nullball League superstar, but I think your dad told me that he played on the Ithaca team for a while before he left for the war. Then I think he played for a season in the minors, the Local L4 Lagrange League for the Hedonia colony team, I think he said. But they weren't great teams or anything."

Trevor only hears that his dad was a Nullball star and cries, "I knew it! I'm not great, but I practice Nullball every chance I get so I think I'll probably get on Ithaca's team. It's not like there's a *whole* lot of competition, but still it's pretty nifty. That's if I stay."

Cesar tells the boy that Nullball is not a bad way to spend his time and they talk for a bit about this year's upcoming Nullball League Playoff Tournament. Since it will be held at Ithaca this year, this is a subject of much discussion at the ranch. Ithaca's team is strong but the Hathor Mining team is the favorite and Manny's Mighties are also heavy contenders.

Regardless, Ithaca is determined to impress the rest of the colonies with the shininess of their orbital. They've all been cleaning and replacing lights and mirrors for weeks. Work finished, now they are just waiting for the games to begin.

That conversation peters out and they walk in silence for exactly ten seconds before Trevor asks, "Did you and my dad ever visit the Rasta Nation?"

"No, those Rasta guys kept themselves pretty quiet. Didn't allow any visitors into that old research station they took over until just a few years ago and by then your dad was out of the loop."

"Where was he?" Trevor wants to know.

Cesar replies after a pause, "I'm not really sure."

Short answers never slow Trevor down. "Did you meet any Rastas during the War?"

Cesar sighs, "No, kid, those Rasta guys refused to take part in the War for religious reasons so I never met any of them during the fighting."

"Oh!" cries Trevor, scandalized.

Cesar explains, "A few of the orbitals refused to take part. Most of them didn't have weapons more powerful than sharpened spoons to throw at the enemy, so it didn't make too much of a difference, but there was some bad blood after the war. Rasta Nation at least would take in refugees from colonies that were hit hard."

Cesar watches Trevor fidget out of the corner of his eye and sighs again. The boy won't give up until he gets a tale so Cesar decides to tell him one. To attempt it anyway.

"We did visit the Poppy Ship. It was really a small colony, but they called it a ship. Before the War, they produced medicines."

Trevor pipes up, "So you knew him before the War, too?"

Cesar shakes his head, trying to get his stories and lies straight. "No, I don't think so. I think we met during the War. I, uh, took a couple hard knocks to the head so my memory isn't great, if you want to know the truth."

Trevor's face takes on the vaguely sympathetic look that teenagers get when someone tells them something tragic that they don't really understand.

"Oh," he says somberly.

Cesar continues, "This time we went to the Poppy Ship was about a year after the War. Your dad was finally healed up from all the hits he took in combat. He started a small trading business with a ship he was able to fix up and the men from his platoon."

Here Cesar pauses, struggles with himself for a minute and then confesses, "Alright, so really it was more in the way of a smuggling business. Your Dad was running black market items to and from Earth."

"Oh," says Trevor, digesting that fact. "But I thought the war was over? How could there still be smuggling after the blockade ended?"

"Well, there's winning and there's winning, as it turns out," Cesar replies, still a little bitter after all these years.

"Plenty of places on Earth were still pretty angry, so plenty of ports were closed. There were others places that weren't officially closed, but Spacers would be gunned down or thrown in some dank prison the minute they popped the airlocks. We learned which was which pretty quick."

"Wow," breathes Trevor. "And my dad's men still wanted to follow him into danger after the War?"

Cesar nods.

The kid makes it sound almost heroic, but at the time it seemed normal.

Those who hadn't headed home would want some employment and he should find it for them. Cesar mutters, "Well, yes. You spend enough years working with someone on the art of not dying and you form some strong friendships."

"Because my dad was a commander," says Trevor, puffing his chest out. "You followed him too? And you snuck in and out under the Earthers' noses going wherever you wanted regardless of the law? Wow!"

"It wasn't glamorous or anything," Cesar protests quickly. "Weeks of boring coasting so they wouldn't pick up your heat signal followed by a few days trying not to attract too much attention buying up all the oranges in town or whatever. Half the time nobody really cared, so we were taken by surprise when some hothead started taking potshots at our ride and we had to make a run for it. And then you make it back and the goons that sent you out want to haggle you down to half the price you agreed on because the fruit has a few bruises."

"Huh," says Trevor, but Cesar can see the boy doesn't quite believe how boring and uncomfortable smuggling was.

Cesar says blandly, "Most of the time we were stuck eating protein bars, when we could get them, and chicken-little when we couldn't."

Trevor wrinkled his nose. "No way," he says, looking at Cesar to see if he is playing a joke.

"Nope," Cesar replies with relish after seeing the disgusted look on the boy's face. "Chicken-little is the main food source for smugglers. You can't eat the food you're smuggling. Too valuable. You ever eat chicken-little, kid?"

"Once," gulps Trevor, looking a little green at the memory. "My mom made me because I wouldn't eat my vegetables. She said I needed to know how lucky I was to have vegetables."

Chicken-little is a bioengineered protein source that, at one time long in the past, was a chicken. If you dig around in the box, you find what is left of its digestive tract and maybe an eye and sometimes a beak.

If you poke it, it twitches and quivers. Cutting off a chunk to eat is not an appetizing experience. In theory, you don't have to cook it because no bacteria will grow on a chicken-little.

Technically, you can survive eating nothing but chicken-little for months, but most people agree that a life like that wouldn't be worth living. It comes in a box and requires only occasional water to regenerate for decades. Most Spacers would rather eat their boots than choke down a serving of chicken-little. It's banned in eight countries down on the Earth.

Cesar replies, "Your dad ate more than his fair share of chicken-little in the War and after. It puts hair on your chest. You don't want to let it touch your skin too much, though. Always gave me a rash."

"Wow," Trevor says again. Then he shakes his head and returns to what, for him, is the important point of the story. "You guys were smugglers? That's so cool!"

Cesar's heart lifts, watching the wiry boy grin gleefully, but clearly this is not the impression he was hoping to make on the boy.

"So we heard about the Poppy Ship and wanted to check it out," Cesar says loudly. "We heard they had been making medicines before the war. Nice boring medicines that healed sick people."

Trevor seems to surface from whatever smuggling daydream he has been swimming in, so Cesar goes on in a milder voice. "They'd been out of touch for a while. We thought if they were still alive and making medicine, we could help them get their stuff out. Trade it for goods and all. Plenty of orbitals were desperate for quality meds."

Trevor grins, "And if they all died, there's probably be a goldmine of medicines left for you to scavenge!"

"Yeah, I guess you're right," Cesar admits, looking at his feet. That was something he'd thought of, too. Trevor is so much like him that sometimes it's downright creepy.

Running a hand through his hair, Cesar says quickly, "But we were hoping they were all alive. Because you always hope for live people instead of bodies to scavenge, even if it means more money."

He looks so sanctimonious that Trevor wipes the grin off his face and nods solemnly.

"At any rate, they were alive, but they weren't so much into making medicines any more," Cesar says, thinking it was time to focus on the story and wondering how to frame this next part. "Or at least, they had decided to focus on just one kind of medicine."

"What do you mean?" asks Trevor.

•

It took Cesar much longer than he planned to find the Poppy Ship. It had wandered pretty far off its course. The truth of the matter was that at some point during the war, the Poppy Ship's chief engineer died of a heart attack and, as far as Cesar was ever able to discover, got replaced by a total moron. When Cesar located the ship, it was slowly drifting off into void space. Not that the people on the ship cared. Not that they noticed.

When Cesar popped his airlock and stepped out, he'd expected a pristine hospital ship with lots of clean people in white lab coats bustling down well lit and clearly labeled hallways. As he looked around, it was clear that at one point he might have found that scene, but that was a long time ago. It was hazy and dim and the air tasted faintly oily. Low mellow music piped thinly through the halls.

"Boys, go check it out," Cesar barked without looking at his crew.

His two best scouts, Dino and Perry, went bolting down a hallway. Cesar turned on his heel and walked back into his ship. He had the rest of the crew repaneling the exhaust shielding and cleaning up the kitchen when the two scouts came rushing back.

"Captain, you won't believe this place!" said Dino, a grinning ex-soldier. Even though he was only few years younger than Cesar, Dino somehow seemed barely old enough to grow a beard, which he occasionally did until someone forced him to shave off the pathetic thing.

"These folks have been sampling their own product, sir," barked the older scout, Perry, as he limped up behind Dino, wheezing slightly.

"That leg still bothering you, Perry?" Cesar asked the man.

Perry shook his grizzled head and straightened up with an effort, "I'm fine, Captain. I think there's a few pieces of shrapnel still working their way out."

Cesar nodded. He did not believe for a second that Perry was fine, but what could he do?

"So they're still making meds?"

"With a will, sir," Perry said, coughing meaningfully. "Looks like mostly, uh, mood enhancers. And I doubt they have any left over to trade, if you know what I mean."

Cesar was catching the gist of it. Before the War, the main products of the Poppy Ship were opium-based painkillers.

"There's all these people in there running around in their underwear, smoking dope and listening to this really calming music," the Dino glee-fully announced to all within earshot.

Cesar arched an eyebrow.

This particular scout was like the human version of an adorable tiger cub, cute and wriggly with surprisingly sharp teeth. Discretion wasn't re-ally a word in the boy's vocabulary and Cesar wasn't exactly thrilled about the whole crew knowing they were in an opium den.

"You boys find somebody in charge?" Cesar asked curtly.

Perry nodded. "She's right behind us," he said, jerking a scarred thumb over his shoulder.

Two hours later, Cesar was trying to maintain his dignity as a Captain while squelching around on the floor on lumpy pillows, eating some sort of drippy rice dish with his fingers. He and a few of the crew were sitting in a large open room while many other people lounged on pillows around them, clad mainly in thin winding cloths and listening to a band play low, discordant music. The haze was thick here due to the number of pipes being passed around.

Cesar was trying to look casual and breathe mainly through his nose in a futile effort not to inhale so much smoke.

The woman in front of him folded herself into a serene lotus position, her long gray dreadlocks streaming down her back and her quite minimal clothing draped artfully around her. Cesar was beginning to doubt this woman was in charge or that anyone was really in charge here. She'd been lecturing him for the last half hour on the glorious enlightenment of the Poppy Ship, which she called the Flower of Hope.

As far as he could tell, the Poppy Ship started smoking their own prod-uct almost as soon as the War broke out and they stopped caring about much else since then. He sent out more of his crew to quietly scout around and they all confirmed this impression. This really didn't bother him.

Medical supplies would have been worth their weight in platinum, but pharmaceutical-grade opium was still worth its weight in gold and a doped-up colony wasn't likely to haggle too much over the price.

Cesar briefly entertained the idea of just taking a whole bunch of the stuff. It was unlikely that anyone here could stop them and quite likely no one would even notice. He sighed and discarded the thought. Repeat business would be lucrative if these people didn't let themselves die first.

Also, his Momma always told him stealing was wrong.

As the woman droned on, Cesar sighed and itched his latest radiation burn. Traveling the stars was a lot less romantic and a lot more uncomfortable than he had imagined.

He really wished the Poppy Ship would embrace the concept of deodorant. Cesar wondered why, of all the things he lost or injured during the War, he couldn't have lost his sense of smell? It brought him more grief than joy, traveling between so many different orbitals, experiencing their smells.

The minute he started feeling light-headed and dreamy, Cesar politely excused himself and commanded his crew back to the ship. Some of them looked ready to protest, but they'd seen that black look on the Captain's face before and they shuffled back to the ship without comment.

Once inside, Cesar sealed the door and gave orders not to cycle the ship's air with the colony. Then he barked a few orders, mainly concerned with confining the crew to the ship, before he shut himself in his cabin and dreamed opium-soaked dreams. It took a ridiculously long time over the next few days, but eventually Cesar located a few people on the Poppy Ship who seemed relatively sane and sober.

It took even longer to negotiate his way to a hull full of opiates and a treaty for regular shipments, but Cesar did it. He spent the entire time dragging his crew away from the delights the Poppy Ship offered and keeping them sober.

It was exhausting.

Truth be told, he was tempted to try the pipe himself, but a captain can't do these things and expect to maintain any kind of order.

Just as they were about to leave, his faithful old scout, Perry stood at attention in front of him. Perry cleared his throat and barked out, "Captain, I think I ought to stay here, sir. I think someone needs to stay behind and keep an eye on this place. I know my way around a colony engine. I'll make sure this old boat gets back to the Lagrange point safe and sound. Can't have a valuable colony like this just drifting off into the void."

Cesar considered this. He looked at thick, red scars running down Perry's injured arm and knew how far down the man's body those scars went. He thought about the limp in Perry's gait and the many times he'd woken up to find Perry walking the hallways, unable to sleep from pain.

Then he said, "That sounds like a fine idea. I need a man I can trust up here. Lord knows I'll have enough problems unloading this stuff."

Cesar clapped Perry on the shoulder to let the man know there was no ill will between them. He was rewarded with the clearest smile he'd ever gotten from the old scout.

Cesar felt a man had to make his own decisions and if what he wanted to do was dream away the pain of life for a while, then it was none of Cesar's business. In Perry's case, the man had more than his fair share of pain.

Cesar was feeling pretty good about that choice for exactly seventeen minutes before Dino scampered up dragging a girl behind him. She had long stringy brown hair and was only wearing what appeared to be several napkins tied around her scrawny frame. Dino himself had swapped his ship coveralls for a long piece of fabric that he'd wound around himself. He had strings of flowers and beads around his neck and ankles.

"Hey Captain!" shouted Dino, because the boy had no concept of volume control. "This is Petunia. We're in love! I'm gonna stay here and marry her and learn how to be a transcendental farmer!"

The Captain also considered this.

Dino gazed languorously at the girl who stared at nothing. They both smelled like they'd been rolling in opium and maybe they had. Dino reminded Cesar of what he thought his son might be some day. Cesar considered what he would do if his own boy wanted to make this choice.

"Mutiny!" roared Cesar. "Boy, how dare you try to shirk your responsibilities? And *where* are your clothes?"

Dino shrank back, bewildered. "Aw, but Captain…"

"No, Dino!" Cesar said in his most impressive Captain voice. "You signed up for a tour of duty, you serve out your term. There's no abandoning your post in the middle of a run. Get back on board this instant!"

"Captain, I'm a grown man! I can do what I want! I wanna stay here and you can't stop me," Dino shouted, grabbing the girl's hand and throwing out his chest.

Cesar was having none of it. He dragged Dino back to the ship by his ear while the Petunia girl trailed listlessly behind. Eventually, Dino stopped howling and Petunia wandered off. Back at the ship, he tossed Dino into his bunk.

"Tie that deserter to his bunk and let's get out of here!" growled Cesar. "And make a note to dock Dino's pay for the cost of his coveralls."

The rest of the crew snapped to it and the ship was flying away in record time.

Sitting in his chair and pretending to go over their planned flight pattern, Cesar wondered if he shouldn't have let the boy make his own mistakes. He knew that he had taken more crew on this expedition than he really needed because he was unable to turn away any of his men who needed a job. He could have spared Dino. But if Dino were his son, Cesar would have never let him set foot on the Poppy Ship.

•

"What do you mean?" asks Trevor again.

Cesar scratches his white beard and wonders how to tell it. "Well, a lot of things changed in the War and the people on the Poppy Ship were making pain killers and sometimes life gets to be a bit much, you see, so they started taking the pain killers. When we showed up, things were kind of weird. I'm sure it was like that here, too. Didn't things get a little weird after the War?"

Trevor shrugs. "The War ended when I was seven. I don't remember how things were before."

"Ah, that's true," allows Cesar as they plod along.

"So what happened on the Poppy Ship?" asks Trevor.

"Oh, nothing too much," says Cesar. "We bought some of their product and sold it somewhere else and made a little money doing it. We had a regular supply run there for a while. Your dad loved you like hell, you know? He talked about you some and I know he thought about you every single day of his life."

"Oh," says Trevor.

Cesar watches as several emotions flick across the teen's face. First there is surprise—that wasn't what he expected the old man walking next to him to say. Next, there is disappointment—he expected epic adventure not mushy parental love stuff. Following quickly after that, there is a rueful grin.

Trevor looks back at the old man, but Cesar has turned his head to study the horizon so Trevor won't see his smile. He has a strong temptation to reach out and ruffle the boy's hair, but he resists. They don't say another word for the rest of the journey.

That is, until the monster attacks.

CHAPTER EIGHT

Back at the ranch, Penelope is sexually frustrated. Or more precisely, she is frustrated because she doesn't want to keep thinking about sex, but somehow she can't stop today. She wants to think about fixing the heating system or finishing the contract for the New Siberia shipment or what she will wear tonight at her party.

Instead, Penelope is thinking about how long it's been since she's had sex. It's been a very long time.

"Surely the urge goes away eventually? How long does it take for the sex drive to die? What do nuns do about this?" Penelope sighs to herself as she oversees the food preparation for the gathering that happens here, without fail, every Friday night.

Usually, Penelope tries not to think about sex on the theory that if you don't think about it, eventually you'll forget about sex and be the happier for it. So far, fifteen years of practice has still not scratched that particular itch. Penelope finds this extremely vexing. And today she just can't keep it out of her mind. She sighs again as her mind is filled with a lurid fantasy involving a warm night in this kitchen with a big bowl of ice cream.

Lupe snaps, "Where's your head today?" as she pushes past Penelope with a large pan of smoked brisket.

"In the gutter," Penelope says, but she puts a bite in her tone to play it off as a joke. A humorless joke.

"Because that's how you could summarize my sex life," Penelope mutters to herself.

Before Lupe can ask her what she means, Penelope sweeps out the door, determined to find some labor so intense that she'll be too tired to think about anything, especially the state of her hormones. She gets as far as the nutrient capture filters on the water lines and spends a pleasant hour banging away on a dented valve with a sledgehammer before Ulixes shows up.

"Heard you could use some help," he shouts over the din she is making.

Penelope looks up into those warm brown eyes, deep and entrancing, looking at her with such caring. He leans forward and puts a gentle hand on her arm to stop her. Penelope can see his hard rippling muscles as the roughness of his calloused palm sends shivers up her arm. She is acutely aware of how rapidly he is improving since his illness. With a few extra pounds on him, he looks more and more like the kind of man she wouldn't mind…

"*Dios me odia,*" cries Penelope with disgust, moving away from him before she did something insane. She is so crazed by some sort of hormone disorder that she is actually getting in a tizzy over some stranger. What is wrong with her today?

Ulixes pulls his hand back as though he's been scalded. "If God hates you, then at least you can rest assured that you're not the only one," he says sourly. And then he chuckles and somehow that makes it all right.

"So, do you want to fix that pipe now or do you plan to go on breaking it, ma'am?" asks Ulixes politely.

Penelope looks at the hammer in her hand and then at the pipe in front of her. Her shoulders slump when she realizes that she really ought to drop the hammer and let Ulixes fix it.

She does, but Penelope hates letting men fix things for her. It is degrading. She ought to be able to do these things. Penelope sits down on the ground and contemplates her many failings while she watches Ulixes grapple the pipe with a large wrench he brought.

They don't speak until Ulixes rumbles, "So Lupe tells me the house will be full of your many suitors again tonight?"

There is a hint of amusement in his voice but also a question. Penelope knows the man has been too sick to notice the other parties in the past few weeks, so this will be the first one he really sees. Penelope waves her hands in the air to deny the word "suitors."

"Oh, that Lupe is wicked," she cries, dusting off her hands. "No, Mr.

Ulixes, they aren't my suitors. Please. Some of them would like to buy me out, sure, but most of them are here for social reasons. There's no real government in the colonies so it's important that we get together like this and talk. So we all know what's going on and can decide important issues together. I'm happy to be able to provide a place for us all to meet. And who turns down a good party with free food?"

This is Penelope's standard answer to questions about her parties, but it doesn't satisfy even herself tonight. She gets up and paces restlessly as she watches him work. Her mind turns over the situation with Wilhelm Asner from the Ex-Austrian Engineering Complex. She is not looking forward to spending time with him tonight. He is one of the men who really does want to have a relationship with her, if only for her fortune. Rejecting him without offending is difficult.

"So how did you decide to start giving these parties?" Ulixes asks, breaking into her inner monologue.

"Oh, gods, who knows?" she replies, throwing up her hands.

And then she decides to let her guard down for once and just tell the truth: "Well, all right, so couple years after the War, I started getting a few hints from men that I worked with. They seemed to think that my husband wasn't coming home and that I couldn't possibly run this ranch by myself so perhaps I ought to find myself a man or else sell out. Hike up my skirts and run back home to my parents."

Penelope snorts indignantly, "My husband disappeared and then my mother-in-law died. Soon after, my father-in-law became too sickly to manage the ranch, you see," she explains.

Ulixes hisses and she turns to look at him. He quickly flaps his thumb and sticks it in his mouth like he's just hit it. She arches an eyebrow at his carelessness but Penelope does not exactly have the handyman moral high ground right now, so she doesn't say anything.

Penelope pushes her hair out of her eyes and stretches her back. "All the men that could went off to the War, off course, so the whole colony was short-handed. That's when my cowgirls started showing up, looking for work. As you see, we get along just fine."

"A few men were very pushy," she continues, not noticing the sudden violence with which Ulixes is clamping the pipe. "I told them I was fine and I didn't want to sell or shack up with some man, but they didn't seem to believe me."

Her words come faster now. She doesn't bother to filter out the fear and worry of these past years.

"When all the men left Ithaca for the War, they took almost all the weapons. So here I was sitting on a goldmine of beef and manure with just a shotgun loaded with rock salt. Anybody who wanted could walk in and take the place and what could I do to stop them? What could I do to protect my son? I couldn't just throw these men out and have them ride back to attack when I least expected it. Sure, we have a bit of a militia now who might look into it if the Vaquero Ranch suddenly had a new owner, but we'd still be dead and decaying in the compost bins, so what good is that?"

Penelope kicks a pipe, but gently in case she breaks something else. As nice as it is to vent a little, she really needs to head back and get everything ready before her guests start arriving.

"So, you went for a bluff then?" asks Ulixes, finished with the pipe and gathering up his tools. "You start inviting all the men with guns over to keep an eye on each other? Because no man would stand for someone else getting the prize? You don't have to worry about defending yourself because you set all the foxes watching each other instead of trying to pick the biggest fox to defend the henhouse?" Ulixes looks at her with disbelief.

Penelope shrugs her shoulders. "Well, yes, I guess I did," she admits. "It's not a great plan, but it's been working for almost six years."

Ulixes laughs out loud and gives her a frankly admiring look.

"Lady," he chuckles. "That's pretty damn clever."

He looks for a minute like he might hug her and Penelope's breath catches just a little, but he just grabs his tools and marches off towards the ranch house.

She catches up with him and says, "But with all these attacks and threats and sabotage attempts on the colony lately, I don't know. I guess if I were smart, I'd sell and take Trevor somewhere safer."

The man walking next to her gives her a long look before replying, "Well, in my experience if we were all smarter, the world would be a lot duller. Besides, there's no place safer. The entire galaxy has nowhere that's really safe. Trust me."

"Hey, how did your trip into town with Trevor go?" Penelope asks, changing the subject. She wonders what it is about this man that makes her so twitchy. Catching her breath like a schoolgirl? It's ridiculous.

"All right," grunts Ulixes, taciturn again.

Then he says carefully, "The boy asks about his father. I don't want to tell him stories that would upset you, but I don't know…"

He trails off, but Penelope is sure she knows what the man is asking. "Oh, you mean all the whoring around my husband did?" she retorts.

His jaw drops, but she just chuckles, "Don't worry. You won't shock me. I've heard dozens of stories about women he got involved with, from one end of the sky to the other. A girl in every port, apparently."

Ulixes drops his tools, looking deeply shocked. He stammers, "No, ma'am, that is not what I meant at all. I just didn't know if it was all right to tell him…"

Penelope interrupts, "It's really no problem. Now, I'll thank you to keep the stories as clean as you can, but if Trevor must keep asking people about his dad then he's going to have to deal with learning what his father was really like. I sure wish I had bothered to ask a few more questions before I married the man."

She bites her lip after that last part. That is a little more truthful than she meant to be.

Ulixes cocks his head to the side, studying her as he picks up his tools. "Ma'am, I don't know any stories about your husband and other women. I was asking about whether you've been telling the boy his daddy was a hero or a villain. I don't want to confuse him or contradict you."

He fidgets for a minute and then continues, "I know your husband sure loved you as much as a man could love a woman. He always wished he were a better man for your sake. But I can see why you'd regret marrying him."

Then he murmurs, "He ran off and left you with all this and a kid to raise and never came back. It's unforgivable."

But he says it like it's a question.

Penelope clasps her hands, suddenly very uncomfortable in this conversation. She says briskly, "Well, does it really matter one way or another if he was faithful to me out there? He's either dead or never coming back, so who cares? To be honest, I barely remember him. Tell Trevor whatever you want."

She strides past him, the conversation over as far as she is concerned. Penelope reflects that the opposite is also true. If he is never coming back, then what does it matter if she is faithful or not? She is tempted to turn back to the man behind her, but she knows it is just her treacherous libido trying to get her into trouble today.

When she gets back to the main house, everyone is in a tizzy about Trevor's near-death experience with a charging platypig.

"What's all this?" asks Penelope loudly, interrupting a much-too-pleased-with-himself Trevor as he holds court from atop the kitchen table.

"I didn't do anything, Mom, I swear," grins Trevor. "This platypig just started charging and he was wicked vicious. I was a goner for sure. Mr. Ulixes here, well, he just popped it one in the snout. He says they got really sensitive snouts. Sent that old pig crying back to its master. Would have ripped my leg off, Mom."

Trevor nods solemnly while a few of the younger cowgirls sighed with admiration. Penelope snorts skeptically, giving Ulixes her best stink-eye for not mentioning this little escapade earlier. He looks embarrassed.

"Oh, well, Mr. Trevor may be exaggerating," mutters Ulixes in the kind of thick drawl that Penelope has only heard from other Ithacans or true Texans. She reminds herself to ask the man where he's from the next time she gets a chance.

"Seems a man was bringing a platypig from someplace swampy to show you," Ulixes says. "I talked to the man who brought it. He said you showed him a dillo-bear the last time he was here and that's what gave him the idea. The platypig thing was running loose and getting all riled up. It took an unreasonable dislike to Mr. Trevor here and, well, in my experience, getting punched in the nose brings everybody up short. That's all."

Penelope gives another "Humph!" and looks at her son.

Trevor widens those big brown eyes of his. "Honest, Mom. He saved my life. It was bigger than a bull and it has poisonous quills," he says earnestly.

"Huh," says Penelope.

Ulixes coughs, "The man said the creature's poisonous quills had been removed, but it does have plenty of claws and teeth and it was awfully angry. I think I'll go see about that heater out back, if you don't mind? Argos said it needed some attention before tonight."

He shuffles off before Penelope can thank him for helping her son. She hugs her boy and then claps her hands, "What are you all thinking, lollygagging around like this? Get a move on! We'll have company here in less than an hour and I need this place to sparkle tonight!"

ESCAPE FROM HEDONIA

Excerpt from Trevor Vaquero's "Tales of my Father" Archive

A tall Asian woman told this story to me. She came up to me in town, stared at me for a minute and told me I was Cesar Vaquero's son. Then she let me record this tale before she disappeared.

—*Trevor Vaquero*

I t is important that you hear some truths about your father, O son of Cesar. It is good you keep these records. There is much about your father that lends itself to legends, but among all the souls in sky, you must know Cesar Vaquero for the man he truly was.

Who am I?

Names are of such monumental insignificance, child. Your father had a most unusual sense of humor. He used to call me "Athena" when he was feeling fanciful, but it's just a string of letters, like all other names. These days, people most often call me "Asia."

I am sure you have heard many far flung tales. The inhabitants of London blow that laser raid all out of proportion. They hardly ever used that bridge, anyway. I know for a fact that your father never did more than shake the hand of that girl on New Siberia who claims to have born his triplet love children. And our involvement in the uprising on Alpha Seti Six was very minor, no matter what the history archives say. That footage was doctored.

You see, Mr. Trevor, I flew with your father, the Captain, on a tinker ship many years after meeting him in the Spacer War.

No, he was not my Captain in the Spacer War.

I was actually fighting against him during the Spacer War and he bested me without ever being aware of my existence. If he had not, the War would have ended in a very different manner, but that is another story.

For years, it was apparent to me that your father was flying as fast and as far as he could from the demons of his youth, whatever they were. I believe he felt he had wronged you and your mother, but he did not confide in me and I do not like conjecture.

About three years ago, he appeared to undergo a change of heart after losing a ship near the Lazar House colony. He spent quite a bit of time building that ship, stocking it with a fortune in weapons. This was just after the uprising on Alpha Seti Six where we lost track of Mike, a dear friend, a good soldier and almost certainly dead. Your father took it very hard and his thoughts turned to those he cherished most… you and your mother.

Please excuse me. I do not make it a practice to think of the past. I have just learned that he has still not returned to this colony. I owe him so much I cannot repay. When I heard you were collecting stories about your father, I became snared by the allure of discharging a small portion of that debt.

So I have come to tell you a story. Please forgive my manner. Telling secrets is not in my nature.

To resume, your father determined to return himself to this colony, but he did not wish to come home empty-handed and we had nothing of value at the time. When he heard there was work on Hedonia, Captain decided to go. I followed, hoping to discharge my blood debt.

I must be indiscreet, but it is important for you to understand that your father and I were never lovers. Some have mistakenly assumed we were because we traveled so much together, but those were not the roles we chose to play.

We went to Hedonia to try our luck as grunts. I attempted to discourage him from menial labor in favor of returning to tinkering, a lifestyle that was more suitable to both our talents, but he declared himself through with the life of a small-scale merchant. He felt his curse made it a fool's errand.

Captain felt he had bad luck, you see. He thought it was a punishment for his actions at the end of the Spacer War. I am sure you have heard about that. They call him Cesar the Scorcher. He felt he deserved all the punishment the world had to offer, but it always seemed to me that he was the luckiest man alive.

The heavens poured their blessings on him. It was just that he gave them all away. I could easily spend the rest of my days naming the lives he saved, but he never saw that. He only saw failures.

So we arrived at New Hedonia and took up work. A charismatic woman named Seersee led a small religious group, truly a cult of personality, to recolonize Hedonia. She was the leader at New Hedonia and her word was law. She preferred to call the colony "Temperance," though outsiders referred to it as New Hedonia.

Her followers saw Seersee as the second coming of Jesus Christ, uncorrupted by the years of Earther influence. It was a bizarre viewpoint, to say the least, but I've seen smarter people do far stupider things in my travels.

Now, let me tell you about Hedonia.

Before the War, Hedonia was a rich man's playground, a high-tech fat farm. People came to eat and drink and make merry and get as fat as a hippopotamus with a thyroid problem. When they were too large to walk or clean themselves, robots intervened to keep them alive. The man who originally commissioned the orbital actually died from overeating, not long after the Spacer War started. His lungs collapsed under the weight of his own bulk, despite keeping the gravity in Hedonia much lower to accommodate the obese colonists.

It was always twilight on Hedonia's habitation level, the hour of possibilities. The agricultural level was totally given over to rare delicacies. What they could not grow, they imported and the cost be damned.

Their orders for pillows and sheets and enormous togas kept the Satsuma Silk Colony afloat in the early days. Vegan Vineyard Colony could have sold Hedonia every drop they made and they would still need more wine. This sort of indulgence is not to my own tastes, but before the War there were many interesting experimental societies built around various concepts of nirvana. To my knowledge, Rasta Nation is the only one to have survived with its original precepts intact.

Not surprisingly, the Hedonians didn't make it through the War. Until it was recolonized, most Spacers assumed Earther military had, at some point, attacked Hedonia and killed all the inhabitants. The new Hedonia colonists found that, in fact, an EMP bomb hit the orbital's hull. The original colonists either drank themselves to death or died in their own filth after their robots broke down.

During the war, China and America had launched millions of the EMP bombs to disrupt Spacers' electrical devices in much the same way land mines are sown in the soil of Earth.

Even today, an unsuspected shuttle will run into one or an old EMP bomb will drift into the side of an orbital and go off. Then they'll be lucky if they don't lose lives or at least significant portions of their non-essential electric systems. Fortunately, most orbitals are equipped with life support systems hardened against the radiation of space, but no one wants to take a chance that radiation hardening will fail to protect them from an EMP bomb. This is one reason is why the junker ships and their endless cleansing sweeps of the Spacer's spheres are vital.

One of the jobs we had on New Hedonia was cleaning up the overindulged dead. However, I quickly negotiated a place for us with the hunters on the Ag Level. It seemed that a parting gift from the original epicureans were roaming packs of tigers, lions and bears.

We never did find out why they wanted to keep predators. The EMP bomb wiped any logs the departed sensualists might have left, if they even bothered. Most of the new colonists thought the dead Hedonians fought the animals against each other to bet on the winner.

I assumed they took a perverse pleasure in eating the creatures. On hunts, the Captain liked to sing a nonsense rhyme about "Lions and Tigers and Bears, Oh My!" He never would explain the obvious amusement he derived from that song.

Hunter duty was one of the better positions for grunts on New Hedonia. Grunts who answered the call for workers were housed in the lowest of accommodations and fed discarded yeast vat growth while the new colonists brought the food manuvats back online. It was not palatable.

However, on hunter duty in the Ag level, you regularly walked through treasure troves of delicacies no longer available on Earth.

While I do not subscribe to overeating and I highly recommend that you avoid it as well, I could spend a lifetime among their mushroom farms. The fungus had run wild and crossbred. The delights I used to be able to scoop up with one hand were truly succulent. And the smell of the jasmine fields alone were enough to transport you to a higher plane of existence.

Whatever other degradations and misfortunes we suffered there, a part of me yearns to return to that idyllic pasture and drink tea among the wild fungus and hear again the growls of carnivores thirsting for my heart's blood.

Within two months, we had distinguished ourselves as being capable people who were best used to the fullest of our capabilities. This is why you must find friends and a partner as you travel the skies, young man. Life is infinitely easier if you band together with others who are as smart and capable as yourself. It is very important, however, to choose your companions wisely. Only allow those who lift you up to attach themselves to you.

You will forgive my impertinence, but you have your father's spark. It is immediately apparent. People will be drawn to you. They will see your ability and your success and seek to bind you to them, to use you for their own benefit. You must be very careful to choose those who do not drain your energies but instead replenish them.

As your father often said, "If you got their back, make sure they got yours or you'll get your ass shot off."

At any rate, your father caught the eye of Seersee herself and she elevated him to chief engineer of the life support systems. Captain immediately named me his second-in-command over her vehement objections.

I assumed it was the typical Caucasian fear of Asians. If you have studied your history, you know that China won the Economy War over a hundred years ago. Although the Worlder Wars and then the Spacer War largely negated the victory, the fear still persists. I do not take it personally, even when they make it a personal attack.

We were comfortable and making a more than adequate amount of money. Captain and I had enough knowledge of Spacer life support systems to get this one running at optimal conditions quite quickly. We were lucky that the original Hedonians had spared themselves no expense on the construction of this vessel.

It was obvious from the design that they wanted a system that needed very little management. Thus, life support and the Ag Level had continued to run relatively smoothly for the years the orbital lay devoid of human life.

We did very well there for several months. Seersee continued to esteem your father and give him access to luxuries that the rest of the colonists did not see. It was not until almost too late that I perceived her interest was more than just professional respect.

I was using my off-work hours to engage in a leisurely perusal of the Hedonia genetic database. I've always been interested in charting transposon drift in closed genetic pools. I believe I have an algorithm to accurately map the effects, but that is just my little hobby.

Your father came to me and said, "Asia, we've got to blow this joint."

One of the things I've always appreciated in a man is the ability to come to a succinct point. As I had not spoken to him in a few weeks, I was unclear whether he desired to leave or to demolish the orbital with explosives.

I awaited an explanation.

"These religious colonists are barking mad," said Captain, scanning our surroundings for those who might overhear us.

Then he looked embarrassed and muttered, "And it turns out their great leader, Seersee, seems to have the hots for me and I'm running out of ways to put her off."

I nodded.

I observed previously that the Captain has, on occasion, attracted the notice of women who see him as a potential sexual conquest. I do not pretend to know whether your father was sexually faithful to your mother. Captain certainly had many opportunities for extramarital conjugal interactions. If he did not feel he would be allowed to return to your family, I cannot imagine what would keep him from seeking comfort of that kind, if he so chose. Unless, of course, he loved your mother enough to remain faithful to her despite the probability that he would never see her again. That is the sort of wildly illogical thing Captain would do, on occasion.

I do know that he did not wish to become intimate with this Seersee woman.

"She's totally insane and not in the fun way," Captain hissed. "I wouldn't let anything I wanted to keep near her nethers. I'm pretty sure hers has teeth."

Those were, I believe, his exact words.

I took his point immediately. In the past few weeks, it was easy to see that the social harmony of New Hedonia was amiss and not a fertile ground for enlightened self-interest. Also, all the women I had met were rather aggressively heterosexual and that was not to my tastes either. Thus I was happy to leave.

We had accumulated enough wealth to purchase a shuttle ticket off New Hedonia and live fairly comfortably for a few months if we were not excessive. Originally, Captain wanted to have something a bit more substantial before returning to Ithaca, but by then he was so sick with longing for his home that he was ready to pull on a voidsuit and swim for it, if that's what it took.

The difficulty was that the shuttles did not come to New Hedonia anymore. All outbound flights stopped a few weeks prior. We heard conflicting stories as to why.

The New Hedonians said there was a problem with the shuttle company and they needed all outbound ships for important colony transport. The grunts said it was because they weren't letting anybody out.

I acted as an unofficial medical advisor to the grunts on New Hedonia since the leaders of the colony did not feel grunts merited access to medical attention, any more than they deserved access to clean water, warm living quarters or fresh food. Thus, the other grunts kept me apprised of conditions throughout the colony.

While we lived fairly well, we were apparently among the few that did. Seersee was very persistent in her attempts to convert all those on New Hedonia to her religion. Those that did not were treated even more poorly than those that did.

There were many who had joined the Temperance cult that also wanted to leave. They had been promised a Utopia of simple living. Instead, they received long work hours and cramped quarters while Seersee and her friends frolicked among the truffle fields and swam in the river of chocolate. It was the typical abuse of power seen during the unraveling of personality cults.

If you have not studied such social dynamics, let me simply recommend that if you should find yourself in a similar situation, try to get out quickly. You don't want to be around for the downfall of a religious figure.

However brief the bloodbath, it is best to be absent when the bullets start flying.

Once I explained to the Captain the current situation within the colony, he set his jaw and got that steely look in his eye. I had seen that look before.

"We have to get out," he said.

"Exactly."

"We can put together a ship easily enough if we bribe a few people to look the other way while we get it together and leave," Captain said.

"The bribes have already been paid."

"We cannot leave these people here to suffer at the hands of that tyrant woman."

"Wait, what?" By my tally, the number of people wanting to leave this vessel was probably in the realm of four hundred. To sneak ourselves out would be the work of a few days. A mass exodus would be impossible and probably get us killed.

"We can't sneak that many out," I told him.

Captain held a hand up, majestically silencing all objections. "We cannot leave these people here to slowly starve to death in the cold, watching their children sicken without care. They came looking for a better life. The Earth may have no pity, but Spacers must be better than that. We need to find a way to get them out."

Perhaps I am paraphrasing. It has been many years. Now, it is in times like these that it is very important to have a thorough understanding of who you are, my child.

Your father was a brilliant man and a leader, but the flawless execution of a truly clever plan has always been my specialty and my passion. I am the type of person who gets things done. Your father was the type of person who decided what needed to be done. Accordingly, I followed your father.

Captain decided we needed to get four hundred grunts and ourselves off an orbital full of hostile religious fanatics?

My job was to get it done.

I explained my plan to Captain and the grunts.

It took me three days.

"The gods are punishing the arrogance of Seersee," screamed the grunts on the first day as a dozen tiny tornados ripped through the jasmine fields, splattering the delicate blossoms across the *foie gras* geese before ripping their cages apart and sending them whirling into the walls.

"God is punishing us for our lack of faith. We must let Cesar and his unbeliever grunts go and return to the true faith," cried the New Hedonia followers of Seersee on the second day, when a scorching heat destroyed the lotus blossoms before they could be stuffed with cheese and fried in truffle oil. It was a main food source for the believers.

"If you don't stop messing with the weather, I will personally rip your fingernails out," Seersee fumed at me on the third day, when rain washed away the chocolate river.

I fell to my knees in front of her and the hidden video filming the entire incident and broadcast it instantly to the rest of New Hedonia and the nearby colonies. Winning a revolution is all about media coverage, child.

"As God is my witness, I know not where these troubles come from. Please let the grunts go so that God will return his favor to New Hedonia. I fear for all of us if the unbelievers stay."

I'd converted to the Temperance cult the minute they asked me. It was my eighteenth religious conversion. When I get to twenty, I'm going to throw myself a party.

Seersee only scowled at me and swept out, giving Captain an evil look as he stood in the doorway, doing his best bewildered and hurt expression.

"On the bright side," he commented after she'd left and I'd rebroadcast the recording on all the local channels and uploaded it to the Ether. "She's stopped flirting with me."

He gave me a thumbs-up before trailing after her to apologize for all the fuss and suggest again that we should go, leaving her and her believers to the creation of her Utopian Temperance. I've seen many Utopias here in the orbitals and I don't recommend them. They are nearly always a disappointment.

At the end of the third day, the shuttles showed up, empty and ready to take us all. People sympathetic to our cause were manning the docking bay. They welcomed the pilots enthusiastically. The pilots said they'd been forbidden to dock by Seersee, but they'd seen our posts on the Ether. All the Spacers were talking about our plight, so they decided to try again.

By the time Seersee and her men came raging to the docks, two shuttles full of grunts had already left and the other two would be full in less than half an hour.

It was tense.

Seersee's men opened fire into the crowd and there were injuries. The Captain roared and flung himself in front of the guns. That stopped them. Seersee glared at us all for a long minute as he walked slowly towards her with his palms raised in submission. Captain leaned close to her and whispered something in her ear. Seersee looked at him sharply, thought for a moment and then nodded once. She and her men retreated.

Captain told me quickly, "Keep loading everyone up. If I'm not back by the time you are done, just go."

Of course, I followed all his commands except that one. We waited. I tried to send the other shuttle on, but the people in there insisted on waiting too, much to the shuttle pilot's discomfort.

After almost an hour, Captain came rushing back. His hair disheveled, his belt unbuckled and his shirt untucked. He looked very relieved to see me hanging out the shuttle door, tapping my foot impatiently.

"She sends us off with her many blessings and hopes we will return when they have made Temperance a shining beacon of austerity," he laughed, tucking his shirt in. "My powers of persuasion finally changed her mind. Well, I'm sure they would have eventually. Only we are pressed for time and she was really pushy so I had to break my rule about punching women in the face. We need to get out of here before she regains consciousness."

I replied, "You have a love bite on your neck."

He rubbed his neck and looked tired. "Yes, well, we all have to do things we'd rather not. Let's go."

He left in the other shuttle. It was to go to Manny's World. My shuttle dropped us off at New Siberia. I planned to meet Captain on Manny's World, but when I got there he was gone.

That was the last I saw of him.

They said the shuttle never arrived. I have hoped that he found peace somewhere in the skies, but I suspect he found only death. Seek a better fate, young man.

CHAPTER NINE

Cesar watches from the door of the sick room as Penelope and her cowgirls flutter on the front porch in their party finery. They are still pink from washing up and their hair is still damp. Most of them literally let down their hair for the night. Cesar can see short curly caps and long flowing tresses, but Penelope shines like a star among these girls so much younger than herself.

Cesar admires the way Penelope pinned up some of her hair for the evening and let the rest flow down around her slim, pale shoulders. She wears a deep blue dress that flows down her body like a rippling river. She looks like an aloof Greek statue. He knows she worked hard all through the scorching day, yet now she looks cool and refreshed. Cesar feels lucky just to be looking at her.

As he leans on the doorway, he wonders what it would have been like if he had returned home right after the War. Cesar doesn't wonder what would have happened if he never left. He knows they'd all be dead. But if he had come straight home afterwards?

She would have raged and screamed. His father would have been furious, but his mother might have still been alive. Cesar would have gotten to say goodbye to his mom.

But would Penelope have eventually forgiven him and let him back into her life? If he had come back before, would he now be standing up there on the porch in an elegant suit, gently helping her with the clasp of a necklace before brushing an errant lock of hair from the nape of her neck?

In his mind, Cesar imagines teaching Trevor to play Nullball and how to drive a skiff. He imagines fighting with his wife while they wash the dishes and making up later in the bedroom. What if he could have lived that life the last ten years? What an awful waste his life suddenly seems.

Cesar thinks about the last three years. They seem to be the most pointless waste of all, yet in his mind, they were oddly serene. It was his last adventure before coming home to Ithaca and his longest. Cesar hopes it was his last ever, but he doubts he is that lucky.

Cesar spent those three years marooned at the Spider House, a tiny little orbital floating just outside one of the Lagrange points. Because he is cursed, what should have been a short shuttle hop from that blighted New Hedonia disaster to Manny's World turned into a desperate ride through a graveyard of ships from the Spacer War.

There was no real plan for when he got to Manny's World, other than keep his head down and hope Manny didn't sniff him out. There were rumors of a bounty offered by Manny for the head of Cesar the Scorcher. Cesar wasn't seriously worried, but any situation that could go wrong inevitably did go as wrong as it possibly could whenever he was involved.

Cesar can still remember vividly the smell of ozone in the shuttle from New Hedonia, the sudden lurch when the shuttle hit some floating space junk and went careening off course. The flashing red emergency lights blinded him as the blaring horns screamed disaster.

He mostly remembers feeling very tired.

•

He'd been through all this before. Cesar saw death seeping in from under every sealed portal, trying to claw in through every microscopic crack. This wasn't the first time he looked around to see the panic of the others around him as they hoped to survive against the cruel and unforgiving statistics of space travel.

It all made him tired. Cesar badly wanted to lie down and die and get it over with, but they looked to him, waiting for him to save them. Why did they always do that?

Cesar wished Asia was there. She always seemed to accept these situations with effortless grace and that dry wit of hers.

But if wishes were horses, then Cesar would be up to his eyeballs in manure right now. So he barked some orders to keep the other passengers busy while he rerouted control of the ship from the charred remains of the pilot's capsule. Then he charted a course through the graveyard of ships and tried to feel enthusiastic about their chances of survival.

Cesar just wasn't in the survival game that day. He still needed to wash the smell of that Seersee woman off him.

The Spacer War ship graveyard they were careening through was the site of one of the most destructive battles during the War. It happened early in the War, before either side realized it wasn't going to be over in a month or two.

Losses were horrific for both fleets. The sheer volume of ordinance expended has not been matched before or since. Most of the ships were destroyed in less than six hours. The rest ran out of munitions before the end of the battle. Both sides still argued they had won that battle, but it didn't matter. Afterwards, neither the Earthers nor the Spacers had the stomach or the ammunition for another epic bloody battle.

After the war, the Spacers told the Earthers they were leaving the floating pile of destroyed ships as a memorial to the dead, but Cesar and every other Spacer knew they didn't have the money to clean it up.

There were junkerships that made a living carting off bits of this war zone to be reused somewhere else. Parts of Cesar's favorite tinker ships came from here. He liked that they had ended their military career here only to be welded together, cleaned up a little and sent off among the spheres again.

Spider House perched on the edge of all this decaying destruction like a child's toy bobbing in a river at the edge of a waterfall. Cesar marveled that they had avoided annihilation in the battle and still never bothered to move. Most orbitals and ships stayed well away from the graveyard. Floating bits of junk were too easily lethal out here.

The Spider House orbital itself was oddly lumpy. Most orbitals were rigid and smooth, precisely geometric metal shapes standing like floating castles against the darkness, vast childish playthings flung into the sky. The outside of the Spider House looked like something organic, like a clump of spores or thick gray bubbles floating in the void. Shiny iridescent strands contrasted sharply with the dull matted modules they held together like twine around balls, like something you might see under a microscope.

If he were less exhausted by his experiences with adventure in space, Cesar might have felt foreboding. Long experience told him there would be something odd or strange or bad about this place and it would make his life more difficult if he miraculously survived long enough to dock at it. They did survive and it was strange.

Cesar didn't care.

It takes all sorts to make a living in the Spacer worlds, but why he had to keep running into the weird sorts was beyond Cesar. Where were the normal people who went to work, came home, washed their dishes and went to bed? The people who did normal things? Did they all stay back on Earth? Was that the deal?

Because normal people don't bioengineer anaerobic vacuum-hardened spiders to spin webs of steel. They used the spiders to construct a home in space. Who were these people? Cesar never found out.

When the current colonists arrived, there was no one left who knew what Spider House had been originally. Cesar suspected the original inhabitants were cocooned in a web somewhere disgusting.

When Cesar came skidding in on that shuttle, Spider House was a tiny world full of spiders that could spin silk, steel, plastic, medicine and even food. The cotton candy webs were said to be tasty, but Cesar never put one in his mouth the entire time he lived there. There were some things he didn't want to experience.

It was actually quite beautiful to see the huge arachnids crawling across the ceiling, spinning cables of steel to shore up whatever flimsy stuff this orbital had originally been built with.

Or it would have been for anyone else, but Cesar was fundamentally done with sightseeing in this life. He didn't want to see new places, experience new tastes and smells, meet new people or have his horizons broadened one tiny little bit. Cesar wanted to go home.

But that was the one thing he couldn't do. Spider House had no ships. No ships came here. Cesar searched for an escape pod or a shuttle or anything remotely spaceworthy that he could use to get out of there, but there was absolutely nothing he could use to build a ship. They had all been disassembled long ago for their raw materials and then "eaten" by the spiders. Even Cesar, who could slap together a ship out of tin foil and bubble gum and who spent all his waking hours trying to find a way off this orbital and back to Ithaca, even he could find no way to put a ship together.

Nearby orbitals had made an agreement with Spider House. They wouldn't blast the whole bug-infested place out of the sky and Spider House wouldn't call them to ask for help for any reason whatsoever. Cesar didn't blame them.

Cesar tried to get on the Ether and convince other tinkers to come pick him up, but as soon they got a look at a spider bigger than their ship crawling around the outside of the orbital, they spread the word and no one would answer his hail. He knew Asia would come, but he couldn't find her anywhere.

So Cesar gave up.

He took over environmental engineering. There wasn't much in the way of organization in the Spider House. Including the ship full of grunts Cesar arrived with, there were less than two hundred people all told. It was Cesar's experience that there were never enough people who knew how to properly route sewage and clean pump filters so he volunteered for that. He knew life in the Spider House would be even more miserable with a disaster in that department.

Spider House was lousy with gene splicers, though. Somehow, the word had gotten out on whatever channel aspiring mad scientists watched on the Ether that this here was the one place in the system where they were just fine with genetic experiments running mad through the halls.

Spacers loved splicers, but even so, most regarded splicing as black magic. It meant there wasn't exactly an Ether study program for gene splicers. So a place like Spider House attracted them in droves, if a couple every year can be thought of as droves. Most people are lucky to meet one splicer in their lives.

Spider House had at least forty. They were nominally led by Calypso. As far as Cesar was concerned it was a clear case of the bat-shit insane leading the bug-nuts crazy, but Calypso gave him a job and fed him regularly, so he kept that thought to himself.

Unfortunately for Cesar, the splicers never seemed to show up on a ship willing to take anyone or anything *off* the Spider House. Sometimes they showed up on wrecks that collapsed five seconds after they stepped off. Sometimes they showed up flying huge butterfly-winged suits sealed against hard vac.

Cesar learned to live with it.

He used the sealant Calypso gave him on all his clothes to protect himself from spider bites, experiments run amuck or random venomous saliva dripping from the ceiling. Cesar learned to plan for hypercolor mold covering the walkways, tentacular fish blocking the water pipes and hunter batrats in the air ducts.

"Nothing fazes you, Cesar," commented Calypso to him one day.

Calypso was short and pudgy with a round, cheerful face. She had a magnificent mane of thick blue hair that she let flow freely down her back. One day, Cesar discovered that her hair also doubled as a great gas mask when one of her experiments went awry. He'd thought she was a goner for sure when that filter frog spat an arsenic cloud at her.

It wasn't so much that Calypso was in charge as people tended to listen and agree with what she said since she was the defacto leader of the splicers, the one they all agreed was the best.

That day, they were both down in the Ag level of Spider House, a dense nightmare jungle of bizarre plants and animals, murky and dangerous. Cesar shrugged and continued pulling what looked like furry seaweed out of a water pump.

It squirmed, squeaked and shot something black and oily at him. Calypso was leaning on a pile of boxes nearby holding a big jar for him to scoop the seaweed thing into.

"I've never seen anybody so determined to be unhappy," Calypso said, keeping her eyes on the creature as he wrestled it into the jar.

Cesar grunted, "Sometimes it's better to just accept what you are. Mind the black stuff. It burns."

Clamping the lid on the jar, Calypso sat back and watched Cesar. He wiped himself off and then went back to the water pump.

"You don't like it here?"

Cesar rolled his eyes. "Oh, how could I not like it? Up to my elbows in slimy creatures with the smell of spiders in my nose all day. It's a bloody paradise."

She nodded while prodding the jar with a toe. The thing inside sloshed aggressively against the side. Calypso took a step back. Looking around, she took a whiff and then wrinkled her nose. "We could do something about the smell, I guess."

"Don't hurt yourself," Cesar snorted in disbelief, but Calypso laughed.

She pulled a meat pie out of her pocket and silently offered it to Cesar. He shook his head so she took a bite herself.

"I love it here," she sighed, leaning against a vine two feet thick and heavy with purple fruit. "It's hard for me to imagine wanting to be somewhere else. This was meant to be my home. I'm glad I finally found it. But that's your problem, isn't it? Your home is somewhere else."

She leaned over and studied him searchingly. "Where is it you want to be, mystery man? Where's home?"

Cesar shrugged again and found a reason to turn his back on her. What was the point of talking about it? He was never getting off this wad of spider spit and, even if he did, the universe would never allow him to actually get home.

"What if I could get you home?"

Cesar scowled and snapped, "You think you can turn 'what if' into… what? A pony for me to ride home on a rainbow? You're a splicer, not God."

Calypso grinned.

"I may not be a god, but I can do a little better than a pony. It depends on how badly you want to get home."

"Don't mess me around."

"I'm not."

It was Cesar's turn to lean forward and search her face. "Could you? Why would you? What do you want from me?"

"Oh, I don't know," Calypso shrugged. It was the light, casual gesture of a happy person who wanted the whole world to be as happy as she was. "I'm bored and bioengineering a spaceship would be an interesting problem. Plus, watching you sulk around the colony every day is totally bumming me out."

Cesar gave a short laugh before he could stop himself.

Calypso looked delighted. "Oh look, you *can* laugh. That's nice. Plus, to be honest, if I actually got you home alive or even mostly alive, I'd have *mad* street cred with the other splicers."

Cesar wanted badly to believe in her, to believe in something again, but he was determined not to get his hopes up. He shook his head and walked away. She followed.

"I have this idea," she said as they walked back to the living area. "But the thing is, there's about eight different ways it could kill you."

Cesar chuckled. "I've been killed before."

Calypso grinned, "I promise you this will be something you've never done before."

Three months later, they stood on a platform in the core as Calypso helped him into a giant bioengineered goldfish that swam through null gravity like it was koi pond. She bragged for a good fifteen minutes about the thrust capacity of the biomechanical creature's expandable solar sail fins. Cesar would never tell her so, but he thought the shiny synthetic space-hardened scales covering the half-machine, half-fish creature were really quite pretty.

"So, just let the amoeba cover your face and try to breathe normally," she said.

"Easy for you to say."

Cesar watched the jellyfish-looking amoeba thing wrap itself around his legs and start working its way up his body. He dimly recalled an old Ether drama about something very similar that digested whole cities on Earth called *The Blob*. He was trying hard not to be embarrassed about being totally naked in front of this woman.

"Don't be a baby," Calypso scolded, slapping his hand away from some sort of slimy tentacle that was poking his belly button.

"Now, the exoskeleton is actually a vacuum-hardened goldfish mod. I turned off its pain centers so it won't hurt to have you crawling around in its stomach, but for chrissakes stop throwing your elbows around!"

He stopped struggling and returned her glare with interest, but it didn't stop her talking. It hadn't occurred to Cesar to worry about the fish's feelings. He thought it was funny that she did.

She didn't even register his discomfort. "This part here that looks like gills are the air and water filters. Ever since Shelly showed up in her hard-vac butterfly last year, I've been dying to try this. My fin design is far superior to those butterfly wings. I was going to do a dragonfly, but then Shelly would say I copycatted her and you know where she can shove that, am I right? Isn't it lucky I discovered you and your wicked death wish before someone else got you?"

Calypso frequently said things like this. It did not inspire confidence in Cesar, but once again he felt that old burning itch to fling himself into some insane idea and this girl sure had plenty of insane ideas. She yanked at something on his back and prodded a spot near his foot.

"Now, I've pretty much reached the limits of integrity on the goldfish, so I can't get it too much bigger. That means you'll have a very limited range before it, you know, dies on you. You should be able to get to one of the nearby orbitals, though. When you get to one, I think you ought to be able to sneak in through an airlock. They probably won't let you just swim the thing into the docking bay because they are a bunch of paranoid jerks. But nobody keeps tabs on airlocks. Not really. If you get in and disappear into the colony quickly, they'll think the airlock was malfunctioning, right?"

Cesar agreed with that logic. "So, I'll fly a goldfish through space?"

"Yep," she said. "We'll practice today with this smaller fish suit in the core where you won't die if something goes wrong."

Cesar had a sudden image of himself swimming through space before getting smashed against the hull of a transport ship like a bug in the grill of an Earther automobile. But it was too cool not to try.

The first suit broke apart after three minutes.

The second almost suffocated him to death.

The fourth flopped to the left at odd intervals and cracked two of Cesar's ribs. Suits five and six tried to eat each other and had to be put down.

The seventh suit seemed to work well, but the amoeba kept trying to crawl down his throat.

"I think this is it," Calypso said on that final day. It was the eleventh suit and they were outside in true hard-vac.

Cesar nodded. She had explained that the final suit would be too big to test in the core. The only way to test it was out in the void and if it failed, well, that was that. But the smaller version, suit number ten, had worked, so why not?

"I'll never find someone else crazy enough to try this, so please don't die," she begged him as they stood on the docking platform.

Cesar felt the amoeba swarm over him. The oxygen-rich slimy amoeba covered his face as the giant goldfish gathered him up and tucked him into its translucent, diamond-hard carapace. Calypso scampered into Spider House's viewing booth and opened the docking bay doors. Cesar flew through space in a giant goldfish.

It was amazing.

If Cesar didn't have an amoeba covering his mouth, he would have laughed with joy. He did two graceful swooping loops around Spider House before stopping in front of the docking bay where he could see Calypso doing a skipping little dance and punching her fists in the air.

"I am a frickin' genius!" she sang into the comm bud in his ear. She'd wanted him to install a comm implant because "What are you a Luddite? Everyone has them."

But Cesar refused and Calypso grudgingly set up the old earbud-style comm system that she repeatedly referred to as "caveman tech" for him.

"Thanks for everything. I'll let you know if I make it!" subvocalized Cesar into the comm, turning the huge fish gracefully through the sky.

Calypso screeched, "Wait! You can't go yet! This was just the test run."

Cesar replied, "Why not? It works. I'm ready. And if it doesn't, my last ride will be a hell of a thing."

Through the comm, Calypso sounded sad for the first time he'd ever seen. She put a hand on the viewing plate, reaching out to him. "But I'll miss you, mystery man."

Cesar knew she couldn't see him, so he flapped the huge fins slowly and said, "I'll miss you too, crazy girl."

He could see the docking bay fill with people; their mouths open with awe. A small child waved and clapped with delight and the others followed. Calypso waved and cried and smiled proudly.

It was a good ending.

The flight of the space goldfish was like a dream, a sticky, oozy, mostly uncomfortable dream. Cesar didn't quite believe it was happening until it was over.

He popped an airlock, dropped into a strange orbital and snuck into the first sonic shower he could find. He watched the amoeba slime on his skin and clothes turn to dust. Then he stepped under the fan and felt them all blow away like a dream.

He accessed the Ether, hoping there was still enough money in his credit account for a meal on this orbital and a shuttle ticket to Ithaca. He was pleasantly surprised to find a large number of credits deposited in his account with a note from Calypso:

"What's the point of having money if you can't spend it on your friends?

No need to tell me where you are going, mystery man. If you access this credit, I'll know you made it. My bragging shall fill the void. Go home. Find what you are looking for."

Cesar might have invested in nicer clothes and some gifts for his family, but already the fever was burning through his body. He guessed the amoeba slime in the goldfish suit hadn't been as benign as Calypso hoped.

He could have asked for medical care, but that would inevitably lead to questions about where he came from, how he got sick and what he was doing in this colony in the first place. Most people didn't have a sense of humor about stowaways and who would believe he flew here in a space goldfish?

They'd never let him go. After lying in a cheap rented room for two days in a clammy sweaty heap, Cesar knew he had to get home before he died, so that's what he did.

Here he is.

•

Cesar opens his eyes to the pretty pomp and frivolous circumstance of Penelope's party on the lawn of his childhood home.

Ithaca.

He still can't believe he is here. He watches the cowgirls giggle while the men flirting with them sip margaritas. It is enchanting, the way they don't seem to realize that death never sleeps, never stops thirsting for flesh.

As more visitors arrive, Cesar watches Penelope graciously show them inside with a smile until another tall, handsome man appears. Cesar watches Penelope let this man link his arm in hers and guide her inside.

Cesar goes into his dark bunkhouse sick room and shuts the door. He will learn to be happy with what he has. He knows he used up all his luck years ago.

CHAPTER TEN

Penelope thinks the party is going rather well until the icemaker dies loudly. She's been through this sort of thing before. The icemaker is quite temperamental. She sends one of the girls off to find Argos.

Argos usually makes himself scarce during parties. Large crowds confuse him.

Meanwhile, Mr. Finomus arrives with his platypig, made docile by copious amounts of lettuce and a nice mud pit to wallow in. Everyone inspects it as the jolly little gene splicer tells them all about how he conjured up the great beast to solve the feral carp problem they were having on his swampy little orbital.

"It also digests chokeweed like you wouldn't believe," he says excitedly as he pushes back his thinning hair.

His hair has a tendency to shoot up from his head like a white halo when he gets excited. Penelope bends forward to get a better look at the beast's billsnout. She doesn't realize until too late that this caused the front of her dress to drop forward and give Mr. Finomus a clear view of her ample bosom. The poor man is bright red and breathing like a buffalo by the time she straightens up.

Penelope takes him inside and makes him sit down to drink a mint julep. Five minutes later, he is still red as a beet and she is worried that the man's heart might not bear the strain. Finomus makes the most of her attention. He clasps her hand and tells her for the fourth time about how his sweet platypig suddenly took a ferocious turn earlier and tried to bite her son.

Penelope doesn't mind.

She thinks Finomus really is a very nice man. He reminds her of Piglet in *Winnie-the-Pooh* a little too much to take seriously. Besides, as far as she can tell, most of the flirting men do at these parties has more to do with their desire to win some sort of competitive flirting game against each other. It is not about her, but about beating the others.

Penelope doesn't take it personally.

She just assumes men are like that and gently reclaims her hand from Finomus' sweaty and enthusiastic grip. She does like him and his courtly ways. Also, Finomus is one of the more mentally stable and productive gene splicers currently in space. He owns the largest orbital factory for making bio-fuel cells and Ithaca could really use a bigger back-up generator. So she looks as attentive as she can while he tells her about his platypig.

"Of course, Piggy's never really dangerous, especially in his swamp. He's not used to the heat and the humidity on your world. I'm sure once he got to know your charming son, Piggy would love him," the little man says anxiously. "I will take this opportunity to once again invite you over to visit my little colony. I flatter myself to think you would quite enjoy the coolness of the swamps."

"I thank you for your generosity, but alas, you know how busy I am here with this ranch and raising my son," Penelope laughs. "And I'm not a very good traveler anyway. I much prefer to stay here on my little homestead than fling myself through the sky."

Penelope moves away to join a group discussing the latest gossip about sending a Spacer representative to the United Nations. The nape of her neck tingles slightly at the approach of someone tall behind her. She turns to see who it is and finds Ulixes striding towards her like she's the only person in the room. He has a look on his face that makes her catch her breath again.

"We couldn't find Argos," Ulixes says, explaining his presence without apology. "Just point me to the icemaker and I'll have it fixed up as quick as I can." His voice sends a light shiver scampering down her spine.

Oh, it is so stupid! All this gasping and girlish foolishness! Penelope frowns sternly at the man, but he looks deep into her eyes and his gaze never wavers.

Penelope turns on her heels and walks quickly to the back of the house. The icemaker is in the laundry room, a little closet right behind the kitchen. It is big enough for one person but close for two. She leads him in and points to the malfunctioning ice machine.

"There is the treacherous thing," she says petulantly. "The grav boosters are a million times more advanced and more important, but it's this stupid icemaker that takes up half my life with its twitchy circuitry."

Penelope sits on a pile of baskets and watches him work. There is no dirty clothing in here because Lupe would die before leaving something unclean with company coming over. She is grateful for a break and a chance to rest her feet for a minute. She has new boots and they are pinching her toes.

Ulixes has to shut the laundry room door to reach the wiring. The sudden privacy makes her chatter nervously.

"I'm sorry to have you doing this so late. Argos hates these parties and he slinks off if he gets half a chance. Lupe too. I wonder where they go on these nights. Into town I suppose," she tells Ulixes as he works.

Ulixes chuckles, "You think maybe they sneak off together and have a little weekend romance?"

"Lupe and Argos?" asks Penelope, totally shocked. "Surely not. I never thought about it. Oh, and now I don't want to think about it. I guess they could though."

She shakes her head to clear out an unwelcome vision of Lupe and Argos locked in a romantic embrace.

Ulixes says with amusement, "Everyone could use a little love in their lives, I guess."

"Oh, I don't know," says Penelope, smoothing her hair while watching the muscles ripple on his back as he twists together two wires. "It seems like love is so complicated and it only ever turns out badly."

The man in front of her turns. Before she quite understands how it happened, he has caught her up in his arms and his mouth is on hers. Penelope throws herself into his rough embrace without a second thought. Or a first one, for that matter.

Her hands curl around his neck and she pulls herself against him. Suddenly her only goal in life is to maximize the amount of his skin she can touch at once. She is absurdly pleased by his quick gasp as she slips her palm up under his shirt and holds it against his warm chest to feel the wild beating of his heart.

Then she realizes what she is doing and pushes herself away from him. How on Earth did that happen? She honestly isn't sure. Feeling like a total fool, Penelope blurts out the first thing that pops into her head, which is: "Wow, that really does feel just like it used to!"

Mr. Ulixes gets a horrified look on his face and then begins apologizing. It is ghastly.

Penelope puts a hand on his arm and shakes her head, "No, it's alright. I shouldn't have said that. It's been so long since I kissed someone, you see. The last man was, well, my husband and that was a good fifteen years ago and I thought I'd forgotten what it was like and…"

But then he is kissing her again and Penelope forgets what she was trying to say. After a few minutes, sanity returns and she tries to apologize again. "I am so sorry. I'm taking terrible advantage. You are a guest in my house and I'm forcing myself on you like this. I don't know what's wrong with me."

Mr. Ulixes barks out a low laugh, "For the love of God, take advantage of me some more. Please!"

He pulls her into his arms. This time, as their eyes flash and their chests heave and their lips meet, their hands also wander.

If it wasn't for the sound of voices getting closer, who knows what might have happened next? Penelope pulls her mouth away from his and rests her forehead on his chest, listening without breathing to the footsteps getting closer and the pounding of his heart. Ulixes holds himself perfectly still.

Penelope listens to his breath slow though his heart still races. Won't it be just her luck to get caught fifteen seconds in to the only forbidden thrill she's had in a decade?

The footsteps stop outside the mercifully closed door of the laundry room and she hears the voice of the last man who had tried to kiss her. Wilhelm Asner of the Ex-Austrian Engineering Complex says, quite clearly, on the other side of the door, "What ever happened to our lovely hostess?"

The man groped Penelope painfully behind a closet door one night a few weeks ago and she's been careful to avoid being alone with him since. Unfortunately, Penelope needs his goodwill right now. The EEC produces the best solar arrays in the colonies and Ithaca desperately needs to replace their aging energy source.

It was fine until a few weeks ago when someone destroyed a whole series of panels, part of the bizarre string of attacks that sabotaged many of the colony's life support systems. Penelope doesn't know why this is happening or how to stop it. All she knows is that if one more array fails before the new ones are delivered, they'll all be fighting some serious frostbite.

Unfortunately for Penelope, the EEC is apparently deep in the production of a massive solar sail array for Uri Mach of the Seven Skies Trading Company. Consequently, they are in no hurry to fill her order. Penelope finds herself trying to encourage Mr. Asner to complete her order without having to endure more groping or worse.

If he opens the door it will be catastrophically embarrassing and potentially damaging to the whole colony, but isn't her life one long trial? Penelope beats her head gently against Ulixes' chest, wishing it were a wall.

He responds by wrapping his arms tightly around her. It is incredibly comforting. She sighs and wallows in the warm safe feeling. Penelope knows she ought to feel guilty and she promises herself she will, first thing tomorrow.

The clear voice of Uri Mach, the owner of Seven Skies Trading Company and her long-time friend, comes floating through the closed door, "She's a busy woman. No doubt she's coordinating some massive political campaign for universal peace on the front porch as we speak."

Uri has faithfully attended these parties for years. He and Penelope were much of the same mind on many aspects of life in the colonies. Penelope has heard rumors of Uri's ruthlessness in business, but she's never seen any sign of that at her parties.

"Did you gentleman get a chance to see my platypig?" she hears Mr. Finomus ask them.

The other two assure him that they have seen the creature and it is quite magnificent. Then they begin chatting about a large order of something Finomus was working on for Uri. Something about prepping for a big project that they didn't have all the base elements for. Finomus is cheerfully telling them he'll get everything prepared so that when they do find the missing elements, they can just inject something into the something else and they'd get the other thing.

Penelope is listening without truly hearing although she does wonder vaguely why Seven Skies needs a splicer like Finomus. Penelope realizes she has been holding her breath so she lets it out slowly. The minutes drag on and the door still remains shut. Penelope starts to worry that she will need to sneeze soon.

The three men shift to talking about progress on something they call the Moon Array. Penelope is slightly surprised to hear that. As far as she knows, nobody does anything on the Moon other than using it as a parking lot for old vehicles and occasionally grabbing moon dust for one purpose or another.

She listens as much as she can while the man holding her slowly and quietly trails scorching kisses down her neck. She bites her lip to keep from gasping.

Asner is apparently slightly behind in supplying Seven Skies with a large order of something. Penelope can't hear what and, to be honest, she doesn't really care right now. He assures Uri Mach that the order will be ready in a week if they can just secure a larger supply of something else. Uri sounds angry.

"You know the faster we get that array up, the safer we'll all be," Uri says significantly.

Even through the haze created by the touch of rough hands on her body, Penelope can't help thinking this is an odd conversation happening on the other side of the door. If this Moon Array is a solar sail like the ones Asner specializes in, it will provide Seven Skies with more energy. That is good, but they could hardly be in any danger from total power loss. Most orbitals are chock full of back-up power supplies. Even Ithaca has a backup generator for its backup generator. Although Penelope spends too much time lately wondering if it will support the entire colony in the event of another sabotage.

Teeth gently, but firmly, nibbling on her ear drive that line of thought from Penelope's mind.

"Well, the extra time will allow you to complete that solar panel order the lovely Penelope has been badgering you for. That should put you in her good graces," comments Mr. Finomus genially. "Perhaps you can convince her to finally sell Uri here the cows he needs."

Wilhelm Asner laughs, "Oh, I think it better to keep a lady waiting and see how much that solar panel order is really worth to her."

Penelope hears the insinuation in his voice and it makes her blood boil. Ulixes' body goes rigid so he must hear it too or else he feels her fingers clench in frustration because he strokes her hair silently. She can't help thinking that he's being awfully protective for a stranger, but she doesn't mind so much right now.

"Yes, well, I need that shipment from you in a week," snaps Uri Mach. "When can you be done with the other project we discussed?"

"Once I get what I need, it will only be a few days," replies Wilhelm Asner sourly.

He obviously doesn't like being lectured by Uri. Finomus suggests they go outside and get some air, as it is getting hot in the house. The other two agree.

"I still think you are wrong to keep its full potential a secret," says Asner as they start to move off.

Penelope breathes a deep sigh of relief to finally hear their retreating footsteps.

Uri Mach laughs, "I find it better to ask forgiveness than permission. The other colonies will find it easier to comprehend the benefits of the Moon Array once I show them. Now where is our missing hostess, do you think?"

That is the last of that conversation Penelope hears. She feels Ulixes' chest shake with silent laughter. She pulls away from him. They stand, looking at each other for a brief minute. Penelope knows she should say something, but instead she takes the opportunity to escape the laundry room before someone else comes along.

Penelope bolts down the hall into the nearest bathroom where she quickly smoothes her hair and pulls her dress back into place. Taking a deep breath, plastering a smile on her face and hoping her laundry room intrigue isn't too obvious, she steps out into the crowd of her guests.

"Why Miss Penelope, you look even more ravishing than usual," cries Uri Mach when he sees her.

Penelope truly hopes she doesn't look ravished, or at least as thoroughly ravished as she feels. She gives her old business associate a hug. Uri has never given any indication that he's interested in anything other than friendship so she finds him to be quite a comfortable companion.

They chat about politics and what ridiculous things the Earthers are up to lately. Mr. Finomus regales them with stories of the platypig's escapades and Penelope obliges him with a few stories about the local dillo-bears. As the evening slips away and her guests begin to say their goodbyes, she finds Wilhelm Asner by her side.

He makes a point of waiting until the other guests are gone. Penelope absolutely does not want to be left alone with the man. She doesn't want to engage in any sort of physical relationship with him and, judging by the way he keeps edging closer and closer to her, Asner has definitely missed her hints on that subject.

As the last of the guests filter out, Penelope squares her shoulders and begins mentally preparing the kind, but firm refusal of his attentions she will no doubt have to make in a few minutes. There are a few raised eyebrows at Wilhelm Asner's proprietary stance. Penelope knows more than a few people will go home with the impression that she is spending the night with Asner. She fervently wishes people would not take such an interest in her life.

Once they are alone, Wilhelm steps closer and whispers, "Penelope, I wish you would accept my offer and visit my colony. You need to get out and see the rest of space."

Penelope edges back and says civilly, "Why thank you, Wilhelm, but you know I don't really care for travel and with a son and ranch to run, I can't get away."

Wilhelm shakes his head and gives her a patronizing smile, "I know you don't think you like to travel, but surely you ought to try it before you reject it? Your son is practically a man. According to Finomus, he fought off a charging platypig barehanded today! The boy doesn't need a mother hovering at his age. And your cowgirls seem to have the ranch well in hand."

As he says this, he takes her hands in his. Penelope forces herself to accept this and not snatch her hands away.

Why should it be that Penelope does not want to touch this man and yet she couldn't keep herself away from that drifter Ulixes earlier? A relationship with Wilhelm would be very advantageous for her, as opposed to stolen kisses in the laundry room with the hired help.

The private army Asner maintains at the EEC would mean her worries about the ranch were over, yet she can't. She just can't do it. For the hundredth time today, she curses her fickle hormones.

She senses Ulixes enter the room behind her. Penelope isn't really sure how she knows he's there, but she does. Perhaps it is his smell—sweat and engine grease and soap. It is intoxicating and strangely familiar.

She wonders if he perhaps smells like some forgotten relative from her home on Earth that comforted her as a child. Penelope turns to him, both grateful and horrified by his presence here.

Ulixes stares resolutely at the floor. "Ma'am, I hate to bother you, but it appears that Argos has injured himself. Miss Lupe is out for the evening and I'm not much of a one for healing."

Penelope takes the opportunity to withdraw her hands from Wilhelm's and say with elaborate regret, "You see? The demands of a ranch never end, do they?"

Wilhelm studies Ulixes suspiciously. "I thought you didn't have any men here," he says sharply.

"Mr. Ulixes is passing through, an old friend of the family, here to see my father-in-law before he passes away, bless him," Penelope says smoothly.

Gesturing an introduction, she says to Ulixes, "And this is my friend Wilhelm Asner. Mr. Asner's Engineering Complex is fixing our solar array."

Ulixes shuffles forward and holds his hand out to Asner, but just then Uri Mach popped back through the door.

"Forgot my jacket," Uri announces. When he sees them standing there, he laughs, "Ah, there you are, Asner! Walk back to the ships with me, I want to talk to you."

Turning to Penelope, he asks, "And who is this man? I don't believe we've met. Hello, sir, I'm Uri Mach of Seven Skies Trading."

Penelope opens her mouth to introduce Ulixes when something happens that Penelope doesn't quite follow. In the span of a second, a look of recognition flickers across Ulixes' face. Then the man seems to expand to twice his normal size. He goes from a broken old man to a large, barrel-chested giant who breathes quiet menace at Uri and Asner. Fortunately neither seem to notice.

Ulixes crushes Wilhelm's hand in a firm shake. "Seven Skies, you say?" he rumbles in a deep gravelly voice. "Wonderful. I trust that keeps you quite busy, sir."

"It does," Uri says quickly, wincing slightly as he yanks his hand away. "And you?"

"Oh, I get around," Ulixes says coldly. "I tinker here and there."

Uri picks up the man's frosty tone although he doesn't seem to under-stand Ulixes' sudden dislike any more than Penelope does. Uri shrugs, dismissing the man with, "Well, how nice. But not all of us can drift around the sky like nomads. I really must go."

Turning to Penelope, his voice changes to a more jovial and gallant tone, "I hope that if you will not reconsider selling me your herd, you will at least reconsider my offer of a trip to the Seven Skies headquarters?"

Penelope smiles, shaking her head.

Uri gives her a charming smile, "Are you sure? I'm prepared to double my last offer. You could buy this whole colony with that and grow all the dillo-bears and minipigs your heart desires."

"And disappoint all my other customers? Sorry, Uri, not even for you," she laughs as graciously as she can.

Uri shrugs and turns but she catches a glint of cold anger in his eyes. Penelope blinks, thinking she must be mistaken.

Uri impatiently gestures for Asner to follow him while Ulixes folds his arms, clearly not planning to budge. Penelope laughs loudly, not sure what exactly the subtext is here, but wanting it to end.

Giving Uri a quick hug and guiding Asner gently but firmly out the door, she says, "Perhaps I will come see your colony, even though you know I've never wanted to travel. I guess I'm just a homebody. Well, I'd better go see to poor old Argos now, I suppose. I hope I'll see you next week? Wonderful! Goodnight."

Before she can shut the door, Asner leans forward and pulls her close to him. "Please do visit. There are things I would very much like to explain to you. Engineering can be more beautiful than you think, my dear."

Then he hisses into her ear, "Beggars are like wild animals. You can feed them on the streets, but let them into your house and they make a mess." Asner scowls at Ulixes significantly before trailing after Uri.

Penelope closes the door, thankful to be done with one problem to-night. Turning she sees Ulixes still standing, a mountain of a man in her living room, his eyes blazing as he watches the retreating figures of Wilhelm Asner and Uri Mach through the window.

"So where is Argos? What happened to him?" she asks, tucking a stray hair behind her ear and smoothing her dress.

Ulixes looks away from the window and loses some of that angry energy.

"I'm sorry, I lied," the man says bluntly. "Argos is sleeping off a bender in his bunk. I thought maybe you needed some help seeing off the last of your guests." He fidgets slightly with something in a pocket and looks suddenly unsure of himself.

Penelope realizes she is grateful for the help getting Wilhelm out the door tonight. It's been a long, very confusing day and she knows the best thing now is to go to bed. As tempting as he might be, Penelope knows that she should not take this man with her and do something she might regret.

Penelope says, as gently as she can, "Look, I have been getting guests out the door on my own for years. I appreciate the help, but I think it's time for both of us to go to bed. Our own beds, I mean. Separately. And sleep."

She edges around the room, not trusting herself within five feet of this mysterious stranger. He nods and moves towards the back door before halting.

"Is that man close to you? A trusted friend?" he asks, pointing to the window.

What is he asking exactly? Penelope says slowly, "Wilhelm Asner has been a good friend and guest in my house for the past five years, but that's as far as it goes between us."

Ulixes nods, his face still turned to the window.

"And the other one?" he asks in the same hard voice.

Penelope almost forgot Uri. She says, "The same goes for Uri, I guess. A friend and a guest. He's fun at the parties and, thankfully, he never pushes for more. Except he always jokes that he wants to buy the whole herd and boil them down for glue. Sometimes he has a gross sense of humor."

Ulixes still frowns. "Hmmm," he rumbles, deep in thought. "And your father-in-law? Is he really bad off?"

Penelope rubs her temples as she replies tiredly, "He is. Larry had a stroke. He stays in his shack at the far end of the property and refuses most company."

Ulixes' frown deepens. Scratching his beard, he says slowly, "With your permission, I'd like to go visit him tomorrow. Your, uh, husband sent me with a private message for the old man if I ever got this way before he did."

Penelope laughs shortly, "Did he really? How interesting. Of course you can go see the old man. Or at least you can try. He's not much on visitors and near lethal with that cane of his."

Ulixes grins, delight making his face look younger. "Is he? Really? That sounds like the father that, uh, your husband described to me. I guess his health hasn't changed him too much then?"

Penelope laughs, "It would take more than a stroke, a blockage in his guts and a bum knee to change Larry Vaquero."

They watch each other warily for a minute before Penelope looks away from the lust in his eyes. The smile fades from her lips. She asks softly, "So Cesar sent a message for his dad, but nothing for me, right?"

Ulixes suddenly looks lost and he starts stammering incoherently.

Penelope says heavily as she moved towards her rooms, "It's fine. Don't worry about it. Really. I need to get some sleep now."

"Sure," Ulixes says quickly, suddenly just as anxious as she is to leave the room, it seems. In the doorway, he pauses to catch her eye over his shoulder. "I won't take advantage of you further," he says, winking and flashing her a wicked grin.

Penelope knows a massive blush is staining her cheeks. She flees to her room, but she does it with a private grin.

VOICES IN THE DARK

Excerpt from Trevor Vaquero's "Tales of my Father" Archive

This is the story I finally got out of Jonas Ulixes, a man who worked with my father after the War. Sometimes, it's hard to convince people to let me record them. I find that breakfast is a good time to get folks to sit long enough to finish a tale.

—*Trevor Vaquero*

What's the recorder for? You want a story?

Holy guacamole, kid. It's much too bright and much too early for you to be so wide-awake and full of questions. Let me drink my coffee first before you start asking me about parties and tales of your dad. Yes, I did enjoy the party last night.

It was quite… stimulating.

No thank you, Miss Penelope, I am not too warm in this kitchen so I don't need to go sit on the porch to finish my breakfast. This kitchen is quite cool compared to other parts of this house. That laundry room for example, gets right toasty.

So, Trevor! You want another story about your dad, do you?

Well I just so happen to have one in mind, so pay attention. About six years ago, your dad and I were cruising around on a trading run in his tinker ship. We knew your dad as Captain.

You know about tinker ships? Smart boy.

Then you know what kind of danger there is out there for a tinker ship crew? No? The short answer is every kind imaginable, including the ship itself.

A tinker ship's fortunes come and go and ours usually seemed to be going, but at the time I am telling you about, we were pretty fat and happy, pulling regular runs between the Hathor Mining Colony and the Poppy Ship by way of a few of the tamer ports of call. Your dad gave up making black market runs down to the planet the third time he got shot with a pulse rifle. He felt it had a poor return on investment once you factored in the doctor bills.

Now, I should tell you a quick thing about the Hathor Miners. They like their privacy. Really like it. They keep to themselves and they are very picky about who they let into their orbitals and ships. And being that they are the oldest, richest and strongest colony out here, they get what they want.

I don't think orbital colonies would have even been possible if Hathor didn't start their deep space mining expeditions out to find all those rare Earth elements that the Earth ran out of decades ago for the computers, mediboxes, and all that other technology nobody wants to live without these days. Indium? Antimony? Gallium? Unobtainium? I never can remember what they are called, but those miners can tell you the price to the microgram. The Hathors are the last of the cowboys, strapping themselves to rockets to drag asteroids back here so we can keep making stuff. They get paid well for it, too.

Anyway, we'd been trading with them for over a year before they let us farther than the launch pad. Also, Hathor miners are mostly men and very into being big hairy manly men. You know the types I'm talking about? Always trying to get to get an inter-orbital football league going or wrestling or something? But no one ever wants to grapple with these guys.

Now, after the War, they were having a heck of a time with their air supply system on account of all the dust. A byproduct of mining is dust and the Hathor mining operation made a special kind of dust that ate through lungs and air filters like it was ice cream on a hot day.

Miners are fantastic engineers, but not every problem has an engineering solution and it took them a while to figure out that this was one of those kinds of problems. They tried everything they could think of, but nothing worked. So finally they put a call out for a gene splicer to see if there wasn't an organic solution.

Eventually one showed up.

A *lady* splicer.

The Hathors didn't think a girl could fix a problem that had them stumped and this lady was the bookish kind. You know the type? Like someone's wound her up a little too tight? She also looked like a good sneeze would knock her over.

Well, you know how rare splicers are so you know that you don't get picky. You pay whatever they want and thank your lucky stars when they deliver. This one was one of the best and she didn't much care for their macho attitude.

So… now this is a big secret I'm telling you Trevor, so you have to swear to keep it private. Can you swear? Good.

So, this lady splicer whips them up a plant that will filter their air and make it pure and sweet no matter how much dust they kick up. But the kicker was, it was roses.

Roses!

Vines of fat roses curling all through the miner ships! Pink and red and white and did it smell wonderful in there? Yes it did.

Like a flower shop. That's one of the reasons the miners don't let anybody in. They think it isn't macho and, believe me, it isn't!

Eventually, they trusted us enough to see them and that's got to be one of the great wonders of man, right there. Roses climbing hundreds of feet through great crushing wheels and pistons and the like.

That isn't my story, though. That was just a side note.

So, anyways, we're cruising along in our tinker ship, minding our own business, when we get a distress call. Tinkers are big believers in karmic debt and any chance to get ahead and have the universe owe you a favor instead of the other way around is a chance we wanted to take.

The distress call said it was from a Hathor Mining Ship bringing home their women's choir. Now, I don't know why this should be, but as hairy and sweaty as Hathor men are, the few women they have are drop dead gorgeous. The ones talking to us on the comm were the cream of the crop: blond, blue-eyed, large, lovely bouncy… Well, you get the idea.

Not as beautiful as Ithacan ladies, of course, but some men go in for that sort of thing. Why thank you, Miss Penelope! I would like some more coffee.

So, we hail them.

Their captain starts telling us all about a cracked turbine that's left them sitting ducks in the shipping lane when your dad gets on the comm and shouts, "Hey there, Hathors, how does your garden grow?" to show them he knows about the roses and thus he's a trusted friend of Hathor people everywhere.

See?

For a minute, the captain of this *supposed* Hathor doesn't respond at all. Even with our crappy, low-res comm we can see the looks on his face and the faces of the girls behind him. They don't know what your dad is talking about. They don't have a clue.

Finally, their captain makes a quick gesture and the most buxom blond of the lot leans over the comm so we can get an eyeful of all her, uh, assets and she coos, "Why don't you come over and bring your stamen to my flower, big guy?"

No, I won't explain what that means. Ask your mother.

Your dad doesn't miss a beat. He says something back, cheerful and flirtatious-like. Then we say that we'll be happy to come help them out and we're on our way.

That was bluffing, though.

Your dad knew there was something fishy so we flew towards their ship as slow as snails, blasting them with every scanner and sensor we have on board. Now, most tinker ships don't bother with too much in the way of detectors, but your dad had been blindsided by too much space junk of both the human and the metal kind, so he had every gadget available crammed into our tiny pilot room.

Turns out they were packing artillery heavier than Hathor singers. You could tell at a glance, they were much too big and armored for us to take on. We had one pulse cannon and it was no good for anything but scaring off the small fry looking to scavenge.

We scrambled our signal and steered clear of them. It wasn't long before we came across a burnt-out hull of another tinker ship with their cargo bays broken open and bits of shattered bodies floating in the debris. That phony Hathor ship was luring tinker ships to their doom with a bogus distress signal. Then they would tear the doomed tinker apart, taking anything of value before they killed the crew.

We reported them at our next port of call and made sure to warn everyone we could, but I know that siren caught at least two more ships. Ships full of good people sent to a hellish end.

How did we stop them? We didn't.

Why, son, nobody stopped them. They were too big and too well armed. Eventually they stopped lurking in the shipping lanes, but I never heard what happened to them.

Why would anybody do that? Set out to trick and murder innocent people just to take their stuff?

Well, as far as I can tell, some people are born bastards. I'm sorry, Miss Penelope, please excuse my language. I meant to say evil. Some people are evil. You need to stay away from them and hope they leave you alone. No, it's not a nice story, is it? But it is true.

I've never been able to forget the captain of the siren ship. I've thought about him often and wondered how a man could lure people to their dooms with such a charming smile. It's a weird story, I guess.

You want to know the weirdest part? I could swear I met that scavenger captain again. It was right here in this house last night.

His name was Uri Mach.

Yes, Miss Penelope, I could very well be mistaken. That is true.

I'm not saying I never forget a face, but that one I remember particularly. So you probably want to keep your eyes open and your exits clearly marked around that man. That's all I'm saying. Now I got to go visit your grandfather today, Trevor, but I'll be back tonight and I promise to think of a better story. It's harder than you think.

Stories about your dad don't have happy endings.

CHAPTER ELEVEN

Cesar plods out to his father's cabin in the sultry morning heat, wondering what he'll find when he gets there. He remembers that last time he saw his father, Larry Vaquero, a huge bear of a man.

They had been going at it hammers and tongs, yelling at each other on the front porch for hours. His father's face was beet red. When Larry peeled back his lips to let loose a fresh wave of angry curses, his eyes got lost in his great bushy beard.

Larry Vaquero was used to getting his way. He'd bullied a miracle before Cesar was born by convincing Earther backers to fund this little ranching nirvana in the sky as an "agricultural experiment." Since Ithaca turned out to be one of the most lucrative investments in farming the solar system has ever seen, Larry has been running Ithaca as his own private kingdom for decades.

Fortunately for Ithaca, Larry was a benevolent dictator. He opted to leave most of the governing to the people. He made sure things were peaceful, fair and run the way he thought they should be run. For the most part, though, he liked to let men make their own decisions. That is, until his own son stood up one day and said he was leaving.

Cesar knew why his dad was so mad that day.

Larry thought Ithaca was as close to heaven as a man could get. He couldn't understand why anyone would want to see other places or try living a different way. So therefore, his son must be suffering some sort of mental breakdown and should be yelled at until he came to his senses. Larry felt strongly that yelling was an integral part of his paternal responsibilities.

"No son of mine will run off and get involved in some fool rebellion!" Larry bellowed when Cesar stormed into his room and started shoving clothes and food into a bag.

Larry Vaquero brought up Cesar's duty to the ranch and his responsibilities to his wife and infant son for the millionth time. They'd been arguing so long that Cesar's head ached and he couldn't remember whether he was arguing to go or stay any more. In the end, it didn't matter. If they were to have a chance at surviving out here when the Earthers started lobbing nukes, he had to fight.

What was the point of arguing about it?

And yet, it is fifteen years later and the argument still isn't over. The shack Cesar stares at now is the decayed remnant of the little temporary cabin his parents moved into when they discovered Penelope was pregnant. They gave the young couple the main house and moved out here until the new ranch they ordered could be finished. When he left, they were just beginning to build. Judging from the ruins, though, it looked like that's all they ever did.

Cesar absorbs this fact and makes the next logical conclusion. His Mom and Dad must have abandoned their retirement home after he left and moved back into the main ranch house with Penelope. Cesar felt guilty for disrupting their life. He is frustrated by that guilt. Because what can he do about it now?

Cesar approaches the decaying shack with the same level of care he would use approaching a lion's den. He steels himself for a frail and weak man on death's door. Probably with a cane, barely able to creep around, blind and deaf.

Cesar envisions himself leaning over the old man's deathbed and begging forgiveness. His father will clasp Cesar's hands, forgive him and say a whole bunch of nice things about him before gently passing away with a smile on his lips. Cesar promises himself he won't cry.

It isn't manly.

"Jesus H Christ on a hotplate, boy! You gonna stand out there using up perfectly good oxygen or you gonna come inside and make yourself useful?" a querulous voice calls from the shack. "My God, you look like hell. I told you not to go. Guess it only took, what? Fifteen years for you to realize I was right? You always was slow."

Cesar sighs. That is his dad in there all right.

"Damn, Dad, you sure turned into a slob in the last decade, didn't you?" Cesar shouts back, picking his way through the various piles of rusting old equipment in the yard.

A great shaggy head pops into view, squinting through the right eye because the left one doesn't work. Just then, a strong whiff of the astringent smell of ethanol slaps Cesar across the face.

"Oh, wow," Cesar says, stopping in his tracks and waving his hands in a futile attempt to waft the smell away from his nose. "You trying to embalm yourself before you die, you crazy old coot?"

Old Larry Vaquero erupts from the door, propelled by a stream of epithets so foul that to repeat them would no doubt cause the very page they were printed on to smolder. It doesn't faze Cesar. He's heard it all before. He actually finds the litany of profanity oddly reassuring.

Cesar watches his father limp energetically towards him and finds the old man's appearance less than reassuring. His father drags his left leg and the left arm dangles uselessly by his side. His dad's face is oddly tilted—the corner of his left eye and the left side of his mouth seem to drag downward. Not that any of that slows the old bear down.

His dad stops right in front of his face and shouts, "You took your sweet ass time getting home, son."

Cesar takes a step back. A lazy smile spreads across his face, "Well, it sure looks like reports of your death are greatly exaggerated, aren't they?"

Larry Vaquero grins. "Ah, she likes to tell all the fancypants at her parties that I'm gonna pop off at any minute. Keeps them from getting ideas about bumping me off or forcing her to do something she doesn't want to do. And it gives me an excuse not to go up there on Fridays! When you get to be my age, you shouldn't have to wear pants if you don't want to."

After dropping that bit of wisdom, the old man pulls Cesar into a fierce hug. Then he grabs Cesar by the shirt and starts dragging him back to the shack.

Cesar allows himself to be dragged, eyeing what appears to be blankets wrapped around his father's lower half. Cesar hopes this piece of clothing is sturdier than it looks. He really doesn't want to see his father without pants today.

Inside, the shack looks like a mad scientist's lab with beakers on burners and tubing running amok. As his dad pushes him into the one chair in the place, Cesar realized what is going on in here.

"So you finally did it? Told the rest of humanity to take a hike and set up a still so you could drink tequila all day?" hoots Cesar.

If he had a dollar for every time his dad swore that Cesar would eventually drive him to this particular state of affairs, he'd be the richest man in the colonies. Cesar felt you had to admire bullheadedness on that scale.

"I certainly admire your sheer cussedness, Dad."

Larry Vaquero grins proudly while handing his son a dented tin cup full of liquor. "It's pretty good too and I'm not just saying that because I drink it morning, noon, and night."

Cesar takes a gulp.

"I think it burnt all the hair out of my nose," he gasps when his vision clears.

His dad claps him on the back and cackles, "That's how you know it's good, son."

While Cesar coughs a few times, his dad pulls up a large box and sits on it, greedily looking at his son. The box clinks with the unmistakable sound of full tequila bottles, but Cesar can't be bothered with those types of details just now.

Cesar opens his mouth to ask a million questions when Larry Vaquero gives a loud whistle and smacks his own knee cheerfully. "Well here you are at last! You haven't told them up at the big house, have you? Hoo boy! I took one look at you and I knew who their mysterious stranger was. Bah. Oh my Lord, that woman is gonna gut you when she finds out! Be sure to let me know before you do it so I can get a front row seat, ok?"

Cesar raises his eyes to the ceiling. He briefly entertains an unfilial wish. Couldn't the stroke have slowed his father's wits a little bit?

He sighs and wishes being a good guy wasn't so difficult. "It's complicated, Dad."

"Bah," says his father. "You say: *'Hey toots, we're married! Hey kid, I'm your dad!'* What's so hard about that?"

He has to admit the old guy had a point.

Cesar holds up his palms. "What can I say? Penelope had a shotgun pointed at me. I panicked."

The old man roars with laughter. He bends over and thumps his good leg. Wiping a tear from his drooping left eye, he wheezes, "Oh that girl has gumption, I tell you. Woo! You're a lucky man. Stupid, but lucky."

Taking a breath to calm himself, Larry adds, "I'll be honest. When you first turned up with Penelope, I wasn't impressed. She was just a tiny little thing, scared of her own shadow and throwing up all over the place before she got her space legs. But little Penelope sure has grown on me."

Cesar does the only thing reasonable at that point. He drains his tin cup and gets up to help himself to some more.

"So, what's going on up there with those parties? Is everything really all right?" Cesar asks his dad.

What Cesar really wants to do is sit and listen to stories about Trevor, but he has to make sure they are both safe first. He also needs to know if Penelope has a man somewhere and what the deal with that Wilhelm character is, but he isn't at all anxious to try asking his dad about that. Penelope *said* she hadn't kissed a man since her husband, but would have she been totally honest with the homeless stranger she thinks him to be?

Larry follows Cesar into the kitchen area, identifiable only by the large stacks of dirty dishes. "You hungry? Lupe brings me big tubs of her food. I never can eat it all."

Cesar isn't and says so, but that doesn't stop Larry from heating up enough food for three lunches. It is barely ten in the morning. As Cesar makes a show of eating, Larry leans back against a stack of boxes and begins to talk.

"Well, your wife throws these parties every week and they all talk politics. For a while, I thought she'd lose her head. Get talked into some crazy quest like you did and want to go charging off, never to be seen again. But, no. She really does see those parties as her way of keeping the peace here."

Larry snorts with disgust. "She's as bullheaded as you. She thinks she can solve things by talking them out just like you thought you could solve things by shooting it out. You two idiots are a match, that's for sure. Like two freaks in a pod."

Cesar grins and forks another bite of enchiladas into his mouth. "But Lupe calls them her suitors."

"Well, that's a little true," allows Larry, helping himself to a tortilla off of Cesar's plate. "Some of them do have designs on her and who wouldn't?

She's young, rich, and smokin' hot. I'd try to get a piece of that action if I were a little younger too. What? It's true, you moron. But don't worry. She puts them in their place. Sometimes she tells them she can't sell because I won't allow it. Me looking like a wreck makes them think I might go at any time and they shouldn't push her. Why risk riling up the neighborhood if I die off next week and they can buy it up fair and square? She's a sneaky one, that girl."

"Guess she had to be, out here all by herself," growls Cesar, ducking his head.

Larry pats Cesar on his head like he is a truculent toddler and says, "She tells people that she can't remarry because she's waiting for you to come home, you know."

Cesar laughs, "Oh, I'm pretty sure that's another lie."

"Well, maybe a little bit," allows Larry. "But maybe it's a little true too. It's better than nothing."

"Huh," replies Cesar, trying to think how to ask his next question. "So she's been here the whole time? Alone?"

Old Larry hoots loudly, "Well if you cared about that, maybe you should have dropped by once in a while!"

Cesar snaps back, "You both made it pretty clear you didn't want to see me again. And that was before what I did with the starship!"

He jumps to his feet and drains his tin cup again, thinking wildly that he should leave.

"Oho, my boy," Larry cries, staggering to his feet and putting a hand on Cesar's arm anxiously. "Don't get in a snit. You knew when you finally came home, we'd be a little annoyed that you took so long. And dropping that uranium-filled mining ship on Mexico... Well, kid, not your brightest moment, but you got the job done and we'd be silly to bawl at you for saving all our lives now. Oh, but your wife is gonna kill you about five times when you finally tell her. Fortunately for both of us, she doesn't seem interested in getting another man. Focus on the important thing here, kid. Sit down and talk to your old father. I've, well... I've missed you."

Cesar's sudden anger drops away and he sits down again.

Larry gets up and refills Cesar's tin cup. Chewing on a bit of tortilla, Larry says almost gently, "Now, whether she's got a bit of tail on the side,

I can't really tell you, but she's got no steady man. Hasn't had one as far as I know."

"Huh," replies Cesar.

He is relieved, but knows he didn't have a right to be. He mulls over what she said last night, but finds he keeps getting sidetracked on the more physical parts of the evening and can't think straight.

Cesar grunts, "That Uri Mach is no good."

"Oh really?" asks Larry, somewhat surprised as he pours some orange juice into his cup of tequila. "The Seven Skies trader guy? What makes you say that?"

"I met him before," says Cesar grimly. "Trust me, he's much more evil than he looks."

He is tempted to add *"and I think he's after my wife."* But he doesn't.

"Well, that's not good," grunts Larry. He scratches himself happily for a minute and then asks, "Did he recognize you?"

Cesar shakes his head. "I don't think he will either, but I won't take any chances."

"You think he means harm to her or the boy?" Larry asks, swirling his drink around thoughtfully.

"Don't know," replies Cesar with a shrug. "Guess I'll stick around and find out."

Cesar's dad sighs deeply and props his feet up on a box of tequila bottles. "Son, there have been a lot of attacks on the vitals of this colony lately. Sabotage. Nobody knows who or why. Whoever it is doesn't seem to want to kill us outright, but they sure do seem to want to make life difficult. It's getting hard to make ends meet with all these expensive repairs."

Cesar says that he's heard about this and maybe they should look into it. Larry agrees and sits in silence for a long minute, his mind elsewhere.

Still swirling his drink, Larry asks casually, "Son, were you planning to come out here and pretend to be a stranger to me too?" And then Cesar knows that age must have changed something after all, because he's never heard his father sound hurt before.

"No Dad," he sighs theatrically. "Fooling you and avoiding an earful was too much to hope for." Then he cracks a grin and gives his dad a big hug.

"You crazy kid," laughs Larry, his big hearty self again. "It's good to have you back."

"You won't give me away, right?" Cesar asks him. "You'll let me keep my secret a little longer until I know what to do?"

"Well, I don't know," Larry says, pulling a long face. "I never was a great hand at keeping secrets and telling fibs like you. Don't keep your secret too long. I'm old. I got a bad memory."

"Dad!"

"Oh, come on. I'm messing with you. Who would I tell?" The only person I see is Lupe when she comes to bring me food and haul off the latest shipment of tequila. I make a bunch of money selling it, you know."

Cesar looks around the squalid little shack.

If his dad makes money, he sure isn't spending any of it here. "Are you sure Lupe's not just pouring it down the reclaimer to keep you from pickling your liver?"

Larry empties his cup of tequila and coughs like he's about to die. "Well, if she's is, she's fighting a losing battle."

They laugh and thump each other on the back for a while before getting down to the business of swapping stories of Cesar's travels and the War and every detail of Trevor's life that Larry can remember—drool, diapers and all.

They even talk about Cesar's mother and her death.

Late in the night, after far too much food and tequila, they also make a few plans.

CHAPTER TWELVE

You kiss a man and he'll always make you pay for it. Penelope is certain of that fact all day.

Sometimes they brag about it to all their friends like it is a game and when you kiss them, then somehow they win and you lose. Sometimes they lure you off with promises of seeing the stars and living in the sky but you wind up raising a baby and feeding cows surrounded by strangers in a dirty metal can, hotter and stinkier than anything back home. Sometimes they get you all hot and bothered in the laundry room and then hint at it right in front of your son the next day, followed by casting aspersions on one of the most upright citizens you know before wandering off without explaining anything.

Men.

She would hate them all with a clear conscience if she didn't love her son so much. For Trevor's sake, she has to keep an open mind about the filthy testosterone-infested creatures.

"God, are you trying to kill the elevator, Mom?" Trevor bursts out, lounging against a wall next to her. "I'm pretty sure one more kick like that will do the trick."

Penelope sighs and stops kicking the elevator. She spends a brief moment trying to justify the kicks on the grounds that men probably made the elevator and therefore it is inherently evil, but even she knows that is too ridiculous.

"Sorry, Trevor. I am not a morning person," she sighs, yanking her hair back out of her face as the elevator shudders and rattles its slow way down to the Ag Level.

"What are you talking about?" snorts Trevor. "You love mornings. Every day, you start annoying everybody at the crack of dawn by singing and shouting orders."

"Yeah, well, not today," she grumbles. "Besides, it's not the crack of dawn. You just want to sleep all the time."

They pass the next few moments in a discontented silence before the elevator finally opens with a groan and a squeak and lets them out.

Finally, Trevor says in an over-casual voice, "So that Ulixes guy seems pretty handy, huh?"

Penelope is horrified. Has the man said something to Trevor? Did Trevor know she was shamelessly making out with Ulixes last night? The absolute last thing she wants to do is talk to Trevor about her love life, however nonexistent it is.

She wants to crawl in a hole and die, but instead Penelope shrugs as nonchalantly as she can. "He seems nice. He sure knows how to fix things around the ranch and he's got all those stories. But you know I don't like to keep men around. It's too disruptive."

"Hey Mom, don't do that. Don't send him away already. He's not disruptive. Everybody likes him and he sure is a big help, right?" says Trevor, now overly enthusiastic. "He's been everywhere it sounds like, even down to Earth."

Penelope snorted, "So what? I was born down there."

"Well, I've never been off Ithaca," retorted Trevor. "I sure would like to see some of the other orbitals like he has. I really want to try flying a cargo ship. Mathis says he'll teach me if I want. Cargo ships aren't as dangerous as tinker ships."

Trevor acts like he hasn't brought this up four times already. Penelope always does her best to ignore or "forget" his dream of piloting.

"No."

"Aw, Mom, come on. I can't stay here forever."

"Yes, you can."

"Mom! Be serious!" Trevor cries, kicking a clod of grass. He seems on the verge of a teenage tantrum, but instead he takes a slow deep breath.

In his most reasonable voice, Trevor says, "You know how much you complain about what the shipping company charges? If I was delivering our stuff in a cargo ship, it'd be cheaper and I'd be home practically all the time. Really often, anyway. It makes sense if you'd think it over."

Penelope thinks it makes sense except for the part where it involves her only child out in the void with only a thin wall of metal between him and death by decompression or pirates or god knows what else.

"You are too young," she snaps.

"I won't be too young forever," he snaps back. "I'm only asking to spend a few days in town each week so Mathis can teach me."

"I need you here," she says with a shake of her head.

Penelope knows she is running out of good arguments. With a sinking feeling in the pit of her stomach, she wonders how much longer she can play the "Because I said so!" trump card. Eventually, Trevor will realize he can leave, just like his father. The thought makes her stomach churn.

"No, you don't," cries Trevor triumphantly. "You've got Ulixes and he's way more useful than me."

"Ulixes is passing through," Penelope protests.

"Oh come on. Passing through to where?" asks Trevor. "He's got no-where to go and he loves it here. You can't kick him out."

"I can if I want to," Penelope replies firmly. "You know I don't like men here. Besides, he seems like a wanderer. Once he's healed and Lupe's fat-tened him up a bit, he'll be off."

"Well, then there will be someone to go with me when I start flying," Trevor shoots back. "Ulixes flew with my dad. He can fly with me."

They arrive at the corral. Penelope never remembered the walk tak-ing this long before. She thinks many unkind thoughts about Ulixes for putting these ideas in her son's head, but eventually cleaning hooves and checking tongues burn the anger out of her.

Penelope realizes that she will have to be smarter than this if she wants to keep her son safe. Threats, commands and arguments didn't work on Cesar, not from his parents and not from her. Penelope winces a little, thinking about him. Cesar is another topic she tries to avoid thinking about. In theory, she'll eventually forget him.

She returns her mind to a safer subject, Trevor. She can't make him stay. She knows that. What can she do?

Penelope mulls the question over all day.

Regretfully, it seems the best course is to let him learn to pilot a ship. It will keep him complacent, at least for a few years. Perhaps that will be enough time for him to grow out of this pilot fantasy and into something safer. If not, better he leave in a few years as a trained pilot than an ignorant runaway.

Trevor works all day in a sullen silence that he doesn't break even when they stop for lunch. Penelope knows her son is giving her the silent treatment as he chews angrily on one of the sandwiches she packed. That is fine by her. It is long past noon, almost sunset, when Penelope calls it quits and they start walking back to the elevator.

"Fine," says Penelope.

"What?" Trevor grunts. He is sure his mom is going to start up the argument again.

"Fine. You can learn to fly," says Penelope, matter-of-factly pushing the button to start the elevator's ponderous trip back to the ranch. "You can go into town and learn from Mathis. How often do you think you should go? Twice a week? I'll ask around and see if we can't get some other pilots to teach you too. It would be good for you to have experience with a variety of ships. And you'll need to start studying astronavigation. I'll download the texts when we get home."

"Mom!" Trevor shouts gleefully, giving her a hard hug. He manages to grind his bony elbow into her side as he does it, but Penelope doesn't mind. "This is awesome! Don't worry about astronav. I passed the competency exam six months ago. Can I get propulsion physics though? Ulixes says I'll need a solid grounding if I ever get stuck with a broken engine."

"Sure," she sighs, still wishing he was a baby and she could cuddle him in her lap.

"So, you'll let Ulixes stay? At least for a while? He knows a lot," Trevor asks, his mind spinning with plans and fantasies.

"I don't know," Penelope replies because she really doesn't and she feels she's made enough mature decisions for one day.

"Then what will you do with him?" Trevor asks, not really paying attention.

It was an excellent question.

CHAPTER THIRTEEN

Cesar is walking the walk of shame. That inevitable stumble home the morning after an evening that involved far too much fun and went much too late, only Cesar is doing it as the sun sets because he's been with his father for a day and a half.

His hair is grimy and his clothes are rumpled. His head feels like it's swollen to at least twice its normal size and his eyes are sticky. His stomach has declared open rebellion against a steady diet of enchiladas and tequila and is now trying to crawl out through his nose.

Cesar concentrates on the most important goal and that is to sneak back into his little room before Penelope sees him like this. His secondary goals involve a shower and bland food, but he isn't sure how to accomplish them without Penelope seeing him. The woman is everywhere. He is bound to disgrace himself in front of her.

There was something to be said for a woman not being so all-fired effective, he thinks.

"Young man, you look like death on a cracker," Lupe snaps.

Cesar whirls to find the little old woman standing behind him, scowling. Women.

They are everywhere on this ranch. He's gone months at a time in space without seeing so much as a hint of one and here he can't walk two steps without them popping out of the grass like… some sort of thing that popped.

"You been back there carousing with that old pirate," Lupe sniffs. "You smell like a distillery."

"That's because he's got a distillery back there," Cesar replies, trying hard not to slur. He considers the possibility that he is not entirely sober yet. He thought he was when he started walking, but now he isn't so sure.

Lupe grabs his shirt and starts hauling him towards the main house. Cesar knows this is exactly the place he doesn't want to go so he digs in his heels like a mule.

"Relax, Romeo, she's down with the herd," chuckles Lupe. "But you only got maybe an hour to clean up and, trust me, you got a lot of cleaning up to do."

"Romeo?" asks Cesar weakly. He allows himself to be dragged now that he knows there will probably be soap at the end of this journey and not a Penelope giving him the stink-eye.

Lupe cackles gleefully. "*Ay carumba, muchacho.* I see the way you look at her. It's no problem. All the men are in love with her."

Suddenly she turns and produces a wooden spoon from one of the pockets in her skirt. Before he knows what's happening, Lupe smacks him hard on the arm with the wooden spoon.

"But she's too good for a drifter like you!" she says fiercely. "So unless you got a gold mine somewhere that you haven't mentioned yet, you behave yourself, *gringo*."

Cesar rubs his arm.

"You just hit me with a spoon." He knows this isn't the most intelligent thing to say, so he tries again. "I know Penelope is too good for me."

That seems to mollify Lupe.

The spoon disappears and Lupe gives a satisfied chuckle, "Yes, she is. But you can still try. She needs a little romance in her life. So go get cleaned up and I'll get you some food. Hurry."

Cesar hurries.

He is tempted to spend the rest of his life in the hot steamy shower, but he keeps having an unsettling daydream in which Penelope discovers him in her shower. Cesar tries hard to make this a naughty fantasy, but he is too practical to expect anything other than horror on her part and embarrassment on his.

Feeling a million times better but still not quite human, Cesar dries off and puts on the clean clothes that Lupe shoved at him. In the kitchen, there is strong coffee and a plate full of *carne guisada* for him. He says a prayer of thanks to whatever gods may be for a woman that can cook.

Lupe keeps up a stream of chatter about all the small doings of the ranch as she prepares vats of food. Between the cowgirls and Trevor's bottomless teenage stomach, dinner is always massive here.

Cesar loves every minute of it. He sighs happily, amazed at how content he can be, sitting in a kitchen listening to gossip over a strong cup of coffee.

Getting up to wash off his dirty dishes, he tells Lupe, "That hit the spot, *abuela*." She turns to him, her hand out for his dirty dishes.

Then her eyes pop open suddenly.

"Cesar!" Lupe screeches.

Then a whole stream of Spanish pours out her mouth, some prayers of thanks to the Holy Father that brought back her prodigal boy and some very dirty curses.

Cesar tries desperately to calm her down before anyone else comes in. Too late he realizes that the clothes she gave him to wear are actually old ones he'd left behind all those years ago. Also, Cesar had called Lupe *abuela* every day of his life before he left.

He sighs. It is profoundly stupid to try and fool your family. Before he knows it, she's grabbed a fistful of his pants and yanked them down hard.

"There! I knew it!" Lupe cries triumphantly pointing at the scar running down his thigh. When he was five, he'd climbed into a bullpen to pet the sharp-horned bull and gotten this scar for his efforts.

"Yes, it's me," he hisses. "Please, don't tell on me yet."

Lupe gasps and crosses herself reflexively. "What are you doing, running off with no word for years and years and then coming home pretending to be someone else? That's not how your *pobre madre* raised you. No, it's not."

She slaps him with a wet dishrag, almost as an afterthought. Cesar wipes soap off his face and watches Lupe warily. Lupe is not a fast thinker, a fact that saved Cesar from many a well-deserved beating as a child. He sees dismay cross her face as she realizes that she just assaulted a grown man. Then a frown appears as she thinks of the decades of slaps that Cesar has missed out on by leaving.

This is replaced rapidly by a look of steely determination as she raises the rag again. Cesar is fully prepared to bolt for the lawn if she tries to dispense fifteen years of accumulated corporal punishment. Fortunately, at that moment they both hear footsteps and voices in the yard. Yanking his pants up, Cesar knows he doesn't have time for a long heartfelt talk right now.

"Lupe, I'm sorry," he whispers bluntly. "Sorry for everything, but please let me tell Trevor and Penelope in my own way. Please?"

Lupe sniffs.

She nods once quickly as Trevor comes walking in with Penelope close behind him.

"Hey Ulixes! Mom says I can be a ship pilot! *Carne guisada* for dinner? Wicked!" cries the boy happily, taking Cesar's plate out of his hand and filling it up with food, talking the whole time about ships, navigation, shipping lanes and solar sails.

Lupe makes a show of turning her back on Cesar.

Penelope stops in the doorway when she sees Cesar, her hand going up automatically to smooth her hair. She walks self-consciously through the room and into the back of the house. Cesar can hear the sounds of her washing up.

Lupe gives him a significant look and whispers, "She's still too good for you."

"You don't have to tell me," Cesar mutters back out of the side of his mouth. "We'll talk later."

Lupe sniffs. "Oh, we most certainly will, young man."

The cowgirls come tumbling into the room with Argos, laughing and chattering. Lupe turns back to her pots and pans while Cesar stands there for a minute, not sure what he should do. Probably, he should go and earnestly tell Penelope the truth, have a long serious talk and hope for mercy.

Instead, he slips out the door and back to his little room with its single bed where he falls into a deep sleep.

CHAPTER FOURTEEN

Penelope desperately needs to throw this guy out of her house. She doesn't need to be worrying about getting caught kissing in the laundry room like a teenager. She doesn't need to toss and turn all night with dreams about rough hands on her body and the coarse feel of stubble on her cheek.

She just doesn't need this.

Accordingly, the next morning Penelope asks Ulixes to help her work on the Ag Level water pump. There isn't anything really wrong with it that hasn't been wrong with it for the last decade, but it is in a remote part of the ranch and she can't think of a better place to talk to this man privately. She is glad when he readily agrees.

•

Cesar knows exactly how secluded the Ag Level water pump is, having snuck out there many a time to smoke cigarettes and drink beer as a teenager.

He thinks this will be the ideal location to reveal his identity to Penelope. Someplace where no one can hear her scream at him and there is nothing lethal she can hit him with. It is also over three miles from the nearest elevator, so she can't run away before he has a chance to explain. It is even farther from the nearest shotgun. Cesar checked.

However much he is not looking forward to the conversation, it needs to happen, so the sooner the better. He sets his shoulders and follows Penelope, determined to hold his tongue until he tells her the truth.

•

As they make their way down the elevator, Penelope's thoughts begin to run along a different path.

Sure, he can't stay. Of course, he can't stay. The man is a drifter and will probably wander off on his own any day now. She has that rule about men staying here anyway and to break it will mean having to admit this man means something to her. She can't have that.

But if he is leaving, then what harm is there in indulging this bizarre attraction before he goes? Penelope thinks about all the Ether dramas she watched in her life and decides perhaps she is being too harsh on herself and on this man. Perhaps she ought to be more open-minded.

If he is leaving anyway, why not steal a few moments of passion before he goes gently into that good night? They get off the elevator and begin walking. The more Penelope walks, the more logical this idea seems.

A good, thorough sexing up will do her good. There are the health benefits to consider. Penelope tries to think of a few beyond a clear complexion and a good night's sleep, but gives up. She has never had an affair previously because her world is so small and sex always came with too many strings attached. But here is this attractive drifter who is obviously interested in her in that way.

Penelope studies the man out of the corner of her eye as he trudges along. He is discreet. She knows almost nothing about him after ten days. So probably the fact that he's made love to the Widow of Ithaca won't come up in casual conversation and rumors won't come crawling back to haunt her. In all likelihood, she can have all the red hot loving she wants with this man and then never see or hear from him again.

The more she thinks about it, the more attractive Mr. Ulixes becomes.

•

Cesar walks without knowing where he goes, so focused is he on coming up with the words that will convince Penelope not to turn him away. There must be some set of words that will make her forgive him. If only he can think of the right way to arrange his thoughts into eloquent arguments so that she'll give him another chance.

Cesar tries to think logically about what he will do if she absolutely throws him out, but he has a hard time making his brain focus on that painful idea.

He can't leave. Surely she can see that?

Cesar needs to find out about the sabotage situation. He needs to know his son and he needs to protect Penelope and Trevor from Uri Mach and his dad obviously needs help. And he doesn't want to go. He really doesn't want to go. He wants to stay here more than he's ever wanted anything. With the force of all his years and any knowledge, experience or wisdom he might have ever gained, he wants his wife to love him again.

Cesar scowls at the ground beneath his feet as they walk on in silence. Penelope must suspect something, he decides. She isn't talking. They've been walking along for an hour in silence. He can see they are almost at the water pump.

This area is one of the prettiest parts of the ranch. Cesar's father planted peach trees here and created a private little grove. Cesar's mother loved peaches. This morning, the peach trees are blooming, throwing their sweet scent in the air like confetti.

Morning glory vines wind around the tree trunks and undergrowth. In the middle of the grove is a little building to house the water pump and the tools necessary for tending the peach trees. As a teen, Cesar had come here to smoke grapevine and use his comm to browse the naughtier parts of the Ether.

Cesar has no eyes for the pastoral scene today. What is Penelope thinking? That's all he wants to know. She is probably getting ready to throw him out for the impertinence of kissing her.

Hell, she probably isn't thinking about him at all. That is a depressing thought.

She is probably thinking about starting an affair with that engineer Asner. That is a more depressing thought.

Cesar torments himself for a few minutes by imagining Penelope slipping into some black lacy nothing for another man, but then gets distracted by the mental image as his imagination takes a lurid turn. Before he can check the impulse, a lascivious smile curls up his lips and he looks at her only to find her eyes on him.

Cesar gulps and knows that the moment has come. He takes her hand in his and moves a step closer to her. Penelope is giving him the oddest look, a curious smile on her lips. He stammers and stutters, not knowing how to begin. All his carefully plotted arguments and persuasive phrases are lost.

It turned out that he doesn't need them. Before he knows what was happening, Penelope is in his arms. Her lips are on his. Her body molds against him like they were made for each other. Cesar feels his eyebrows practically leap off his face, but he is no fool. He kisses her passionately.

They are lost to all but each other for quite a while. At one point, Cesar takes a deep breath and tries to say something, but Penelope holds a finger to his lips.

"Now is not the time for talking," she whispers.

Well, Cesar never liked to contradict a lady.

As they fall into the thick grass, Cesar tries to tell her he loves her, but before the words form, she nips his ear gently with her teeth and then trails sizzling kisses down his chest. After that, all he can manage was a groan.

Much later, they lie together on the grass, watching peach blossoms drift from the trees. He runs his hand lightly down the small of her back, marveling at the soft, almost velvety skin.

Cesar no longer trusts himself to speak. He is content to feel her gentle breath across his chest as her cheek lies against his shoulder. He finds himself half-hoping that she already knows. That this is her way of letting him know all is forgiven. Wouldn't that be wonderful? To get exactly what he wants without even having that awful awkward conversation.

He sighs. No, he isn't that lucky.

Life is never that easy.

On the other hand, judging from the noises she was making earlier, Penelope is probably in a very good mood right now. If Cesar is going to tell her who he really is, now is a great time. She'll probably be pretty happy to find out that instead of making love to a stranger, she's actually made love to her husband.

Cesar turns his head to speak to her and realizes Penelope is softly snoring. She's fallen asleep there against him. His heart melts and he tightens his arms around her. Not enough to wake her, just enough to feel her heart fluttering against his ribs. Then he frowns, returning to his previous thought.

If Penelope doesn't know who he really is, then she's just made love to a stranger. Cesar does not like the idea at all. He might have gotten in a serious snit about it except she is so warm and soft against him that he falls asleep too.

•

Penelope wakes up with a start and realizes she is drooling on a man's chest. This is definitely not how she is accustomed to waking up.

She closes her eyes, remembering the joy of the afternoon. With a thoroughly satisfied sigh, she stretches luxuriously before looking around for her clothes. She sees them scattered here and there around the grove, but makes no move to retrieve them yet.

Penelope has no idea what she's been missing in the last fifteen years. She really must have forgotten how much fun sex was, because if she'd known it was like that, she'd have been doing it with every other man she saw.

Realistically, probably not.

Penelope's gut instinct tells her that it is not like this with every other man. Fortunately, making love to this stranger was stunningly similar to her dim memories of making love to her husband.

Maybe it is the same with all men? That would be a big letdown. She's been saving herself all these years and the whole time, any random guy could have been scratching this itch. Penelope could have given the Whore of Babylon a run for her money if she'd known it would be good with any man, but she hadn't. Is she just dumb?

The truth is, Penelope has long suspected that most men aren't any good at sex or, at least, not any good at making it fun for her too. She suspects that good lovemaking requires brains in a man. He has to be smart to know how to make love to a woman. And there is something else.

She isn't really sure what.

Whatever it is, she'd found it two out of two times and those were pretty good odds. She's never been interested in seeing anyone else naked except for her husband and he'd been quite good at sex too. After some practice, anyway.

Penelope figures it was just her luck to fall in love with one of the few men good in bed and then he went and abandoned her here for whatever reason. But she could have sworn Cesar really loved her. Or maybe what she thought was love was only lust? It certainly felt like the real thing. Or at least, at the time she couldn't imagine wanting anyone or anything else more. Perhaps that was simply lust though.

Right now all she wants to do was wake up this mystery man and explore some long held fantasies. That sure sounds to her like pure lust. Penelope lies on her back and stares into the sunless sky above her. She obviously doesn't pick men based on their ability to stick around and make a life together. If that were the case, she'd have married Wilhelm Asner or Mr. Finomus or half a dozen stable, successful men who have been interested in her over the last fifteen years.

She must have terrible taste in men, because instead of any of them here she is with this drifter. Someone she knows nothing about.

Penelope turns to look at her sleeping mystery man as he lies on his side, turned away from her and snoring softly. Penelope admires the curve of his biceps and softness over his belly and hips. She molds her body to his back, pulls her arm across his chest, and stops thinking. He sighs and rolls over to pulls her into his rough embrace without opening his eyes.

Any thoughts she had about sending this man away could wait for another day, Penelope decides. Already her mind turns to likely spots for future trysts. The ranch house is tricky. Her room is private enough, but too many people could see him coming and going. This little grove is lovely and outdoor sex is fun, but a girl does like a bed.

There is the room she shared with her husband. She locked that door the day he left and it's been closed ever since.

No, she isn't going back in there now and definitely not with a new lover. Penelope sighs and abandons thoughts of anything but right now as he turns over and draws her to him again.

A few hours later, they walk back to the elevators grinning like fools. Once, Ulixes stops to brush grass out of her hair and steal a kiss. Later, Penelope helps him straighten his collar in the elevator and runs her hands down his body.

He pulls her close and whispers, "Let me come to you tonight."

She blushes and agrees, pulling away from him before the doors open.

Back at the ranch, Ulixes slips away to help Argos. But not before he gives her one last lingering look as she heads into the house, carefully not watching him walk away. Penelope showers quickly, smoothing her hair and trying to scrub the glow from her cheeks. Then she goes to help Lupe with dinner.

Lupe looks her over and sniffs loudly, but says nothing. Nothing in English anyway. She mutters in Spanish about people trying to get away with things they shouldn't. Penelope decides to ignore it as Lupe bangs pots and pans, punishing them for her worries.

How she gets through the rest of the day, Penelope never knows. The hustle and bustle and warm good cheer of dinner is like a distant parade to her. Thankfully, Ulixes shows up only briefly to collect a plate of food that he takes back to his bunk without looking at her.

Penelope hears Lupe say something rude to him, but she knows that if she even looks in his direction, she'll give everything away. Penelope always thought of herself as a good liar when lying was required, but this feeling is too big to keep inside. It's like a fire radiating heat out of her very pores. She almost asks Argos, sitting next to her, if he can feel the warmth of it.

Penelope excuses herself as soon as she can, mumbling something about a headache. She goes to her room and flops down on her bed, fully clothed. Pulling out her customary braid, she finger combs her hair, spreads it across the bed, sighing at the pleasure of letting it loose.

Wouldn't it be nice to let go of all the other bindings of her life? No, this is a good life. She knows that. Others have it much worse.

She has her son, friends, work she likes and plenty to eat and relative safety. Whatever bindings chafe her, they aren't that bad. And yet... This life is so far from where she started. She could have ended up so many other ways. Penelope's mind turns to the choices she made to get to this most unlikely place.

CHAPTER FIFTEEN

During the Worlder Wars, a debutante in San Antonio lived as sheltered a life as a girl can lead on a thousand acre ranch run mostly by robots. Half the time, Penelope was sneaking off to help her brothers break horses, brand cows and castrate steers. Not that they ever actually did anything more than watch the robots wield the lasers while they chewed stolen wads of Daddy's new-baccy and spit and pretended to be real cowboys.

The other half, she was being sewn into dresses so elaborate they required magnetic hoverhoops to keep their shape. Penelope would complain to her mother that if she was so ugly it required anti-gravity devices to make her look attractive, then maybe she should stay home.

"Penny, you know you are pretty, you spoiled girl," Penelope's mother would sigh, as though her daughter exhausted her. "Why are you always complaining? You are one of the luckiest girls in the whole world. It is your responsibility to your family to attend these balls and make yourself pleasant. Charm your father's business partners and maybe one of them will marry you. Then you can go live on their ranch where I can't hear all your complaining."

Penelope could never understand why her mother bought into all that patriarchal crap. It was almost the twenty-second century, for the love of God. Girls could do whatever they wanted now. Half her father's business friends were women. Well, a quarter anyway. More than half the population was divorced, remarried a dozen times or in some sort of not-quite-monogamous arrangement. It was just her luck that Penelope would get born into one of the last families in the world that still thought getting married was the be-all, end-all point of female existence.

Just her luck.

So Penelope would dutifully paste a smile on her face and charm her father's business partners in Spanish, English or whatever other language they preferred. She spent her young life learning to be charming and she was good at it.

Afterwards, she would slip back to her room and download another veterinary textbook. She had this elaborate and possibly nonsensical fantasy that involved becoming a certified veterinarian and traveling far away where nobody knew her father.

Penelope knew that when she grew up, she'd wear jeans and ratty shirts with fringe music bands on them for the rest of her life. She'd travel the world and maybe even visit those orbitals too. She'd stay up all night dancing and spend all day outside in the dirt with the animals.

What could be better?

Penelope knew the minute she saw Cesar Vaquero that she was easy picking's for this boy. She might as well have embroidered a welcome mat across her chest and flung herself at his feet.

Penelope always hated the way she wanted Cesar. It made her feel powerless. It scared her. She kind of hated him for it. She was sure she couldn't trust him with her instant and unconditional love. It was almost a relief when he finally broke her heart.

She'd always known he would.

Ever since the day Cesar Vaquero showed up with his father at one of San Antonio's endless parties. She saw him through the crowd before he saw her. Tall and handsome, he had hair so red it practically glowed. Cesar looked around the room like he was on safari and they were a herd of giraffes.

That wasn't what caused all the gossips to titter and whisper, though. It was his clothes—the grav boots, the spacer pants with all their pockets, expensive real-leather cowboy hat, and the gaudy shirt that he must have picked up somewhere in town, mistakenly thinking it made him blend in. It all gave him away.

He was Spacer. A real live Spacer.

Penelope knew every girl at the party and quite a few of the married women were lusting after this boy, so she felt no qualms about joining in the gossip and the sidelong glances. It was harmless fun.

In all likelihood, he'd never even see her. His father was handsome too, in the rough-and-ready way they were all used to out here on the edge of the "civilized" world. Within minutes of departing their shuttle, every member of San Antonio's high society was gossiping about the handsome Vaqueros.

They talked about how the father, Larry Vaquero, had inherited one of the richest and oldest ranches in Texas, only to sell off everything and gamble it all on this colony in the sky. It had been a big scandal twenty years ago. Everyone had been sure that he'd come to a bad end.

Much to the disappointment of the gossips, Larry had not squandered away his wealth on a foolish dream, but instead built a Spacer empire and raised a child. Then he hadn't done much else of interest until he'd decided to come back for a visit and bring his handsome young son with him to see the old country. The members of San Antonio high society were very much attached to the idea of being part of the Vaquero's "old country."

"Big hat, no cattle," Penelope whispered to her best friend as they eyed Cesar talking to a group near them.

Her friend smothered a scandalized giggle. It used to be something people said in Texas about out-of-towners who pretended to be ranchers, but it had turned into a joke about the size of a man's private parts, on the level of *"All talk and nothing in the sack."*

"He's from the Ithaca colony," her friend whispered back, pointing towards the sky. "That ranch up there. His dad owns it. He's got lots of cattle, actually. Space cattle."

"Figures," laughed Penelope, throwing her hands up with mock disappointment. "Cows. Always cows. It's too much too hope that we'd get anything really exotic, like a Spacer that builds lasers or mines asteroids with robots or something."

Her friend's eyes grew to the size of saucers. Penelope turned to see why and found Cesar Vaquero standing right behind her with a mischievous grin on his face.

He looked right at her and drawled in a gravely grave voice that sent shivers down her spine, "Ma'am, I can build a laser."

Penelope blushed and that made her angry. She said hotly, "So you play with lasers while your daddy tends to business? They have dilettantes in space too, I guess."

Then she bit her lip. That came out so much meaner than she'd wanted to be.

It was his turn to blush. "No, I don't," he said with a frown. "I know how to build a laser, that's all. If that makes me a dilettante down here, then I guess the Earth is a lot weirder than I thought."

"I'm sorry," Penelope rushed to say, aware that she'd been rude and there were many eyes on her right now. "What I meant to say was: Hello, my name is Penelope. Welcome to Earth."

She curtsied formally and smiled at him brightly, hoping to cover her slightly-too-rude remarks.

He laughed and made an attempt at a formal bow.

"It's nice to meet you, Penelope," he said with delighted civility. "My name is Cesar. This is a very nice little planet you have here."

"Can I help you to some refreshments, Mr. Spacer?" Penelope replied in her best giving-the-visitors-a-tour voice.

When he nodded, she slipped her hand onto his arm and they stiffly walked to the refreshment room where he acquired punch for them. They both delighted in pretending to be formal adults instead of rowdy teens, loose at a party.

Penelope asked him questions about the Ithaca herd with regards to their health. Since she was interested in veterinary medicine, the differences between Spacer cows and those on Earth was a fascinating subject for her.

Penelope took no offence to his initial surprise that there was anything factual floating around in her pretty little head. She was used to that. Nobody ever expected her to have two brain cells to rub together. What stole her heart was how quickly Cesar got over it.

They plunged into a long conversation about the effects of gravity on bovine gastric motility and how to counteract the increased rates of hypernatremia found in the Ithaca herd. Later, Penelope would wonder whether it was the smell of him, his deep earnest eyes or the joy of a stimulating intellectual conversation that made her want to tear all his clothes off and run her tongue all over his body.

Whatever it was, Cesar must have felt it too because he dragged her behind a tree and kissed her thoroughly the first chance he got. She responded enthusiastically, but eventually Penelope knew she'd have to get back or she'd get in trouble.

"Is there someplace we can go? You and me?" whispered Cesar raggedly, trying to pull her back into his arms.

"Looking for a bit of fun on vacation, Spaceman? Something you can brag about to your friends back home?" Penelope asked as she gently pushed away from him to catch her breath.

She laughed to cover the reproach in her words. She threw up one of her hands and sighed, "There are Earth girls that are easy, but I'm not one of them. I'm sure you'll have no trouble finding another girl in this crowd."

"No," Cesar said, looking frustrated. "I like *you*. I want to see *you* again. Can we go somewhere, now, just to talk? Are you hungry? Is there a place to get food or something? I only want to talk to you. You're fun."

He looked at her with eyes that melted her soul.

Oh, how much she wanted him, wanted to believe he could feel the way she felt!

While she was mostly busy getting caught up in the romance of it all, there was a part of her brain wildly trying to think of someplace private they could go so she could let this boy do what he liked with her. Another part was trying desperately to remember why she might want get away from the temptation he offered. In the end, they snuck out and ended up at an all-night coffee shop near the old university.

They were wildly out of place in their party finery. Over the stares and whispers of the five other people in the shop that night, Penelope and Cesar talked desperately and disjointedly, both distracted by their frustrated desire to touch each other.

She talked about all the places she wanted to visit, all the sites she wanted to see and sounds she wanted to hear, all the experiences she wanted to have. He talked about all the things he wanted to do and to be. Penelope never could remember what she actually said or what they really talked about, she only remembered marveling at the eloquent arguments and the insightful monologues that their unfulfilled attraction inspired.

Perhaps it was like that for everyone.

She didn't know.

When it was far past the time she should have gone back, they decided to walk instead of take a drone cab home. They took advantage of every possible dark corner and private nook on the way. And, of course, they wandered all night, got lost, and eventually called a drone cab. Penelope knew she would be in such incredible trouble when she got home. She didn't want to go, but every moment she avoided it was another day she'd be grounded or worse.

"I probably won't be able to see you again," she whispered as Cesar held her close.

It was a typical San Antonio night, sticky and hot. All she wanted to do was crawl out of this close little car, shimmy out of her scratchy dress and lie, naked and panting, on the cool grass that rolled past the window.

"No," Cesar insisted, wiping sweat from his brow and folding her hands into his sweaty ones. "I'll talk to your father. I'll apologize for keeping you out so late. I'm here with my dad for another week. We can spend it together."

Penelope gave a short laugh. "A week? That's all? Then what does it matter if I see you again or not? Next week, you'll be gone and it will be like we never met at all. Better to end now than prolong the agony."

She smiled to take the sting out of it. Kissing her palms, Cesar shook his head. "We'll be together for as long as we have. And then I'll come back for you. You'll wait for me. You'll wait for me, right?"

His eyes went adorably puppy-dog big, willing her to believe that it would be like that. It sounded so very right and yet so much like every pathetic teen love story on the Ether. The ones that never ended well for the girl.

Penelope shook her head. "You won't come back."

Pushing away from him, Penelope smoothed her hair and took a deep breath, trying to end this dream without tears and also trying to brace herself for the coming fight with her parents. Cesar wouldn't let her. Pulling her back into his arms, his eyes blazed.

"Then I'll take you with me," he declared.

Even at the time, it sounded like so much stupid teen drama, but somehow it hadn't been. He'd been totally serious. Penelope never could quite understand that part.

Somehow, instead of dropping her off at her house to face the wrath of her father, Cesar came in with her and had taken the brunt of it. Somehow, they'd spent the next week together and at the end, they were standing in front of a clerk signing a marriage license.

Of course, as soon as she told her family and her father stopped cursing and her mother stopped weeping, they prevailed upon the Vaqueros to extend their stay another two days. Then there was a hurried little wedding in the church that every member of her family had been baptized in since they started building churches in this part of the world. Penelope wore one of her cousin's old wedding dresses and almost tripped over it when they walked down the aisle. Her cousin was four inches taller, but there'd been no time for alterations.

Penelope really had no idea how all this had happened. It seemed like the right thing to do at the time even though it felt like she was playing a part in an Ether drama more than it felt like her actual life. Cesar seemed so sure about everything, so sure that this was what they should do.

Penelope admitted only to herself that she wasn't so sure, but she couldn't seem to stop, couldn't bear not to reach for this dream she suddenly desired so desperately. Thus she found herself sitting next to Cesar, her brand new husband, and his highly unimpressed father, Larry Vaquero, on a shuttle bound for the stars.

Cesar swallowed three blue pills and fell asleep. He'd offered some to Penelope but she wanted to watch their escape from Earth through the tiny window.

"We'll visit every star in the sky," Cesar whispered to her drowsily. "I'll take you everywhere you ever dreamed of going. Together we'll see more than the world, we'll see the galaxy."

"Do you really think we can?" asked Penelope for the fourth time that day. "It seems like it ought to be impossible to actually do the things you dream."

"Not for us," slurred Cesar, puffing out his chest to make her laugh. "For you, I can do anything. Anything in this galaxy! For you, I can spin the sky."

Then Cesar squeezed her hand, closed his eyes and began to snore.

Penelope figured most of what he said was drug-induced euphoria, but she found that she liked him saying it anyway. She had no idea she would be such a sap about all this romantic stuff. Penelope watched Cesar doze for a while and then turned to see how his father was doing.

"My wife is gonna kill me," the old man kept muttering while taking swigs from a flask and tucking it back into his jacket.

Penelope wanted to soothe him but she'd never reassured an adult in her life. She gave it her best shot.

"My parents didn't kill me," she pointed out.

Larry Vaquero looked at her, really looked at her for the first time in this whole crazy week.

"Honey, you may come to regret that," he said. "The sad truth of it is that your parents are much nicer people than my wife. I wouldn't have it any other way, of course. But sudden changes make her cranky. So she may not be her normal sweet self when you meet her or for a few months after that, frankly. And I apologize, but this shuttle ride is gonna make you wish you was dead."

Penelope shook her head and chirped, "Oh, I'll be fine Mr. Vaquero. Don't worry about me."

Cesar's dad held out the flask. Seeing the expression on his face, Penelope took the flask and swallowed as much as she dared. It felt like someone was dry-cleaning her lungs.

Coughing, Penelope asked the old man, "What was that?"

"It's really better not to think about it," Larry said.

She did keep thinking about it, but it didn't matter. After five minutes in the air, whatever Penelope swallowed from that flask was spewed inside the vomit bag she clutched like a lifeline. In another five minutes, Penelope became convinced that she must be a dangerously unstable moron to ever think that this was a good idea. Circumstances since then tended to support that conclusion.

•

Penelope blinks away the memories of yesterday and tries to go to sleep. She knows it's silly, but she keeps waiting for the door to creak open, revealing the shadow of her mystery man intent on ravishing her all night long. Turning over, she tells herself to relax and go to sleep. Nothing that interesting is going to happen tonight.

As it turns out, Penelope is wrong.

A mere ten minutes later the door flies open to reveal shattering plates and pictures. The ground beneath her shudders and shakes. Penelope lurches into the hallway to find Trevor already running for the front door.

They bolt to escape the swaying house as the whole orbital makes a horrible crunching sound.

CHAPTER SIXTEEN

"**S**o, now I'm having an affair with my own wife," Cesar tells the ceiling. The ceiling is unsympathetic.

Cesar Vaquero stretches out on the stiff mattress of his tiny bed in the bunkhouse sickroom and sighs. Looking at the ceiling, he seeks to sum up his current situation in a way that sounds more mature and understandable.

Sighing again, Cesar says aloud, "I am an idiot."

He can't help laughing at himself and then he keeps on chuckling quietly. The residual joy from an afternoon spent in unexpected intimacy with Penelope comes bubbling to the surface at the slightest opportunity.

Then the ceiling drops on him.

Cesar is momentarily stunned, first from the fleeting feeling that the room is passing judgment upon him and then from the sharp pain of having the roof cave in on his face. After a dazed moment, Cesar realizes he is bruised but otherwise unhurt and also that the colony is in serious structural peril.

Crawling out from the rubble, Cesar sees the silhouettes of screaming people running through the night before the ground gives another terrific heave and throws them all down. Cesar has never heard or felt anything like this.

It is like Ithaca is tearing itself apart.

Staggering towards the house, he sees Trevor and Penelope streaking towards the private elevator, both carrying more ammo and guns than they can really handle. Penelope has a comm unit and is shrieking orders into it. Cesar bolts after them. He isn't the only one. Argos and the cowgirls are following close behind.

"We're under attack," Trevor tells him when he catches up, passing him a gun without slowing down. The boy's lips are white with worry.

"Invasion?" asks Cesar tightly, ripping off the gun's faceplate and cranking up the stun settings to a lethal dose. He's seen slave ships before. His family isn't getting on one today.

Penelope answers Cesar on the move, "No. Thieves. Someone is trying to steal the herd."

"The herd?" Cesar cries, disbelief making him hoarse.

"Yeah, that's what they are telling me," she replies over her shoulder, waving at her comm unit meaningfully. Penelope turns to look at him, bewilderment and shock all over her face.

Argos has been following them closely. He calls out, "So, wait. If they are just trying to steal the cows, what's happening to the colony?"

A huge mirror comes crashing down much too close for comfort, spraying shards of glass and leaving Argos and several of the cowgirls with bloody gashes.

Penelope cries in frustration, "Don't know. I guess they did something to mess us up good. Let's hope it's fixable."

Trevor shouts, "Maybe they sabotaged something to keep us busy while they steal the cows?"

"Maybe they sabotaged something to kill us while they steal the cows," Penelope replies grimly. "The engineers say they have everything under control up there. They say whatever the problem is that it's coming from the Ag Level. They think something is attached to one of the walls down there. So that's where we're going and you all better hope we can fix this because there aren't enough vacuum suits down there for all of us."

They reach the elevator before the cowgirls can really get over the shock of the situation. The women look around in a daze while Cesar, accustomed to dire circumstance, keeps scanning the ceiling for more falling debris. When Penelope gets to the elevator, she immediately pushes the button to lock it in place so they won't have to worry about it squashing them. Then she pulls ropes and harnesses out of the emergency closet next to it and starts passing them out.

Cesar has lost count of the times his father drilled him on how to use rappelling ropes down the elevator shafts during emergencies. So he remembers how to cinch the belt and thread the rope even though he's never actually done it during a real live emergency. Penelope obviously kept up the drills because they all start strapping in without comment.

Cesar briefly wonders where his father is right now. Probably drunk in his little cabin. Hopefully not smashed to death by a falling mirror. If he survives this, Cesar is going to check on his father as soon as he can.

"Have they breached the vacuum seal?" pants Trevor.

"No, thank God. Not yet, anyway."

"Are they still here?" questions Argos. "Maybe they haven't got the herd yet."

Penelope throws her hands up. "I don't know. How about we focus on fixing the stationquake issue before we all die?"

Cesar hopes the thieves are still around. He'd love a chance to punch someone right in the mouth for this assault on the safety of his family. Except that would mean the bad guys are still around to do more damage. Cesar moves to help Penelope get the rest of the crowd ready to jump down to the Ag Level.

In a low voice, he asks her, "Shouldn't you stay, you know, up here with the boy?"

She gives him a quizzical glance without slowing down, "I assure you, we can handle this."

Cesar wants to stuff her in the box next to the elevator and sit on it until the danger is past. Trying to think of something that might convince her to stay, he barks, "During a battle, the commander sends in the troops while he waits in safety. Shouldn't you be safe? The boy?"

Penelope gives a short laugh. "Nice try, but you aren't getting rid of us."

She clips her belt into the loops on the elevator and turns to face him with an impish grin. "I bet you thought life on a farm was dull, didn't you?"

Then she steps into the shaft and starts falling two miles into the darkness. Cesar hopes there is something down there when they get to the bottom and promptly flings himself after her.

The ropes keep them from killing themselves, but they fall nonetheless. Cesar swallows the urge to scream, but Argos doesn't. Listening to the man screaming like a little girl for ten minutes has the rest of them tittering.

They fall forever, it seems. He begins to worry that there really is no Ag

Level left and they'll fall right out into void space, but then he sees light and feels the harness pull on the ropes as it slows them down.

Staggering out into the sunlight, Cesar follows Penelope as she coolly strips off her harness and begins scouting the landscape. Cesar hurries to catch up, but he sees that the rest of the group isn't quite ready yet.

Argos flops onto the ground and lays there, breathing heavily. Trevor leans against the elevator shaft and groans, "I think I threw up."

Shani, the blond cowgirl, wrinkles her nose, wipes her pants and snaps, "Next time, be a man and swallow it. Gross."

A low rumbling thud and distant gunfire bring everyone back to fight-readiness. Penelope quickly explains where the engineers said the disturbance is coming from. Cesar grabs Argos and a dark-skinned cowgirl whose name he can't remember and announces they'll be scouts. He bolts off towards the disturbance, pushing the other two in front of him before Penelope can protest or Trevor can try tagging along.

Trevor follows him anyway. Cesar hears an angry oath from Penelope but he doesn't stop for fear that she'll want to come too.

"How do you think they are doing it?" the boy whispers loudly as they quickly and, with the exception of Trevor, quietly make their way through fields, orchards and pastures.

"Doing what?" grunts Cesar, busy scanning the horizon for movement. The ground beneath them gives a series of little shuddering heaves but no one falls.

"Making the colony shake like this," Trevor says, almost shouting over a loud metallic groan that emanates from below their feet.

Cesar shrugs without looking at the boy. "I'm guessing they attached some kind of transport ship to the sidewall of the colony and cut their way in. The outer wall beneath us is thick, not even considering the six feet of dirt between our toes and the wall itself. A sidewall, though, is like the top of a tin can. There's no dirt and it's a bit thinner. That's where they will attach themselves, so that's where we are going."

"Oh!" cries Trevor. "A ship stuck on the side of the colony."

Cesar can hear the excitement in the boy's voice and it irritates him. The boy thinks this is some Ether adventure tale to impress girls with later. Doesn't he know he can get killed? Cesar has a sudden insight into his own father's insistence that every gray hair on his head came from yet another one of Cesar's insane exploits.

"But that won't cause the earthquakes, will it?" is the next question Trevor comes up with.

Cesar sighs. The cowgirl hisses at Trevor to shut up.

The boy looks crushed.

This time Argos answers, "Not like this. But maybe if they are randomly firing their thrusters it will throw the colony rotators off and cause problems with our gravity."

"They'd need a pretty big ship with really big engines," comments Cesar.

"Maybe they are smashing bombs against the wall just to break it," the cowgirl says grimly.

Cesar remembers that her name is Julia. Cesar thinks that name is better suited to a girl who doesn't look quite so comfortable wielding the enormous knife she keeps strapped to her back under her shirt. It flashes into her hand every time she thinks she hears danger.

Cesar doesn't think bombs are the cause. He thinks the intruders wouldn't do that while their ship is still attached, but afterwards is another story. He is about to say so when he hears another gunshot; this time it is close.

The four of them crouch low and run quickly towards the end of the Ag level closest to the wall. They run through a small vineyard, taking cover amongst the vines. Cesar can see there is, in fact, a large rectangular hole in the side of the wall where it meets the ground wall and there is some kind of ship attached. Since they aren't all getting sucked out into the void right now, the ship must be sealed pretty well to the colony wall.

In front of the ship, there are about half a dozen men shouting angrily, trying to push cows into the hole and onto their ship. The cows aren't having any of it. A thousand pounds of beef doesn't have to go anywhere it doesn't want to and the cows aren't about to leave their sunny pastures for a dank hole.

One man shoots a cow in frustration. It limps and bellows and still doesn't go into the ship. The other men yell at the shooter. Argos snickers. The rest of the crouching Ithacans have enough experience with cattle to know why.

"That's never going to work," snorts Trevor, giving voice to their amusement. "These guys don't have a clue about cattle."

Cesar can also see that they have thousands of cows gathered here. "Jesus, are they trying to take the whole herd?" Julia says scornfully.

"That's only about half of the herd," Argos replies.

"Still," Julia mutters. "What are they going to do with that much beef?"

Cesar wonders that too, but all he says is, "Well, that transport ship they have can fit a lot more. They could take the whole herd if they wanted."

Trevor points to a man dressed all in black who is currently rolling on the ground, clutching his foot after a cow stepped on him. "Somehow, I'm not too worried about these guys," the boy snorts.

Julia snaps, "Then you better start. They all have guns. And don't forget they are destroying our home right now."

They are far enough from the intruders that Cesar doesn't worry too much about being overheard. Even so, he whispers, "They must want these cows pretty badly to bring a ship that big and all these guys. I spent plenty of time on ships and, let me tell you, it's not easy to land against a turning wall like that. It's really not easy to drill and seal on an unsuspecting orbital. Either they are death-wish crazy or they are paid well enough not to care."

Argos whispers back, "If they are so all-fired keen on cow, you'd think they'd bring someone who knows how to herd the critters."

This thought occurs to Cesar too.

Cesar leads his group around so that they are hiding along the sidewall closer to the invader ship. They are making plans to attack when another tremor whips past them, throwing Cesar to his knees. A low rumbling sound begins behind them. As it grows louder and louder, the dust at their feet shakes and then the gravel bounces around like water in a hot pan.

Something big is coming.

They turn to look as the intruders hop into two moon buggies and take off into the Ag Level.

"Oh, God," Argos cries when he realizes what is making the noise.

"It's the other half of the herd."

All four of them unconsciously back up against the wall as thousands of cows come thundering towards them. Cesar spies a service ladder just as Trevor leaps for it. Trevor scrambles up the elevator with the girl close behind him. Argos is pinned to the wall with fear, so Cesar grabs him by the shirt and thrusts him up the metal rungs. With his old injuries, Cesar has a hard time climbing, but the herd bearing down on him is a powerful motivator. He is barely high enough to pull his feet out of the way when the first cow races beneath him.

The sound of their hooves roars louder than a hurricane as their bovine eyes roll wildly with fear. The ground shakes so hard that Cesar has a hard time staying on his feet and Trevor stumbles to his knees.

The invaders in the moon buggies whoop and fire their guns to keep the herd running. Cesar can see that the invaders are trying to turn the herd into the ship, but the herd is moving too fast for that. They smash into the cows standing by the ship without slowing down.

Two thousand cows crash and flail. The service elevator shakes ominously and Cesar fervently prays to whatever gods may be that the bolts will hold until the danger passes.

Cesar sees a steer hook one of the moon buggies with a horn and fling it like a child's toy. The two men inside are lost in the angry herd. Cesar can hear muffled cries of pain. He doesn't think their chances of survival are too high.

The main crush of cows has passed, but even now Cesar can barely think straight with all the noise and confusion so he decides this is an excellent time to reduce the number of intruders. He hops down from the ladder and pads his way towards the strangers. The men are so bewildered by the stampeding cattle, they don't realize he isn't on their side until he walks up and calmly shoots three of them as Argos, Trevor and Julia scramble down the ladder and after him.

There are two more close to the ship. Argos wrestles one to the ground and then methodically punches the man in the face while the other aims his blaster right at Cesar's chest. Cesar throws himself to the ground while raising his gun. Trevor comes flying out from behind a bush and tackles the man, grabbing the man's gun, unable to wrench it out of the intruder's grasp. Cesar flings himself towards them.

Suddenly, everything moves with unbearable slowness.

Cesar sees the man bring the blaster up as he struggles with Trevor. Cesar's heart breaks as he watches the intruder turn the muzzle towards his son's head. He sees the man's eyes squint as his finger tightens on the trigger.

Cesar screams incoherently and waves his hands.

He knows he'll never get there in time. He only hopes to draw the man's attention. He'd rather die than see his son take that blast.

Julia appears behind Trevor and the man with the gun, her knife flashing. Blood spurts across Trevor's face and shoulder as the man gives one gurgling scream and collapses to the ground. Trevor stands and dazedly watches the man die.

Cesar rushes up and pushes the boy away from the corpse, uttering every curse word he knows. Trevor lets him. Julia wipes blood off her knife. It disappears back under her shirt.

Cesar grabs the boy by the shoulders so he can more effectively shout in Trevor's face. "Never, ever take a chance like that again," Cesar bellows. "You could have died. Don't you have any brains, boy? Christ, I thought I was going to have a heart attack."

Trevor responds by throwing up on Cesar's shoes. Julia laughs and claps Cesar on the back. Watching Trevor heave, she says companionably, "That kid is just full of puke, isn't he? Come on."

Argos hogties the last remaining bad guy to a tree and dusts himself off. However, Cesar can see two other moon buggies with three or four men apiece. They are still trying to herd the cows into the transport ship. They succeed in organizing the cows into one large group that immediately begins running away from the hole in the wall.

As the cows race off, Cesar sprints over and throws himself onto the closest buggy. This one has three armed men in it. Cesar pushes one man off and, seeing Julia closing in on him with her knife, thinks no more about him. Cesar punches the driver as hard as he can. The man's head whips around, pulling the steering wheel hard left. The buggy careens onto its side, throwing all three of them into the dirt.

Cesar sits on the dazed buggy driver, pulling a zip cord out of one of the pockets in his pants to tie the man's hands and feet. He looks up to see that Trevor holding the other man while Argos ties him up too. Cesar nods approvingly. They don't know how many invaders there are so better not to waste stunner shots or blaster power on these when a piece of cord works too.

He stands up and sees the last moon buggy turning to follow the herd. It's too far for him to catch. That's when he sees Penelope burst out of nowhere. She leaps through the air and onto the buggy, fists and boots flying. The rest of the cowgirls swarm over the buggy and drag the invaders to the ground.

Cesar winces at the brutality of the invaders and cheers the ferocious response by the women. By the end of the melee, the invaders lay still, but so do a few of the cowgirls. Penelope is bruised and bloody, but looks too angry to be seriously hurt. Cesar and Argos leave Julia and Trevor to watch the transport ship and the men on the ground.

Cesar doesn't want to leave the boy, but there is no time to argue and he can't see any invaders still conscious or alive. Argos helps Cesar push the buggy nearest them back onto its wheels and they take off towards Penelope.

She sends cowgirls to get the other two buggies and starts driving towards the herd like a bat out of hell. Cesar chases after her as fast as he dares go in the flimsy little buggy. It looks like the herd is picking up speed. They crash through fences and fields, unstoppable now. The noise is deafening.

"What the hell is going on?" Cesar shouts when he catches up to her. That isn't what he meant to say, but he's just so happy to see her alive.

Penelope slows down enough to shout back, "Apparently, our thieves aren't too good at it. They put both herds together and the colony can't take that. Two hundred tons of beef are running wild and throwing off the orbital rotator's momentum. We'll spin out of control if we can't stop them."

Cesar knows the herd will be very difficult to stop now, like a pipe bomb rattling around in an electric clothes dryer. He shouts back, "So, just to be clear: Incompetent cattle rustlers have caused a space stampede that's tearing the colony apart?"

Argos laughs but Penelope simply nods.

"I'm going to stop the herd," she barks. "You stop the rustlers. If they take off and leave that huge hole in the wall, we are all dead."

She tilts her head, looking into his eyes with a gaze that pierces his heart. "Try to leave a few alive so we can figure out where they came from," she ordered with a fierce smile.

Cesar wants to tell her he loves her.

He wants to tell her everything.

He wants to keep her safe while he saves the day so he can spend the rest of his life looking into those eyes. There isn't time for any of that so he pulls her close and kisses her hard.

Cesar hears Argos gasp from the buggy behind him and, pulling back, he sees Penelope's eyes are wide and dazed. Her jaw drops slightly, lips red from the pressure of his mouth on hers.

"And *I* thought life on a farm was boring," she laughs shortly, running a hand through her hair. Then she gets back to business.

"Come on, Argos," she calls as her buggy goes barreling after the stampeding herd. The man gives Cesar one quizzical glance as he guns the engines and follows Penelope.

Cesar runs back to the transport ship. The other two buggies full of whooping cowgirls race past him heading towards Penelope. He runs faster than he'd thought possible, pausing only to collect guns. Almost back to where he left Trevor and Julia, he leaps over the fallen body of a cow and soars through the air.

It is exhilarating, almost like flying. Cesar knows this is very, very bad. The Ag level is losing gravity. The rotators are grinding to a stop.

They don't have much time left.

CHAPTER SEVENTEEN

Penelope concentrates on driving the buggy after her stampeding herd. She needs to keep her mind on the task at hand. She needs to not kill herself driving this buggy like a speed racer in an Ether game. She needs to stop a stampede before it cracks her home open. She does NOT need to be worrying about her son back there with that Ulixes man.

Careening around a fallen tree, she takes a deep breath and grips the wheel harder as she pulls up in front of the rushing tide of panicked animals. She has to turn them, but how? Penelope zigzags in front of them, trying to slow them down even a little. She knows this is a great way to get trampled to death, but she has to try something while she waits for the other buggies to catch up.

Swerving to avoid a utility shed, her buggy bounces over a small hill and flies into the air. Penelope braces herself for the crash for a long moment before she realizes she's been in the air far too long. When she does land, it is far too soft. The Ag level is losing gravity.

Looking back, she can see the herd slowing down. They feel it too. They are suddenly too light.

She can see a few heifers leaping and gamboling like spring calves. The rancher in her worries more about injured cows than the utter destruction of a stampede.

The other buggies catch up. "Look, boss, I'm flying," calls Shani, jumping high, her pigtails floating above her head.

Penelope doesn't have to do more than shout a few orders to coordinate them. She has drilled the cowgirls well enough on emergency herding that they know how to slow the rushing animals. Of course, they've never had a full stampede and never dreamed that they'd have to work the whole herd at once.

After all, they keep the herd separated for this exact reason. There isn't an orbital in the sky built to withstand two hundred tons of beef moving at the same time.

Penelope never had a good head for physics, but she is pretty sure that if the stampeding herd has stopped the colony from spinning, that's bad. She can't really grasp what will happen to the colony, so she thinks about all her best dishes at home, floating around and shattering everywhere. That simply will not do.

Turning a critical eye on the herd, she thinks out loud, "If the herd running this way makes the orbital stop spinning, what happens if we run them the other way?"

Shani puts a finger to her lips. "The colony speeds back up and we get normal gravity?" she guesses like it's a game.

Penelope shrugs and frowns. "Or we mess things up worse than they already are. Maybe it would be better to split the herd and get them back in their fences?"

One of the other buggies turns too sharply, but instead of spinning out in the dirt, it spins through the air before it crashes into a cow. The confused heifer also spirals off into the air, kicking wildly. The two cowgirls inside the buggy scream their lungs out, but Penelope hears more fear than pain in their voices. The other cows shift and rumble as though the animals know something is not right.

"Boss," says Shani in a low serious tone. "I think we better try something. If we don't get grav back soon, we're going to have a flying stampede on our hands and, as cool as it sounds, I don't want to actually see that."

"I take your point," Penelope replies briskly. Raising her voice, she calls, "Alright, ladies, let's turn this show around."

Infinitely slowly, they get the cows turned and start them moving in the opposite direction. At first, it's more like the cows are swimming through the air, but this actually helps them gain speed.

Penelope allows herself a relieved sigh when she feels the weight return to her body and watches everything gently fall back to the ground.

It worked. Gravity is returning.

Now how will she stop them before they swing to the other extreme and gravity pulls the colony apart?

CHAPTER EIGHTEEN

Cesar finds Trevor a moment before the crazy kid attempts to boards the intruder ship. "What are you doing?" he roars.

Julia is right behind Trevor. She turns to look at Cesar blankly, her knife in her hand. "Killing the enemy," she replies. "Why? What did you want to do? Play poker? Have a sandwich? Take a nap?"

Cesar sputters incoherently for a minute. "Wait for me," is what he finally comes up with.

He passes out the guns he's collected to Trevor and Julia even though Julia rolls her eyes and puts the gun in her pocket. Then Cesar positions himself firmly in front, grumbling about getting stuck with two insane infants and repeatedly ordering them not to shoot him in the back.

Inside the massive cargo hold, their footsteps echo loudly. They don't see anyone, but there are plenty of signs that these strangers are preparing to moving a very large number of cows. Cesar looks down as he steps up to stand on a large metal platform. He's wondering why these pirates think cows need a large metal platform until he realizes that the platform is actually the Ithaca outer wall, dropped onto the cargo hold floor after it was cut. The thieves must have cut the hole and simply laid down the thick metal wall right here.

Cesar grimaces.

They must not have planned to put it back. How could they with a thousand cows standing on it? If they pushed it in instead of letting it fall out and into the hull like this, it could potentially be repaired and they'd have been able to fly away much faster without several extra tons of this metal in their hold. Cesar taps his foot thoughtfully and wonders why some people are such jerks.

It worries him. This is a fairly elaborate and well-funded plan to steal a bunch of cows. Why? Surely anyone with this much money and ship could just fly down to the planet if they want steak so badly?

Julia begins running lightly towards the stairway that heads up to the catwalk above the ship's hold. There are two doors up there that must lead further into the ship. Trevor scampers after her and Cesar follows, wheezing in exasperation. He resolves to exercise more if he survives the heart attack Trevor is hell-bent on giving him today.

Cesar manages to get to the door just before Julia opens it and puts his hand out to block her.

"What are you doing?" he hisses as quietly as his anger will allow. "You want to die? Take it slow. Check it out before you go barging around an enemy base."

"There's no time," she growls through clenched teeth.

Cesar grits his teeth. He is old enough to hate working with youngsters. Behind Julia, he sees Trevor peering at them. Cesar understands the eager expression on Trevor's face, excited and reckless. It is the look of someone in the middle of their first experience with real danger, before the full weight of death and mayhem has had time to settle on them. He's been a fool to leave his son on his own all these years.

How had the kid lived this long? Cesar clears his throat and tries to clear his head too.

"There's plenty of time if you don't die first," Cesar says slowly, since his patience isn't working too well today. "Now, let's think a minute. What do we need to do now?"

"Find the bad guys," Trevor volunteers while Julia glowers and fingers her blade.

Cesar shakes his head. "No, think. What we need to do right now is pry this damn ship off the side of Ithaca without blowing a hole that will kill us all. So we actually don't want to find any bad guys. Because that would slow us down."

Julia shrugs.

Trevor frowns as he utters an involuntary "Oh."

"So how do we do that?" asks Cesar, scanning the hold. Julia and Trevor look around too.

"The bad guys must have had a plan for leaving," comments Trevor.

"Most likely they planned to just detach their ship and leave this hole, venting the Ag level into space," observes Julia. Her eyes are still on the two doors, but she obviously hasn't missed the implications of Ithaca's wall lying on cargo floor below them.

"Surely they wouldn't do that," replies Trevor, walking over to examine the control panel covered in buttons, knobs and what looks like a joystick. "Whatever they used to make the hole can unmake it. Right?"

"Aren't you cute," snorts Julia. "Must be nice to grow up somewhere that let you be so naïve."

Trevor looks outraged. He turns away from the console he is prodding. Cesar sees the boy opening his mouth to protest and quickly cuts him off. "Argue later. Be quiet and solve the problem now. Julia, you got these doors covered, right?"

The girl jerks her head down once.

"Good," Cesar says curtly. "Don't neglect the front door." Here he gestures to hole in the side of Ithaca. "I think we got all the guys out there, but you never know. Trevor, you're with me. We need to close this hole."

Trevor points to the huge machinery hanging from the ceiling. "Look. That's a welding laser. A big one. It must have cut this hole in the side of Ithaca," he tells the rest of them. "And that over there is a high-pressure crane. After they cut the big hole, that's probably what they used to lower the huge metal slab to the floor of their cargo ship."

"See there?" Trevor says, pointing. His natural enthusiasm for ships gets the better of his flight-or-fight response for the moment so Cesar breathes a little easier. "They'd have to have put plenty of force there to keep the orbital's internal pressure from blowing the slab right through their ship once they pierced the wall."

"So we can use it to prop the slab back into place over the hole," replies Cesar.

"Right," says Trevor with a kind of giddy despair. "Except the panel is locked." He gestured to the control panel in front of him.

Cesar laughs, "Kid, Spacers are too lazy for good security. Look."

Bending over, he reaches under the console and yanks out two wires. Twisting them together, he straightens up as the lights on the console flicker on and a fan begins to whir. "It's the classic case of a huge padlock on a flimsy door. Can you work this thing?"

Trevor reaches out to test the joystick. The crane overhead groans and twitches in response. Looking uncertain, Trevor takes a deep breath, squares his shoulders and steps up to the console.

"Good, because I imagine we are going to attract some bad guy attention pretty soon," Cesar says, clapping the boy on the shoulder and pulling out his gun.

The crane screeches loudly as Trevor lowers it to the slab. It scrapes against the slab once, sending deafening shudders through the hold.

Trevor looks at Julia and Cesar sheepishly, but both of them are crouched down, covering the two doors, waiting for bad guys to come pouring out. When they don't respond, Trevor pushes up his sleeves and goes back to work.

Propping the slab up and fitting it back over the hole goes agonizingly slow, but Cesar notes with pride that his son works wonderfully under pressure. Trevor is just positioning the laser to weld the hole shut again when the ship door closest to the console opens.

Cesar doesn't even wait for the door to fully open. He sees it edge open a crack and he fires off a few rounds. The door slams shut.

Julia giggles, "Oh, you might have let one in for us to play with. All this waiting is giving me a cramp."

"You are one scary little girl," Cesar replies. "You'll get a chance with that knife later. We'll have to go in there to move this ship."

Just then, there is a muffled thump and the other door pops open. A man in a flak suit leaps out and starts firing. Cesar flings himself in front of Trevor and returns fire while Julia creeps catlike through the shadows.

Another gun pokes out of the open doorway and starts firing too. Cesar wings the first man so that he stops firing just long enough for Julia to reach him with her knife. Cesar hears a thick gurgling cry and sees Julia dive from the fallen body through the doorway. The second gun stops firing and Julia comes back through the door, slamming it shut behind her.

"There were just the two for now, but think I hear more of them out there," she announces, wiping blood on her pants.

Trevor stares at her, his hands limp on the console. Cesar watches Trevor. The boy looks like he is about to throw up again.

"Son, you're driving a laser right now. You might want to pay attention to that," Cesar says brusquely.

Trevor looks around in a daze for a minute. "I'm not sure I have the right settings," he mumbles at last, wiping a hand across his neck. "I don't want to screw it up."

"So practice on something first," recommends Cesar. "Like that door."

"The door?" Trevor asks with a frown.

"Yeah, that one," Cesar replies pointed at the door with the dead man lying in front of it. "If you melt it shut, then you have the right settings, yeah? And if you don't, you blow a hole through their hull. Either way, that's good for our team."

Trevor's eyebrows shoot up, but he nods, slaps on some protective goggles, and starts moving the laser.

Cesar calls out, "Julia, get away from the door." She obliges immediately when she sees the laser swinging her way.

With one quick hot flash, the door melts into slag. The corpse in front of the door is too close and it roasts as well. Cesar touches his face lightly. It feels sunburned.

"God, that smells awful," complains Julia, looking at the charred dead man in front of the smoldering door. "Like you used an engine block to barbeque a squirrel."

Cesar wants to ask her why a melted man makes her think of squirrels, but doesn't think he'll like the answer.

Trevor wrinkles his nose and eyes the door critically. "Yeah, that'll work if I adjust the spectrum and crank up the power," he decides, turning back to the console. The laser swings around and points back at the hole in Ithaca's outer wall.

Cesar wants to hug the boy. First for calm under pressure. Second for knowing how to work a welding laser at all. He promises himself that he'll spend the rest of his life thanking Penelope. She's obviously raised this boy right.

For now, Cesar covers the remaining door, his mind on how they'll find the flight deck and steer this ship away from Ithaca. He hopes everything inside the colony is going well.

The laser does its work. The hold gets very, very hot.

There is only one pair of welding goggles to protect their eyes and Trevor obviously needs them the most. Cesar and Julia keep their eyes shut, but eventually it gets to hot so they hide on the other side of the remaining door. They hear voices, but no one comes to investigate.

The laser is so loud that Cesar almost misses the telltale low rumbling of engines firing up. Someone is about to move the ship. Cesar's blood pressure shoots through the roof. He yanks the cargo hold door open and sees the ship's outer doors closing. The light of the laser sears his eyes even though he squints and avoids looking anywhere near it as he races to Trevor.

"We've got to get out of here," he shouts, tugging Trevor's arm hard enough to get his attention but not so hard that he jostles the laser.

"I'm almost done," Trevor yells back without turning from his work. "The doors stopped halfway so I have room to finish."

Cesar doesn't look to see how close Trevor is to being finished. The laser is killing his eyes even without looking at it. It feels like another minute in this heat and his whole body will burst into flames, but just now he doesn't care. He has to get the boy out before the ship takes off and vents this cargo hold to space.

Cesar feels the metal catwalk under his feet jerk and shudder. He knows there was no time for arguing. He grabs Trevor and throws him through the door. Then Caesar flings himself through the door too, knowing there is no time to be pretty about it. With a deafening roar, the seal between the ship and the colony snaps. Julia slams the hold door shut and bolts it as the vacuum of void space snatches at them with its icy fingers.

"Did you finish?" shrieks Julia, jittery with the adrenaline of cheating death.

"Get off me," is Trevor's muffled response, but he is talking to Cesar.

Cesar rolls off the boy. Trevor groans and clutches his hip. Fixing Cesar with an outraged stare, Trevor grumbles, "I might not have sealed it. I don't think I did, you moron. And then you squashed me."

Cesar yanks the boy off the floor and hugs Trevor before he can stop himself. Then he remembers how angry he is. He gives the boy a good shake and bellows, "I saved your life, you ungrateful brat. You had it almost done. That'll have to be good enough. The orbital can cope with a small gap. The welding you did will keep the whole thing from blowing. So quit your yapping."

Trevor pushes Cesar away, eyeing him uncomfortably. "The part I didn't finish is more than a foot across. You think that will work?"

Julia breaks in to say firmly, "That's small enough that the electromagnetic envelope will cover it. They'll be able to seal it pretty quick with the outer wall dronebots now that this pirate ship isn't in the way."

Cesar takes a deep breath and thinks about what will happen next. "The bad guys will send someone down to make sure we died when they vented the hold."

"How many of them do you think are left on this boat?" Trevor wants to know.

"Can't be too many, but it would still be better if they thought we were dead," replies Cesar.

Quickly and quietly, they sneak down the hallway until Julia finds an unlocked door. They duck inside a small storage locker with just enough room for the three of them to cram into. Trevor and Julia are silently shoving each other over whose elbow is jammed into whose windpipe when they hear footsteps echoing through a vent above the door. They stop moving and listen hard.

They hear the footsteps rush past their door and a voice call, "Come on, you big baby." It is the deep voice of an older man comfortable with command.

The voice continues, "Anybody in the hold is now a corpesicle frozen to our bumper, so you can quit your whining. Nobody would waste bullets shooting at you anyway." The brash voice chuckles like he's just said something really witty.

Another set of footsteps follows, decidedly less hurried. "I should be monitoring our escape to make sure we remain undetected," whines the second man. He has a much softer, more nasal voice.

Trevor shifts and Julia pokes him. Cesar knows they are dying to see the men in the hallway, but there is no way to do that without opening the door and exposing themselves. Cesar isn't willing to do that. Not yet.

"Don't be silly," booms the first voice, striding to the cargo hold door. "I've done this a million times. After a snatch and grab, everyone is too busy scurrying around like ants to chase after us. It's stupid, but there you are. Now come and make sure the hold is sealed so I can open the door."

"Yes, you are the big bad pirate who raids his way across the stars year in and year out," grumbles the second voice. "I am the nerd who makes the tools that let you do it. How lucky I am to have the brains to open doors for you."

It is a mild voice with a hint of some sort of Eastern European accent. Whoever it is has a very precise way of speaking, totally unlike the jovial wickedness so evident in the first voice.

They both sound faintly familiar to Cesar, but he can't think why. He looks at Trevor and Julia, arching an eyebrow, but doesn't dare make a noise. They just stare back at him blankly. So much for nonverbal communication.

"Don't be such a whiner, Asner," commands the first voice. There is the sound of buttons being pushed and the sigh of a sealed door popping open. Evidently, the cargo hold is repressurized enough to open the door.

The first voice continues, "Cheer up, you sourpuss. Tell you what. If you ever manage to solve the lubrication problem and we finish the lasers, I'll let you take a turn at the controls. You can fry whoever bothers you. Maybe then you'll lighten up."

Asner sputters angrily, "Solve the problem? I solved the problem! But you can't stop being a pirate long enough to just buy the stupid cows, can you? No. You have to go charging around and almost kill everybody on Ithaca and for what? Do you see any cows in this hold?"

"Ah, you just want to get into little Penelope's pants," scoffs the first voice. "It's never going to happen. We should go back and slice open that colony like an orange. It would be so much easier to scoop up the cows when everyone is dead."

Asner snaps back, "I told you. We need the cattle alive so we can inject them with that serum to make them produce the necessary lubricants. How many times do I have to say it? You just like destroying. Any child can destroy. It takes a man with a mind to create something."

The bickering goes on, but the three in the closet don't hear it because the door to the cargo hold door slams shut behind the two men. Julia flings the closet door open and pulls herself out, breathing deeply.

"You two have some seriously bony elbows," she gasps.

"Asner!" cries Cesar, his eyes on the cargo door. He claps a hand on Trevor's shoulder and jerks his thumb in the direction of the cargo door. "That guy was at the ranch. He's some kind of engineer?"

"I know him!" Trevor yelps as he rubs his knee. He flattens himself to the wall's edge and cautiously looks down the hallway in the opposite direction. "He's always trying to be nice to me because he's got a crush on Mom. What a jerk. He could have killed us all."

"We need to get out of here," Julia says, straightening up, going on alert.

"The command center has got to be this way," Cesar decides as he jogs quickly and quietly down the hall, his gun drawn and ready.

They find it quickly. They don't even have to threaten the pilot. The little man takes one look at their weapons and their grim expressions and holds up his hands.

"I can go sit over there," he says helpfully, pointing at a bare spot on the floor. "Or I can take this ship anywhere you want to go."

"You got to appreciate a sensible man," chuckles Cesar. "Trevor, you cover this guy. Make sure he takes us back to Ithaca. Shoot him if he tries anything funny. Julia, you are on lookout."

Cesar isn't too worried, though. The door bolts from the inside so even if there were a hundred men out there, they'd still make it back to Ithaca. He doesn't relax his guard, but he does allow his mind to turn over other problems.

Addressing no one in particular, Cesar asks, "So, why did they want all the cows? Asner said something about lubricant? They need live cows to make some kind of lubricant?"

The pilot is busy keeping one eye at his flight controls and the other on Trevor's gun pointed at his head. He shrugs his shoulders without looking away.

"All I do is drive this boat," the pilot mumbles. "They wanted something big enough to hold two thousand cows so they got this boat and me to drive it. That's all I know."

"That's almost the whole herd," growls Julia. "Why do they need a whole herd? That's a lot of lubricant. Who needs that much lubricant?"

The pilot shrugs again, saying nothing. Trevor prods him with the gun but that only makes the little man's hands shake.

"I can't think of anything that isn't really perverted," comments Trevor. Cesar snorts.

Julia giggles, "Thanks Trevor. Now I can't either."

"Your mom will know," Cesar says with conviction. "What the real use is and it won't be, you know, pornographic. We'll see her soon."

The churning terror in his guts that started with the first tremor on the orbital begins to ease. He will see Penelope again soon. A man could get used to that.

Cesar idly opens and closes doors in the command room, making sure there aren't any secret entrances. He always had one in any ship he captained. You never know when you'll need a back entrance into the control room.

You'd be surprised how many perfectly good pilots will lock themselves out after being at the controls for a good long haul. From what that first bad guy said, this outfit was in the habit of raiding. Pirates are sure to have boltholes and back passages too.

Cesar finds it under a control panel for the air filtration system. If he crawls, he can fit in there, but it wouldn't be a happy thing. He peers down the shaft, but doesn't see anyone in it. He stands up to report this find to the other two and feels dizzy.

Cesar has to put a hand out to steady himself. Looking over, he sees Julia slumped against the door. Trevor is blinking as his gun arm keeps slipping down. The pilot's head bobs as though he can barely keep his eyes open.

Looking up, Cesar sees a faint smoking gas curling out of the air vent in the ceiling. Cesar swears and immediately drops to the ground. They are pumping poison or sleeping gas into the command center so they can get in. He should have thought of that.

"Trevor! Get over here! Now!" Cesar barks as he shimmies into secret passage. The pilot takes advantage of their confusion to race for the door and undo the bolt.

The main door bursts open and he hears gunfire, but it is too tight in the shaft. Cesar can't turn to find out what is going on. He thinks he hears Trevor behind him so he throws himself down the narrow passage, looking for a place to turn around.

The passage drops him into a small storage room. Cesar immediately spins and looks behind him down the shaft, but Trevor isn't there. He can see that the door to the passage is shut. There are no signs of anyone following him. Panic claws at his guts again.

Where is Trevor?

Cursing, Cesar dives back into the shaft and quickly crawls up to the command room, his gun drawn. If Trevor is hurt, there will be hell to pay.

He doesn't let himself think about any other possibilities. When he gets to the little door, he hears Asner and the other voice on the other side, arguing again. Cesar pauses to listen.

"We will not kill this boy," Asner says loudly. "We will not."

"Why not?" the unknown voice growls. He sounds annoyed. "We can't just drop him off at home to blab to all his friends and neighbors about us. And he's cost me a pilot, to say nothing of the rest of this fiasco."

"You shot the pilot," replies Asner. "You didn't look at what you were doing. You just fired off a few rounds into the room. It's lucky you didn't break something we need to get us out of here."

"Well, you shot this girl," the other man points out. "So don't play like I'm the only loose cannon here. You get to clean up all this blood and haul her body over to the airlock."

Asner snaps, "Fine, but you have to clean up the pilot. And you can't kill the boy. We'll put him in an escape pod and fire it back towards Ithaca. Now let me get the ship reprogrammed to the proper coordinates before we crash into something."

Cesar's vision blurs for a minute. Julia is dead. Poor little Julia, with her knife and her smile, is all gone.

He wonders who she was and if there is anyone to cry for her. No matter how much senseless death he sees out here in the void, it never stops getting to him. Cesar takes a silent slow breath and focuses on the important thing: his son.

Trevor is still alive. He has to stay that way.

Cesar takes stock of the situation. He has the element of surprise. However, squirming out of the cramped compartment under a control panel will put him at a severe disadvantage. Should he burst out now and start shooting before they have another moment to hurt his boy or should he wait for a better opportunity? Cesar has to make the right choice and he has to do it quickly, while Asner and the other man are still fighting.

"Uri, the boy hasn't seen us. He doesn't know anything," says Asner. "We'll just send him off in an escape pod. It will be easy and they'll be sure to find him."

Uri's name is like a punch in Cesar's stomach. Cesar listens hard. It doesn't sound like they know he is on the ship. He hopes that will come in useful.

"Why bother?" grunts Uri as he lifts something heavy, probably the pilot's body. Cesar tenses, preparing to fling open the door and start shooting.

"If the boy dies, all opportunities to negotiate with the mother will be gone," replies Asner in that precise way of his. Cesar hears him tapping at the control panel.

"She won't know he's dead," argues Uri. "And once we get the lasers up, we won't need to worry about who finds out and whether they like us or not. You are always going on about how we need the goodwill of the colonies, but with a huge fuck-off laser that can fry New York right off the planet, we won't have to care what anybody thinks. That's the whole point."

Cesar hears Asner give a long-suffering sigh. "We don't have it yet, so we have to play nice. Besides, I have a plan," says Asner. "Perhaps we can salvage something from this disaster and still stay on schedule."

"You always have a plan," grumbles Uri, but there is grudging admiration in his voice.

"I will go back and 'find' the boy and take him home," Asner explains. "His mother will be grateful."

Uri scoffs, "And then she'll finally sleep with you. Sure. How does that help me?"

"I'll explain that bad evil men who will stop at nothing are after her herd and, if she wants to keep her family alive, she'll sell them to you," Asner replies calmly. "It's the truth. I know you don't like the truth very much, but I think in this situation it will work."

"There's something in that," Uri finally admits.

For the next several minutes, Cesar hears only the sounds of men mopping up blood, bickering over the best way to go while typing coordinates into a navigational system, and hauling bodies into the hall.

"If you have a better way to achieve our objective, I am listening," Asner says in a neutral voice. "It's just that we need to stay on schedule and time is running short."

"I know, I know," declares Uri. "All hail the hallowed schedule. Well, fine. The kid lives and you get to play hero with the widow lady. Hope it's fun. Help me get him into a pod before he wakes up. If your plan doesn't work, we can always try my plan: blow up that stupid ranch and scrape the cows out like freeze-dried blood pudding. Yes, I know. We need them alive. My way still sounds better."

Cesar edges back down the little passage as silently as he can. His mind is whirling. It appears that Trevor is safe for now, but what should he do? Should he still try to attack these men? They are obviously still a threat to Penelope and Trevor in ways he doesn't completely understand right now.

Trevor is much safer floating in an escape pod out in the void than he is here. They aren't planning to hurt Trevor now. If he attacks and the boy is harmed in the crossfire... Cesar gulps. He doesn't like that plan.

And if Cesar dies here, there will be no one to protect Penelope from these men. If he waits until they send Trevor off, can he find a way off this ship without being detected? Cesar decides to risk a little reconnaissance.

He shimmies slowly backwards down the narrow passage. Reaching the little storage room, he quickly takes stock of his surroundings. The storage closet leads out into an empty hallway. Cesar has been in enough ships to know which way the escape pods and airlocks will be.

If he can find a small cruiser, or even a repair skiff, he can escape in that. There is probably another escape pod at the very least. At the worst, he can just hole up and wait for them to go wherever it is Uri and Asner planned to go next. But Cesar does not think that is a great idea.

On the one hand, as a stowaway he'll probably get more information about these men and what they are planning. On the other hand, his chances of escaping and getting back to warn Penelope will substantially decrease. He doesn't want Trevor anywhere near these men, especially not to get "rescued" by Asner. He's also not enthusiastic about leaving Trevor alone in an escape pod for any longer than necessary.

Cesar wonders what these pirates are up to with their lasers and lubricants. Why are they targeting Penelope, Ithaca and the herd? It seems too strange, but the Spacer orbitals are nothing if not bizarre.

Lasers big enough to fry New York doesn't sound like a good thing for these guys to get their hands on. Cesar wouldn't normally bother worrying about something like that. It sounds so ridiculous and impossible that it couldn't be real, except Uri and Asner discussed it so casually. Like it is a done deal.

That can't be good.

Cesar puts it aside. He doesn't need to go looking for trouble. He just needs to find the landing bay. He has to get off this ship. Quickly and methodically searching, he finds it while avoiding Asner and Uri as they head towards the starboard escape pod. There isn't anyone else on the ship right now.

When Cesar discovers the cruiser, he almost cries tears of joy. It is a little ship barely big enough for two people, intended for short trips. Large lumbering cargo ships use these cruisers for repairs or retrieving things near the ship and also for visiting colonies they are too big to dock with easily. The little cruiser is equipped with a maneuverable claw for repairs that he can use to grab Trevor's escape pod if he can find it.

Cesar isn't sure how far the cruiser will go, but he doubts they are very far from Ithaca right now and he'll just have to take his chances. Another bit of luck is that the little cruiser is stored right next to the cargo hold so they might think the cruiser deployed in all the excitement earlier and thus miss his escape.

Cesar needs to get out before they get back to the control room and notice the cruiser is gone. He doesn't think Asner will try to chase him or that Asner is even a good enough pilot to catch him in the little cruiser, but why take chances?

Cesar straps in and powers up. He thinks about Trevor and hopes the boy is all right. Cesar tells himself that if they get back to Ithaca alive, he will personally teach Trevor every trick he ever knew about flying. Look how useful that kind of knowledge is. But first he has to go rescue his son.

Shooting out of the massive cargo ship, Cesar begins searching for Trevor's escape pod as fast as he can. His heart is in his throat the entire time. Where is Trevor? Is he alive?

As he scans for Trevor, Cesar notices that the pirate ship is equipped with huge thrusters that would propel the cargo ship much faster than normal. A retrofit like that is expensive. Only a rich, well-organized group could have a ship like that and he doesn't like to think about anyone that powerful deciding to use their cargo ship the way it was used today. He is glad to be pulling away from it.

When he finds the escape pod hurtling through void space, Cesar lets out a breath he didn't know he was holding. He feels briefly overwhelmed by all that happened today and the six or seven miracles he is still counting on to get his son back home safely. Cesar focuses on what he needs to do right now and that is to snatch up the escape pod and get the hell out of here.

There's nothing like adrenaline surging through your system in a crisis to make you a genius for survival and Cesar is no exception. He seems to have an instant understanding of the grappling claw. Although his hands shakes and sweat pours into his eyes in the freezing cold little cruiser, he grasps the pod with the claw.

Cesar doesn't think about anything but using every drop of fuel on the cruiser. He constantly monitors for signs that the cargo ship is chasing them, but there is nothing. He scans the little escape pod to make sure it stays warm enough for Trevor. He'd feel better if he can monitor the boy's vital signs, but there is only so much the little cruiser can do.

It can tell him what he doesn't want to hear though, which is that the escape pod has a leak. It is slowly but surely venting oxygen into void space. Cesar scans and rescans the pod a dozen times. He runs the calculations four times before he finally lets the truth sink in.

Trevor isn't going to make it back to Ithaca.

CHAPTER NINETEEN

Penelope feels like the walking dead.

She really doesn't understand how her body is still standing. She suspects that the only thing keeping her from collapsing is curiosity. Just how long she can keep going before her legs finally give out? It is much farther than she would have thought.

It took hours to finally stop the herd and get them secured. Hours in which she was sure they were already dead and she was only stopping the herd just to have something to do before the end. She drives everyone else until they drop. They separate the herd and get them penned as the colony continues to rattle and shake. They dodge falling lights and collapsing buildings. Tremors occasionally throw them to the ground, but they dust themselves off and trudge wearily onward.

Then she helps care for the injured and puts together work crews to repair the worst damage. Eventually it sinks in that she isn't going to die today, but Penelope still doesn't stop moving. One foot keeps finding itself in front of the other. Her hands move wearily from one task to the next.

"They're gone," Argos tells her, keeping his sad eyes on the floor at her feet. "Trevor and Ulixes and Julia. They aren't on the colony. Not even bodies. They are gone."

That's what finally does it. She feels something hit her cheek and realizes it's the floor. Then there is darkness.

Penelope wakes later to Lupe sponging her face with cold water. "Where's Trevor?" she asks groggily. Argos was saying something stupid earlier. She must have heard him wrong.

"You need to sleep," hisses Lupe.

SPIN THE SKY ›› 179

"Where's Trevor?" Penelope repeats, more urgently.

"How about some of my soup?" Lupe suggests.

Penelope sits up to glare at Lupe. "Where's my son?"

Lupe fusses with the wet rag she was using on Penelope's face. "Everyone is looking. They'll find him soon."

Penelope's vision goes white and fuzzy around the edges. The room spins a little, but she swings her feet around to stand up anyway. Lupe puts her hand out, gently urging Penelope back into bed as she prattles, "The damage was really not so bad, those engineer men say, *mija*. And they've got the hole all sealed up now. Isn't that good?"

Penelope pushes Lupe's hand away and stands unsteadily. "Who else is missing?" she asks too loudly. Her voice echoes through the room and hurts her head.

Lupe sighs and hovers over Penelope, wringing her hands. Talking rapidly, she admits, "Trevor, Ulixes, and Julia. Everyone else accounted for and no dead! At least, none of ours. Some of your cowgirls will be laid up for a while, though. We were very lucky. A million to one, us pulling through with so few casualties and damage. That's what the engineer men said."

Penelope's sight swims and her knees buckle. Lupe catches her before she can fall and hit the bed stand.

Penelope gets angry. She needs to find her son and her body is betraying her. She kicks the bed stand viciously.

"Trevor and Julia and Ulixes were all together," she spits out, furious with herself and her powerlessness. "I sent them to go after the rustlers. I told Ulixes to go after them. I sent them." Then Penelope is crying and she can't stop that either.

Lupe sighs and her shoulders slump. Low and quick, she says, "Someone got on that ship. The ship that attacked us. Someone got on and sealed the hole from inside their ship. Well, almost sealed it. And then the ship flew away. That's all we know. There are no bodies. Not in here, not floating out there. That's all we know."

Her voice cracks as she sits down on the floor to cry with Penelope.

Penelope sobs until her lungs hurt and her eyes run dry. Then she gets up and makes coffee. They clean the house in a daze. When a group of suitors arrive, Penelope is standing outside, throwing the broken shards of

Cesar's mother's favorite plates into the trash.

"Outworlders," she thinks dully, more interested in the shattered plates.

Penelope pushes her hair off her face and feels the grittiness in it. She wonders when her last bath was and suddenly realizes that she smells like cow. She also realizes that these men coming towards her are from her parties. Powerful, rich men in expensive clothes.

She really doesn't care.

Penelope invites them in. They fill up her front room, surrounding her in an awkward silence until Wilhelm Asner comes rushing in. He looks anxious and annoyed at finding so many people already there. Pulling off his elegantly tailored coat, Asner ignores the others and steps close to Penelope, wrapping his warm coat around her.

"Penelope, come sit down," he insists, soft and earnest. She allows him to guide her to the porch. The other men follow, staring at her, fascinated by her pain apparently.

She still doesn't care.

Mr. Finomus uncaps a flask and passes it to her without comment. Penelope gives him a grateful look and takes a generous swig. Wiping her lips and shivering from the burn of the alcohol in her throat, she remembers her manners. She can't remember what manners are for just now, but she does remember them.

"What can I do for you gentleman?" she asks in her politest voice, looking from one face to the next.

"Penelope, you poor woman," says old King Manny's trained lapdog, Castor. "We are here to see what we can do for you, what aid we can offer."

Penelope has a few ideas on that score. Through gritted teeth, she asks, "Can you find the men who did this? Can you bring them here? Because I have a few questions for them."

The men in front of her shuffle their feet.

"None of the captives survived the interrogation and they didn't talk. I saw to it personally," says Asner. He edges into her personal space again and says soothingly, "Several of us have ships out scanning local space, but there's been no sign of them so far."

"And my son and… the other people missing? Can you find them?" asks Penelope, her hands curling into fists of their own accord.

Asner asks quickly, "So there's been no sign of him? Nothing? Your people are scanning for everything? Even escape pods? I mean, in case he escaped that ship?"

Penelope looks at her hands in her lap and shakes her head.

"They still haven't found him," she replies. She's been calling the docking bay every thirty minutes just to make sure.

Penelope clenches her jaw to keep from crying again. Again, there is that uncomfortable silence as they all shake their heads and look everywhere but at her. Penelope sighs and knows she should stop torturing them now. So she uncurls her fists, takes a deep breath and says, "We will need help rebuilding."

"That we can help with," Castor pipes up eagerly. "I brought a team of our engineers to help repair your lights and structural damage and such."

The others also brought various people and supplies. Penelope discusses with them the damage to the colony, the injured and what Ithaca will need. It helps clear her head, dwelling on these details and not on the million and one horrible things that might be happening to Trevor and that poor Ulixes man. She should have known better than to think there could be love in her life.

Castor asks quietly, "What about the herd?"

"What about it?" Penelope replies, twisting the ring on her left index finger. Her mind is still wandering, no matter how much she tries to stay here in this conversation.

"Don't you think it might be a bit much for you right now? Dealing with such a large herd during this time of crisis?" he asks gently.

Asner leans in to put a hand over hers. "You should be concentrating on yourself now, not bothering over such a large herd. I worry about you. Whoever did this didn't get what they came for. They will come back. They won't stop. You have to protect yourself."

Asner looks into her eyes and smiles at her, but she can see his desire and it makes her wary. Penelope can never figure out exactly what it is he lusts after. Her body? Surely not.

What is it he wants from her? He doesn't want the herd, but he always seems to be pressuring her to sell it and leave here. Why? Penelope often suspects that she is just a game that he wants to win. Penelope blinks hard and tries to think practically.

Asner sounds sincere. They all do, but they are only here for the herd, these men. All their solicitous good will and helpful donations are just to butter her up so she'll sell out.

What a bunch of vultures.

Fortunately Lupe creates a distraction when she comes bustling in with a tray full of drinks and snacks that she hands around, whether anyone wants them or not. She keeps wiping her nose and muttering Spanish prayers and in general, disrupting the scene as much as she can. It gives Penelope a chance to think.

What if Trevor doesn't come back?

She finally allows herself that thought. Without him, what is the point of all this? Maybe she *should* give up, sell out, and go away. Maybe she should go find wherever it is all the people in her life keep going. What is it that was so interesting out there?

The truth is that she still yearns to travel. That wish never died, but she's been tied to the ranch all these years. She's had to stay safely at home because she knows that if something happens to her, there was no one else out there as psychotically obsessed with getting Trevor to adulthood.

But she failed anyway. Penelope feels exhausted. She feels a million years old. She doesn't want to fight any more. Penelope slowly pulls her hands away from Asner. She carefully keeps her face blank as she edges away from him.

"So you think I should sell the herd?" she asks them loudly. But for Lupe's outraged gasp, there is nothing but stunned silence. Then the men all start talking at once.

Penelope almost laughs to hear them tripping over themselves to make polite but definite offers. She lets them bid against each other for a while before saying, "Thank you for your generous offers. I appreciate it more than I can say, but how am I to choose? Do I sell to the highest bidder? Do I sell the ranch and everything or just part of the herd?"

"Whatever you want, Penelope," says Asner, standing too close again and giving the other men sharp looks, like a dog guarding a bone. "I am not bidding, of course. I am only interested in your welfare. But I know Uri Mach will make you a very generous offer if you need to have some of this responsibility taken off your beautiful shoulders."

"Thank you, I'll keep that in mind," Penelope snaps before she can stop herself. Why must he always be crowding her?

She pastes a smile on her face and says graciously, "Gentlemen, I have had a very long day and much to do. I see the value of your counsel, but I will need time to decide how to settle my finances."

"Of course," says wily old Castor smoothly, kissing her hand while Asner scowls. "Take all the time you need, my dear."

Then he pauses and, as though he just thought of it, Castor says, "But Ithaca is to host the next Nullball Tournament, isn't it? Surely you do not need that responsibility on top of everything else? Manny would love to host. We've got that huge stadium he built and we hardly ever get a chance to use it."

Penelope may contemplate selling her home and her life's work, but she isn't about to tolerate the suggestion that there is something Ithaca can't handle. The man is practically insulting her colony right to her face! She doesn't need Lupe grumbling behind her to know that.

"No, thank you very much," she says in a clipped tone. "We will be more than ready for the Nullball tournament. The damage was really quite minimal and, as you know, Ithaca's team is quite strong even if they got banged around a little today." She smiles at Castor, but it feels more like she is baring her teeth.

"But the tournament is only days away," protests Castor. "Surely you won't be ready by then."

As sweetly as she can, Penelope says, "I would hate for our team to beat yours as badly as I think they will on your home court. We'd better keep it here."

The other men chuckle and begin moving off. Penelope made a good show of convincing them that both she and Ithaca are going to be just fine.

Asner steps close again and Penelope wills herself not to flinch. With an intense look, he asks, "Will you have made up your mind by then? Will you sell?"

Penelope feels her shoulders slump in defeat. Biting her lip, she nods. "Yes, I'll sell. I'll choose at the tournament."

"Perhaps you should sell to whoever wins," laughs Finomus, trying to make light of this sad affair in his own excitable way. "We could make a bet."

Penelope peels back her lips and forces herself to chuckle, "Then I bet my team wins the tournament despite this vicious attack today. If I lose, I'll sell my home and my life's work to the highest bidder."

There is an awkward pause. Penelope isn't very good at hiding her feelings just now. But they still shake her hand and take the bet.

"If you win, I'll give you a platypig," cries Mr. Finomus, enthusiastic and sweating more than a little. "And if you lose, you can come live with me. You'll love the swamps."

Penelope laughs with the others and tries to be genial as she ushers them off her land. When she can see them no longer, Penelope sits down and puts her head in her hands. What will she do now?

If those men were to see the fell light gleaming in her eyes, they might reconsider the wisdom in pushing a woman who just lost everything she loves.

Lupe sits down next to her. "I got something I should tell you," she mumbles, twisting a rag. Then she starts sobbing again, her round little body quivering.

"What is it?" asks Penelope without interest.

"It's about that man. Ulixes. The drifter," sniffles Lupe. "You are going to be so angry and so sad."

Penelope really doesn't see how it matters now, but Lupe is family, so for her sake Penelope persists, "What about him?"

Lupe opens and closes her mouth a few times without a word. Penelope's interest is piqued. Lupe never has a problem saying what is on her mind. Usually her problem is quite the opposite. Then Lupe sighs theatrically, "I have to go tell Larry first. This will kill him for sure. Just kill him."

With that, Lupe rushes off the porch and into the dimming light. Penelope watches her go with a furrowed brow.

What in the spheres was that about?

CHAPTER TWENTY

Trevor's fragile escape pod is losing pressure.

Cesar knows these pods often sit for years unused. Even a good crew can forget regular maintenance on escape pods. It is only to be expected that they develop a few cracks here and there. The harsh void of space finds every single one. Trevor only has about an hour until the air leaks out and the cold seeps in to end him. The little cruiser won't go fast enough to get him to Ithaca in time.

Cesar frantically tries to figure out how to load the escape pod into the cruiser, but there is no way. It just won't work. Not in the time they have left.

There must be a way to save his son.

He presses his hand against the viewscreen, over the image of the tiny pod, willing Trevor to survive. Cesar blasts the empty space around them with every scanner and distress call he can find. He doesn't care if Asner's pirate cargo ship finds them now. Anything for Trevor.

The blip on the radar is like a sign from God. A ship close by! It has a strange radar signature, but Cesar doesn't care as long as it has people on it that will let his son aboard. Carefully he steers towards it, hailing them on all channels. He doesn't pause to breathe when he finally sees the ship with his own eyes. He won't relax until Trevor is out of danger. He just keeps scanning and rescanning the pod, deciding how he will get Trevor safe as fast as possible.

Cesar notes the huge solar sails flung out from the ship without interest. At another time, he'd be carefully scrutinizing the massive nets full of old satellites and rocks. He'd try to figure what it all meant about the people inside.

Today, he only cares for one thing.

Cesar carefully loads the escape pod into the rescue bay. It's rare for people to survive space disasters, but Spacers are nothing if not optimistic about that sort of thing, so most orbitals and ships have a bay for escape pods to dock with emergency facilities right there.

It takes Cesar almost two hours to finally stumble out onto the strange ship's rickety docking platform. He forces himself go slowly. He can't afford to make a mistake. He doesn't have enough fuel for a do-over. The entire time, he is tortured by visions of Trevor lying unattended in that tiny ship. When the final gear clicks into place, Cesar leaps out of the cruiser.

There are two people, a man and a woman, waiting on the docking platform to catch him. Otherwise, Cesar would have dropped to the floor with exhaustion. He pauses only long enough to balance himself and then begins looking for Trevor.

"He's alive," says the man, holding Cesar steady with a hand on his shoulder. "Your son is going to be just fine."

Cesar turns to him. The man looks younger than Cesar but he has dark, close-cropped hair and a few wrinkles around his eyes. The man is speaking in the firm, gentle way that kind people do when they are helping a distraught stranger or calming a wild animal. When Cesar looks him in the eyes, the man suddenly squints, his gray eyes darting over Cesar's face like he's looking for something.

Remembering his current set of lies, Cesar opens his mouth to protest that Trevor isn't his son, but he just doesn't have the energy for lying right now and can't remember why he started in the first place.

Instead he asks, "Where is he?"

The woman takes his arm and says, "This way."

Cesar wastes no time in following her. She has brown hair coiled in braids around her head and she is wearing a soft faded blue coverall with plenty of zipper pockets. The man is wearing something similar, but in a dark red.

They have already moved Trevor to a sick bay. The boy lies on a stretcher with an intravenous line pumping fluids into him. Cesar looks the boy over as Trevor groggily opens his eyes. There is a nasty bruise across the boy's jaw and an ugly decompression burn down one arm. Cesar winces when he sees the cracked and puckered skin.

Trevor turns to Cesar, looking confused. He tries to rub his eyes, but the IV drip stops him.

"What happened?" Trevor asks, his voice thick and hoarse.

Cesar blinks. A wave of terror-induced nausea crashes over him. Looking away from Trevor, he finds the man in the coveralls staring at him with a frown. While Cesar clears his throat to cover his sudden discomposure, the woman brings Trevor something to drink. It seems to wake him up a bit.

The man and the woman keep darting expectant glances at Cesar, waiting for him to tell his story. Cesar opens his mouth to start explaining, but then shuts it again. He doesn't want to have to introduce himself as Ulixes and go through the whole charade again, but these people are going to start asking questions soon.

Cesar is suddenly exhausted. He slumps against the wall and stares at Trevor for a while, overwhelmed. He finds it soothing to do so. The boy is alive. Trevor looks pretty banged up but he is basically in the same condition that he started the day in. Meanwhile, Cesar's son thanks the woman politely and asks where they are. He is delighted to find himself in a junker ship.

"I've never actually been inside one before," he says, craning his neck to look around, although the room is the same nondescript tan plastic you find in almost any ship sickbay.

Junker ships make a living cleaning up space junk. The thousands of dropped hammers, broken ships, and general garbage floating around the Spacer's spheres add up. It was a problem back in the beginning of space exploration and now that the orbitals around the Earth are filling up with people, junk collection is practically an industry.

Junker ships have special solar sails to catch debris and funnel it into the nets trailing behind the little ship. Most orbitals pay to have a junker periodically sweep the space around their orbital to keep it free of hazards. The junkers, in turn, sell their catch to ironworkers and other people who can reuse it.

"It's a living," laughs the woman. "Not exactly high status, but it lets us sail wherever we want with our kids and that's what we like."

She smiles at the man and, smiling back, he takes her hand.

"Well, I guess you can tell we've had a spot of trouble," Trevor says ruefully as he prods the burn on his arm. "I wish I could tell you more about it, but I think I was out for the really exciting part."

Cesar is looking at the floor, but he can feel three sets of eyes on him.

"Trouble isn't following us," he says lowly without looking up. "You needn't worry about that."

Cesar knows he's stalling. He just doesn't want to talk about what happened. He wants to pretend it was all a bad dream and go take a nap. He's had a very long day and it is, apparently, far from over.

Trevor breaks the awkward silence by introducing himself. The man the woman are delighted to meet Trevor Vaquero of Ithaca and take turns gently shaking his good hand.

"I'm Jane, by the way. I'll get the kids up to meet you in a little bit. They'll be so excited," he woman says warmly to Trevor. "My husband here flew with your dad. He's told them quite a number of stories."

Cesar snaps his head up, his eyes darting up to the man. The man stares back, grinning at him. With a jolt, Cesar realizes he is looking at Mike, that crazy Earther kid from his tinker ship days. Mike has aged, but he looks happy. Cesar finds himself grinning back.

"You knew my dad?" Trevor asks Mike.

Cesar feels the grin on his face fade away.

This is going to be awkward.

Without taking his eyes off Cesar, Mike says, "I heard you ask everybody for stories about your dad. That true?"

"I do," Trevor replied eagerly. "Geez, look. The recorder on my comm still works. You got a story about my dad?"

Cesar gives Mike a hard look, trying to threaten the man with his eyes. Mike sees the look and only grins wider, looking more like the insane kid Cesar remembers. Back then; Cesar frequently wondered what would eventually kill this kid. Mike's whole personality was tied up in his incredible death wish.

How could Mike have lived long enough to turn into this family man? Cesar feels like killing him right now.

Mike gets that death-defying gleam in his eye and says, "Son, I got stories about your dad that would curl you hair."

"Tell me the worst," Trevor dares him.

So Mike does.

WHERE THE ONE-EYED MAN IS KING

Excerpt from Trevor Vaquero's "Tales of my Father" Archive

As told to me by Mike, the junker ship captain, right after the time I attacked pirates and mostly won and almost died.

—*Trevor Vaquero*

S o I used fly with your dad back when he was a tinker ship captain. That was some good times. Well, dangerous and unpredictable and frequently hungry times, but there was good in there too.

Lot of people come and go on a tinker ship, but I must have flown with your dad almost three years before I lost track of him. He was the best there was. Ever.

The thing about flying with your dad, Trevor, was that he made you feel safe. You knew he was going to be doing his job the best he could all day every day and you didn't need to worry about getting ordered into a suicide run. There are enough ways to die working a tinker without a moron captain or one who will freeze up in a crisis.

Some do that. Lots do that, actually.

Captain liked to keep to himself, but there were plenty that flew with him for as long as they could. There was Asia, for one. She was sort of the unofficial second-in-command and practically your dad's shadow. Then there was Nomie, just about the best pilot I ever flew with. That girl was fearless.

Oh, you met Nomie? She's settled down to raise a family out in New Siberia? Well, how lovely!

Honey, we'll have to go by when we're out that way. You'd like Nomie.

But let me get on with my story.

This particular time I'm thinking of, we had a full crew and no troubles for a couple of months. We'd been doing really well with medical runs between a couple orbitals. Your dad had a deal worked out with the Poppy Ship that kept us pretty busy. When trouble showed up, at least we had full stomachs and a good night's sleep.

So we get a hail through the Ether from some orbital we never heard of before. You'd think I'd remember the name of that little hellhole, but the truth is I don't.

They put in a high bid for antibiotics. That's a kind of rare medicine that you only take when you got something nasty eating your privates off and the medibox doesn't know what to do with it. They're expensive and hard to come by, but we had some.

Asia checked out the Ether gossip about the place and there wasn't much, but what there was in the gossip didn't worry us either. Apparently before the War, it used to be one of those fancy training facilities that a few of the richer countries tossed up here. This one was built by an American outfit to be an ultra-tech, high-grav, oxygen-rich colony for training athletes for the Olympics or the pro leagues or whatever.

At first, the Earthers tried to make it illegal for athletes to come up to those places, but eventually they gave up. After the War, it wasn't so much of an issue. Nobody had the money to pay athletes to train in space.

The Captain and I spent a little time trying to remember what sport was in off-season when the War started. We were wondering whether it was footballers or figure skaters that got stuck up there when the bombs started dropping. Regardless, according to the Ether, they mostly kept to themselves except for exporting a little wool and cheese and mutton.

Them being on the shy side didn't worry us. Most Spacers kept to themselves anyway and if they exported then they had some money or something to trade so we wouldn't be showing up to a colony that was hoping for charity. Tinkers are too hungry for charity. We like getting paid.

So off we go.

Now, the Captain didn't want to go. I should tell you that. This colony had put out a hail for a large order of these special antibiotics and we didn't have the full order. We had about a third of what they were asking for. Captain wanted to go scrounge around and get the full order together before we went. The rest of us talked him into it.

That colony was offering a great price and marked the hail as urgent. Most of us, myself included, felt like we should head over there with what we had. First, we could make sure they had the cash to afford the full order. Second, we could make sure there were still people alive to pay us when we came back with the rest of their meds.

So off we went.

We get there and dock up with no problems. Since they were asking for the antibiotic equivalent of a nuclear bomb, we boarded in full hazmat suits. My Momma didn't raise no fool. Still, I was one of the first out and there was this giant on the docking platform waiting for us.

Literally, a giant.

You wouldn't believe how big this man was. He was probably eight feet tall, at least, and built like a miner ship. You know, solid. Dense. Scary. He had a thick black mop of hair and clothes that looked like they were stitched together from old bed sheets by a five year old.

The giant starts talking in this thick, deep voice. He was welcoming us. It was obviously a prepared speech and he hadn't prepared too well because he kept stopping to remember bits and had to start over a few times.

All of us were mesmerized, but Asia pulled me aside and whispered, "Second generation on a high-grav athlete training facility. That kid can't be more than fourteen. Do you think he can see at all?"

As soon as she said it, I realized that this kid had something wrong with his eyes. His eyelids were only cracked open a slit and oozing green pus. It was disgusting.

Asia was cursed with an over-abundance of brains. I never could figure out what she was doing on a tinker. Some said she was hiding out from a military coup gone bad or a jealous lover. Some thought she was a spy. I heard she is running a colony somewhere, but I've also heard she went down to Earth and died of a plague. My favorite story is that she has a stealth ship that she sails through the spheres, picking up and recording all the signals like some superhero, listening for the small cries for help. I think it's better not to know.

"I thought spinning a colony at high grav was supposed to make people shorter," I said to Asia out of the corner of my mouth.

Real quiet, without taking her eyes off the giant, she said back, "Yes, the increase in body weight typically means elastic supportive tissue is compressed more, resulting in a height decrease, but this is the athlete training facility. No doubt that boy has been taking growth hormones and steroids since birth. He may even been genetically mutated to be taller." Or something like that. Asia used lots of big words.

Anyway, she must have messaged the Captain on her comm, because he popped out of the ship double quick, with a hazmat suit on of course. The Captain always liked checking things out himself. The giant kid wanted us to follow him somewhere, but Captain wasn't having any of it. We'd been burned too many times for that. We stayed with the ship when in a strange orbital.

It took a while for Captain to get the point across to the giant, but once the thought was firmly lodged in that huge head, the boy lumbered back down a hallway. He kept one hand on a wall at all times so I guessed he couldn't see too well.

Captain had us pull out a carton of the meds. The kid showed up with a half a dozen reinforcements and we found out that he was apparently the runt of the litter, with the exception of an old guy who was only about seven feet tall. The giants were all blind or at least they had the same funk in their eyes that the kid did.

We knew that because they had canes and kept their hands on the rails. Not that old guy though, he had one bright blue eye that didn't miss a thing and a grubby patch over the other socket. Despite the long white beard and bald head, the old guy was still stacked in the muscle department.

"The Brick," breathed Captain, stepping forward to vigorously shake the old guy's hand.

It turned out that the old guy was some famous boxer from before the war. In the ring he was known as *The Brick* on account of that's what his fist felt like. I guess it was off-season for boxers when the War hit.

Captain charmed The Brick up and down the block by recalling a few of his fights, but the giants still jumped us the second the old guy was sure we actually brought the goods. Before we knew it, we were face down on the floor, trying to breath with a giant sitting on each of our backs. The crew that was still in the ship locked the doors and took off about five seconds after a giant clamped the Captain in a headlock.

Now, we've been through this routine before so we weren't too upset. It was standard procedure to take the ship out of a situation like that. Plenty of people think they can save a few bucks by scamming a tinker.

That's why we don't deliver until the credits clear our account and if we are doing a trade, we give up one box of our goods for every one box of trade goods. It takes more time, but better safe than sorry. We forgot that some folks are just stupid or crazy.

These guys were both.

The Captain talked a mile a minute, trying to make them understand that what was in the box was maybe a tenth of the order and the crew wouldn't ransom us for the rest because we didn't have the rest. He kept explaining to them that we only had another two boxes of their meds, but these giants were not bright and real grouchy.

Meanwhile, Asia sat next to me, whispering that the bug that's gunking up their eyes was probably in the water and probably crawled up their eyeball nerves to get in their brains and made them nuts. She had a name for it, but I'm not too good at remembering that stuff. I just remember being glad the bug wasn't airborne because all our suits got torn open when the giants jumped us.

"How do you know all that?" I asked, because if it was anybody but Asia, I'd be thinking all that was just the space hysteria talking.

"Used to be a doctor," she replied.

"Really?" I asked.

To be honest, I was thinking about winning the ship betting pool with that little tidbit. I know I should've been paying attention to the situation in front of me, but there were a lot of free beers riding on what Asia used to be.

"Yeah," she grunted, keeping her eyes on the giants. "But don't spread it around. I don't want to get stuck here."

I saw her point. If these guys would jump us for a carton of meds, what would they do for an actual doctor?

That's when all hell broke loose.

One of the younger crew members, some kid who'd been flying with us less than two months… I don't bother to learn their names until they've survived at least a year. The kid had been mouthing off to the giant holding him for a good fifteen minutes and I guess the giant just couldn't take any more.

The giant grabbed the kid and just smashed him into the wall. He crushed the kid's body a few times, until that poor boy was just so much meat. Brains everywhere. Totally disgusting.

Now, I know it's gross, but remember you asked for the worst and this was it. The next thing I know, that giant, the one who just smeared this kid across the room, ran one finger through the brains dripping down the wall. Then he licked his fingers and laughs. The other giants started laughing too. It was the most horrifying sound I ever heard.

So, of course, we knew that we're all dead. There was no way those giants were going to let us go.

The Captain figured that out too because he turned around and punched the old guy right in his one good eye. The Brick dropped to the floor, howling and clutching his eye. The giants heard their king fall and went ballistic. It provided just enough of a distraction for a few of us to wiggle free and start fighting. Asia jumped up and did some sort of ninja stuff, kicking the crap out of the giants nearest her. They were big but slow.

I did my part too. I always kept a few knives handy under my hazmat suit, still do. Those of us that could bolted down a hallway, but not everyone made it. We heard the crunching of bones and screaming. No matter who you are or what you do, make sure you wear solid footwear, kid. You never know when you'll need to run fast.

We ran like hell.

Captain was in front, leading us on. I could hear people behind us, but I didn't look back. Eventually, Captain ducked down a hall into a large bay, slammed the door and locked it from the inside. We stood there, panting and looking around for some way out of this mess. Since our hazmat suits were shredded in the fight, we ripped off the remnants so they wouldn't slow us down. Nobody was thrilled about that, but Asia repeated what she told me about the bug being in the water and we all felt a little bit better.

"How do we get out?" asked Asia. She always was one for getting right to the point. I looked at the Captain because I sure as hell didn't have an answer.

Now this orbital wasn't your basic spinning can. It was a fancy one with a lot of globes strung together like beads on a necklace. We were talking about why they built it like that when we docked. Captain thought they did it so they could spin each globe independently to change the gravity and have a bunch of different environments to train in.

"Well," said the Captain after a minute. "If we can find anything to get us out into the void, the crew will pick us up."

"How do we find a ship or even a suit without finding more of… them?" asked Asia.

Captain nodded.

"They have bad eyesight," he stated, scratching his head.

"And thus poor depth perception and poor hand-eye coordination," replied Asia. "Also, I imagine whatever infests their optic nerves causes a fair bit of pain and thus renders higher cognitive functions difficult for them."

I tried to get in on all this heavy thinking. "They are blind and stupid. So we can sneak around and they won't notice us?" I said.

Captain shook his head. "They'll just turn on the cameras in the hallways and have the computer look for us."

Yeah, I didn't think of that.

I tried again with, "So we fake out the cameras?"

Asia got a faraway look. "They are all giants. If it were me, I'd set the computer to look for short people. I don't think they are sure how many of us there are."

And that's why we jumped the first giant we saw and wore him like a backpack. It wasn't the most pleasant experience.

He was heavy and he smelled.

It was lucky these guys favored large loose clothes. I was down one pant leg and Asia was down the other. Captain was on his back, under his shirt.

At first, the plan was to knock him out, but he started crying and we just couldn't do it. Actually, Asia tried to wallop him anyway, but I stopped her and Captain didn't stop me stopping her.

Our giant was kind of on the slow side, mentally speaking, but once he figured out what we wanted to do, he played along like it was a funny game. He complained an awful lot about us pulling his leg hair and the Captain digging boots into his back hair, but he didn't stop going where we wanted him to go.

We tromped along like that for a while before the giant rumbled, "Look, what is it you are trying to steal? Let's just go get it and then you can leave me alone."

"We aren't trying to steal anything," I protested. "You guys jumped us.

We're trying to get out of this asylum."

Captain filled the giant in on what had happened.

The giant let loose a huge sigh, and muttered, "The Brick and his boys are such a pain in the ass since the funk struck us blind last year, but what can you do? The whole colony is falling apart and we don't have the money to pay for a real medical team. How about I take you to the ship bay? Steal something in there and get out of here."

That sounded like a fine idea. We worried about a double-cross, but didn't have a better plan. Twice the giant ducked through a door to hide from a gang searching for us. Lucky for us, there were a lot of bathrooms in that joint. We had to go through the docking bay, so we saw what happened to the rest of our crew.

Apparently the giants had anger management issues because bits of our crew were smeared all over the place. After Asia said it looked like they'd been eaten, I stopped looking. We finally got to a ship bay and with a little work, I managed to hotwire a small ship.

The giant waved to us sadly. The Captain asked him, "You want to come with us?"

It wasn't my favorite idea. The ship we were taking was going to be mighty cramped with just the three of us and I didn't know how to rig any of the larger ships in that bay.

The giant looked like he was thinking it over, but then shook his head reluctantly. "I got family here and those meds you guys left may help."

Captain shrugged and turned back to the little ship. Asia paused in the doorway and then told the giant, "The bug is in your water supply."

She told him how to shock the water using sheep urine as a basic homemade bleach to kill the bug. I was itching to shut the door and get out of there, but experience taught me to let Asia do whatever it is she wanted to do.

Finally, she stopped jawing and came in. Right before I closed the door, the giant asked Captain, "Who are you?"

Captain gave him a pitying look and said, "Jonas Ulixes," because that's the fake name he always gave to people when he didn't want to say his real name. Your dad always was shy about his past.

What's the matter, kid? You just got all green and queasy looking. If you have to be sick, do it in that bucket next to your bed.

Anyway, I slammed the door shut and we got out of there, only to find the rest of the crew didn't wait for us. They'd taken the ship and hightailed it. I never did find out what happened to them, our ship and all my stuff. I had the most wonderful pillow I lost on that ship. Sometimes I still dream about that pillow.

I heard through the local Ether that the giant's colony eventually got help, but most of them were permanently blind and stupid afterwards. They might have been stupid before. You never know. It seemed that a benevolent dictator set up shop and taught them all to play Spacerbase and they've been dominating Spacerbase League ever since. They even have their own dedicated reality site on the Ether. Last season, it was more popular than mini-pig racing.

It was hard times for us, though, getting that little puddle jumper to a real port, but we made it. We were definitely a few pounds lighter and a lot scruffier by then, though. Eventually, the three of us cobbled together another ship and started tinkering again.

I rode with your dad for almost another year after that, until we got separated in the uprising on Alpha Seti Six, but that's another story.

CHAPTER TWENTY-ONE

If Mike hoped for applause at the end of his tale, he is sorely disappointed. Trevor stares at nothing, meditatively chewing a thumbnail. Cesar is memorizing his shoes while feeling his stomach digest itself. He wonders if he will finally get an ulcer from everything life keeps throwing at him. The grin slides off Mike's face as he looks from Trevor's ghastly expression to Cesar's discomfort.

Cesar knows it is time for him to do something.

Drawing himself up, Cesar gives Mike a grin and a firm handshake. "It's good to see you again, Mike," he says, clapping him on the shoulders. It is, too.

Mike grins back at him uncertainly as Cesar says smoothly, "As you can guess, we are in a bit of trouble which, I promise, we will not bring down on you. You certainly saved our bacon today and I thank you for that. You always were a good man, Mike, and I'm happy to see you so settled. I'll be happy to fill you in on the details and figure out how to get out of your hair without putting you out any more than we already are, but first I need a few minutes alone with my son."

"Of course, of course," Mike says jovially. "So glad to know you're alive and your boy there! Well, he's the spitting image of you, sir."

Mike allows himself to be guided out. Cesar shuts the door firmly behind Mike. He suddenly realizes that no matter how absolutely horrible it made him feel to disappoint his parents, that is nothing compared to disappointing his son. Given the choice between getting boiled alive in hot oil and turning towards his son to see the rejection and disappointment he knows is on that boy's face, he'd rather strip down and deep fat fry himself any day.

"Stories about my dad never have happy endings, huh?" Trevor asks quietly.

Cesar looks at his son. Trevor picks lint off his blanket with the kind of concentration usually reserved for brain surgery or advanced mathematics or video games.

"I didn't mean for you to find out this way," Cesar stammers. "I didn't mean for things to be like this."

Trevor frowns, gulps and switches his attentions to prodding the burn on his arm. How can he ever apologize? Cesar sighs. What can he say? There are no excuses for being a terrible dad.

"So you're my dad?" asks Trevor slowly, his eyes on the burn. Cesar thinks his heart might break, hearing the pain in the boy's voice.

"I thought about you every day," Cesar finally says. "Every day I thought about you and your mom. I just couldn't come back. You've heard the stories. Death, destruction, violence. That's all I ever had to offer. I couldn't bring that home to you. I've been in your life a few days and look where we are, for God's sake."

Cesar slams his palm into a wall to relieve his frustration. It doesn't help.

Trevor smiles wryly. "Well, I guess that's why you keep hugging me," he says with a quick glance at Cesar. "That's good. I was starting to worry you were like the guys from Lavender Lambda Orbital and had a crush on me."

Cesar laughs, "Ah, no. Definitely your dad. Definitely not gay. Got a serious crush on your mom, though."

It is Trevor's turn to laugh and the awkward tension stops sucking all the air out of that room.

"Good luck with *that*," he chuckles. "She was planning to boot you out, you know, and that's before she knew who you were. She's gonna be so pissed at you. It'll be nice to see her mad at somebody else for a change."

"Yeah," replies Cesar, running a hand through his hair. Penelope is one too many problems for right now. Holding her in his arms seems like eons ago. "Fortunately for me, we have more pressing issues just now."

Cesar starts talking. He methodically goes through everything he remembers from the pirate ship. He has to go through it a few times before he gets it straight in his mind. Adrenaline isn't the best thing for the memory. He mumbles through the part about Julia.

Trevor swallows hard with Cesar watching him anxiously. He doesn't know how hard the boy will take it.

"They killed her?" Trevor asks in a small voice. "You're sure? Maybe they just captured her? Maybe there's a way to save her?"

Cesar shakes his head grimly. "No, they killed her. Then they dumped her body out an airlock. I'm sorry, son."

"But it's not right," Trevor mutters, looking as though he is trying to find some solution, some way to undo the girl's casual murder. Cesar has been down that road many times.

"Son, uh, Trevor. Sometimes people we really like die. The worst is when they die suddenly and terribly for no reason. You keep thinking that it's wrong. That there is some way around it, but there isn't. The best way to mourn them is to survive and win, to try and find a way to make their death meaningful."

Trevor looked down at his thumbs and nodded sharply a few times. "Yeah, I guess," he muttered, grief putting the years on his face, making him look more like a man than a child. "In those stories people tell me about you, lots of your friends die and, most of the time, it happens quick and brutal and you don't have a chance to stop it or say goodbye or anything. I just thought it was part of how stories go, but it sucks. I forget that they are real people in those stories."

Cesar patted his son's head gently. "Real life usually sucks, kid. But it beats the alternative. So let's figure out how to get out of this mess and get back home."

Trevor swallows a few more times, but then he asks Cesar to continue. Cesar is happy to talk.

He rambles on; trying to describe every detail and not notice while Trevor sniffles and wipes his eyes with the back of his hand. Cesar wants to rip Mach and Asner apart, not only for killing Julia but also for making his son so sad. Cesar's memory is blurry and the conversation he thought he heard seems so unlikely as he recounts it now.

"So Uri Mach from Seven Skies Trading and that Asner guy from EEC are trying to get the herd for some sort of lubricant for a laser that can fry a whole Earth city," Trevor summarizes.

"Yeah, it sounds crazy, doesn't it?" replies Cesar, feeling old and tired. "No one is going to believe us."

"They might believe you," Trevor suggested. "You are Cesar the Scorcher. If you worry about some guy with a big laser, other people will probably worry about that too."

Cesar gives him a sour look. Then he remembers dimly overhearing Asner and Mach talking at Penelope's party. He hadn't been paying too much attention because Penelope was entirely too distracting, but he remembered one thing.

"I overheard them another time talking about a Moon Array. So, a laser that needs lots of grease on the Moon? That sounds even more bizarre, doesn't it?"

Trevor's brow furrows. "That would have to be a really big laser. They couldn't hide a laser like that, could they? I mean, someone would notice that, right?"

Cesar didn't have an answer.

Trevor points out, "It does sound crazy, but on the other hand, we just escaped from their pirate ship and we know for a fact they were trying to steal the herd. I've heard Mach trying to convince my mom to sell him a thousand head before. Then there are all these attacks on Ithaca, ever since she refused to sell. It's crazy, but maybe that's what they are up to. They are up to something, at any rate."

"If they need a thousand cows worth of grease, that's a really big laser," comments Cesar, still mulling it over, looking for the best answer to this riddle. He is pretty stumped, though.

"They think I'm dead," Trevor points out.

"And they don't know about me at all," says Cesar. "There's got to be a solution to this problem in there somewhere."

Trevor sighs, "Like what?"

"Well," Cesar says, clearing his throat. "First, we've got to decide where to go next. I know your mother wouldn't like this solution at all, but I think it's better if you don't go back to Ithaca right away. Let the bad guys think you are dead a while longer. It will give us some time to figure out what our next move is."

"You're right," laughs Trevor. "My mom would hate that idea."

"Yeah, she would," agrees Cesar, rubbing his chin thoughtfully. "It just seems like we don't really know what we're up against so we should exploit what few advantages we have. If you have a better idea, I'm open to it, but otherwise I'll go talk to Mike and see how far he's willing to take us."

"Sure. Whatever," says Trevor, lying back, exhausted from the effort of deciding what to do next.

Cesar reaches out to hold Trevor's hand, but the boy turns onto his side, away from Cesar. Cesar pulls his hand back and looks at his son for a long minute. Straightening his slumped shoulders, he says quietly, "You get some sleep. I'll go talk to Mike and see where he can drop us. Sound good?"

"Yeah, sure," Trevor says without turning.

As Cesar opens the door to leave, Trevor turns to Cesar and calls, "Hey, uh, Dad?"

Cesar tightens his grip on the door but keeps his voice level as he says, "Yes, Trevor?"

"It's nice to meet you."

Cesar feels tears in his eyes again. Fatherhood is turning him into a big weepy baby. Clearing his throat, he looks at the tentative smile on Trevor's face and feels like singing. "It's nice to meet you too, son. It's… very nice."

Then Cesar flees the room before he starts crying or singing in front of his son. The poor boy has enough to deal with already today.

CHAPTER TWENTY-TWO

Penelope is rethinking that whole *"resist the urge to despise all men"* resolution she made. She was young and naïve when she thought that a Y-chromosome couldn't really negate all possible redeeming qualities in a human.

That was before she had to deal with sixteen Nullball teams bouncing around her orbital when the whole place is held together by duct tape and hope. The testosterone cloud surrounding the player housing area is practically generating its own climate.

Penelope tries to tell herself that the teams are co-ed and the women are just as rowdy, loud and ridiculous as the men, but it seems to be only the men that have a particular genius for getting on her very last nerve.

Last night, for example, some of the players from the Seven Skies team apparently conducted a "panty raid" on the local Sisters of the Sword nunnery and came away with serious injuries for their efforts. Now she has to deal with outraged knife-wielding nuns, players spurting blood everywhere as well as leaders from other colonies screaming to know how this could happen and that it's Ithaca's fault their team can't play today, so she better fix it right now. The whole thing gives her a throbbing head-ache.

Trevor has been gone for nine days. Nine days.

Penelope feels she's done a decent job of keeping herself together and working for the good of the colony. They performed a miracle just by get-ting things functional so quickly. Ithaca was late on a few shipments in the last week, but they fulfilled every promise, even if it meant working around the clock fueled by insane determination and nonstop caffeine.

Not only that, but they are as prepared for the Nullball Tournament as they are ever going to be. So what if she spends the few hours Lupe forces her to rest just staring at her ceiling? So what if the entire point of her existence was suddenly snatched away?

She will soldier on, even if she no longer knows why.

The worst was yesterday when her insane father-in-law, Larry, finally came careening onto the ranch to make his grand appearance. He was magnificently drunk. The old man worked himself into a pathos of tragedy that even the most dedicated Shakespearean actor could only dream of bringing to Hamlet.

"The end of my line!" wailed Larry, while actually rending his garments and tearing his hair.

Penelope was fairly sure that he spent over fifteen minutes developing a line of reasoning that ended with "All is lost and ruined." But she blocked out the end of it by getting drunk, purely as a defensive mechanism. Her in-laws stressed her out in the best of times and this is most assuredly not the best of times.

It did not help at all that Lupe went for Larry's feast of tragedy like it was an all-you-can-eat buffet during the early-bird special. She wailed and bawled and matched the old coot shot for shot on that moonshine he made out there in his squalid little shack.

Penelope wasn't really surprised, but she was disappointed. Lupe has been mostly incoherent since Trevor disappeared. She keeps mumbling about having to confess to Penelope something about the drifter, but then the old woman bursts into tears and rushes out of the room.

Penelope tells herself it is for the best. If she has anyone to lean on right now, she'll probably collapse like a house of cards.

Even Argos is less than his usual stalwart implacable self. He's disappeared for most of the last few days and just mumbles about helping Mr. Larry when she asks. Penelope can't bring herself to lecture Argos right now, so she just ignores his absences and tries to do everything herself. Exhaustion is a sort of escape right now anyway.

At first, she tried to understand Lupe's behavior, but now Penelope is getting annoyed with her oldest friend. She wonders at what point she started considering Lupe a friend. Somewhere in these long years, the old woman and her Spanish cursing has become necessary to Penelope, just as her son…

She won't think about that. She'll think about getting the plumbing fixed in the athletes' quarters before they start some sort of juvenile water fight or exhibitionist bathing in the street.

Yes.

Penelope has also firmly put that drifter into the part of her memory she tries not to visit. He still manages to intrude on her thoughts more often than she really feels necessary for someone she barely knew and spent so little time with, but it's better than thinking about… other unpleasant losses.

Later, Penelope trudges back to the house after far too many hours spent dealing with various petty problems and overseeing the final preparations for the tournament. She is heartily sick of Nullball and would like nothing better than to be done with the whole stupid event. At least it keeps people from asking her if she's heard anything new about Trevor and the other two.

Finomus, Castor and Asner have been by her side so much in the last few days that Penelope is surprised not to find one of them at her elbow when she rolls over at night. Even now, she's only alone because she lied and told them that she has urgent private business.

She is sure Finomus is just a nice little man, anxious to help and excited that his team made it into the tournament. It's the first year they've managed to qualify. Penelope also knows Castor is looking to recommend himself as the best buyer for her farm, but he does so with charming sincerity.

Asner she isn't sure about.

He spends far too much time hanging around, getting in her personal space. Asner also spends quite a bit of time telling her she should sell the ranch to Uri Mach at Seven Skies, but she can't understand why. Perhaps he thinks to ingratiate himself into her life by telling her how to run it? It isn't working.

"God, could I be grouchier?" Penelope asks herself with almost a laugh. Probably not. At least, not until she sees who is sitting on her front porch.

Penelope notes a shadowed figure sitting on her porch and observes it without much interest as she trudges home. She was hoping for an empty house and a hot bath. Whoever this is, it isn't her son and is therefore unwelcome. After a minute, her curiosity wakes up.

Who can it be? It isn't Lupe's round shape or Larry's hunched profile. She left Asner, Finomus, and Castor back in town sampling the local beer and barbeque. Maybe Argos? Why would Argos wait for her on the porch? More bad news, probably.

Then the figure stands and steps into the sunlight. Penelope's breath leaps in her chest.

Him!

She is half running, half staggering with shock. How can it be him? Ulixes has a joyous smile spread across his face as he limps towards her.

He catches her up in his arms and she luxuriates in his warm safe embrace for exactly half a second before twisting around to look for her son.

"What happened? How did you get here? Where's Trevor? Is he hurt? Where's my son? Where have you been?" The questions tumble out of her mouth too fast to make sense. She isn't even sure the words are in the right order as she rushes to get them out.

Fortunately, Ulixes answers the most important question first. "He's safe," the man whispers in her ear, tightening his arms around her.

Penelope forces herself to breathe through her nose, slowly and calmly, the way her mother taught her to do when she needed to calm herself. She desperately wants to believe this man, but she can't relax until she sees her son with her own two eyes.

Pulling away from him, she inhales his distinctive smell. Something about the way the man smells makes her want to tear his clothes off every time she gets near him.

Shaking her head to clear it, she asks suspiciously, "Where's my son?"

He laughs. It is a slow comfortable chuckle.

"Trust me, he's safe. He's a little banged up. We had ourselves quite a little adventure, but Trevor is fine," Ulixes says.

"Where is he?" Penelope persists. "Why isn't he here telling me this himself?"

Ulixes sighs, pulling away from her and sticking his hands in his pockets. "Well, to make a long story short, there are dangerous men who will try to kill him if they know they didn't succeed the first time. So we thought it would be better to hide him for a while."

Penelope eyes him critically. "You have some explaining to do."

"I think so too," he agrees. "Let's go into the house. I could use a cup of coffee."

An hour later, Penelope is staring at the man in front of her as he talks. He says Uri Mach and Asner and possibly even Finomus are in a plot to steal her herd and boil them down for glue or something, all so they can complete some sort of secret project on the Moon that involves lasers that can fry Earth cities.

He tells her these men she has known for years are launching a secret weapon so they can take over everything. That they tried to kidnap and kill her son, but this man in front of her rescued him in the nick of time.

Ulixes informs her that he snatched Trevor from the jaws of death and now has him hidden away somewhere, safe as can be. This man in front of her also says he is going rescue her from the villainous forces trying to destroy her and Trevor.

Penelope isn't buying it. This man is obviously deranged and talking a whole lot of crap.

He also tells her that poor little Julia died in the most senseless way possible. She asks him about it several times because she can't believe the girl is gone. Penelope always expected the knife-loving, man-hating Julia to eventually join the Sisters of the Sword nunnery. Penelope cries for the girl, feeling guilty that she has little energy for grief. She is too busy worrying about her son.

"Darling, I thought about you and Trevor every day," Ulixes says tenderly. "I'm so sorry. But I'm here now and I will do everything I can to keep you and Trevor safe."

Like suddenly he's totally in love with her and wants to be a father to her son after a few weeks of hanging around helping out? Oh, yeah. He's nuts.

She tries to be open-minded and take his story seriously. After all, the last time she saw Ulixes, they were fighting off pirates in the middle of a space stampede. That would sound pretty unbelievable if you weren't there. And with Trevor's obsession about stories about his father, she's heard more than her fair share of unlikely tales over the last couple of years.

While she assumed most of those stories are just fairy tales or the dreams of oxygen-deprived tinkers, that doesn't mean that really bizarre, improbable things can't happen to people or that the stories don't have a grain of truth to them. What this man is saying did sound like a big pile of lies though. It's just too much. Penelope hopes this is just hysteria inflating the actual rescue of her son who really is safe somewhere right now.

She nods mechanically while studying Ulixes as he goes on and on and on. How on earth did she sleep with this man and not realize he's totally insane? It's really depressing to know that she is still so utterly incapable of figuring people out. This right here is what they mean by the exception that proves the rule. Penelope understands that now.

She decided long ago that sex is not worth the risk and the first time she breaks her own rule, what happens? She goes and sleeps with a mentally unstable drifter suffering from hallucinations. The only thing she isn't sure about now is how to get this maniac out of her house without a fuss.

He reaches for her hand and Penelope snatches it away and gets up from the kitchen table.

"I need to think," she stammers, pacing around.

Penelope realizes that she is in her own kitchen and there is a bottle of tequila on the top shelf. She decides she can think better with a drink and pours a shot of tequila straight down her throat. The fire in her stomach clears her head remarkably.

"I understand," he says, watching her pace anxiously. "It's a lot to throw at you all at once."

Now that she studies him, Penelope realizes that Ulixes actually looks a bit like Cesar. If her long dead husband had a much older, wiser schizophrenic cousin who had been thrown in an industrial-grade meat grinder once or twice, he might look like this man in front of her. Perhaps that's why she was attracted to Ulixes in the first place? The thought makes her feel sick.

Penelope takes a deep breath and reminds herself to think clearly. Even if he is insane, the last time she saw him was with Trevor.

"Where is Trevor now?" she asks carefully.

"Lazar Colony," he replies promptly.

Penelope closes her eyes and takes another slow calming breath. "Why would my son be on the Synthlep colony? How did he get there?" she asks patiently. She tries to be patient, but Penelope can hear the anger and total disbelief in her voice even if he can't.

The man starts talking, but it is more insane gabble about a war buddy on a junker ship and saving some Synthlep sufferers from imminent death and other nonsense.

"Can we call him? Can I talk to Trevor?" she asks eagerly, trying to remain calm. She has to know if her son is still alive. If there is any possibility of that, she'll listen to a million crazy stories from the poor man. He's obviously broken with reality long ago.

"Sure," replies Ulixes anxiously.

She hands him the comm and he dials through the Ether. She watches him tap away for a minute, surprised at how effective insane people could be. The man has no problems getting through the Ether. He nods once or twice, typing diligently before he winces.

Taking off the comm set, he looks at her mournfully and shakes his head. "We can't talk to Trevor right now. Apparently, Lazar House is in the middle of a Sectarian riot right now and Trevor is caught up in it."

"Great," Penelope sighs.

More loony stories. The guy is totally bonkers.

BETWEEN SCYLLA AND CHARYBDIS

Excerpt from Trevor Vaquero's "Tales of my Father" Archive

Ever since the word got out on the Spacer Ether that I've been collecting stories about my dad, I've gotten some seriously crazy crap sent to me. I would have just dismissed this next story as the ramblings of another nutter out in the void, except it is from the infamous Aeneas, the *ronin* captain of the Ex-World Fleet, a wandering army clinging to their precious honor, despised by those who hire them to die in their stead. The Worlders sent their fleet to kill us and afterwards the Ex-World Fleet couldn't go back to Earth. Since they hang out in the L5 Greek Camp, they are just a myth to those of us who live in orbitals from the L4 Trojan Camp. I figure that Aeneas wouldn't bother making up lies to send to a boy he doesn't know.

—*Trevor Vaquero*

Dear Mr. Trevor Vaquero,

Please excuse the informality of the following communication. I am not sure what the correct format would be for sending messages to the son of one of your dearest heroes and greatest adversaries. I will proceed as best I can.

I may unreservedly say that meeting your father changed my life... saved my life. Which is ironic because from the time his ship appeared as a blip on my radar until the time his ion trail disappeared across the horizon, I was sure he would die spectacularly at any minute. In fact, I can honestly say that I followed the man around for no other reason than to watch him die. I long hated him for besting me in the Spacer War and he behaved so much like a man thirsting for death that it seemed impossible he would not slake his thirst and, in doing so, Death would give me a show better than the highest-budget Ether blockbuster.

Death owes me that and much more, but he's a stingy bastard. And Cesar Vaquero is a man Death flees, I think, but only because Cesar leaves a river of blood everywhere he goes. I will not shield even his son from the truth—that Cesar Vaquero bought himself a thousand gifts from Death by giving the grave millions of lives.

By the grace of God, I have also committed many souls to the hereafter so I cannot judge your father. Judging men is God's job in any case. I confine myself to doing the work the heavens have given me, no matter how much the good Lord requires me to consort with assholes and idiots.

I have always wondered why the astronomers assumed that we in the orbitals parked in the largest stable points around Earth, the L4 and L5 Lagrange Points, would be hostile to one another. They named L4 "The Greek Camp" and L5 "The Trojan Camp."

Why?

I can only assume it was because astronomers are the most incredible nerds. Excuse me, Mr. Vaquero, if you have an inclination towards that branch of science, but many troubles would have been averted if the L4 and L5 orbitals did not have a predisposed distrust of each other brought on by stargazing Earthers' fanciful names.

Yes, I am an Earther. But God decided that the spheres would be my home and I am not sorry.

Certainly, your L4 Greek Camp fared better than our L5 Trojan Camp during the Spacer War and I flatter myself to think this was primarily because my fleet focused our efforts on the Trojan Camp. I destroyed every orbital I was ordered to attack in the Trojan Camp.

Let me begin the tale properly.

On star date 30060.04471080678, I led the Ex-World Fleet to the end of the Trojan Camp closest to the entry point, the point where a visiting fleet of tinker ships from the Greek Camp would most likely enter our region of the spheres. My intelligence officers had heard quite a number of rumors on the Ether about an armada of tinkers, heavily laden with all the civilized amenities we in the Trojan Camp lacked—coffee, silk, chocolates, etc.

The Trojan Camp hadn't had any trade vessels from outside our Lagrange point in two or three years. The dangers in our area of the spheres are not exaggerated. The Trojan Camp did not hold on so well to civilization after the Spacer War as those in L4 Greek Camp. The war cost the orbitals there too much. We of the Ex-World Fleet sold our protection and experience to all who needed it at the most reasonable price we could, but few trusted us enough to hire us. None offered us the permanent settlement we craved. Such was the lot the good Lord had given us.

No fleet from the Greek Camp would have crossed to the other side of the sky if they knew the horrors awaiting them. The orbitals of Scylla and Charybdis hung at the gates of the Trojan Camp like sentinels at the gates of Hell. So the Ex-World Fleet flew out to rescue this Greek flotilla from its own folly.

"Admiral Aeneas? There is an incoming fleet of small merchant-class vessels, sir. We count twenty-three ships in all," the petty officer on duty reported. "They are approaching the gateway, but have not yet come within range of either Scylla or Charybdis."

"Signal them at once!" I ordered. "Explain the danger they are about to encounter and offer our services at the usual rates."

I was confident this Greek fleet would hire us to guide them through. Our fees were cheaper than the energy and time they would lose going around Scylla and Charybdis.

Charybdis was what remained of a Chinese military orbital. I'm not really sure what went on in there. Both their airlock and Ether uplink were one way trips, as far as I could tell. I'm not even certain there were any live souls aboard. I only know they had a powerful tractor beam that they loved using at every opportunity. Even we were not immune. The Ex-World Fleet simply stayed out of Charybdis' range.

Scylla, on the other hand, I knew too well. Its furry mutant inhabitants loved talking on the Ether. They never said whether their radiation shields were too thin or their genetically engineered filter bacteria went haywire, but something caused all of Scylla's inhabitants to suffer from severe hypertrichosis i.e. excessive hair.

Personally, I think God was punishing them for their wickedness, but if divine justice were the cause he surely would have blighted them with something that kept them from producing so many insane Ether clips about the glories of becoming a furry psychopathic post-human who preyed upon anyone passing by with their harpoons. Their orbital was originally built as a docking station for some kind of space gun that launched cargo from Earth, so Scylla was able to move their orbital around quickly and fire their harpoons to snag any cargo the gun fired up. Unfortunately, they never really got the gun on Earth working, but Scylla was designed perfectly for attacking small ships that ventured too close.

Before the Scylla and Charybdis went feral, there were other orbitals close to the gateway, but they moved rather than deal with such vicious neighbors. After a few skirmishes, Scylla knew better than to try their tricks on the Ex-World Fleet, though.

"Sir, the L4 tinker fleet declines our services," the petty officer reported a few minutes later.

I frowned. "Did you explain the dangers?"

"Yes sir. In some detail. Also there is the wreckage in this area from their previous victims."

Sipping my customary 09:00 cup of caffeine water, I pondered the implications. "Do you suppose they did not believe you?"

"No, sir," the petty officer replied. "They said they knew about our S&C issue beforehand."

"I see. Then they will try to go around," I muttered, mildly irritated to lose a potential contract and seriously concerned that these fool tinkers had traveled halfway across the spheres to get themselves destroyed because they were too cheap to hire us. "Well, since we are out here, let's go through a few training exercises and keep an eye on them."

I wasn't going to push them. The Ex-World Fleet never descends to thuggery, no matter what they say about us. I wanted to argue though. Those rickety, pieced-together ships were already too close to Scylla for my tastes. People underestimate how fast that monster can move when she wants. I figured we'd be getting a call pretty soon to wade in and rescue those fat little merchants. For that, we charge double.

The Ex-World Fleet prides itself on staying tight, so we ran through two mock battles as easy as putting on our shoes in the morning. I had plenty of time to watch this tinker fleet and wonder if they had real coffee on one of those boats. I was going to be pretty peeved if they got themselves killed and wasted perfectly good coffee while I had nothing better than caffeine water rations for the last six months.

I thought those tinkers were fools, but I didn't dream they were damned suicidal fools. I couldn't believe my eyes when they took their entire fleet and flew it straight at Scylla, right into the monster's mouth. I'd have insisted on protecting them if I'd known that was their plan.

Scylla waited until they were good and close before flinging out all six of her massive harpoons at once. Six ships were struck. The smallest practically exploded when the harpoon pierced it. As the other five struggled against the barbed hooks slowly reeling them towards the doom of Scylla, the merchant fleet scattered.

A black ship, too small to be anything but a single pilot fighter, appeared out of the tinker fleet. I didn't see which tinker it came from. The black fighter slipped through the mayhem of fleeing merchants and fired a precision shot that neatly severed the cord on one of the harpoons, freeing the round ship it had speared.

"Well, they have one man out there with some brains," I snarled to no one in particular. "Too bad he waited until it was too late."

I watched as the newly liberated ship fired one of its thrusters and went spinning off at a crazy angle, so eager to get away from Scylla that it forgot the other danger of this passage. The freed ship was only able to celebrate its survival of Scylla for about two minutes before Charybdis captured it, pulling the doomed ship into its inescapable gravity well.

The stars behind Charybdis warped and shimmered as it activated the fell technology that allowed it to suck down entire ships without pause. There was always that strange moment before the ship disappeared where it warped, almost fading out of existence. You can't ever record it clearly. I've tried.

"Sir, the Scyllans are broadcasting a live feed of their attack," the comm officer reported to me unnecessarily. The Scyllans always did that. They liked to brag about their brutality. "Do you want to patch it into your comm?"

"No. Offer sanctuary to the survivors, but don't hold your tongue if you feel like lecturing them," I replied, already weary of watching the tinkers flounder and die. I tapped the power button to switch off the comm implanted in my right temple and enjoyed a few hours of peace in my bunk.

"Admiral Aeneas, the tinker fleet continues to decline our protection," reported the petty officer on duty when I returned to the bridge.

"Really?" I asked, my interest piqued. "All of them?"

The petty officer frowned thoughtfully. "They let one of the captains speak for the lot of them. He says they had arranged payment to the Scyllans in return for safe passing, but the Scyllans double-crossed them. He was very angry, mostly at himself for not guessing that Scylla would betray them."

I might have tried something similar if I hadn't known the Scyllans. "I see. And who is their leader?"

The petty officer had the brains to look ashamed. "I don't know, sir. The others just call him *Captain*. He was the one flying the black fighter."

Having nothing better to do in this region of the spheres, we followed the tinker fleet into the Trojan Camp and picked up a job escorting a Hathor transport ship. It was a straight babysitting job and there were no complications. When we were done, we came across the L4 tinker fleet, this time they were preparing to head back to their part of the spheres.

"Offer them our services," I ordered, confident they'd had plenty of time to see reason.

The answer came back within an hour. "They decline, sir. But Captain wanted to know if you were still our commander, sir," the comm officer told me. "He asked if Admiral Aeneas is still the leader of the Ex-World Fleet."

I raised an eyebrow. "And what did this Captain say when you affirmed it?"

The comm officer had the grace to look embarrassed as he relayed Captain's response. "He wondered how the great Aeneas could sleep at night with two monsters on her front doorstep. He seemed to think you must be getting on in years to let something like that slip."

Years of experience in command kept me from choking on my caffeine water, but only just. Before I could voice any of the blasphemous responses in my mind, the comm officer hurried to finish his report, "The tinker Captain also wanted to know if we could procure for them a Class C8 cargo hull? He said they'd pay premium rates."

Well of course we could procure a Class C8 cargo hull. We had more than half a dozen of those bloated cargo ships beached like whales around a destroyed orbital not too far away. Class C8 cargo ships were used to transport entire armadas of the Worlder Fleet at a time. If we had known the Earthers only planned for it to be a one-way trip up, we may not have bothered saving them.

"Tell them we'll have to look around. That such things are hard to come by," I grumbled.

The comm officer cleared his throat. "Captain said to tell you he had twenty pounds of the freshest from Columbian Coffee Conglomerate. Dark roasted. I could hear him drinking it. I could almost smell it, sir." The man was dangerously close to whining and I sympathized. Ex-World Fleet missed its coffee.

Two days later, the tinker fleet had their cargo hull. "Tell them it will never work," I growled at the petty officer as he poured more water into my coffee press. "No, don't. If those hubris-blind dolts think they can sneak between Scylla and Charybdis inside the dead body of a cargo ship, they deserve what they get."

I decided it would make a good training exercise for the Ex-World Fleet to fly far around Scylla and Charybdis just in time to meet the tinker fleet on the other side, if any of them made it that far. I doubted they would. I'm not the sort of monster that would deny my crew what promised to be a good show.

We were getting bored when the cargo ship lurched into view. They must have rigged up a remote steering mechanism, but even in its prime the C8 drove like a pig. The tinker fleet had to be inside steering it. There was just no other way to get that boat to fly. You could practically hear the Scyllans slavering through the void. I settled down with a fresh steaming mug of coffee to watch the show.

As soon as the cargo ship blundered its way between Scylla and Charybdis, the Scyllans let their harpoons fly. I noted that they had fixed Captain's damage. All six harpoons sunk into the side of the C8. The lines went taut, pulling the cargo ship slowly towards Scylla. I waited for the inevitable tide of escaping tinkers to flow out of the bloated ship. Scylla would be too smart for that trick. She'd reel the cargo ship in fast and snap up a few tinker ships before they could get away.

Instead, four harpoons shot out of the cargo ship away from Scylla, towards Charybdis. I clutched my coffee mug with shock, scalding my palms as I stared with disbelief. There was a strange spark on Charybdis as the barbs sunk into it and held tight.

"Well, that was interesting," I gasped. "But now the fool is just double damned. Does he think he can fly away with both of them in his back pocket? They'll just tear him apart. Sweet Mother of God." There were no replies from my officers. They were too busy watching the action on their comms.

There were four wide-eyed officers on duty with me and several more who had found various reasons to loiter on the bridge, so the roar of surprise was almost deafening when that fat cow of a cargo ship started spinning like a Russian tether. The harpoon cords wound around it, reeling in both of those cursed orbitals.

Just before Scylla and Charybdis crashed together into the cargo ship, that tiny black fighter shot out of the cargo hull.

Then all hell broke loose. Literally.

The cargo ship exploded, shredding Scylla like a paper ball. Charybdis fizzled and warped and shrank into itself. The resulting gravitational wave rocked the whole fleet back. My coffee mug shattered against a bulkhead as I flung a hand out to steady myself.

The black fighter was flung out into voidspace. I ordered my command ship to follow it. As we retrieved the black fighter, my officers informed me that the tinker fleet was picking its way through the wreckage and readying for their long trip home to the Greek Camp.

"But they want their Captain back," my comm officer reported with a grin. The Ex-World Fleet is uniformly of the opinion that the next best thing to fighting a good battle is watching one.

The black fighter was in a tumbling free fall. The death blast of Scylla and Charybdis had knocked it hard. Fortunately, we quickly gathered it into our modest flight deck and extracted its pilot alive.

That day, I watched one man in a tiny black fighter destroy two monsters that I thought too large to even contemplate attacking directly, much less destroying utterly in a single blow. I commanded the Ex-World Fleet to the best of my abilities and that day I realized I had been failing them. My best wasn't good enough. We spent years sailing around the Trojan

Camp, hoping that if we showed we were pious and honorable, some orbital would take us in and give us a home.

This man showed me that I needed to act as though anything were possible. Instead of wandering in search of a home, we needed to make our own orbital, found our own empire in the spheres. Of course it was many years and many wild adventures until our story ended, but in my mind the path finally became clear that day. He was my greatest hero and I eagerly rushed to meet him on our flight deck.

But you don't want to hear my story. You want the story of how I met your father.

I stood on the flight deck in my threadbare full dress whites, my spine so straight it hurt. Two of my men gently helped the black fighter's pilot out of his ship.

"Well, my girl *Surprise* is banged up, but she'll keep flying. Just like me, I guess," I heard the pilot say to my men as he limped towards me.

Even with the scars, the white hair and the limp, I recognized your father. I spent so many nights studying all the files I could find on my great adversary that I could pick Cesar the Scorcher out of a crowd. My mind reeled. My new hero was my old enemy.

Your father stopped two feet in front of me, snapped to attention and gave me a crisp salute. What could I do but offer him my hand?

"It is an honor to meet you, Captain Cesar Vaquero."

If hearing his true name surprised him, the only indication was a slight twitch of his left eyebrow.

Gripping my hand and shaking it enthusiastically, Cesar the Scorcher, replied, "The honor is mine, Admiral Maria Aeneas." He bowed low and kissed the back of my hand before returning to his ship without another word. The tinker fleet collected him quickly.

After that, the tinker fleet regularly traveled between the Greek and Trojan Camps, but your father was never with them again. I checked every time.

May God Watch Over You,
Admiral Maria Aeneas

CHAPTER TWENTY-THREE

Trevor is standing on a strange orbital alone with practically nothing but the clothes he is wearing. Almost everyone he knows thinks he's dead. There are rich and powerful men after him who will stop at nothing to kill him if they know he is still alive. He is still weak from surviving a near-death experience and mourning the death of a beautiful girl. Holding his throbbing burned arm tight against his body, Trevor walks slowly into town alternatively gulping back sobs and wanting to sing.

Trevor represses the sudden desire to skip and makes an attempt to feel traumatized again, but it just isn't working. He wonders if his weird attacks of good mood are the after-effect of almost getting killed. Some sort of survivor's euphoria, maybe?

Trevor makes a mental note to ask Cesar about that.

He would know. Cesar, the guy who used to be Ulixes who is his dad.

Trevor still isn't totally sure what to think about that. Instead, he thinks about how starving he is.

Mike and his wife Jane stuffed him full of food before dropping him off, but Trevor is always hungry these days. He went back for second and third helpings once Mike assured him that they had plenty of food.

While he wolfed down some sort of curry-spiced bean and rice soup, two small boys watched his every move with eyes wide as saucers. Trevor grinned at them and they shyly grinned back and ducked under the table, but that was all he knew of them.

If there were more time, he'd have asked a million questions about life on a junker and how the ship handled and what they ate and how they washed their clothes and everything. But Trevor needed to sleep an awful lot and they were in a wicked hurry.

He and Mike and Cesar went over the plan at least half a dozen times before they dropped him off. It was a fairly straightforward plan.

"You need someplace to hide out until I can signal that all is clear," Cesar told him. "Al and Arete are great people and the last time I saw them, they seemed to think they owed me a favor. You go and ask if they will put you up for a week or two until things get more settled."

Mike chuckled, "They do owe you a favor. You lost a ship helping them."

"That wasn't their fault," objected Cesar.

Trevor perked up. It sounded like there was a story here. "What happened?" he asked.

"It doesn't really matter," Cesar said with a wave of his hand and a warning look at Mike. "Now, they have a little girl named Nausicaa, real sweet kid and very independent. Why when I first met her, she didn't come up to my belly button and they'd leave her in charge of the family laundry business all by herself! See, son, Lazar House is a textile orbital and Al and Arete run the laundry."

Mike broke in, "Lazar House is also a Synthlep colony."

During the Worlder Wars, someone came up with a synthetic version of leprosy that was easier to catch that the original disease and, without the medication, progressed towards the skin-and-fingers-falling-off phase much faster. Synthlep is a fluid-borne disease that still doesn't have a cure, but with the right medication, infected people infected can live a normal life. Without the medication, Synthlepers die a slow, excruciating death, but it takes almost a year to reach the end stage.

"So what?" asked Cesar with a frown. "They are good people."

Mike raised his hands up defensively and then pointed at Trevor. He said, "Hey, the kid needs to know what he's getting into."

"He has a point, uh, Cesar," Trevor spoke up. "I need to know what I'm getting into."

Cesar relented.

Mike explained, "So we were bringing meds to Lazar House a while ago. There are some shipping companies that won't go there. The fools think they'll catch Synthlep just by docking."

Cesar wrinkled his nose with disgust for such squeamish behavior and muttered, "Little Nausicaa developed a rare manifestation of Synthlep. That sometimes happens to kids born with the disease. She needed special meds to fix the problem and they were willing to pay a premium."

"Captain dragged us all down to Earth and made us deal with the dirt-lovers to get those meds," Mike said, remembering with a grin. "Almost got our butts shot off. We didn't want to go, but Captain said the kid would die without our help. Seemed real keen on helping her. We all figured it had something to do with, well, his kid. You, I guess. Also, when Captain sets his cap to do something, it's better just to fall in line or else get out of his way."

Trevor looked at his dad. Cesar was picking at his fingernails and looking like he'd like to shove Mike down an airshaft.

"Yeah, well, we had the meds," Cesar said gruffly. "We show up to drop them off and Lazar House is screaming on every channel of the Ether. Long story short: Al and Arete had taken a puddle jumper over to Satsuma Silk World to negotiate a trade for some silk. Lazar House makes cotton and they wanted to do something with silk. I don't remember what."

"Cotton silk blends," Mike broke in promptly. "They breathe like Egyptian cotton and have excellent drape."

Cesar raise an eye at Mike and the man blushed bright red before mumbling, "Bought some dresses for the wife last year and she's always going on about 'em."

"Anyway," Cesar said loudly, still eyeing Mike suspiciously as though the man might suddenly make them talk about shoes. "Al and Arete and a half a dozen others were on this runaway puddle jumper, about to smash right into the side of their own orbital. Lazar House isn't built sturdy like Ithaca. An impact like that could have vented the whole colony into the void."

"And like always, we jumped into the fray," Mike broke in with a grin. "Your dad was awesome. He goes all cold and steely and starts barking orders. It's a sight, kid."

Trevor looked at his dad. "I've seen it," he said.

Mike ran on with his story while Cesar shared a smile with his son.

"And then we come swooping in and catch them up like fish in a net," Mike was practically shouting, holding his hands in the air like they were ships to show Trevor how it was. "I've never seen anyone like your dad with a ship. I swear ships just love him. They do whatever he wants. They sit up and sing if that's what he asks them to do."

"I didn't ask that ship to crash, Mike," Cesar said mildly.

"Yeah, but that old clunker practically broke itself to pieces because you asked it to," Mike answered. "Too bad you had to abandon your little skiff. You should have seen his skiff, Trevor. Shiny and slick and as fast as anything, but we lost it out there. So then we got everybody into the escape pods with barely enough breathing room. Yet your old man still remembers to grab that box of meds before he fires us off, seconds before the ship goes careening out of range and out into deep space."

Cesar remarks with a faraway look in his eye, "And we landed on Lazar House with a box of meds and nothing but the shirts on our backs. Flat broke and hungry again. Why on earth did you crew with me so long, Mike?"

Mike replies, "Cuz it was fun as hell."

"I remember you always were crazy," says Cesar as he and Mike grinned maniacally. "Now, back to the current situation. Al and Arete did right by us back then. Gave us a better than good deal on the meds and then bought what was left of the tinker for scrap metal. They put us up for a week, fed us up and even sent us off with a change of clothes. I hate to ask them for favors now, but there's no one else and Lazar House is close."

"Their girl sure took a shine to your dad," Mike told Trevor. "Little thing followed him around begging for stories and made him show her how to fly. She kept telling us all she was going to marry him and go be a pirate too."

Mike chortled, "That girl had spunk. You give her a hug from me if you see her again."

"So," said Cesar, slapping Trevor on the back. "We'll drop you at Lazar House. You go see if Al and Arete are still there and ask if you can stay with them for a little while. You tell them I will pay them back with interest as soon as I can and you be on your best behavior. If that doesn't work out for whatever reason, call your Mom and get a shuttle back home. You've got enough credits?"

"Sure do," Trevor said, holding up his right thumb, the one he usually swipes to pay for things. "Mom may be a hard ass, but she isn't stingy with the allowance."

"Good," grunts Cesar. "Because I'm broke. I don't know how I will ever repay Mike here for his incredible generosity."

Mike waved away the thought, "Don't worry about it, Captain. Least I can do."

"No, I promise I will compensate you for your time and generosity," insisted Cesar.

Mike growled, "An I'm telling you I won't take a dime from you. Just accept it, say thank you and don't forget to tell me where you end up."

They bickered back and forth about it. Trevor nodded off. By the time they docked at Lazar House, Cesar must have told Trevor to be careful about a million times.

"I'll be fine. Jeez, you're worse than Mom," Trevor finally cried with exasperation as Cesar hovered over him anxiously giving advice while his pulled on his boots to leave.

"I don't want to leave you here," admitted Cesar, shoving his hands in his pockets.

Trevor hugged his dad and it felt good, but he also wanted to go explore and have a little time to himself to think about suddenly having a dad. After all the stories he'd heard, it was hard to think of this guy standing in front of him as an actual person and yet, he was just too... real.

Trevor always wondered if finally meeting his dad would be a let down. If he'd be a jerk or a liar or just boring. He isn't any of those things. Cesar is real. It is a little overwhelming.

Trevor looks around at the Lazar House orbital. This is his first time alone on a strange colony. Hell, this is his first time off Ithaca. So far, Lazar House looks like the town part of Ithaca, but more brightly colored and packed closer together. He starts walking; following the directions his dad gave him.

There are more people on the streets than Trevor expected. At first, he just thinks this part of Lazar House is more crowded or has more people, but then he realizes that there is something going on, some kind of gathering.

Trevor hears a crowd roaring to the left.

Maybe there is a tether tantrum game going on? Is it time for the Nullball Tournament? He's been out of sorts the last few days and can't remember if the tournament has started yet or not. Maybe there is a group watching it on a vidscreen down there.

Trevor can't remember ever hearing of a Lazar House team in previous tournaments, but that doesn't mean they aren't watching the game. After debating it in his head for a whole half a second, Trevor decides to go investigate.

As he gets closer, Trevor realizes there is something wrong with this crowd. This isn't some kind of celebration. That isn't cheering he heard.

These people are angry.

The roar of the crowd has been one of rage. As he walks down a street mobbed with people, he can make out someone speaking over an amplifier to the jeers of the crowd.

It's a girl.

She looks about Trevor's age, maybe a little younger. She has long brown hair curling down her back like a river of caramel. Trevor thinks she is cute, but she's also the first foreign girl he's seen that isn't a cowgirl working for his mom. She has a nose shaped just like a pinto bean and bright green eyes. But why is someone so young up in front of this mob and why are they so angry?

She is saying in a dramatic, clear voice that echoes across the little courtyard jammed full of people, "Like you, we seek to live in peace here on Lazar. We want only to make you welcome, but we cannot accede to these demands. Lazar just doesn't have the facilities. We must learn to live together. If you set yourselves apart, it will only end in disaster for all of us!"

Trevor thinks she should maybe tone it down a little, but he remembers getting carried away when making a speech himself. There was one time, after a truly spectacular Spacerbase win, that he went on for ten minutes about the sanctity of defensive snipers. He gets the impression this girl is worked up about something slightly more important, though.

"None of your threats, leper!" a man near Trevor screams at her.

Trevor sees the fuming man is wearing long flowing white robes and an orange headband. Looking around, Trevor sees that most of the men and women are wearing loose white robes or saris and orange headbands are very popular. They all tend to be shorter and darker than Trevor and many of them are holding long ropes of prayer beads.

The girl speaking to the crowd looks totally out of place, even without her pale skin and blondish hair. She has on Spacer pants, grav boots and a depiction of the six-armed Hindu elephant god Ganesh playing drums on her chest.

He recognizes it as a concert shirt for *The Angry Yogis*. He likes their music too. Trevor knows he looks totally out of place too. He is also wearing grav boots and a too-big set of Mike's old gray coveralls. Some of the people in the crowd are eyeing him and muttering irritably.

Trevor knows he should get away from this crowd and head towards the house Cesar sent him here to find, but somehow he finds himself edging toward the girl at the center of the courtyard. She continues to speak to the crowd. She pleads with them to disperse peacefully, but they don't seem inclined to do it.

Trevor is no more than five feet from her when the flaming bottle comes flying out of the crowd. It hits the girl squarely in chest. He sees her look down in shock and pain before flames engulf her.

He doesn't even think before he leaps forward. He snatches a jacket from a woman next to him and throws it over the burning girl to smother the flames as the crowd roars and surges. Trevor realizes that if these people choose to attack, there is precious little he can do to protect himself or the girl. Fortunately, the crowd as a whole hasn't wound itself up to a murderous pitch yet.

Still, they are tossing Molotov cocktails, so its time to get out of here. Hands reach out to pinch and push him, but Trevor grabs the girl and starts pulling her away from the center of the mob.

There are more flaming bottles, followed by shouting and what sounds like muffled gunfire from the opposite end of the courtyard. The crowd roars and surges away from Trevor.

He doesn't stop moving. Trevor has seen what flechette bullets can do during gun practice at home. He doesn't want to feel them. A spray of hard rubber bullets pelts the crowd behind him. He's thankful that the maniac firing into a crowd was at least smart enough to use non-lethal rubber bullets. But then again, Trevor imagines that no one was eager to draw blood at the Lazar House.

Trevor just keeps his head down and continues dragging the girl. The jacket is still over her head and her clothes are still smoking. She squirms, driving bits of broken glass into Trevor's leg and arm. It hurts. He is starting to get annoyed.

Who does she think she is? Gandhi? Why on earth does she think antagonizing an angry mob is a fun thing to do? Stupid girl.

"Look, stop wiggling," Trevor snaps at her. "Just keep moving and we'll be out of this soon. Then you can go throw yourself out an airlock or something."

"What?" she cries. "Who the hell are you?"

The girl pushes the jacket off her head and stares at him with outrage, but Trevor doesn't even slow down as he drags her along. There are entirely too many people still following them.

The sound of breaking glass is followed by screams and muffled shots from someplace close by. The crowd around them scatters. Trevor takes advantage of the confusion and ducks down an alley. He grabs her shirt and yanks her after him. Her shirt catches around her throat and the girl gives an indignant squawk. Twisting to check behind him as they lurch along, Trevor doesn't see anyone following them.

It's getting harder to hold onto her now that she is pummeling him, but Trevor isn't ready to slow down until he finds someplace secluded to catch his breath. Letting go of the girl becomes a more and more attractive idea, however.

Then he spies an open doorway leading into the kitchen of a little diner. A large swarthy man listlessly scrubs a pot. He raises his eyebrows at the pair, but makes no other indication that he cares about their existence.

Trevor pulls himself into a confident posture and nonchalantly walks to the tables at the front of the diner. He shoves the girl into a seat and then collapses into the chair opposite her. The girl glares at him like she thinks her eyeballs are lasers and the fact that Trevor's head isn't melting away right now is a personal affront.

Trevor catches his breath, trying to think of the best way to open up a conversation with this crazy girl about what he just wandered into out there. He is hoping she'll just start explaining, but instead she keeps glaring.

With a sigh, he gives her his most charming grin and says, "Well I think one of us owes the other lunch right now. We just have to figure out which is which."

The girl's jaw drops.

Her brow furrows as her mouth forms a shocked pink ring. Trevor finds himself grinning because she is just so wicked cute. Then she frowns, straightening up. She looks just like Lupe when the old lady is about to start yelling and smacking him with a dishrag. Trevor looks for the exit. That's when the swarthy Bonalu man from the kitchen lumbers up, muttering something about ordering or getting out.

Trevor could have hugged him.

She orders chai, dal and roti. While Trevor orders coffee and samosas, he thinks of a new way to start conversation. As soon as the waiter guy trudges away, Trevor leans over and asks her, "Are you hurt?"

This elicits the type of response Trevor was hoping for. The girl smiles at him and then quickly pats her hands over her hair and her arms while giving a little wiggle.

"Oh, I think I'm pretty good, actually. Couple of bruises. Missing some hair, I guess." She holds up her charred hair sadly.

Trevor says solemnly, "Well, I'm sorry about that, but it could have been worse."

It is a pity. Her hair is definitely missing some chunks and no longer has that shiny bounciness he admired earlier. Trevor still has a few bits of broken glass lodged in nasty oozing cuts on his arm, but he doesn't really want to make them into conversation pieces just now.

The girl gives her face a quick scrub with the napkin on the table. Trevor decides to move the conversation towards more important topics.

Leaning forward, he asks casually, "So what was all that just now? An angry mob almost immolated you. You trying to earn style points with the martyr crowd? Do they not have Ether on this orbital and you got bored?"

On some level, Trevor knows he has what his mom likes to call "a smart mouth." He knows it gets him into trouble. He just can't seem to turn it off.

Fortunately, the girl doesn't frown or yell at him. Her eyes get round as saucers and she sighs dramatically, throwing what is left of her sooty mane over one shoulder. "I was trying to prevent a riot and save our community from a violent war, actually," she half-whispers to him, nodding for effect.

"Huh," says Trevor.

"And you rescued me," she breathes as though she relishes every word. "I totally owe you lunch."

Trevor grins. He was hoping she'd come to some conclusion that involved eating. He's starving.

The waiter appears rather abruptly by their table for a man so large. He dispenses plates and cups and leaves, mumbling about going out back for a smoke if they need anything.

Trevor sips his coffee. It is surprisingly good.

He can feel the caffeine do its jittery-jangly dance down his nerve endings. He isn't sure how much he should tell this girl about himself.

Fortunately she's too busy talking to ask him any stressful questions.

The girl inhales a plate of beans and flatbread while explaining to Trevor that, during the War, Lazar House took in hundreds of refugees. She had Trevor pegged for a foreigner immediately. Most of the refugees were from Betel Bonalu, a nearby Hindu orbital that produced the best betel and betel-related products in the spheres before heavy action in the War rendered it a slowly venting death trap. These particular Hindus are very passionate about their religion and their caste system.

The Bonalus took to cotton farming and the Lazars took to their Hindu food and ideas on reincarnation. After living together in relative harmony for over a decade, the original Synthlep Lazar colonists and the Hindu refugees are having issues.

Recently, the Bonalus have been agitating for separate water supply and food processing plants so they won't catch Synthlep. The original Lazars feel that after creating an entire little world to accommodate their affliction, they don't really want to go changing everything for a bunch of uninvited houseguests. The Bonalus insist this is their home now too and the whole conversation degenerates from there along predictable routes until today they are throwing flaming bottles at each other in the streets.

Trevor eats his samosas and the plate of curry he orders after that and also what she doesn't finish on her plate. The girl is very pretty and her cheeks flush when she gets excited about her topic. It's slightly distracting, but Trevor feels he's following the gist of the thing. She was out at a rally, the crowd turned against her and that's how they ended up here.

"I'm Nausicaa, by the way." She announces, wiping one hand on her shirt and stretching it out to shake his.

"Really?" he replies, one eyebrow arching. He shakes her hand. "Is that a common name here?"

His dad told him about some kid named Nausicaa. What are the odds?

Nausicaa shrugs and sips her chai. "Don't think so. Never heard of anybody else with the same name. Why? Is it common where you're from? Where are you from, anyways? Not here, obviously."

"No," says Trevor. "It's just that my dad sent me here to see some people, Al and Arete I think he said, and they have a little kid named Nausicaa. I guess you don't know them. I hope they still live around here."

Nausicaa grins. "They do live here and I do know them. My folks are Al and Arete."

"Oh," says Trevor, at a loss. "I thought you were six years old or something."

"No. Sixteen."

"Oh. I'm seventeen."

"Oh."

That seems to be enough conversation for the pair of them and they lapse into covertly glancing at each other over their cups and blushing furiously. They keep that up until the waiter starts hanging around their table, muttering about folks who take up the good tables for hours and don't leave tips. He makes an unconvincing show of wiping off the tables near theirs with a greasy rag.

Nausicaa pops her eyes wide and shakes herself like she's waking from a nap. "We should go back to my house," she decides, swiping her thumbprint over the credit strip before Trevor can even offer to pay his half.

"Is it safe?" asks Trevor, peering out the window at the front of the diner. There are people milling around, but they don't look like an angry mob.

"Well, I think so," says Nausicaa, peering out as well. Then she thinks of something important.

Turning to him, she asks, "Hey, why are you looking for my parents?"

Trevor blushes and shuffles his feet. When he got off the junker, he was dying to tell someone about his adventures, but now that he has the opportunity, he finds he doesn't want to go through it all.

Trevor shrugged and says, "Things are a little dicey at home right now and my dad thought maybe I could stay with you guys for a little while until… things get less dicey, I guess. He met your parents a few years ago when he was a tinker ship captain delivering meds and they were on a runaway ship or something."

Nausicaa gives a little gasp, "Oh my gosh! Your dad is Cesar Vaquero? Wow!"

Trevor inhales sharply. She knows his dad's real name. His dad didn't give her and her family a fake name. A pang of jealousy shoots through him.

"Yeah, I'm Trevor Vaquero," he mutters.

"Oh, wow!" she says, bouncing with excitement. "My folks are so gonna want to meet you. Let's go!" She grabs his shirt, pulling him into the street.

"So, you're from Ithaca then?" she calls over her shoulder as she drags him along like a bull with a ring through its nose. She doesn't wait for him to answer.

"We've heard about all the attacks and sabotage on Ithaca," she announces, stopping to peer down an alley. "Everybody in the spheres is talking about that pirate attack last week. If they can do that to Ithaca, what does it mean for the rest of us? People are really scared. I think that's part of our troubles here too. But if your dad sent you here, it must be even worse than we thought."

She stops again and says dreamily, "Your dad is awesome, by the way. He taught me to fly."

Trevor is getting more jealous and tired of being yanked around. He pulls his shirt out of her grasp. "Yeah? Well, I wouldn't know. I met him for the first time a couple weeks ago and he only told me he was my dad a few days ago," he says sourly. Trevor wonders if Mike didn't say something, would he still think of Cesar as some stranger?

"Oh," gasps Nausicaa. "But he was going home! Mr. Cesar left here six years ago on his way home. That's why he told my folks who he really was. He wanted their advice about how your mom would take it."

Trevor shrugs, feeling a little better.

Her eyes go round as she says, "I wonder what happened to him. He really wanted to go home."

"Well, he sure took his time," snaps Trevor, knowing he is being a jerk right now but not really caring. "Is it far to your house?"

There is a muffled boom from behind Nausicaa and they both jump. They turn to scan the horizon, but see nothing.

"Let's go," she says, walking quickly in the opposite direction. Trevor follows.

After a few more blocks, they run into another mob, chanting as they burn a straw man with a sign on its chest that says "Synthlep Dalit." Nausicaa looks like she wants to jump into the fray, but after she glances up at Trevor's pleading face, she grabs his arm and ducks down another alleyway. As they watch the crowd move away from them, Nausicaa explains that *dalit* is the Bonalu word for "untouchable" or "unclean."

"To heck with this," she says with exasperation. "The whole colony is buzzing like a kicked-over ant hill. Let's go up to the core and wait for things to calm down."

Trevor thinks it is an excellent plan. Like Ithaca, the core is at the center of the colony. Since it's mostly storage space, there won't be too many people there unless a ship is loading or unloading or the kids are playing tether tantrum or Nullball.

On the way, Nausicaa sends a message to her parents, letting them know she has Trevor with her and where they are going and why.

"But who knows when they'll get it?" she sighs, enjoying the strangeness of all the turmoil. "The local networks are all jammed with people talking about the riot. I hope no one is hurt."

Nausicaa leads him to a large storage space that her family owns. It's stacked high with pallets of laundered clothing, but otherwise empty. Nausicaa has the pass code to the small office in the back and so they have drinks and snacks and a ball to toss around while they wait.

Trevor picks glass out of the small cuts on his arm and cleans up the blood. Nausicaa gives him antiseptic wipes and wound glue out of a little emergency medical kit she has in her pocket. She looks a bit queasy at the sight of blood.

"Since the Bonalus came, everyone carries this stuff around with them," she explains when he asks if she usually carried around the medical kit. "We have to be careful about the virus."

Then Trevor and Nausicaa talk about everything and nothing over the next three hours. Nausicaa wants to be a gene splicer and travel around fixing things like Synthlep and seeing all the different orbitals and the people in them. She wants to try out new foods and have all kinds of new experiences. Trevor tells her about his studies on ship engineering and his plans to be a pilot.

They find that their favorite bands and video games and Ether dramas are stunningly similar, or at least, similar enough to be remarkably exciting. He and Nausicaa pool information on the latest Ether scandals and roundly denounce the most recent celebrity to leave a loving wife and children to go live with his mistress on Vegan Vineyards. They also share the same ideas on what is wrong with the colonies and how they would fix them if they were in charge of anything.

The storage spaces are kept cold, so eventually they decide the best thing to do is to huddle together for warmth and then conversation drops off somewhat as they listen to each other's hearts racing. They wonder why their throats are suddenly dry and their palms sweaty.

Trevor keeps reminding himself that she has Synthlep and he can't kiss her unless he wants to take medication for the rest of his life. Would she want to get kissed by a stranger like him?

Finally, Nausicaa's comm bracelet jangles with a slew of incoming messages. The local networks are working again and the streets are clear. Nausicaa's parents heard of her public immolation and have been sending frantic messages all day.

"We better get home," she says after listening to the first few.

Al and Arete lavish parental concern on Nausicaa and adoration and praise on Trevor while they bring out an endless variety of food to urge on the teens.

Arete is tall and willowy with kind gray eyes and white-streaked blond hair cut in a short curly cap. She wears a Hindu sari in muted blue colors. Al is dressed in Spacer pants and boots under a long white collarless shirt. Their home is warm and comfortable, simply decorated with the kind of well-made, sturdy things that are so expensive in space.

"You saved our girl! Are you sure you won't have another slice of the spice cake?" asks Al for the fifth time.

Arete smiles at her daughter and her new friend fondly, but concern wrinkles her forehead when she sees them shooting each other coy glances. After Trevor explains how Cesar sent him to ask for shelter for a few days, she makes him tell them everything that happened to him and to Ithaca in the last few weeks.

When Trevor tells the story of the pirate ship attack and how they snuck aboard the pirate ship and what happened to him there, Nausicaa gasps, twining her fingers around his.

When Trevor tells them about Uri Mach and Asner, Al swears loudly, "Mach! I might have known! He got his start as a pirate during the war. Supposedly he went clean when he started Seven Skies Trading, but once a pirate always a pirate."

Al pounds the table angrily, "We used Seven Skies to transport cloth shipments, but they kept hiking up the protection fees so we decided we'd be better off on our own. Then some of our ships went missing, only to turn up later empty with a dead crew. We never could prove it was Seven

Skies, but I know it was them."

Trevor nods, but he is careful not to move, lest Nausicaa remember that they are holding hands and that she should probably get hers back. He replies to Al, "We weren't sure who else was in on the plot. That's why I came here. I didn't want to put my mom and Ithaca at risk by showing up. Mach and Asner might think I know more than I do. I can't tell you how much this means to me, you all letting me stay here."

Trevor takes the opportunity to look at Nausicaa significantly. Arete frowns at that, but her face shows only kind concern for her daughter and her new friend.

"And your father explained about Lazar House?" she asks. "You understand that you are staying in an Synthlep house? Fluid contact could infect you. We know how to take the precautions, but you must always be on your guard. If you get Synthlep, you must take the medicine for the rest of your life and, if you ever leave, you will be reviled everywhere you go as a plague carrier?"

Trevor shrugs. He doesn't want to think about that, even as Nausicaa tenderly untwines her fingers from his.

"I have no place else to go," he mutters, hating the uncertainty in his voice. He stands up abruptly. "If I am intruding, I should go."

"No, no!" cries Al, jumping to his feet. "No, please stay. It is the very least we can do."

Al does not stop talking until Trevor promises to stay at least three times and takes another slice of spice cake, although how it will fit in his stomach, Trevor has no idea.

They turn on the Ether so Trevor can call his mother and let her know he is fine. That's when they find that she apparently called earlier that day. Trevor starts calling her back, but then he gets distracted watching a recording of Nausicaa's speech with its abrupt flaming ending. In the recording, it looks like she must be dead. Trevor thanks his lucky stars that smoke from the fires obscures him on the cameras. He's just a blurry image in the corner of the screen when he jumps to grab Nausicaa.

The footage has been playing on all the major news sites and has gotten millions of hits. The comments and sympathetic notes number in the thousands. Al begins thanking Trevor all over again.

Nausicaa wants to make an announcement on the Ether that she is alive and uninjured. She wants Trevor to be in it too, but he declines since he is supposed to be dead. He takes a shower instead, a real one with actual soap and water. The junker only had a sonic shower.

Trevor is happily drying his hair in the little bedroom they offer to let him stay in when Nausicaa comes bursting in. "The Bonalu leaders have called off the riot!" she cries. "They want to talk! I'm supposed to sit in on the negotiations."

She gives him a hug that leaves him gasping and then flops on the bed, running her fingers through her hair dreamily. Arete appears in the doorway, but she only arches one eyebrow and pointedly pushes the door wide open. Trevor understands. His mom wouldn't let him hang out with a girl alone in a room with the door closed either, even though he is practically a man.

Trevor watches Nausicaa with a bemused smile. He tries to push his wet hair down while she tells him, "It's because I wasn't mad about getting set on fire. I said I would rather die by fire than see conflict destroy our colony. Also, they think I must have powerful mojo or something. No one seems to remember you dragging me off and patting out the flames."

Trevor laughs, sitting on the bed next to her.

"Well," he says. "I guess watching you negotiate peace will keep me amused until it's time to go home."

Nausicaa grins and sits up. "You could also learn to fly the ship."

"What ship?"

"Your dad's ship," she says and then smacks her forehead. "Oh, duh. I forgot to tell you. We found your dad's old ship. Well, *we* didn't, but it got found and now we have it. It's this shiny little skiff that would be excellent for one or two people who wanted to go tooling around in the spheres. My dad was always hoping your dad would turn up so he could give it back as a proper thank you, but since you're here we can give it to you."

Trevor's eyebrows must finally shoot right off his face because Nausicaa giggles.

"Yeah," she says, "One of the transport ships found it floating around out there in the void and towed it back. We took possession of it because it was registered to Jonas Ulixes and we knew your dad would want his ship back. Who doesn't want their ship back?"

"Wow!"

"Yeah," she says again. "My dad takes me out in it every now and then so I can practice flying, but we are careful not to mess it up or anything. We haven't even opened the holds so his stuff is still in there. Unless it's food. Anything food wouldn't last this long."

"This is awesome!" cries Trevor, dreams of piloting almost too thick for him to see as he stumbles down the hall to ask Al about the ship.

Al is happy to talk about it and Trevor is thrilled to listen. "Yes, it runs perfectly. I maintain it regularly, in case your father comes back. I've checked all the engines and systems, but the holds were locked and I did not want to go poking through them, out of respect," he tells Trevor eagerly.

He questions Trevor thoroughly about the boy's knowledge of space flight and his studies so far. Then, looking thoughtful, Al scratches his beard and says, "A few days should be plenty of time for someone with your background to learn to fly it. I don't pretend to know more than the basics of piloting, but that should be enough to get you home whenever it is time for you to go. You can return the ship to your father on Ithaca. How does that sound?"

Trevor thinks it sounds like the best idea ever. He collapses into bed that night with his head full of thoughts about the ship, the events of the day and Nausicaa, so full that he completely forgets to send a message home to his mom to let her know all is well.

He remembers late that night. "Oh well," he yawns. "I'll call mom to-morrow morning."

Trevor promptly falls back to sleep.

CHAPTER TWENTY-FOUR

Penelope always thought that losing your mind would be fun, a relief in many ways.

She's often thought that running mad through the streets sounds like a great solution to the many trials and tribulations involved in living a good life, paying bills, raising her son and eating well-balanced meals. Today, Penelope is pretty sure that life has finally driven her insane, but she isn't enjoying it nearly as much as she thought she would.

Penelope has not seen Ulixes since the day before yesterday when he finally left to go "gather intel." It wasn't that difficult to get rid of him. She just kept repeating that she needed time to get used to all this. She made a mental note to ask him about the best way to go insane.

He would know.

Ulixes said something about organizing a resistance when he left. She knows she should call people to warn them that a crazy man is running loose, but it's just too awful to think about so instead she crawls back into bed and stays there, nursing a large pitcher of mint juleps.

She stares at the ceiling for hours on yet another sleepless night, trying to find a solution to this catastrophe. Where is Trevor? What really happened after he and that Ulixes man vanished into that mystery ship? What should she do now?

Penelope goes through the motions of preparing Ithaca for the semifinal round of the Nullball Tournament. Normally Ithaca felt spacious and relatively empty for the ten thousand people living in it. This last week, Penelope feels like they are up to their armpits in overhyped fans and unruly Nullball players, eating them all out of house and home, doing their best to destroy everything in the place.

Her first order of business is to contact the Caribbean Coffee Conglomerate and beg for an express shipment of anything edible. The semifinal games are today and the finals are scheduled for tomorrow, but at this rate, the players will be peeling the biosteel girders off the walls by noon and the fans will start eating them.

Penelope feels her temples throbbing just thinking about it. Fortunately, she has long been friendly with the folks at CCC so she knows they will help her out, especially with a hefty profit to look forward to.

Penelope finishes strapping on her boots. Then she sits on her bed, staring listlessly at an empty wall. She sighs. She realizes that she's sighed about six times already.

The only thing for it is to get up and trudge through another day. Penelope dimly realizes that, depending on how the game goes; she is supposed to sell off her ranch, or at least, the cattle tomorrow. She tries to care about that, but can't manage it.

Stomping out the door, she wishes Lupe is around to yell at, but the old woman has made herself scarce again. And where is Argos? She knows he hates crowds and the whole Nullball Tournament is making him so miserable he can't stand himself, but if he wants to keep his job, he is going to have to show his face eventually.

Opening the door, she beholds a most unwelcome sight. Asner is sitting on her porch with a bouquet of flowers.

God, what is it with this guy? Penelope sighs again and that only makes her angry. Asner looks at her hopefully. She sits down next to him and he hands her a dozen red roses, so fresh they must have just come off a ship from Minerva Gardens. Penelope takes them unenthusiastically. Then she has an epiphany. She can just ask.

Turning to Asner, she asks, "Did you attack my colony with a pirate ship and try to steal my herd?"

Asner gapes at her and stutters something that sounds like, "Uuhhhh."

"What about killing my son?" she asks matter-of-factly. "Did you do that?"

Asner's face twists like it is trying to express too many emotions at once. "What? No! Who have you been talking to? My God," he blurted, looking around like perhaps there is a hidden camera. "No, I didn't kill your son."

She just looks at him and waits.

Asner takes a few deep breaths. Then, quick and low, he says, "I would never harm Trevor. I only wish I knew what happened to him." She believes him.

Penelope nods thoughtfully. She suspected as much, but part of her was hoping he would say he kidnapped the boy and is holding him ransom. Part of her wishes there was a way, any way, to get her boy back. "And I guess you don't know anything about the attacks and the pirates?" she asks.

Asner fidgets. "Well," he says at last. "I may know something about that."

When he sees the look on her face, he throws up his hands defensively. "Whatever I may or may not know, the truth is that it will be in your best interest to sell that herd and get rid of it. That's why I've been pushing for it."

He takes her hand. "My main concern has been to keep you safe."

Penelope hears the tenderness in his voice, but all she can focus on are the facts. The last time she saw her son, he was getting into that pirate ship. Asner knows something about that. He will tell her what he knows or she will end him.

"Tell me what you know or I will break your face," she says calmly, removing his hand from hers.

Asner looks shocked. Rubbing his hands together, he thinks for half a moment. "You are distraught. But it would be better if I could just explain it all. Yes. If I could just explain what I know, you would understand. It would be easier."

He stands up and glances around, distracted. "Come with me," he said. "I will show you. I wanted to tell you before, but... Just follow me."

Penelope gets to her feet. She thinks about trying to find a weapon or calling someone, but looking at Asner, she decides against it. It's like he collapsed into himself in the last five minutes and he wasn't a particularly impressive man in the first place. He looks like a scared mouse, caught in a trap. Whatever he knows, she can hear it and then decide what to do.

And really, what can he know? The man is an engineer on the most boring colony in the skies. This whole act could actually be just a ridiculous ploy to impress her and thus cause her to fall madly in love with him or whatever it is he wants. Engineers are strange.

Asner sets off towards town and Penelope follows. Before long, she hears the roar of the crowd as they get closer to the public elevators. There were long lines of fans waiting for the elevators that will take them all to the core for the semifinal Nullball match. The streets are crowded with laughing, excited people. She sees a few people she knows, but Asner isn't stopping and she doesn't feel like chatting right now anyway.

Penelope hears someone calling her name as she threads her way through the crowd. On the other side of the walkway, she sees Argos pushing towards her. He looks upset and he is waving at her frantically, but Asner grabs her hand and pulls her into a ten-ton elevator that will take them up to the core with at least fifty other people. The huge elevator is usually reserved for freight, but they've been using it for crowd control during the tournament.

Looking back, she sees Argos get swept away by the crowd, still calling to her. He seems distraught about something, but there is little she can do about that now. The comm systems have been overwhelmed all week, so she can't just call him. She will go find him as soon as she sees whatever it is Asner wants to show her.

As the elevator goes up to the core, Penelope feels lighter with every breath. It is hard to feel dead inside this tidal wave of happy humans, but Penelope feels she is managing it pretty well. She enjoys the brief feeling of safety in numbers.

When they reach the core, Asner insistently guides her to the docking bay. The crowd turns in the opposite direction towards the Nullball arena. In the docking bay, there are only a few people milling around the ships.

"Why if it isn't Asner and Penelope!" cries Uri Mach, ever jovial. "Just the two people I wanted to see!"

Penelope smiles at him. "Why Uri, what are you doing here? Shouldn't you be over in the arena, cheering on your team? I know they are the favorites for today's match, but I hear it will be a close thing. You must be so proud."

Uri chuckles, clasping his hands behind his back. "Ah, yes, Seven Skies is very proud to field a Nullball team in this tournament, but work never stops, does it? Now, are you here to finally let me take all the bovine weight off your shoulders, my dear?"

Asner interrupts. "She wants to know about the attacks. The truth. She deserves to know," he said, moving to place himself slightly between Penelope and Uri.

Uri takes a step back, "Ah? Well. Yes. The attacks. The truth is difficult to know, isn't it? But if you are selling to me today, those attacks need no longer concern you. That, I can promise."

He rubs his hands together and looks from Penelope to Asner speculatively. There is a sharpness to his look that his jovial manner cannot mask.

Penelope feels her pulse leap as she remembers what Ulixes insinuated. That Uri Mach is a pirate who preys on unsuspecting tinkers. It seems too unbelievable. The man has eaten at her house.

Uri has a tendency to get food in his beard and then she always has to decide whether to tell him that he has cheese stuck to his face or just ignore it, trying not to laugh while he goes on about the deplorable working conditions on the Hathor asteroid mine or something.

Well, perhaps he used to be a bad man before he settled down to run Seven Skies. Well, so what? Everybody has a few skeletons in their closet, right? Even if it is true, then maybe he knows things through his ties into the black market. Perhaps he's heard something at the pirate bar, playing pirate poker with other dastardly men who kill people and never wipe their upper lips.

"We should tell her what we know," Asner insists. "If she understands…"

Penelope can't imagine what it is these guys know, but the longer she stands here, the more important it appears to be.

Stepping forward, Penelope tries appealing to the man's compassion. "Uri, I just need to know what happened to my son. After that, I don't care what happens. If I could get him back alive, I'll sell you my herd or whatever you want."

Uri looks deeply annoyed. "But what if you don't get the answers you want? What if you never hear from him again, just like your husband? You made a bet to sell your herd tomorrow to the tournament winner. This is business."

Penelope rubs her neck, wondering what all this weirdness is about. "Look, Uri, we've known each other a long time and you know how important my son is to me. You must understand that I can't make any decisions until I find my son. I'm sorry."

"But what about your bet?" he cries. "You lose and you sell the herd."

Penelope rubs her eyes. "I know we shook on it, but I am grieving for my child. I just don't know what to do. I can't think straight. This bet seems silly."

Uri clasps his hands behind his back and thoughtfully looks over Penelope's head for a minute. Then he sighs deeply. Penelope thinks it is just a day for sighing.

"You know," Uri says, his voice dropping from its hearty tone to a low menacing growl. "Life would be so much simpler if everyone would just do what I want them to do."

Looking back over Penelope's head, Uri makes a quick gesture and she sees stars. A sharp pain explodes in the back of her head and she drops to the ground. Penelope suddenly realizes she's been an idiot today. She hears Asner yell while the room spins and rough hands grab her. Someone throws her over their shoulder like a sack of potatoes.

Blackness descends.

CHAPTER TWENTY-FIVE

"What do you mean?" roars Cesar. "You saw Penelope heading towards the core with Asner and you just let her go?" He stares at Argos incredulously.

Argos looks like he wants to crawl under a rock and die. His shoulders slump and if he ducks his head any further, he'll be a hunchback. He mumbles, "Well, I called out to her, but there were lot of people and, well, they're probably just going down to the match, right?" Argos trails off at the end and sticks his hands in his pockets.

Cesar wants to shake Argos like a terrier shakes a rat. How could he watch Penelope wander off with that evil little engineer and not stop her or follow her or something? Does Argos not realize how much danger there is down in the core? It's right next to the docking bay!

For that matter, why was Penelope going anywhere with Asner in the first place? Cesar knows he impressed her with the seriousness of the threat that Asner and Mach represent. He curses himself for leaving her alone. She just looked so overwhelmed. That's why he stopped short before revealing himself to her. He genuinely wanted to tell her that he was her long lost husband, but he sensed the moment just wasn't right. Cesar thought a day to herself would let her get used to the whole bizarre predicament.

Penelope deserved that for the calm and levelheaded way she took the news of Trevor's adventures and the betrayal of her friends. What a woman!

Cesar had plenty to do anyway. He needed to decipher the threat to Ithaca and help prepare the colony for whatever comes next. After leaving Penelope at the ranch, Cesar went to his father and told the old man everything. The more Cesar talked, the older and paler Larry looked, until he heard that Trevor was safe on Lazar House. Then the old man jumped up and did a shaky little jig.

"Wahoo!" the old man cackled, almost falling over a box of bottles. He picked himself up before Cesar could help him, shaking off his son's concern about bruises or broken bones impatiently.

"You need my help more than I need yours today, son," Larry declared merrily, his face pink. He rubbed his hands together and started mumbling about rocket blasters fueled by tequila.

"Dad, let me finish," Cesar kept saying to his preoccupied father. Finally he was practically shouting: "Listen to what I am saying!"

Larry stopped in mid-rant, raised one eyebrow and waited.

In a slightly calmer voice, Cesar said, "When I called to check on him, the lines at Lazar House were all out. There was a message about some kind of Sectarian riot. Trevor may not be so safe after all."

Larry clamped his lips shut, squinting his eyes the way he did when he was furiously thinking. Finally the old man waved his hand. "Well, we'll just send someone over there to see what's going on. The rest of us have to work on Asner and Mach. Now that we have names, we should be able to find out the rest."

Irked by Larry's cavalier attitude, Cesar snapped, "You lost me there, Dad. What is your plan? Because I don't know what to do now."

Larry grinned, clapped his son on the back and said, "Boy, you got lucky the last time you stopped a war. You saw that nuclear starship was a trump card and you played it before they even knew you had it. This time, we do it smart."

Then the old man slapped on a comm so ancient and huge, it was practically a helmet. Larry started shouting into it. Shortly after that, people showed up and Larry shouted at them too.

Eventually, Larry turned to Cesar and asked, "So, you told Penelope all this? Including all about who you really are?"

Cesar nodded. "Well, pretty much. I mean, I think she understands."

Larry squinted at him skeptically. "Really? But you still have all of your original limbs. Did you run real fast afterwards? Are you sure you really explained it? You didn't use some complicated metaphor or something, did you?"

"Nope. She took it really well." Cesar grinned at his dad even though he was stretching the truth more than a little. It was just so nice to see his dad flummoxed. Cesar was tempted to add some instructive advice on dealing with women, but decided not to push it.

"Huh." Larry scratched his chin for a minute. "Well, every day is a new opportunity for surprise, I guess." But he sounded doubtful.

Further discussion was cut off by the torrent of angry people coming in, demanding answers. They asked Cesar endless questions before they left again, some shuffling and some stomping. Cesar recognized many of the faces, memories from his youth.

All their expressions were the same shade of angry disbelief and worry. By the time Cesar thought he couldn't possible say another word without his vocal cords committing suicide, Lupe arrived to hand him a steaming bowl of tortilla soup and mug of coffee.

More people came filing in. Cesar realized after a while they were the same people as before, only now they talked instead of listening.

Larry shouted even louder.

The scene became like one of those bar fights where the music is too loud to really understand what's going on and everybody is shouting but no one hears a word. Cesar knew by the glances he was getting that these people expected him to play a part in this unfolding drama. He tried to look stern and keen, hoping that will suffice. His mind felt stuck in a loop of questions about Penelope and Trevor.

Cesar made an effort to focus on what was happening around him, but it all seemed just further confirmation of what he already suspected. Uri Mach ran the Seven Skies Trading Company fleet of cargo vessels all over the skies, but no one knew where their base colony was located. Seven Skies was shady at best and little more than a gang with ships at the worst.

Lately, Uri had been saying that Spacers needed to arm themselves against the Earthers, that maybe it was the Spacers' turn to own a piece of the Earth.

People showed Larry and Cesar reports, receipts and Ether messages. The Ex-Austrian Engineering Complex has been behind on its work lately and outright refusing jobs, saying they were too busy. The EEC was working on something big, but no one knows what. They were making large orders for equipment, but no one knew why. One man reported that his cousin was complaining about a large order of industrial lubricant that Asner bought and then returned, screaming that it was inadequate.

Equipment has been seen on the Moon and signs of a settlement, but any ship that came in for a close view saw nothing out of the ordinary.

The Moon had never been colonized. Cesar tries to remember why. Before the Spacer War, no one would think of violating the Moon Treaty for fear of antagonizing the Earthers. The Moon Treaty was created to limit the size of military bases in the sky and leave the Moon for all humanity.

In practice, that old treaty only kept permanent bases off the Moon. Many colonies used the Moon as a dumping ground for old vehicles or obsolete projects that they might want to pick up later for spare parts. The Earthers complained that the Moon glittered with Spacer trash. In the orbitals, they maintained that a true Spacer wouldn't know what the Moon looked like from "down there."

After the War, there wasn't any reason not to put a settlement on the Moon other than having to wade through all the trash, but nobody tried it. If they thought about it, Spacers would probably consider putting a colony on the Moon to be rude. The Moon was there for all of them. Also, there was that old urban legend about how anything done to the Moon would cause the tides on Earth to go all wonky and kill everybody. Most Spacers didn't hate the dirt-lovers *that* much.

More people wandered in and out.

Cesar kept trying to call Trevor, but Lazar House communications had gone from repeating a pre-recorded message about riots to being totally offline. All he got was static. The Ether rumors said the riots on Lazar House were over and negotiations were going really well, but that didn't make any sense to Cesar. Why would they turn off their Ether?

Cesar looked around and realized there were more than a hundred people milling around outside Larry's shack. Until that moment, he assumed they were talking to all the crackpot conspiracy nuts on Ithaca, but there were too many people and the whole thing was way too organized.

In an effort to make sense of what was going on around him, Cesar listened to the angry conversations around him. He learned that there were mutterings on Earth about how belligerent some of the Spacers have been lately. Like maybe the Spacers have something new, something that will turn them from a stubborn set of strange beggars into a threat to be reckoned with.

Then a sweaty anxious little man showed up with two large Ithaca farmers half-dragging him into the room. The little man looked around anxiously. Cesar knew this guy looked familiar, but it took him a minute to place the face.

"Look, I just sold them some nukes. That's all," protested the little man. The name "Finomus" popped into Cesar's mind. This was the man with the platypig. Cesar remembered the conversation he overheard that night he kissed his wife for the first time in fifteen years. Cesar stepped forward. He wanted to hear what this Finomus man had to say.

Just then, old Mathis appeared in front of him, exuding a cloud of alcohol-soaked breath and looking pleased with himself.

"Found your kid," the old man cackled. Then he shook a grubby finger in Cesar's face. "And don't think you fooled me, sneaking into Ithaca like that, young man. Not for a minute. Old Mathis doesn't miss a trick."

Cesar was almost positive that Mathis was totally fooled by his re-entry into Ithaca, but doesn't say so. "Where's Trevor?" he asked instead, steadying the old man with a hand.

"Oh, he's up at Lazar House," the old man replied breezily. "Saw him myself. He's learning to fly some old wreck and flirting with a little plague girl. Trevor's fine."

Cesar closed his eyes, saying a silent prayer for patience and then asked through his clenched teeth, "And why didn't you bring him home with you?"

Mathis scowled back at him, not appreciating the tone. "Don't get snippy with me, young man. I'm not the one that dumped him off on the Synthlep colony, am I?"

Cesar apologized, asking after Trevor again.

Mathis looked more inclined to go wandering about the room to see what was going on. He dismissed Cesar's question with a wave. "Trevor said he was coming home in your ship. He'll be here in a few hours."

That was all Cesar could get out of Mathis. The old man shook him off with a curse, stumbling off to where Larry was holding court by the tequila still. Cesar watched his father interrogate Mathis briefly before turning his attention back to the crowd. Well, if Larry wasn't concerned then Cesar could wait a few hours.

A group of cowgirls hustled in with a man in a Nullball jersey, hogtied and covered in lipstick. People swarmed around the Nullball player angrily. Cesar could make out the Seven Skies logo on the player's jersey.

He wanted to get closer to see what they would do with the player, but that's when Argos showed up talking about how Penelope went off to the Nullball Tournament with Asner and wasn't he their new arch enemy?

Cesar tries to get information out of Argos while ignoring the whoops and screams behind him as they question the Nullball player. Cesar realizes he is clenching his jaw so hard he can taste blood. He forces himself to stop.

Trying for a calm tone, he asks Argos, "Would you just tell me everything you saw? Did Penelope look worried or upset? Was Asner maybe pointing a gun at her from under his clothes?"

Argos scratches his chin and thinks hard. "Well, now that you mention it, she did look pretty upset, like maybe she'd been crying again. And he was kind of dragging her along."

Cesar feels rage burning through his veins like a shot of whisky for the soul. It drowns out all reason with the throbbing song of madness.

Asner has taken his wife. The man dares to kidnap his woman? This ends now.

CHAPTER TWENTY-SIX

Penelope feels awful when she wakes up, groggy and disoriented. All she can think is that she must have done something truly stupid to feel this bad. Her head feels like something crawled in there and died. Her eyes aren't quite tracking the way she'd like them too.

She stares blearily at three Asners and really doesn't want to see any of them. She closes her eyes but the spinning doesn't stop.

"I figured it out, Penelope," Asner is saying. "A way to end war. I actually made a machine that will end war."

She squints in his general direction and the three Asners do a crazy dance through her field of vision.

"That's very nice," she tells him. "Now, how about you let me go?" For emphasis, she pulls against the tape holding her in the chair, but Asner is in full rant mode and not paying attention to the comforts of his audience.

The low gravity isn't doing her skewed vision any favors. The small room she's held in has the classic industrial strength bioplastic fittings you see in mass-produced Spacer ships or orbitals. Homemade projects might have bac-wood or biosteel. Penelope lets her mind wander around with those facts, but it doesn't get anywhere with them. This bare little room looks like typical ship's quarters. It is a small room with a fold-up bed, pullout sink and collapsible toilet. She could be anywhere.

Her hair drifts into her eyes and she reflexively tries to reach her hand up to push it away before remembering that her hands are bound with tape. Penelope looks at Asner, trying to decide if she can find a way to get him to at least free her hands. Asner continues droning on about something or other, but it's just giving her a headache. She blows at her hair until it drifts away from her eyes.

Asner looks more than a little crazed right now so she decides she'll just wait until he pauses to bring up the whole "incarcerated against my will" topic again. That will give her some time to pull herself together.

"You were always against the War, against violence," says Asner. "I admire that about you. And I agree there should be no war. My family was killed when the Earthers attacked. Earther soldiers butchered my brothers and their families. That should never happen again, Penelope. I figured out a way to do it."

Penelope feels the throbbing pain on the back of her head that says someone hit her hard enough to scramble her brains for a bit, hopefully not permanently. She has a strong feeling that she is no longer on Ithaca. It just smells wrong. Foreign. Perhaps she's on a ship? No, there is definitely some gravity. Could she be on a foreign orbital? How long was she out?

Asner continues on, "They always say the best defense is a good offense. We'll have the Moon Array online within days and then the Earthers won't be able to stop us. They'll pay for what they did."

Penelope swallows a bitter laugh. The first time she leaves Ithaca in almost two decades and she does it bound and gagged. It figures. At least Asner removed the gag.

Pacing, Asner says, "The hardest part was building something that big without detection. We are still so vulnerable. But as soon as we have the final ingredient, Spacers will never be exposed again. And not just from Earth. You never know when aliens might show up. They could be a threat, too."

She's been trying to ignore him, but that is too much. Penelope glares at him so hard that he finally stops talking and really looks at her.

"What?"

"Seriously, Asner? You are trying to tell me that assaulting and kidnapping me was necessary for Spacer defense against *aliens*? Seriously?"

Asner scowls. "You are looking at this incorrectly, my dear. I am disappointed." Penelope rolls her eyes, but he's pacing again and doesn't see her.

"Look," she says, as calmly and persuasively as possible. "My head is killing me and I may throw up. This chair is incredibly uncomfortable. I want to listen to you, but I can't concentrate like this."

Penelope licks her lips and hopes she looks as pathetic and vulnerable as she feels.

"Well, if I am to make you understand then I must let you listen," Asner says gruffly, his eyes lingering on her chest. It makes Penelope's skin crawl, but he pulls out a blade and cuts the tape.

Before she has a chance to bolt for it, Asner quickly retapes her hands to the bed frame. Taped to a bed is not her preferred location in any room alone with Asner, but it is considerably more comfortable than the chair. Twisting her wrists just slightly, she feels confident that, given enough time, she can get out of the tape around her hands. She focuses on this task.

"So," she says brightly, desperate to keep Asner's mind off the bed. "Tell me about what you are making. I guess you and Uri are making... what? A weapon?"

The man smiles. "Yes, exactly. It is necessarily a secret project so that the Earthers do not try to stop us before it is done. Also, it will be easier to explain to the other colonies once we have it working and they see the benefits of it."

Penelope asks, "But what exactly is it?"

"I call it the Moon Array," Asner says dramatically. Penelope does her best to look impressed.

He sits down on the bed and keeps talking, "I mostly design solar sails, but my true passion is lasers. I designed some portable lasers for Uri. We started talking about how to defend Spacers against another Earther attack. You know it will only be a matter of time until they covet our freedom again."

He pauses, before confessing, "Uri maintains a covert base for his Seven Skies Company on the Moon. A very private person, Uri Mach is. Regrettably, he is also a very ruthless and selfish. But is not the whole idea of true peace that the lion shall lie down with the lamb? Uri is a lion and we must learn how to tame him if we want peace."

Penelope nods and makes encouraging noises while twisting her wrists slowly back and forth. She wonders if there is such a thing as space madness, because everyone around her is going totally crackers this week.

"It became apparent that Uri and I were of the same mind," Asner says. "Except he thought the answer was to produce a great many of the mobile lasers I made for him. I showed him how we could focus them for even more power."

Asner explains that he made Uri a dozen or so robot-controlled laser cannons mounted on moon buggies to patrol the Moon near Uri's base like high-tech guard dogs. Uri hid his base on the dark side of the Moon to avoid detection by Earthers. The robots swarm out to attack any ships that get too close.

Apparently, Asner also designed a polycarbonate lens as a focuser for all those lasers. The laser buggies will line up and fire at the focuser, combining the strength of all the small beams to make one extremely powerful laser capable of scorching a hole practically through the Earth.

"The only hindrance in construction of the focuser was finding a large amount of lubricant for the torque iris lens needed to concentrate the laser beams," Asner admitting, like this was a personal failing. "We tried everything, but the only thing with the right properties that holds up in hard vac is modified beef tallow and, Penelope dear, you have the only source of beef tallow in the spheres that will work. Finomus says there's something about the genetic make-up of your cows that makes them special."

He went on to say that Finomus whipped up a batch of genetically modified bacteria that, when added to beef tallow, will produce the required lubricant, but they needed practically the entire herd to have enough to finish.

When Uri initially approached Penelope about buying the herd, he didn't want to alert her to what they were really after. When she refused, they tried to order the lubricant from Earth, but the quantities they needed and the genetic component raised too many questions. Now they have to get the weapon up and running before the Earthers find out what they are up to.

"From the beginning, I wanted to explain it all to you," Asner says, a note of pleading in his voice. "You are a Separatist. I knew if I could just explain, you'd understand. You'd want to be a part of such a magnificent project. But Uri refused. And only now can I tell you everything. I am sorry it has to be like this. I know you'll be able to forgive me."

Penelope smiles even though it makes her head pound. If she ever gets the chance, she'll show Asner exactly what it feels like to get hit on the head so hard you lose consciousness.

Then maybe she'll work on that whole forgiveness concept. It isn't high on her list of things to do, though. Asner doesn't need to know that right now, she decides. Penelope concentrates on looking sympathetic and thoughtful and not so much like she wants to spit in his face, even though it's her first impulse.

Over the ringing in her ears, Penelope can barely understand Asner as he tells her about his plan to put the focuser in place and align the lasers during the next lunar eclipse. While the Moon is covered in the reddish brownish darkness of the Earth's shadow, no one on Earth or the other orbitals will be able to see what they are doing until it is all over. The next lunar eclipse is tomorrow night and will last for about two hours.

"That's barely enough time to move the herd, harvest their fat and process it so they can assemble the final weapon, but I think we can do it," Asner says, sounding entirely too confident for Penelope's liking.

Than Asner startles her by crying, "When we have a weapon that powerful, there will be no more war because no one will dare defy us for fear of bringing down the wrath of our Moon Array."

Before she can stop herself, Penelope asks, "But isn't that the same logic the makers of the atomic bomb used? That nukes were so awful no one would ever use them? Look how that turned out."

There are parts of Earth that won't be habitable for another thousand years for anyone but the six-legged bunnies. Asner doesn't appreciate the comment.

"This is different," he snaps. "Only we will have this weapon."

Penelope snorts, "And you are going to let Uri be the guy with his finger on the trigger? Do you really think that's such a great idea? Uri, the guy who just beat up and kidnapped one of his oldest friends?" she shoots back before biting her lip. Arguing with this maniac isn't going to get her out of here. She needs to be smarter than that.

Penelope wonders how long she was out. How far from Ithaca are they?

"If you had just sold him the cows we required, none of this would have been necessary," huffs Asner. "But you refused and delayed. Personally, I am sorry that we must detain you here, but Uri can get excitable when he doesn't get his way. Still, it will be safer for you to be here with me while his men raid Ithaca. I do not think his men will try to minimize the casualties this time. It is regrettable, but the time for caution has passed. We will have to secure the goodwill of the other colonies after we are finished. They will understand. Omelets and eggs, you know."

"We're on the Moon?" she asks with despair.

"Yes. The ship docked an hour ago."

"Wait, what?" She is so shocked to find herself on the Moon right now that she almost misses the part about the raid.

Asner suddenly becomes very interested in straightening the collar of his shirt. "Yes, you gave him the access codes while you were delirious. I am sorry for that. He was not kind. His men had already infiltrated Ithaca as part of the Nullball crowd. Most of the Seven Skies team is only there to make sure that, one way or another, they leave with the necessary bovines. They are loading the cattle as we speak."

Penelope sucks in her breath. She didn't remember giving any access codes, but now that she thinks about it, there are several places on her body that hurt beside her head, particularly the crook of her arm. She looks at her arm to find a bloody gash like the kind a needle might make if you were injecting something into an unwilling subject. Penelope shudders.

Asner pats her leg while she works hard not to flinch. He is sitting so close that his leg is touching hers and she can feel his breath on her cheek.

"It will all be over soon," he murmurs.

Penelope does not find that at all reassuring.

"What an amazing plan, Asner," she says, praying she doesn't sound as sarcastic as she feels. "But if Uri's men are raiding Ithaca, won't that tip your hand? The colonies won't understand your, uh, grand vision. They may attack. Won't that stop you?"

Asner waves his hand. "No, they'll never find the Moon base in time. And if they do, the laser buggies will slice them to ribbons before they can possibly get close."

Penelope's heart sinks. She sees no way to free herself and no way to save Ithaca, much less stop these madmen with their lunatic laser weapon. She isn't going to give up, even if her brain is momentarily stunned.

Penelope blurts out, "So, what you are saying is—you turned the Moon into one big giant weapon."

Asner smiles modestly, "Well, I am an engineer."

"It's just so... impressive," she stutters, suddenly wondering if she should try to sound more impressed so Asner will keep talking while she tries to escape. She twists her wrists again as she says, "Old Manny is going to be so jealous."

Asner makes no effort to be modest this time. "Do you think so?"

"Oh, wow, sure," she says, nodding vigorously. "Of course he will be. Who wouldn't be? You're a genius. A visionary."

Asner moves closer, giving her a heated look as he rubs her knee rather awkwardly and vigorously. Penelope eyes him, uncertain what the man will do next. Asner lurches forward so that he is practically on top of her. He smears a kiss across her face as she pulls away from him.

"Oh Christ, are you serious?" she cries with exasperation.

Asner steadies himself on a wall, sweating heavily. "Don't you think you'd better be nicer to me?" he asks nastily. "Would it not be logical to give in to my desires so that you live? Wouldn't you be willing to do anything to see your son again?" The man eyes her, smug and leering.

Penelope replies by spitting in his face. Asner snarls and slaps her hard. She spits at him again. The engineer uses one hand to grab her hair, yanking her head back agonizingly while his other hand flies up and back, ready to hit her again.

Penelope kicks him hard, grateful that no one thought to remove her thick anti-grav boots. Her right boot connects with his knee. Asner slams his elbow into her while twisting her arm painfully.

Penelope keeps kicking. In the cramped room, Asner can't easily get away. Judging from his high-pitched screech, her foot must have connected to something really painful. Asner grabs her hair again and uses it to slam her head into the wall. Now she is bleeding from the lump on the back of her head and a gash over her eye.

Adrenaline and fear give her strength she never knew she had. Twisting, she pulls her foot up and kicks it directly into his face as hard as she can. She feels something crunch, probably his nose.

Asner lets go of her hair and pushes away from her. Penelope still manages to land a few more kicks, including another face shot. After that, Asner collapses onto the floor whimpering.

Breathing hard, Penelope wrenches her hands out of the tape and leaps up off the bed, every muscle in her body tense. Asner twitches a little bit, but otherwise doesn't make any sudden movements.

Penelope bursts into tears. "Well, I could have handled that a little better," she groans to herself. Wiping her eyes and taking deep breaths, Penelope feels the blood trickling down her ear and more stinging her eyes. Cautiously, she leans over Asner but doesn't touch him. She can see he's still breathing.

Spying the roll of tape he used to bind her, Penelope goes to work. Taping Asner to the chair reminds her of a sheep-shearing contest she watched a few years ago. She wonders what the record is for how fast you can tape a person to a chair.

"At least I'm not kicking you in the head anymore, you big stupid jerk," she tells Asner's limp, drooling form when he moans. She sure isn't getting any points for gentleness, though.

Penelope quickly searches Asner's pockets and is rewarded with his passkey. Clutching it like a talisman, she leaves him there. Penelope hopes the engineer has access to the docking bay. She also hopes there is something there she can use to get as far from Uri and his Seven Skies goons as possible.

Someone needs to know what Uri's goons are up to out here. Someone needs to stop the Seven Skies raid on Ithaca. Penelope goes racing down the corridor, catlike and quiet, looking for a way out.

A few times she has to duck into a supply closet or down a garbage chute to avoid someone. The endless gray halls are quite disorienting and Penelope is horrified at the thought of getting lost. Eventually she finds the cargo bay, breathing a small sigh of relief when the passkey opens the door.

Slipping into the busy cargo bay, she ducks behind a pile of equipment and crouches down. There are lots of people in here, milling around. She's gotten this far, but where to go from here?

The only thing to do is sit tight, hope no one notices her and look for an opportunity to get out. Penelope crouches there long enough to feel her knees go numb before she hears the telltale drumming of a ship outside entering the airlock and the grinding of the pressurization doors. In a minute the docking bay doors will open to let a new ship in. Another ship will probably mean even more people in the cargo bay. Will that make it easier for her to slip aboard an outbound ship or will more eyes make it impossible for her to escape unnoticed?

Penelope isn't sure she can fly a ship if she manages to steal one. She played a few flight simulator games over the last couple of years, but that was mostly because Trevor wanted to play. She never was very good at them. She hopes those robotic laser guards out there aren't as good as

Asner seems to think. Maybe she can find a comm or Ether connection and at least get the word out? She figures she has, at most, another hour or so before someone discovers Asner, then Uri's men will start looking for her. What can she do?

Then there is a muted thud as everything the cargo bay pitches hard to the right from some enormous impact to the base. Penelope falls over and throws her arms over her face, trying to protect her head from flying cargo boxes. The people out on the floor go sliding across the floor and stacks of equipment tumble around. Alarms blare over the screaming and chaos. Another thud follows and then another. She hears the sounds of explosions and disaster. Armed men pile into interceptors while others load the ship guns. Penelope realizes what is going on.

Someone is attacking the Moon Base.

CHAPTER TWENTY-SEVEN

Cesar races towards Ithaca's core with the beat of rage pulsing through his brain. He feels as though he is standing still while the world around him races past in a blur, chasing something that has nothing to do with him and his rage. There is nothing but the goal: Find Penelope.

His eyes scan the environment around him, looking for tools to accomplish the goal. His legs move mechanically, marching to the beat of his pounding heart. The only thing he really has to concentrate on is breathing. He seems to be having trouble with that just now.

He pushes through the crowds in town to get to the elevators. Cesar hears people behind him muttering, cursing his rudeness. He can't be bothered with that now. Where is she? He keeps looking, hoping he is over-reacting, wishing she'd come walking along to tell him to stop being a fool and trust her.

When he gets off the elevator at the core, he has to make a choice—the tournament or the docking bay? Cesar stops, staring at the two diverging paths. It is far more likely that Asner lured her to the Nullball arena on some pretext and she went, thinking there would be safety in the crowd. But if Asner is dragging her then she might not be following him willingly. It would be much easier to hide an unwilling pillar of the community in the docking bay than in a sports tournament.

But what if Argos was mistaken? The man isn't exactly sharp of mind and keen of intellect. Cesar knows he has to allow for observer error, too. People frequently remember things wrong. They are actually much less likely to correctly remember a high-stress event like a ship crash or a robbery than some mundane chore like washing dishes. You would think it would be the other way around, but that isn't the case.

The tournament is more likely. Except it will take him far longer to locate her in that crowd than searching the docking bay. Also, if Penelope is at the tournament, she is in much less danger than if she is at the docking bay. But what if he chooses incorrectly? Cesar feels the steady pounding of his heart, thudding the seconds away as he stands there, paralyzed by indecision.

"Hey, Dad!"

Cesar whips his head around, looking for the source of that clear call. His eyes finally pick out Trevor's buoyant grin and enthusiastic wave. Cesar frowns, momentarily confused by his son's appearance.

"Dad, I'm back!"

Trevor comes bouncing forward, gleefully dragging an equally chipper young girl along after him. There aren't many people in the hallway, but the few that are move out of Trevor's way lest the gangly boy trample them in his haste to get to Cesar.

"Trevor!" cries Cesar.

He knows he has no time for it, but Cesar is so ecstatically relieved to see his son that he has to touch the boy just to make sure he's really here. Cesar moves forwards to greet his son, but he is brought up short when he suddenly recognized the girl.

"Nausicaa!"

Her grin gets even wider. "Hi there, Mr. Vaquero! I thought I'd bring your son back."

Trevor punches her lightly on the arm. "You wish."

Turning back to his father, Trevor throws himself into Cesar, giving him a crushing hug while bragging, "I flew us here all by myself. They had this old ship of yours and we brought it back, me and Nausicaa, all by ourselves!"

Cesar releases his son but keeps a hand on Trevor's shoulder, unwilling to break that connection just yet. "That's great, son. Really great. All by yourself?"

He starts to quickly explain about the trouble with Penelope, but then his brain processes what Trevor just said.

"What did you say?" Cesar asks just to make sure he heard the boy correctly.

"I flew here all by myself. Well, all right, so Nausicaa helped. Al showed me. They found that ship you lost back when you saved her folks and we brought it back. Cool, right?"

Cesar agrees that this is very cool. It changes everything. Carefully, Cesar looks at Nausicaa for confirmation. After she gets through punching Trevor for taking all the credit, she bobs her head in agreement. Cesar hardly dares to breath. Can he be that lucky?

"You found the *Surprise*?"

They both shout, "Yes!"

"And flew her back. So then she's flight ready?"

They nod again, grinning widely.

"What about the weapons? Are they still intact?"

The grins disappear and get replaced by frowns. Nausicaa pipes up, "What weapons, Mr. V?"

Cesar feels like his whole body was inflated by helium and he just popped like a balloon. Well, so they found the ship minus the weapons. Still, that's better than nothing.

"Were they in the cargo bays, these weapons? Because they never opened those," Trevor says, watching Cesar's face closely enough to see the spark of hope that flashed across it.

Turning to Nausicaa, Trevor asks, "That's right, isn't it? You never opened the cargo bays."

Nausicaa nods, also looking at Cesar anxiously. She says quickly, "The cargo bay seals are intact and we left them that way. Thought you'd have a bit of a late Christmas present when you got them back."

Cesar's heart sings, but he can't get ahead of himself. The goal is Penelope right now. Grimly, he fills them in. "Argos saw Asner dragging your mother down here. We've got to find her."

Trevor asks tensely, "What should we do?"

Finally Cesar knows. Pointing towards the arena, he says, "You two go look for her at the tournament. I'll go to the cargo bay."

Trevor tells him where the ship is docked and then goes bolting off towards the roaring crowds of Nullball with Nausicaa chasing after him.

"It was nice to see you again, Mr. Vaquero!" she calls to him over her shoulder.

The rage has Cesar in its claws again and he is already blazing towards the cargo bay. Once there, he finds it mostly deserted and quiet, technically open for business except everyone is off at the tournament. Cesar finds the calm to be highly offensive. His wife is missing. There should be alarms. It isn't a large dock so it takes very little time to confirm his rising fear. She isn't here. He doesn't see any sign of Asner either.

Pouncing on the first dockworker he sees, Cesar frog marches the poor man over to a comm and makes him read through the list of ships docked twice.

Then Cesar has the dockmaster look up ships that have departed in the last hour. The man rattles both of them off, flinching at the black look on Cesar's face when he says, "Seven Skies shuttle, owner Uri Mach."

There are no other ships that he can connect with Asner or Mach besides this one that is already gone. Cesar knows his wife's life might very well depend on what he does next. He has to be sure of his next move, even if it means delaying a few minutes.

"Pull up the security footage for the last hour," he commands. The dockmaster protests. Cesar's glare combined with the pain from his vice-like grip on the man's shoulder convinces the dockmaster to do as he is told.

He speeds through the recorded footage until Cesar sees Penelope arrive in the little camera's view with Asner. Cesar hisses as he watches the man with the crowbar sneak up behind Penelope while she shakes her head over and over. Both Cesar and the dockmaster gasp in outrage when the man with the crowbar brutally attacks the small woman. Cesar watches with horror as she crumples to the floor and is then carried into Mach's shuttle.

Then Cesar doesn't stop moving until he is pulling his old ship, the *Surprise*, away from the dock. He almost pauses when he hears the dockmaster squawking into the emergency speakers. It is some garbled version of "Penelope Vaquero has been kidnapped!" but Cesar has other fish to fry. And fry is what those slimy bastards will do.

As he listens to the hum of the engines powering up, Cesar slips back into the role of tinker ship captain like it is a second skin. A tinker ship captain has to be good at many things. One of those things is making a ship out of the wreckage of other ships. Cesar built the *Surprise* at the peak of his largest fortune and he did it with years of experience and plenty of time.

He runs a hand along its console. It almost broke what was left of his tired old heart to lose this ship all those years ago. To be honest, if he had known he would lose it, Cesar wasn't so sure he would have dropped it to save Al and Arete.

He'd kept what shreds of sanity he still had out there in the black by lovingly polishing her hull while she sat in the docking bay of his big tinker ship with its loud and frequently irritating crew. To find her again after so many years seems like a sign. It lifts his spirits and gives him hope. Cesar has his *Surprise* back and, judging from the smooth hum of her engines, she is good as ever.

The rocket engines blast him back into his seat as he shoots off in pursuit of Mach's ship.

Running through the diagnostics, he can't believe how well everything survived on his little skiff. Cesar made her small and lean, an easy ship for a man to pilot alone. He carefully hollowed out traditional solar thrusters to hide the fastest and most expensive chemical rockets he could find. Then he moved heaven and Earth to collect a nice little hoard of rocket fuel, if it is still stashed in the cargo hull.

He spent weeks reconfiguring the fins and ballast so she could turn on a dime. And then he lovingly strapped all the AI-missile launchers and neutrino beams he could fit under her ballast. The *Surprise* was his baby and she is one mean little bitch.

Mach and his little gang of bandits will never know what hit them. For all their talk about secret projects and lasers, Cesar isn't impressed. You hear a lot of big talk from Spacers. But really? What can they possibly have?

CHAPTER TWENTY-EIGHT

As fast as their anti-grav boots can take them, Trevor and Nausicaa shoulder their packs and go careening through the halls to the Nullball Tournament.

Trevor yells apologies over his shoulder as they crash into people left and right, pushing their way through the crowd.

"I'm calling your Grandpa, Trevor," shouts an old man as he shakes a fist. Trevor thinks that is a great idea, but he can't stop to chat. His eyes scan the crowd for a glimpse of his mom.

Trevor explains to Nausicaa as best he can, "She's got long black hair, usually in a braid. She's real short and usually she's yelling at someone or at least looks like she's about to. She'll have on anti-grav boots, but who doesn't right now?" Usually Trevor loves the lack of gravity on the core level, but today it just annoys him.

"Oh man, do I hope your mom is OK," mutters Nausicaa, trying to catch her breath as she follows in his wake.

There must have been a goal scored because the crowd roars. It momentarily distracts the guards so Trevor and Nausicaa can slip into the arena.

"I wish we could stop and watch the game," Trevor apologizes, but Nausicaa just shakes her head.

She says cheerfully, "Never been much of a fan, but it does look fun. Maybe if we find your mom and she's OK, we can watch a bit later,"

Trevor wonders if she can play with her disease and all, but doesn't ask. He isn't sure yet how they should talk about her Synthlep. He's still happy that she came with him back to Ithaca.

•

Mathis, Larry's old drinking buddy and the ever-vigilant sentry of Ithaca, showed up at Nausicaa's house, growling about lepers and insisting Trevor go home with him because his granddad was worried. Things moved pretty fast after that.

First, Trevor had to explain to Mathis five or six times that he was just fine. Al and Arete helped him explain to the old man that the main comm link for Lazar House got hit by space junk and destroyed right after the riot, but it wasn't related to the riots and they should have it back up and running in a few days. Just random bad luck.

Mathis was deeply suspicious of Al and Arete and, to Trevor's embarrassment, rather hostile until Al poured him a large glass of something amber-colored he called a "restorative." It made Mathis cheerful and chatty and suddenly in no hurry to go anywhere. When he arrived, Mathis refused to sit and seemed afraid to touch anything, but after his drink, he sprawled in a chair and rambled happily about all his important duties on Ithaca.

Trevor didn't want to go back with Mathis. He was in love with the idea of piloting Cesar's old ship home. For starters, he'd left as a victim and this way he would return triumphantly with this sweet ship. Also, he was really hoping his Dad would decide that he didn't need the ship any more, so Trevor could have it. Trevor didn't want to let the ship out of his sight.

At first, Al and Arete thought Trevor should go home with Mathis. They didn't want Trevor's family worried. Nausicaa helped him argue that Trevor, after spending every waking hour of the last day or two on the little ship, could fly it anywhere. She'd spent most of those hours with him on the ship.

After a second glass of restorative, Mathis decided it wasn't really important that Trevor come right back and, if it would only take a few hours to outfit, there was no reason the boy couldn't fly this other ship back. Mathis was not the kind of man to think you should leave a perfectly good ship behind if you could take it with you. When Al insisted he take the bottle of amber-colored liquid with him, Mathis was only too happy to leave Trevor behind and toddle back to his ship.

"I hope he takes a little nap before he leaves," Arete fretted.

Al put an arm around her shoulder and squeezed. "Unless I miss my guess, that old man has plenty of practice doing things blind drunk. He should be fine, honey."

Trevor admired how gracious they were to the drunken old man. He turned and smiled into Nausicaa's luminous eyes. Over the last few days, he'd come to realize that she was quite possibly the prettiest girl in the solar system.

Nausicaa smiled back at him in that glorious way she did, but then her mouth twisted and her face crumpled. She burst into tears and fled the room.

Trevor gaped at her retreating figure. He got up, wanting to follow her. "What did I do?" he asked Arete, bewildered.

She smiled at him gently. "It's time for you to leave, Trevor. I think my daughter is getting a head start on missing you. Let's give her a little privacy. I'm sure she'll come out to say goodbye."

Al packed up a change of clothes for Trevor as he quickly cleaned himself up. As Trevor and Al left for the docks, Arete handed him a package of food and a water bottle and gave him a gentle hug. Trevor strained to hear Nausicaa, but there was silence from the direction of her room.

"It's really too bad you are an outworlder," remarked Al after they had trudged in silence for a quarter of an hour. "It will remind Nausicaa that there's a whole world out there but she's so much safer here, where we can control her condition."

Trevor understood what Al was saying and he also understood the gentle warning beneath it. Nausicaa had Synthlep and there wasn't any getting around that. Trevor still glanced back a dozen times, hoping to see her running up to tell him goodbye. He knew they couldn't kiss even though he was dying to try it, but at least he could hug her one last time and feel her heart beating against his chest.

Nausicaa didn't come.

Al went through a final check of the ship with him, then said goodbye. "You and your family are always welcome to visit," Al said sincerely. "And be sure to tell your father again how much I esteem him."

The man walked off. Trevor dawdled with powering up the engines, packing away the food and clothes, tidying up the ship, and rechecking all the systems. Finally, he knew he was just wasting time. She wasn't coming. Trevor walked over to shut the outer doors and suddenly there she was.

"Permission to come aboard, Captain," Nausicaa called, grinning widely. She snapped off a jaunty salute and walked past him into the cabin.

Dumping her pack in a chair, she turned and asked, "Well, what are you waiting for? Let's go!"

"Uh," he stammered. "I thought you had to stay here."

She flapped an unconcerned hand at him and sat down in the co-pilot chair while putting on a comm. "My mom said it was fine. I'll get a shuttle back tomorrow. You need my help in case something crazy is going down at your place."

She said it like it was no big deal, so he guessed it wasn't. Trevor shrugged, sat down at the comm and strapped himself in. The trip was pretty uneventful until they ran into his dad. Since then, his heart has been pounding a disco beat in his chest.

As they weave through the crowd, there's no sign of his mom and Trevor is getting worried. He'll see long black hair out of the corner of his eye, but when he turns there's no hint of his mom. He keeps spotting a glimpse of someone who looks like her, but it never is.

While they look around, Trevor sees enough of the Nullball game to realize that it has only just begun, but it's going to be epic. Both teams are playing their hardest, determined to win. There are amazing shots and unbelievable saves. The crowd is hyped up to a fever pitch.

The faces all seem to blur after a while. Nausicaa points to women and asks Trevor if that's his mom, but she's doing it less often and the hope has fallen from her voice. Trevor keeps going, but he's more and more sure that he's looked at everyone in the arena and his mom just isn't here.

At last, Nausicaa asks if they can stop at one of the vendors selling drinks and liquid snacks in null-grav sippy cups.

"I don't think she's here," Trevor admits as he swipes his thumb to pay for two hot chocolates.

Nausicaa sips her drink appreciatively. She looks tired but her cheeks are flushed pink. "So what should we do?"

Trevor thinks about it. His first impulse is to go home, but what good will that do his mom? She isn't there. He could tell his Grandpa Larry or Lupe or Argos, but he can't imagine what they could do. Mathis went on for forever about how Grandpa was organizing the whole colony for war, but that was after two large glasses of Al's "restorative" and Trevor has a hard time seeing his old Grandpa doing anything other than chucking tequila bottles at bad guys.

"I guess," he says, taking a long sip. "We should go back to the docking bay and see what Cesar has come up with."

Nausicaa brightens up. "Yeah, good idea. If your mom isn't here, she's probably there and they might need our help."

They go racing towards the docks. The docking bay is almost completely empty. There is no sign of Cesar or Penelope. There's just a group of dockworkers that Trevor doesn't recognize loading a large cargo ship in the back.

After they walk around the third time, Nausicaa cries, "Where is everybody?"

"I don't know. I guess they are all at the tournament, but where'd Cesar, I mean my dad, go?"

Nausicaa throws her hands up and looks just as frustrated as Trevor feels. He decides to go ask the dockmaster if he's seen Cesar.

Trevor jogs over to the dockmaster's station and pushes the door open. There's a strange woman in there talking into the dock's comm. She has a hard jaw, buzzcut hair and she's wearing an Ithaca dockworker coverall but Trevor knows she's not from Ithaca. He knows all the dockworkers. As she turns towards Trevor and Nausicaa, Trevor looks past her to see the dockmaster's crumpled, bloody form curled up on the floor.

Nausicaa screams. Trevor shouts. The woman lunges for them with a snarl. She grabs the front of Trevor's shirt and cocks her other arm back, making a fist that means business.

Nausicaa smacks the woman full in the face with her backpack so hard that her head snaps back and the comm implant over the woman's temple cracks loudly. The woman looks stunned, but only a little. Her grip on Trevor loosens enough for him to yank his shirt out of her grasp. He looks around for some sort of weapon and spots a heavy metal wrench.

The woman turns on Nausicaa. Nausicaa whacks her with the backpack again, but it doesn't have the same impact as the first time. The woman hits Nausicaa hard. The girl's whole body jerks back as she lets out a pained yelp. Nausicaa would have gone flying if her boots didn't keep her locked to the floor. Trevor doesn't even think twice about picking up the wrench and bringing it down on the woman's head.

It isn't hard enough. Screaming curses, the woman pounces on him, her fingernails gouging thick rivers of pain down his arm. This time he hits her as hard as he can with the wrench, but that only makes her move her grip to his neck. She squeezes cruelly. Flailing around with the wrench, Trevor yells and twists, but he starts to weaken. He drops the wrench to claw at her feebly, his vision going dark.

All at once, Trevor feels her grasp on his neck disappear. Gasping for air, he pulls away and goes scooting across the floor, getting as far away as fast as he can. After he's several feet away, his vision returns. The strange woman is lying in a heap. Nausicaa stands over her, breathing heavy and holding a hammer as a cloud of spherical globules of blood whirl around her.

The hammer is bloody, but Trevor only sees the naked fear all over Nausicaa's face. "Are you dead?" she stutters. She has to try twice before she can get the question out.

"Not yet," he replies, raspy and hoarse. His throat feels like he's been gargling with bleach.

"I don't think any of this blood is mine," comments Nausicaa, sounding a little dazed still. "That's lucky for you guys. No risk of infection."

Trevor frowns at her. "It's also nice that you aren't hurt," he points out.

Trevor grabs the dockmaster's duct tape and quickly tapes the woman's arms and legs. As soon as he is done, the hammer slips from Nausicaa's shaking hands and gently twirls in midair while she collapses to the floor. When Trevor goes to her, she waves him away.

"Go check on that guy in there," Nausicaa insists.

Dino, the injured dockmaster, is groggy and keeps mumbling about a terrible headache. Trevor asks him, "How many fingers am I holding up?"

Dino just calls him a very rude name and tells him to get out of the way.

"Whatever that *puta* was trying to do, she's not getting away with it on my watch," swears Dino, his fingers flying over the comm.

Trevor and Nausicaa hover in the doorway, alternating between exchanging worried looks and scanning the docks for trouble. Trevor retrieves his wrench and Nausicaa plucks the hammer from the air.

Finally, Dino punches a fist into the air. "Ha! I don't think so!" Turning to Trevor, Dino shouts triumphantly, "Those bastards think they are gonna rustle cattle out of *my* docks? Let's see them try it with the outer doors sealed and all the cargo elevators jammed."

Nausicaa claps and cheers.

"Won't they send someone else to beat up on you?" asks Trevor, his mind going to those dockworkers in the back. He hasn't seen them for a while and that is making him nervous.

Dino's hand goes to his bleeding scalp but he stops before touching it. Trevor winces just watching him.

"Yeah, I hope not," Dino says, prodding his wound gently. "I'll put out an emergency message and then lock the door. From what I saw before that *pendejo* beat me half to death, those guys were heavily armed. We are going to need help."

"Did you see Cesar Vaquero?" asks Nausicaa.

Dino's eyebrows shoot up. "Did I what?"

Nausicaa repeats her question.

Dino answers before Trevor has a chance to explain and his voice takes on a reproving note. "Listen, miss, if Mr. Vaquero were still alive, there's absolutely no way he'd be involved with these jerks, stealing and attacking people."

"Dino, my dad is back," Trevor says urgently. "He was here just a while ago, but he's not with these guys, he's trying to save my mom from them."

This time Dino gasps and, fumbling for his chair, sits down quickly. "He's here? Alive?"

Gesturing to the woman taped to the chair, Trevor says, "I think these guys may have taken my mom and dad came here looking for her."

"Oh!" cries Dino, looking flustered. "That was your dad? Wow. That explains a lot. I'm sorry Trevor, that knock on my head must have really rattled my brains. I was here before when he came looking for Mrs. Vaquero. Yes, they took your mom. Seven Skies. I was just putting out an emergency call about it when that stupid woman over there pulled open the door and started hitting me."

Dino stops as though he's had a sudden thought and starts tapping on his computer.

"We should go get help," Nausicaa whispers urgently.

Trevor likes that idea.

"Your dad took that ship you guys came in on," Dino says.

Trevor nods, "Good, then he went after Mom. Wait. Did you say cattle rustling a minute ago?"

Dino responds by getting on the comm, blaring out emergency calls on every frequency. Ithaca is under attack from within. Trevor knows that what he needs to do right now is go protect his family's herd. He doesn't know what he's going to do exactly, but he does know that he can't do it here.

Trevor and Nausicaa sprint towards the elevators near the stadium, but the explosions and gunfire start before they make it out of Ithaca's core.

CHAPTER TWENTY-NINE

After the third or fourth blast knocks Penelope on her now thoroughly bruised bottom, she decides to stay down. Unfortunately, the sliding storage bins and falling equipment in the cargo bay make that difficult.

Penelope spends a few minutes curled in the fetal position under a pile of discarded hazmat suits before pulling one on. Ships rush in and out through the pressure locks, making the docking bay icy and cold. Then she spies the little repair skiff sitting neglected in the corner, its grappling claws tucked up under it like a sleeping crab. They will miss it after the action when they want to fix the damage, but she'll be long gone by then.

Perfect.

With all the people running around and all the sirens going off, Penelope decides it is time to risk it. It isn't too difficult to grab a mask hat and pull it low over her face after stuffing her hair up inside it. Mask hats are shaped like tall baseball hats with an oxygen mask that pulls down over your face and attaches to your hazmat suit for limited vacuum protection. They only have maybe thirty minutes worth of oxygen in them, but they come in handy during emergencies so they are common headgear in docking bays.

Penelope keeps her head down and avoids eye contact as she briskly walks across the large room to the little repair skiff. She almost reaches it before she hears Uri Mach bellowing across the cargo bay.

"Get every ship with a gun out there and hit that bastard!" he roars.

Penelope's heart sinks so fast that it lands right on her stomach and she has to swallow back a gulp of bile. She stops walking for only a second, and then hurriedly dodges behind the wheel of a large fuel tanker. It is unlikely that he spotted her, but it's not like she can trust her luck. Not today.

She peers around the edge of the tire to find people in flight suits surrounding Mach, keeping him blessedly distracted.

Someone is asking Mach, "Why aren't the lasers working? They should have fried the attacking ships before it got close enough to hit, right?"

"The lasers are working just fine," snaps Mach, sounding even angrier. "It's just one ship. This guy is too small and too fast for them to burn. They can't get a lock on him. The lasers need to stay focused on their target for a moment to heat it up enough to burn. He's got some kind of reflective armor on that thing."

There is general muttering before Mach snarls, "It's just one little ship! Go get him!"

People scatter. Penelope takes the opportunity to hurry closer to the skiff she has her eye on.

"Just one ship?" mutters one of the pilots getting into a ship near Penelope's new hiding place. "Where's Asner? He's been talking about how nothing can get through the laser field for months and one little ship gets through to do all this damage?"

Penelope wonders who is out there giving Uri such hell. Whoever it is will get a big kiss of gratitude from her for providing this distraction, if she ever meets them.

People back at Ithaca might have noticed she's gone by now, but that is doubtful. It will be hours, maybe days, before anyone figures out what happened to her. She isn't even sure there is anything to see. Asner and Mach could have erased them or positioned themselves so that the cameras failed to record her little kidnapping.

The person climbing in behind the first pilot replies, "Asner? Never around when we need him. Figures. He'd only say he designed the stupid lasers to take out big military ships or some crap like that. He'd say small ships are our problem. He's always putting it on us."

Penelope hopes this means no one has found Asner yet. It will give her more time to escape. It takes her a few tense minutes to get the door open and climb in. She fumbles through powering it up, praying that she remembers how to do that correctly from that flight simulator. She wishes she paid more attention during those lessons. She wishes she hadn't taken them so long ago.

Penelope sighs, feeling the profound embarrassment she's been ignoring since she woke up. How could she have let herself be taken so easily? What kind of fool walks right into that kind of danger? She might as well rub herself down with bacon, pop into a tiger's cage, put her head in its jaws and then act shocked when it bites her.

The worst of it is that she was warned. That Ulixes man warned her about Mach and Asner and she dismissed him as a raving lunatic. Penelope feels very stupid. Actually, realizing he was right about that means he may have not been totally mad.

Penelope feels so exposed, sitting in the cockpit of the little skiff. The clear plastic front of the cockpit gives almost everyone in the docking bay a view of her sitting here. She can see Mach in the extreme right-hand side of the window, warped where it curved to meet the metal walls. People surround him as he barks out commands.

Her hands shake while she waits for the engines to power up. She can only hope that, with all the other ships jostling to get out and into the fight, they don't notice her sneaking off in the skiff. She eases the skiff into flight and prepares to make a break for it.

There is a flash from the right. Penelope sees people running towards her and the little skiff. She turns to see Mach glaring right at her. They found her. Penelope reflexively winces, causing the little skiff to veer suddenly to the left before she guns it hard, pushing for the doors.

The skiff lurches forward to the sound of small pings against the hull. They are shooting at her. Penelope knows it's all over, but she is damned if she will stop fighting.

There is a large blue ship blocking the door. Penelope flies the skiff up, seeking a chance to slip out over the lumbering thing as it moves into the airlock.

No good. The huge blue ship swerves up and she narrowly avoids getting flattened like a bug against the roof of the docking bay, to be scraped off later. Then the inner door slams shut, ending all hope of escape.

Penelope pulls the skiff back and looks around, desperate for a way out. She knows they'll probably just shoot her down the second she breaks free of the bay, but she doesn't care. If this thing had guns, she'd make sure that at least she takes out Mach.

Penelope flies the skiff in circles around the ceiling as they lob things at her from below. She is sure each *thunk* against the hull will be the last. She uses the claws to pry a pipe from the wall and fling it at Mach.

Steam shoots out of the broken end of the pipe as Uri beats a hasty retreat out a door. Penelope scowls at his disappearing backside, wishing she could take one more shot at him. Then the walls shake and Penelope sees stars.

Literally.

The inner doors rip open with a searing explosion that burns against the glittering backdrop of stars. Penelope watches as everyone and everything left in the cargo bay gets sucked into the void. Something has blown open the doors. The skiff banks hard at the sudden pressure change, grazing against the ship next to it.

The large blue ship blocking the door goes zooming out. There is a flash. Penelope sees the back end of it go shooting off at an angle that can only mean ruin for the big ship. Two other ships go out afterwards, but Penelope doesn't see what happens to them, other than flashes of light. Everyone else is either sitting tight in their ships or they are already dead by decompression.

Penelope watches the debris drift around for a long minute before she realizes that she can get out of the cargo bay now. Before she tries it, Penelope decides this is a good time to recheck the seals on her hazmat suit, just in case. Seeing all those decompressed corpses makes her want at least another layer of protection, however flimsy, between her and the vacuum.

As Penelope yanks the suit on, she sees a small black ship slowly nose its way into docking bay. It is bristling with missile launchers. It looks tiny but lethal, a wolf sneaking into a barn.

Penelope slowly eases the skiff into a corner of the bay, hoping to go unnoticed. The strange shiny ship sets down. The missile launchers swivel every which way, but mostly point at the doors Mach disappeared down just moments before. Penelope decides this is probably the ship attacking the Moon base, but she can't afford to be wrong, can she?

Penelope decides to risk it. Turning on the short wave, she calls, "Who are you?"

She listens to static for a long moment before the answer comes.

"Penelope?"

Jesus. It almost sounds like…

"Ulixes?"

This time she only has to wait a few seconds before she hears a heavy sigh through the crackling static.

"You could call me that."

"Uh." It isn't her most eloquent moment.

"Where are you?" he wants to know.

She waggles one of the skiff's claws back and forth by way of a reply and hears an amused chuckle over the comm. "What are you doing here?" she asks.

"Looking for you."

It is monumentally preposterous that he should be here, but he is here so…

"Can you give me a lift?"

"That's what I'm here for."

Penelope sets the skiff down quickly on the floor of the destroyed docking bay. She double-checks the seals on her hazmat suit and then lopes the short distance to his gleaming little ship as fast as her grav boots will let her. It is a much longer, more harrowing experience than it should be. Sliding pieces of the bay almost hit her as she dodges floating debris. About halfway there, she trips over a corpse and slides along the floor unsteadily as she untangles the dead body that has wrapped itself around her legs. Getting up, Penelope brushes little red crystals of what she is fairly sure is frozen blood off her facemask.

Penelope never thought she could fall in love with the sound of an airlock hissing open, but she does. Sure enough, Ulixes is standing there waiting for her with a mug of something hot. She is still surprised.

As she staggers into the vehicle, Penelope notes that the man shaved off his thick white beard at some point since she saw him last. He looks about two decades younger. Really, he doesn't look much older than she is. In fact, the man looks rather attractive, but perhaps that is because he just rescued her in a most heroic fashion. Penelope catches herself smoothing her hair as she stares at him.

"It really is you," she says, taking the steaming cup he is holding out to her.

He grins. "In the flesh."

It hits her all at once, that grin. It is the same cocky devil grin from a million years ago, from a cute Spacer stranger at a party when she was a girl. The same smile that shone through the dark night the first time she made love to her husband. The same grin on the face of Trevor's father the very first time he saw the boy. This is Cesar. This is her husband standing in front of her.

Penelope slaps him so hard he almost falls over. To be fair, the look of shock on his face says he wasn't expecting it.

"What the hell?" he sputters, rubbing his face and scrambling back. He throws up his arm to protect his face, so Penelope settles for punching his stomach as hard as she can.

"Where the hell have you been?" she shrieks. She winces at the shrewish tone in her voice, but can't help that right now.

Cesar is no fool. He takes refuge behind his chair. "Jesus!" he cries while dodging kicks. "It took me a while to get through that laser field, alright? You know those maniacs have automated lasers mounted to moon buggies out there? That's not easy, what I just did."

Penelope feels hot tears sting her cheeks. Gulping, she remembers they are still in the enemy base. She cries, "Get us the hell out of here!"

Cesar is more than willing to comply. The *Surprise* spins before it shoots out of the mangled docking bay door. Cesar sets a course that will get them as far away from the Moon base as fast as possible. As the ship pulls up and away from the Moon, Penelope collapses onto the floor behind him and catches her breath as gravity falls away from her.

When she sees the ship's direction, Penelope sits up to put a quick hand on his shoulder. "We can't leave yet," she says urgently.

Cesar eyes her quizzically. "Of course we can. I'm doing it right now."

Penelope shakes her head. "No, listen. Asner built Mach some kind of focuser thing for the lasers. It sort of bundles all the little lasers together and makes one superlaser that can destroy Earth cities or entire orbitals."

Cesar raises a skeptical eyebrow. "A laser bundler?"

"Physics isn't my thing," she yells. Waving her hands for emphasis, she says, "It's a huge colony-destroying laser he built out here. We need to break it before they get it running."

He looks slightly less skeptical so Penelope stops yelling. She says, "Asner was telling me all about it. They need the herd to make this huge laser

Moon base. Something about a special lubricant you can only make out of cow fat."

The ship's comm starts beeping about an unidentified object just as a huge dish looms into view. Penelope points at it triumphantly. Cesar's jaw drops as he taps through the scans of this vast piece of mostly-finished construction. The he whistles low and turns back to Penelope.

"Those guys really turned the Moon into a Death Star," he says to her, his voice full of awe.

Penelope frowns. Cesar sounds more like a teenager ogling his first laser rifle than a man about to seriously destroy a dangerous weapon.

"I noticed that on my way in," he muttered. "How come nobody else noticed it? It's pretty hard to miss."

"Asner said they were getting ready to power it up during the lunar eclipse tomorrow night so maybe it was hidden and they only uncovered it today. Who cares? Shoot some of your missiles at it and let's go already," Penelope commands.

Cesar rubs his chin thoughtfully. It's still red from that slap earlier.

"I don't know that we need to do that," he says, looking at the huge dish. "I demolished a whole lot of those laser moon buggies. I doubt it will work now anyway."

Penelope folds her arms and cocks a hip. "Yeah, and when they get it fixed up, who will be the first people they aim it at? They know where I live."

"Good point," replies Cesar. "The thing is, that dish is kind of big and this ship is pretty small. Destroying it won't be easy."

"I have confidence in your ability to figure it out."

Cesar stares at the huge dish. "But if they need the herd to finish it, then maybe we don't really need to worry," he mutters absently, tapping at his comm. Half of his mind has wandered out of the conversation.

Penelope explains, "Asner said that they have a gang of Seven Skies men in Ithaca, hiding in the Nullball tournament crowd, even in their team. Mach gave them orders to take the herd by force and they have enough ships that they could do it. They are raiding Ithaca right now. Best not to take any chances."

Cesar swears a violent, filthy curse and turns to stare at her with disbelief. "There is a gang of murderous thieves attacking Ithaca right now? Trevor's back there! He got off this ship about an hour after they took you!"

Penelope grabs his arm frantically. "We've got to go back. Now! Screw the dish."

Cesar turns back to the ships comm, but then his hand stops over the screen. "No. First, we need to blow this focuser up," he says grimly.

Penelope wants to argue, but the part of her brain that isn't totally filled with terror says he might be right. She tries to apply logic to the situation, but her thoughts are too jumbled and a small sensible voice in her head just points out that arguing will only take up more time. She settles for screaming obscenities as she straddles the only other chair in the ship's command room and starts firing the small defensive laser cannons at the dish. The effect is much the same as one would get shooting a skyscraper with a slingshot. She doesn't do any major damage to the evil thing, but it makes her feel like she is doing something.

Cesar taps away at the comm quietly. Over her muttered curses, he warns her, "You better hold on, this could get rocky."

Penelope stops blasting the dish long enough to strap herself in. Cesar turns once to make sure she is secured before dropping into his seat and strapping himself in as well. He never stops working away at the comm.

The ship zooms up and away from the focuser. Then it banks hard, pulling them deep into the high-backed seat cushions as the ship turns sharply. Then the ship shoots off, aiming directly back towards the floating dish so fast that the ship whines and shudders, protesting the speed. Penelope opens her mouth to ask what the hell Cesar thinks he's doing when the ship suddenly spins so fast her jaw would have cracked if her mouth had been open.

The thrusters roar behind her. She can feel the heat building up inside the cabin. She starts worrying they will burn up, but then Penelope suddenly understands what is going on. Cesar maneuvered so that their ship will fly right along the curve of the dish, across the widest part. Then, just before they get close enough to touch it, he quickly turns them so that the biggest weapon on this little ship, the thruster rockets, scorches the dish as they go skipping along it like a stone across water. A flaming destructive stone.

There is a nasty crunching noise. They are too close to the dish. Penelope is shoved deep into her seat cushions by the angry arms of gravity as the ship tumbles out of control.

Well, if she has to die this is a very cool way to go.

They move quickly, thanks to Cesar's incredible control of his ship. Finally they slow down, released from the wild ride. As soon as she can lean forward easily, Penelope throws up all over the floor in front of her.

Cesar chuckles.

Penelope's first impulse is to make a rude gesture at him for laughing at her, but then endorphins flood her brain. Joy screams from every nerve fiber in her body. Penelope starts giggling hysterically.

"We lived!" shouts Cesar, pumping his fist in the air.

Cesar passes her a rag. He turns back to the controls and scans the damage while Penelope cleans herself and the floor up.

"Oh, thanks be to the powers of physics," Cesar breathes. He gestures with relief at the comm screen. "I thought we might have to do that again."

"It's finished? Definitely wiped out?"

Cesar gets up and walks around the cabin while Penelope sits in his chair, using his comm to check the scans herself. He was right. Penelope can see that a large chunk of the dish broke off and is now floating gently away. The rest of the dish crumbles as the scorch marks slowly spread. She starts to tell him he is brilliant but she sees that cocky devil grin on his face again.

Just as Penelope is searching for an appropriately snarky comment to make, something big crashes into the ship and they are both thrown to the floor. Penelope's head smacks against the chair hard while Cesar crashes against her knees painfully. She wonders how much more head trauma she can take in one day before turning into a drooling moron. She can feel the little ship do a herky-jerky dance that can't be good.

Cesar scrambles back to his seat, glued to the comm.

"We've been hit," he tells her unnecessarily.

"By what?" asks Penelope, clutching her head. She has disjointed thoughts about a loose piece of the dish hitting them.

"A missile," says Cesar grimly.

"A missile?"

"Yeah."

"Is it bad?"

There is a long pause. Penelope's brains aren't so scrambled that she misses Cesar's quiet cursing.

"Not too bad," he says finally. "Not yet anyway."

His fingers fly over the comm as the ship goes careening off, making sudden twists and rapid turns that push and pull Penelope across the tiny room to crash into just about everything. Finally, there is a brief pause. She quickly, but carefully climbs back into her chair and straps herself back in.

"The ship that hit us is sending a hail," Cesar tells her. "It's probably Mach. You want to listen?"

"Is he going to hit us again?"

She can only see a sliver of Cesar's face from where she is. The protective seat cushions hide the rest of him. He looks thoughtful.

"No," he says slowly. "Not right now, anyway. I have us hidden behind the focuser wreckage. He'd have to start taking shots at this thing and even then, probably won't get us. There are a few of those automated lasers on the Moon's surface firing this way, but they won't be strong enough to burn through this big hunk of junk to get to us. If he sits there and shoots rockets at us, eventually he'll get us, but I'm hoping he isn't that angry."

Cesar's head moves like he's just shrugged his shoulders.

"Yeah, sure," says Penelope. "Let's hear the hail."

Cesar flicks it on.

Uri Mach appears on the main screen. "Whoever you are, you ruined a perfectly reasonable plan to put Spacers in control of the human race. I was going to be a benevolent dictator, but you screwed it up," he screams. There is another seven minutes or so of cursing and ranting. Penelope and Cesar trade bemused smirks.

Mach froths and rages, but then pulls himself together at the end to wrap up with, "Well, you might have blown up billions of credits of equipment and killed half my people, but at least you killed that moron Asner before I got my hands on him. It doesn't matter. I'll be able to start over anywhere with my brand new herd of cows." The man winks evilly at the screen and the message ends. The screen blinks off.

Penelope and Cesar stare at the empty screen wordlessly.

Finally, Cesar asks, "Did you kill Asner?"

"I don't think so. I beat him up pretty good, but he was mostly alive the last time I saw him. Maybe I did, though."

Cesar looks her up and down like that's the hottest thing he's heard a woman say in years. "Huh. Well, good riddance."

"So, is Uri hanging around to shoot at us some more?" asks Penelope.

"Looks like he's pulling away," replies Cesar.

Then after a while, he follows that up with, "Yeah, he's definitely headed out. There are three large ships moving off together."

"I can't believe he left a gloat message."

"Yeah. That's so lame," agrees Cesar. "He might as well have cackled like a bad Ether drama villain and threatened to make us rue the day we crossed him."

Penelope smothers a giggle, before worry sobers her. She blurts out, "He is, though. He's threatening our Trevor. We have to get back right now."

"We are going as fast as we can," Cesar says grimly as the ship pulls away from the cover of the broken dish.

Penelope digs her fingernails into the chair cushions and asks urgently, "You know that's where Mach is headed now, right? He's off to meet up with his men on Ithaca and take off with the herd. Can we catch them?"

Cesar turns to her with anguish written all over his face.

"We can't."

CHAPTER THIRTY

"What do you mean we can't catch that ship?" cries Penelope, pulling herself out of her chair.

Cesar shrugs, his eyes on the comm screen. "That hit we took damaged the main thruster. I can get us up to about sixty percent capacity, but that's it. We'll get back to Ithaca in about fourteen hours. Mach will get there in less than eight hours." His voice is glum.

Penelope starts pacing. "There must be something we can do."

Cesar shrugs and sits back in his chair, staring despondently at the comm screen. "Even if we had full power, we'd have a hard time catching him. I guess we ran out of miracles for today."

Penelope throws her hands up in the air. "But Trevor!"

"I know."

Penelope looks at the slumped figure in front of her. He looks deeply depressed. That is no good. She needs him in top form so he can save Trevor.

"Did you set the course for Ithaca already?" she asks.

"Yeah."

Penelope paces briskly some more. "Well, then you look like you could use some food and I could use a vat of coffee. Is there food on this thing?"

Cesar looks momentarily distracted. "You know, I have no idea." He gets up to go investigate.

Down in the tiny kitchen, they rummage around and find a few packets of noodles and some instant coffee, the kind that will last until the sun goes nova. To pass the time, Cesar tells Penelope about the origins of the ship. Then Penelope grills for details of Trevor's encounter with the pirates and he tells her as much as he can remember.

Blowing on her boiling coffee, Penelope mutters, more to herself than him, "So Trevor's been on Lazar House these last few days and he was fine the last time you saw him."

Around slurps of noodle soup, Cesar replies, "Yes. Don't you remember? I told you all this a few days ago in the kitchen back at the ranch. Did they knock you around that badly?"

Penelope waves her hand, dismissing the question. "No, I remember that talk. It's just that I thought you were some poor wandering nutjob with delusions then. I wasn't paying too much attention after about ten minutes."

Cesar sits back. "Delusions?"

She shrugs, looking only mildly apologetic. "Well, you have to admit it all sounded pretty farfetched and you dumped a whole lot on me all at once. Don't worry. I'm over that. Now I *know* you are a wandering nutjob with delusions, dear husband of mine."

Cesar looks offended for about half a second before he snickers. "And here I was telling myself you took it so well. I should have known better."

Penelope sits up straight, outrage lengthening her spine. "And what does that mean?" she demands.

Cesar just shrugs and goes back to his noodles. He hunches slightly and keeps darting looks at her like he expects her to throw her coffee at him and he is trying to finish the noodles before she gets to that point.

Penelope feels her temper flare as she watches him. Just like a man to overreact like this. Her temper isn't so bad. And he provokes her severely.

"Don't just sit there," she snaps. "We've got to find a way to save Trevor."

Cesar sighs, "If I could make this bucket of bolts go any faster, I would."

"This defeatist attitude is starting to seriously irk me," she grumbles. Penelope stands up and begins pacing again. "Then... Oh, I know! What about the Ether? We can call for help. At least we can warn Ithaca that Mach is on his way and in a murderous mood."

Cesar blinks in surprise. "I didn't think of that. Good idea."

"Men," she says, snapping her fingers. "They never think about calling for help."

Now Cesar looks annoyed. "Maybe I didn't think of it because the ship only has a short-wave comm and there's nothing down this close to Earth except that Moon Base we just destroyed. They probably won't let us tap their Ether connection."

Penelope pinches the bridge of her nose, trying to focus. "Well, then, we can use the short-wave to send out a distress call. At least we can try to let someone know what's going on."

Cesar shakes his head. "If any of Mach's men are still around, they'll hear it and come shut us up."

"We have to try," she insists.

Cesar finishes his noodles, wipes his mouth, and then says, "Yeah, I guess we do."

She follows him back to the comm screen. They record a message explaining about Mach and the Moon Base and the attack on Ithaca. The message ends with both of them begging.

Cesar clears his throat a few times before he states, "I am Cesar Vaquero, sometimes known Jonas Ulixes. My son is Trevor. Please go now and help my son. Save Ithaca. Stop Uri Mach."

"Please help us. Please, if you can hear this, go to Ithaca and save our colony. Help our son," adds Penelope desperately.

Afterwards, Cesar is very busy programming the comm and clearing his throat. Penelope decides it's better to leave him alone for a little bit. They send out their message on every channel and every wavelength, knowing it will probably go unheard.

Then they have nothing to do but stare at each other and hope for another miracle. Cesar sets the ship to spin just slightly to give them a little bit of gravity. Small thrusters on the hull of the ship spin like them bullet out of a rifle. This is another trick Cesar personally built into the little ship. It only got up to half Earth gravity and they both have on anti-grav boots, but he wants Penelope to be as comfortable as possible.

After that he prowls around the cabin restlessly. Leaning against a wall, Cesar eventually asks, "Well. What do you want to do now?"

Penelope decides she wants to pace some more. Her head is pounding and it feels like her stomach is trying to digest itself. How in space will she be able to wait fourteen hours? She will go mad.

Cesar spends some more time on the comm. Penelope assumes he is checking over the ship to make sure it is fine. Then he flops into a chair and watches her pace.

"Wearing a hole in the floor isn't going to help," he says gently.

Penelope scowls at him. Rage floods through her, impotent rage boiling through her bloodstream. "Like you'd know anything about what would help," she snaps.

Cesar's face takes on a strange expression. It reminds her of the time she watched Argos crawl into a steam tunnel to find out what was blocking it. She was watching from above the tunnel when he discovered the blockage was a huge nest of blood wasps. Cesar's face has the look of a man who has just realized he is in a confined space with something very dangerous. He scans the room like he is looking for an escape route. It really pisses her off.

"Where the hell have you been, you bastard?" she yells. "Do you know your son still asks every damn person he meets for stories of you? As soon as he was old enough to talk, he started asking where his daddy was. And where were you, you useless jerk?"

Penelope slowly advances towards him. She knows she is not looking her prettiest right now. Her face is red. Her eyes are bloodshot and leaking tears of powerless rage. She doesn't care. Cesar opens and shuts his mouth a few times, but makes no sound.

"He keeps a file of all the stories people tell him, you know. Do you know that? I listened to all those stories of you traipsing all over the place," Penelope says, her voice rising.

Cesar starts to look like a kicked puppy. It makes Penelope feel mean, but she can't stop the words pouring out of her. "That's what was so important? Saving other people's families? Having mad adventures with exotic women? But could you even call once in a while? No! You have never been there for us once. Not once!"

Cesar scowls and takes a step towards her. Penelope feels an odd sense of satisfaction at having finally succeeded in making him mad too.

"Are you kidding me?" he bellows. "I demolished an entire country for you. I dropped a bomb that made Hiroshima look like a cow fart and killed millions of people just to keep you and Trevor safe!"

Penelope jumps to her feet. "Oh yeah? Big whoop-de-doo, asshole!" she screams back. "Where have you been since then? You left me there! I put up with your insane family! I changed Trevor's diapers! You owe me at least five thousand diaper changes. And don't get me started on lost hours of sleep spent with a sick kid. And vomit! Who knew one little kid could be full of so much vomit?"

"Oh. Right," says Caesar, his righteous indignation momentarily derailed.

He flounders here, but then he thinks he might still have a chance at regaining the moral high ground. Drawing himself up, he screams back at her, "Then that… MAKES US EVEN! So stop bitching at me!"

Penelope blazes. She looks like she might tear his head off and eat it. Caesar experiences a moment of genuine fear before she does the utterly unexpected.

She laughs.

"I'm so angry at you I could bite your head off, you stupid jerk," she giggles helplessly, covering her mouth with her hand, but laughter escapes between her fingers.

Caesar finds himself suddenly and inexplicably exhausted. He still feels like screaming but all enthusiasm for this fight is gone. In the back of his head, Cesar is still holding out hope that there is some way this scenario plays out to end in passionate make-up sex. That's how it happens in the Ether dramas and every time he played this scene out in his head.

Cesar has no idea how you get from here to there, but he can't help being an optimist. So he does the only thing he can think of. He kisses his wife.

Penelope stiffens when he first pulls her close, but then she slowly melts into his embrace, letting him gently kiss her.

"You are not even remotely forgiven," she whispers against his lips, but she also doesn't stop kissing him.

"That's fair," he murmurs back.

The kissing takes a long time. Cesar is starting to have ideas about what they can do next instead of fighting when the alert on the comm starts pinging loudly. Against all odds, someone has replied to their distress call. Both heads swivel in the direction of the alarm. Penelope glances at Cesar to see if he wants to go listen to it, but he is already moving in that direction.

When Cesar taps the comm, the face of a tall, beautiful Asian woman fills the main comm screen. She looks practically luminous with joy. She is wearing a plain gray jumpsuit and holding the biggest gun Penelope has ever seen. Penelope doesn't understand how someone so thin can even carry that monster. There are streaks of white in the Asian woman's hair but her pale face is smooth and unlined except for the tears coursing down her cheeks.

"Oh Captain. My Captain. I am coming."

That is the whole message.

Penelope turns to Cesar. "Who was that?"

He runs a hand through his hair. "It's a long story." He doesn't continue, but Penelope sees the tension drop from his body. Whoever she is, Cesar is very relieved that she is coming. It gives Penelope hope.

"How did she find our message so fast?" she wonders. "How was she able to send back a message? You said we shouldn't be able to get anything out here."

Cesar holds his hands up to show he has no idea.

The comm pings again. Another message.

The jovial face of Mr. Finomus fills the screen while he twists his hands anxiously. "Penelope, I hope you get this soon. I am so sorry. I had no idea what Asner and Mach were up to. I am so very sorry. Ithaca is fighting back. They were holding their own when I left. I am on my way back there with troops right now. I was able to get out and let people know what was going on there, so the other colonies are sending help. Your distress call is all over the Ether. It's on every channel. It's everywhere. I've never seen anything like it."

Penelope breathes a tiny sigh of relief. She only wishes Finomus had said something about Trevor. At least Ithaca is getting help. Cesar hugs her. Over the next few hours, they get a steady stream of messages.

For the next message, the screen is filled with a face that looks as though it was carved from ebony. Hundreds of intricate braids fall down his chest over a colorful woven shirt.

"Rasta Nation hears the plea of Cesar Vaquero," the man says stonily, his arms crossed forbiddingly over his chest. His tone is flat, but spoken with a lilting accent. "It is not our policy to become involved with the violence of outsiders. But we owe Cesar Vaquero a blood debt for returning home the bodies of our brethren and sons, Mingo and Fishtrap. We send a ship of marijuana bombs to Ithaca now and pray it brings peace to your colony."

Cesar whispers to Penelope, "I actually have no idea who that guy is."

But he salutes the man on the screen anyway.

Penelope cleans herself up the best she can with what the ship has, grumbling about Cesar's hygiene habits. Then she rummages around for more noodles and coffee. Cesar sits at the comm, waiting for more news.

Eight people in uniforms deliver the next message in unison. Apparently, they are the eternal revolutionaries of Alpha Seti Six and they are suspending their everlasting leap forward long enough to send three platoons to Ithaca to "liberate Ithaca from their oppressors and praise the resurrection of the great leader, Cesar Vaquero."

Penelope arches an eyebrow at Cesar. He blushes and looks at the floor. In between the pings of incoming messages, they talk. Penelope asks him how true some of the stories Trevor collected are and Cesar does his best to explain. She asks how he managed to show up here or there and how he ended up in various situations. Cesar tries to remember.

In the next message, Monsieur Marceaux of Vegan Vineyards elegantly informs them that he is sending their militia over to Ithaca right now and that "the lovely Penelope must not fret so. She will get the worry lines and mar her perfect face." Monsieur Marceaux also expresses delicate regret that Penelope has actually located her errant husband and implores her to call him if she should ever need another.

"Another husband?" Cesar asks her, bemused. Penelope blushes and shrugs.

"He's such a flirt."

While the ship steadily gets them closer and closer to Ithaca, Cesar listens raptly to stories about the ranch and about Trevor growing up. Penelope laughs and says he can't possibly want to hear about every bruised knee and scraped elbow, but Cesar assures her he'll never get tired of it.

Old King Manny sent a rare personal message: "I can't say I'm happy to hear little Penelope got her man back and I won't apologize for maybe ordering a hit on you a couple years ago, Cesar, but we're sending our people to help out Ithaca," the ugly old man barks. "We need a military for this kind of thing, don't we? Can't have raiders upsetting Nullball like this. Well, I guess it's up to me to get a real Spacer police force going."

Then the old man grins impishly, "And who knows, maybe this time *I'll* win *your* war. That'd be nice. No hard feelings, Vaquero." He cackles as the message ends.

The Earth city of Barcelona is also sending a ship of supplies and engineers to help with rebuilding whatever damage was done by Mach's men in thanks for Penelope's help "in that most delicate matter a few years ago."

Penelope tells Cesar she'll explain it some other time because just then another incoming message pings.

This time, a plump woman with luxurious blue hair and an anxious expression appears on the screen.

"Mystery man, you made it home!" she cries with a grin. "But it sounds like you sure do need some help. The Spider House is always happy to lend a hand. I programmed the bees to follow directions from anyone from your genetic profile. Just make sure your family understands that killer bees have very tiny brains even with the swarm mentality thing. So make your commands very clear and very brief."

It takes a long time for Cesar to explain Calypso and the Spider House to Penelope. She doesn't buy it at all.

"Giant space goldfish, indeed," she hoots. "Do I look that gullible?"

"God knows what she'll have sent," mutters Cesar. He scratches his head meditatively and mutters "*killer bees*" a few times before the comm pings again.

In the next message, a scarred old man jubilantly tells Cesar that the Poppy Ship is alive and well and they are back to making a full line of medicines. He says they are sending a ship of medicine and paramedics to Ithaca, but that Cesar has to promise to be godfather to his new son. The scarred face splits into a grin of delight as the man on the screen tenderly holds up a tiny baby, so swaddled in blankets that they only see a tiny fist and a pair of bright blue eyes.

"We named him Cesar," the old man says proudly before the message ends.

"Look at that!" Cesar cries happily. "Old Perry has a kid! I never thought he'd live this long. Just goes to show you, I guess." He tells Penelope all about Perry and the Poppy Ship.

The next message is from some very large and angry Hathor miners who roar that they are on their way over to Ithaca right now with all the 'roid rockets they could strap to their ship to "sort out that bastard Mach."

"I hope all these helpers don't get overexcited and obliterate Ithaca," mutters Cesar.

"Me too," agrees Penelope, mentally picturing the miners rolling through Ithaca like raging buffalo, destroying everything in their path.

They silently stare out the window at the emptiness of the stars for a minute before Cesar gently says, "It's been about eight hours. Mach's ships should be at Ithaca now."

Penelope has no idea how the next agonizing hour passes. They both just wander around in a fugue. She cleans things listlessly, just to keep her hands busy.

Finally, she throws down her cleaning rag and slaps a frustrated palm against the wall next to her. "I just wish I knew what was going on there. I mean, you just know your dad is going to get himself killed, lobbing tequila bottles at Mach's band of thieves."

Cesar is about to tell her what Larry was up to when he left, but the comm pings and they both race for it. Cesar sees that it's from Mike's junker ship. Before he went chasing after Penelope, Cesar sent a message to Mike. He wanted to let the junker ship family know he and Trevor were fine but that there was trouble brewing on Ithaca.

Mike's face fills the screen. He looks worried and tired, but cautiously pleased. He immediately starts talking:

"Well, buddy, I'm sorry to report I didn't do like you asked. We didn't stay away from Ithaca. I don't know when you'll get this, but I just wanted to keep you posted. Me and the other junkers got to talking and we decided a bunch of us should hang around Ithaca just in case. We formed a blockade around the orbital the minute Finomus sent out the message about the raiders attacking. We're holding off three big ships with Seven Skies markings right now. They've got a lot of firepower and they seem pretty determined to get through, but we've got plenty of help from Hathor and New Siberia and a bunch of other people. You guys have friends, that's for sure."

Mike chuckles and then continues, "They are still trying, but I think we've got them contained. No word yet on what's going on inside Ithaca. Their signals are still jammed, but nobody is trying to get out yet. If or when they do, we'll have 'em. So don't you worry about anything but getting on home, man."

Cesar rubs his eyes. "Well, that's good news I guess. Trevor is probably safe, Penny."

She appreciates his attempts to help her calm down, but it isn't going to work. Penelope chews on her nails, a habit that, until just now, she successfully kicked as a teenager. She knows she won't be able to relax until she sees Trevor and Ithaca with her own two eyes.

CHAPTER THIRTY-ONE

Trevor and Nausicaa are pinned down by gunfire and the crush of the mob. The shooting started when they were almost to the elevators. They don't exactly know where the invaders came from, but they came heavily armed.

"Never a dull moment with you around," laughs Trevor as he crouches behind a piece of blasted shrapnel from what used to be the Ithaca Nullball arena.

Nausicaa peers cautiously around the edge of their cover. She doesn't look at him, but slaps his shoulder by way of a reply. Then she bolts out into the hail of gunfire. Trevor feels his jaw drop with disbelief. Is she trying to commit suicide?

Trevor crouches low and sprints through a hail of bullets after her. His nose and throat are clogged with stinging smoke and burning bioplastic. He can barely see through the haze of destruction. He really hopes Nausicaa knows what she is doing, charging out into all this. Because he has no idea where they are going, except into an apparently short and brutal death.

It isn't so much the bullets or explosions as the fact that they all keep ricocheting crazily on and on, bouncing around the core like burning, deadly pinballs. The smoke clears just enough for Trevor to see the stairwell door that Nausicaa is running towards. An explosion behind him singes his hair and tells him they left that cover not a second too soon.

Agony flares through his left calf with a bizarrely quiet splutchy kind of popping sound and a spray of blood. As he tumbles through the air, Trevor can see Nausicaa dive into the stairwell before turning back towards him.

The lack of gravity helps him. Trevor goes skidding across the room to her. Something explodes to his right and shrapnel sprays his neck, clawing into his skin. Trevor curls into a ball as he flies into Nausicaa. The door slams shut behind him as they both crash against the opposite wall.

"Oof," groans Nausicaa.

"Sorry," apologizes Trevor, rubbing the hole in his calf. Whatever did it burned its way through. There wasn't even that much bleeding. Their anti-grav boots click into place on the stairs and Trevor uses that to pull himself upright.

The running and lack of gravity has caused Nausicaa's shirt to float up and it is very obvious that she is not wearing a bra under her shirt. Trevor looks away, embarrassed catch himself staring at a time like this. He watches her pull her shirt down out of the corner of his eye.

"God, are you hurt?" asks Nausicaa when she sees the blood all over his pants and neck. Trevor shrugs. She runs her hands over her body, quickly checking to make sure she wasn't hit too before rushing over to repeat the process on him.

Trevor blushes and pushes her hands away. He doesn't want her to pat him down *everywhere*.

"Oh!" cries Nausicaa when she sees his calf. She bends down to get a better look. Trevor looks down to find Nausicaa's pink lips a few inches from his pants' zipper and almost passes out. He pulls away from her with a groan and leans against the wall.

"Be careful," she cries, jumping up and putting her arms around him. "You've lost a lot of blood. You could pass out. You'd better sit down."

Trevor thinks it's about to get weird and awkward in this stairwell, but then there are shots and voices on the other side of the door. Nausicaa and Trevor climb away from the core as quickly and quietly as they can. It is going to be a long hike, even with no gravity.

Trevor's leg has gone numb and his vision is going white and fuzzy around the edges. He takes deep breaths, but doesn't stop, feeling normal gravity return to weigh him down with every step. It makes his leg bleed faster and that gets kind of nasty after a while. Finally they make it to the habitation level.

Nausicaa insists on looking out first. Trevor can only nod and focus on not passing out. She peers out and then disappears for a very long minute.

Trevor listens to faint crashes coming from the direction of the core, but it doesn't sound like anyone is following.

Nausicaa reappears with a grin. "I think it's safe."

She helps him out onto a deserted platform. This is one of the less-used stairways in the city, at the end of Ithaca near the loading docks. Trevor sits down and eats the protein bar Nausicaa pushes into his hand. After Nausicaa insists he drink a thermos full of juice, Trevor feels better. Not great, but better.

Nausicaa sees him grimace, "What? Does it hurt bad?" she asks anxiously.

Trevor shakes his head. "No, it's just that we're a long walk to my house. I can't think of a better plan than trying to get home, though."

"There isn't a medibox close by? At home, we have public mediboxes all over the place."

Trevor winces. "Yeah, that's a good idea. There are some in town."

"Oh. Good. Only there will probably be raiders in town too," Nausicaa says, looking around like she is trying to think of an alternate plan but not coming up with anything.

Then she sees the blood oozing out of hole in his leg and gasps, "When did that happen? How come you didn't say anything?" She pulls out her little medical kit and reaches towards him, but then snatches her hand back and begins vigorously rubbing her hands down with antiseptic wipes.

"I don't want any chance of accidentally infecting you," she says, her voice trembling. "I wish I had some latex gloves."

Taking the medical kits from her shaking hands, Trevor follows her directions to cover and bind the wound as best he can. It feels much better when he is done. Trevor really wants to kiss Nausicaa as she wipes her tears and hiccups a few times, apologizing the whole time for almost infecting him. Instead, he struggles to his feet and starts limping towards home.

"Well, let's get going," he says as nonchalantly as possible. He manages to dredge up a smile just for her. Nausicaa beams at him and curls her fingers around his arm.

"Anywhere you want to go."

They almost make it.

The town is disturbingly quiet for most of their hobbling walk through it. It practically emptied for the tournament and that was before the elevators shut down. By now everyone will have heard the emergency message and be hiding in their homes, hitting the Ether to see who won the big game.

"Where are all the tourists?" whispers Nausicaa as she pokes her head around a corner nervously.

"Good question," Trevor whispers back, limping along as fast as he can. "Still down in the core probably. Can't imagine there are having too much fun down there, but I doubt the elevators are working or else they'd be up here."

At the edge of town, violence seems to erupt out of the dirt right in front of them. A large pack of men in Nullball uniforms toting huge guns suddenly appears at the end of the road they are walking along. They open fire immediately. Trevor and Nausicaa dive down an alley.

Fortunately, they aren't the gunmen's targets. Moon buggies with large guns mounted to them come barreling down the streets, full of livid screaming Ithacans. Argos is driving the lead buggy and screaming angry taunts at the men in Nullball uniforms.

"Run home, you pathetic excuse for pirates!" shouts Argos as he speeds past.

The men in Nullball uniforms take cover and spread out with military precision. Nausicaa pulls him back into the shadows, but Trevor catches a glimpse of his grandfather Larry leaping off a moon buggy, draped with bandoliers of grenades and waving a gun bigger than his leg.

"Stop firing and we may spare your worthless lives, you stupid thieves!"

The thieves in Nullball uniforms apparently don't appreciate this suggestion and they open fire again. Trevor and Nausicaa are safe for now, but it's loud and more than a little scary. Trevor hears jeering hoots as the buggies go bouncing past, firing back at the raiders for all they are worth.

"Run or die, you bastards!" old Larry screams as he shoves a grenade into the gun he is holding. Trevor hopes that gun is actually a grenade launcher and his old granddad isn't just over-excited and about to blow himself up.

As he aims the launcher, Larry screams, "You ain't getting my life or my cows today. Nothing. All you bastards get today are grenades." Then the old man falls back as the gun goes off.

The grenade smacks into the side of the building and kicks up a shower of rubble. Judging from the yelling down there, Larry has actually managed to hurt someone. Trevor laughs and cheers, coughing through the thick pungent smoke that the grenade leaves behind.

Larry turns at the sound. When he sees his grandson, a huge grin spreads over his face.

"Trevor!"

Trevor waves.

"Trevor, you're alive!" his granddad crows. Then the old man glances around and wipes the joy off his face, replacing it with fear and consternation.

"Trevor, what are you doing here? Get home now! And don't breathe in any of that smoke. You're too young. That was one of my special grenades. Got it from my Rasta friends."

Trevor wants to explain about his leg, but he can't yell loud enough over the gunfire. He sees Larry hop back onto the buggy and shout an order to the driver of his buggy. It begins making its way towards where Trevor and Nausicaa hide.

Unfortunately, the Nullball fighters have grenades too. One of them catches the rear wheel of Larry's buggy and the explosions sends the little vehicle slamming into the wall of the building next to Trevor's hiding spot.

Trevor sees his grandfather get up and shake himself dazedly. The buggy's driver bleeds heavily from a gash, but at least he is conscious and moving. Turning to look back at the enemies, Trevor sees a man taking aim at Larry. Before he has time to think about it, Trevor leaps out of the alley. He throws himself in front of the bullet aimed at his grandfather.

Trevor hears Nausicaa's scream from far away. He wishes he kissed her before. He hopes that this will save his granddad and not be just a stupid stunt that gets him killed. He also hopes dying doesn't take very long or hurt very much. Trevor watches the man pull the trigger, the bullet racing through space and time to end his life.

CHAPTER THIRTY-TWO

High above Ithaca, an army buzzes angrily. Mostly the buzzing comes from the killer bees. Or at least Cesar imagines they buzz although he can't actually hear them. The bees showed up just a while ago, much to his delight.

Calypso could have been talking crazy when she sent that message earlier. You never know when its just talk and when they actually do something at the Spider House. In Cesar's experience, splicers are a bunch of braggers. The bees add a certain amount of insane festivity to the tense standoff between Cesar's impromptu hodgepodge army of supporters and the menace of the three large and heavily armed Seven Skies vessels that Mach commands.

The bees are about the size of a closed fist and apparently totally fine flying through hard vacuum on little retractable solar sail wings. Cesar doesn't see how they can fly so fast, but they do. They swarm around the ships like an angry rain cloud before forming a funnel-shaped cloud that pours itself into Ithaca.

This is probably a good thing since the Seven Skies raiders inside Ithaca have control of the docking bay. Meanwhile, Cesar's friends effectively keep the Seven Skies ships from landing on Ithaca, but they can't seem to push them away once and for all.

"God, why doesn't he just give up and go?" screams Penelope with frustration after they watch the fighting for over an hour. "He won't be able to take off with the herd now. We won't let him land and, even if he did, we'd just send someone to follow him while we regroup."

Cesar has their little ship bobbing and weaving through the crowd of ships, striking small hits on the three giants. He makes a rude gesture at his comm screen as, once again, another ship blocks what would have been a solid hit.

"There are too many people out here," he replies. "We'd be better off if some of them went home so I could kill these guys and go take a shower."

Penny laughs bitterly. She is strapped into the copilot chair and taking shots at the enemy ships with a neutrino blaster whenever she can. She is surprisingly lethal for a woman who has never fired a weapon larger than a shotgun and hasn't set foot on a ship in fifteen years.

The comm crackles and then the speakers hiss out Mach's malevolent laugh, "Well, this is fun, boxing with the rabble like this. I'd love to stay and play, but I'm bored now and I think we've made a big enough mess for you. Sorry about your colony and all."

Penny falters for a minute as Mach chuckles satanically. Cesar can see the color drain out of her face when Mach says, "My men tell me they've killed the crap out of Trevor and Larry Vaquero. Oops! Guess Ithaca will have fewer mouths to feed. Too bad since we slaughtered all your cows for you."

The comm beeps off. Cesar watches Penny. She's like a shipwreck unfolding before his eyes, grisly and mesmerizing. Her lower lip quivers and her pale hands tighten on the trigger. Cesar knows what she is feeling. Waves of nauseating despair crash against his heart. The taunt about slaughtering the herd barely registers after what he said about Trevor and Larry.

"He's lying," Cesar croaks.

Penny nods vacantly.

"He has to be."

Penny nods again, but Cesar doesn't think she is listening. She's not really in there right now. That's fine. Cesar isn't in a talking mood anymore. He's in a *"killing Uri Mach"* mood. And he means to make the most of it.

Cesar banks the ship hard and it darts forward past the fray of small ships surrounding Mach's three larger.

"We may die now," he tells Penny.

"Thanks for letting me know."

Then the rage takes over, pounding its heartbeat rhythm through him. It makes his movements sharp and defined as his thoughts all bend to a single goal. The ship moves like an extension of his lethal rage, performing every screaming death wish shot with pinpoint precision.

•

When it's all over, the wreckage is everywhere and the screaming on the comm is deafening. Cesar is well and truly spent. He stares at the destroyed remnants of Mach's ship, listening to the other ship captains howling in triumph as they fall back, allowing the junker ships in to clean up the debris.

"You are a god!" screams the Hathor pilot. "Only a god could have brought down Mach's fleet with one tiny ship!"

"How did he do it? I was sitting here watching and I still don't understand how he did it!" came pouring in on every channel.

The team from Rasta Nation comment, "I would not have thought to use a grappling gun to spear our pallet of marijuana bombs and sling it into the enemy ship like that."

"He had some help!" huff the revolutionaries of Alpha Seti Six in perfect unison.

"Once again, Cesar the Scorcher stops the fight by being the most ruthless bastard in space!"

They praise his bravery and insanity. Their words fall on deaf ears. Cesar stares at the burning wreckage, all that remains of Mach's three huge ships, with unseeing eyes.

Ithaca is safe, but Mach's voice replays in his head. Trevor is dead? Larry is dead? The man must have lied. The alternative is unthinkable and yet Cesar can't turn his mind to anything else.

The words whirl around in his brain long after they lose all meaning for him. Cool hands slide over his, gently pulling him away out of the pilot's chair.

"Cesar, let's go," Penny whispers to him.

Her small cool hands pull his face around so that Cesar is forced to look her in the eye. There is so much he needs to tell her, so much they must talk about. He has to find the words that will make her love him, even though Cesar knows that with Trevor dead, all is lost.

Penny pulls him into a hug. He slumps against her, feeling her heart beat against his chest. Her breath moves in and out, warming them both.

"Cesar, we should go," she whispers again. "We should go down to Ithaca."

"No," he murmurs back.

He doesn't want to go down there. Not if he is going to have to see Trevor and Larry dead. Then Penny will slip away from him and that will be it. He'll have lost everything after all. Cesar just doesn't want to do it.

Penny gently wraps her hands around his face and pulls his chin up, forcing him to meet her eyes again. She smiles at him through tears.

"Come on, husband," she says gently. "Let's go home."

Cesar pulls away, shaking his head. He's going to run, hide, anything. He can't go down there.

Her palm stings his cheek sharply when she slaps him. Hard. Cesar whips his head back and sees her pulling back her arm to do it again.

"Pull it together, Cesar," she growls when he grabs her arm to stop her. "Get your rear in gear and get me home. I need to see my son," Penny orders in a voice full of steel and menace.

Cesar sighs.

She has a way of making her point. He drops back into the pilot seat and turns the ship towards Ithaca without a word. The comm crackles. He really needs to reset the thing so it stops playing every incoming message. All the ships in the air seem to want to chatter at them all day long.

"Mom? Dad? Are you guys alive up there?" Trevor's voice floats over the blackness of the void.

"Trevor!" cries Penny, flying to the comm in front of Cesar even though there is one sitting right in front of her.

Pushing Cesar out of the way, she calls joyfully back: "Trevor! Trevor! Tell me you aren't hurt!"

"Uh, well. I'm a little banged up, Mom, but it's fine."

Cesar doesn't mind being pushed in the slightest. He is busy dancing for joy listening to Trevor's repeated assurances that he is doing just fine. When Cesar hears Larry growling and cussing, he experiences a moment of nausea as his entire digestive tract unwinds, relieving tension he didn't know he'd been carrying. His stomach has been one big knot since the last time he saw his son and it's finally untwisting itself.

It takes a few minutes to set the course for Ithaca's dock, but once he does she joins him in dancing around the tiny cabin with joy. They kept repeating to each other that it's over. Larry says they have all Mach's men in Ithaca rounded up. Mach's ships are utterly destroyed. Trevor is safe. It's over. For Cesar, it hasn't sunk in yet.

He pulls Penny close, wanting the solid feeling of her body against his. That, at least, he can understand. She stiffens as he wraps his arms around her.

Pulling back, he looks at the frown on her face.

"What?" he asks.

"Exactly," she says, folding her arms across her chest. "Now what? What happens next?"

CHAPTER THIRTY-THREE

"The bullet would have killed me, but Argos stepped in front of it," sobs Trevor over the man's lifeless form.

Nausicaa holds his hand and sobs with him. Penelope is miserable over the death of a friend so close. Argos was unquestionably family. It's awful.

Penelope is also miserable over how distracted she is by questions, mainly about this strange girl clinging to her son. She is crying about Argos, but she can't stop glancing at Trevor and that girl. She wants to hug her son about eight or nine thousand more times to assure herself he is actually alive and well. This girl is in her way.

"I'm just fine," roars Larry from a cot across the room. Lupe stands over the man, pushing him back onto the cot every time he tries to get up.

Since Larry actually dislocated his shoulder firing grenades at Mach's men, getting pushed back onto the cot by Lupe hurts him quite a bit. He grimaces to cover the pain, still trying to insist he can get up now. Lupe says he can't and she's winning the argument. Larry is also trying to grab the tequila bottle Lupe pried from his hands. He is just as unsuccessful at that.

Lupe wipes away her own tears and shushes him. "Stop your silliness, old man. Lie down. Let them mourn poor Argos in peace."

Penelope hears him loudly whisper back, "I don't need to lie in the cot like an invalid. I just need a drink to clear my head."

Lupe hisses in reply, "You've had five drinks already and they haven't cleared your head. *Madre de dios*, you've had a lifetime of drinks and they haven't done your head any favors, Mr. Vaquero."

Penelope hears nothing more from Lupe and Larry for a long time. She notices that Trevor is favoring his right leg and she's itching to check out the left leg. Sprained ankle? No, too much blood.

Trevor is covered in blood and this Nausicaa girl sticks to his side as though they are married. Trevor doesn't look so bad that Penelope is really worried but enough to make a mother want to build a tower and stick her kid in it. If Trevor needs stitches, Penelope wants him in the medibox as soon as possible. And then he needs a haircut. And who is this girl?

Then she hears her father-in-law grumbling, "If you'd ever start calling me Larry, maybe I wouldn't need to spend so much time drowning my sorrows in alcohol."

Penelope glances back just long enough to see that Larry has taken Lupe's hand. Lupe is using the other hand to sob into a lacy embroidered handkerchief the size of one of Penelope's skirts.

Larry asks Lupe quietly, "Did you love him?"

Lupe makes a gulping noise. "Oh, Argos was a good friend. He will be missed."

"So he was just a friend? Nothing more?" presses Larry urgently.

"No, but a good man," sniffles Lupe.

"I'm glad," Larry says gruffly. "I would hate to see you hurt."

Lupe snaps, "Oh like you care about what hurts me."

"What?"

Penelope has to really fight to keep from turning back to stare at Lupe and Larry. Their conversation is much too interesting.

She hears Lupe spit out, "All these years I haul food out to you in your stupid shack and you never so much as give me a second glance. I know you are mourning the loss of your wife and that's as should be, *que Dios la tenga en la gloria*, but I am not made of stone."

Larry sputters, but Lupe is having none of it. "No! I'm done. I can't stand silently by as you drink yourself to death. I'm out. While I'll never love anybody but you, I'm sure I can find a hell of a lot of fun out there. Mr. Cesar will tell me where to look. Sounds like he found all the good spots."

Penelope smothers a giggle. Standing next to her, Cesar makes a strangled sound like he is doing the same thing. They share a look as they choke back laughter. Penelope doesn't dare look behind her. She hears the cot creak as Larry jump up and clutches Lupe.

"You silly woman," he cries passionately. "I started having feelings for you about a year after my wife died. I moved out of the main house because I knew it was wrong to feel this way about an employee and I did not want to impose upon you. Because I knew you could never feel the same way about me, a tired old wreck. You deserve a strong, healthy man and I won't push myself on you. I only want you to be happy."

The room is dead quiet. You could hear a penny drop on the Ag Level it is so quiet. Then there is the wet sound of an ardent kiss. Penelope is surprised at how disgusting the sound is when you aren't one of the people involved in the kissing. She decides it is high time the Vaquero family got back to the ranch.

Making quick arrangements for Argos' funeral, Penelope herds her family out the door, smacking Cesar hard on the back when he looks like he might crack up laughing at Lupe and Larry, arm-in-arm. He swallows his laughter and pastes a fake smile on his face.

Then she has to practically drag Trevor over to the closest medibox to get the bullet hole in his leg cleaned and the shrapnel dug out of his neck. When the machine starts laser-fusing the wounds, he complains at top volume until it gives him a big shot of the Poppy Ships' finest painkiller. Then he keeps chuckling like he thinks getting his leg lasered shut is the funniest thing ever.

Cesar hovers over the boy the entire time, alternating between looking green and bilious or pale and light-headed.

"I don't know how you survived this long," Cesar confides to Penelope. "That kid gives me a heart attack every three hours. And I think my hair would go white all over again, trying to keep him from throwing himself out the airlocks all day long, or so it feels like. How do you do it?"

Penelope laughs, "Oh, I have my fair share of white hair from Trevor's antics. And worry lines and the rest. Just think if we'd had more, though."

"How do people do it?" Cesar shakes his head, overwhelmed by the mere thought.

"I have no idea," Penelope admits.

As they walk back, suddenly Penelope can't seem to find anything to talk about.

"So what did you do with those bees?" she finally asks Cesar as she slows to give the others plenty of time to get ahead. She doesn't want to overhear Larry and Lupe talk love to each other because that's just gross.

She also doesn't want to overhear Trevor and Nausicaa right now either, because she might have to jump in and be a mom and she just isn't feeling up to it.

"I ordered them to go down and hang out in the Ag Level for now," replies Cesar. "They seem happy with that. No doubt there is militant and highly effective pollination going on down there right now."

Penelope laughs. "Space bees," she giggles. "My life is totally ludicrous."

Cesar's asks, "Did you know my Dad had such an arsenal hidden out there?"

"No!" she cries, remembering to be shocked about that. "God, if I had known… No. I had no idea he was making that much money from that tequila still of his and I definitely didn't know he was stockpiling Spacer War Two back there in that empty lot."

Penelope says this loudly enough for Larry to hear her. He chuckles loudly and calls back, "Just because you don't believe in violence doesn't mean the rest of us have to play like Gandhi, darling. Talk is all well and good, but people tend to listen a lot better when they know you've got some fuck-off huge guns."

Lupe swats him playfully and then starts lecturing Larry about his language in front of "the children," but she does it gently. She goes on to nag him about walking around with a dislocated shoulder. There is mention of her special soup.

"So now what?" asks Cesar. He wants to know what happens next with them, but if Penelope understands that, then she isn't ready to answer yet.

"Well, I guess we'll have to do something with all the people who showed up to help us out," she replies, dodging the question.

Cesar nods and they continue walking.

"And I guess, we'll need to get together with some of the others and go back to the Moon to make sure the Seven Skies base is totally defunct," Penelope says. Cesar agrees that they should, but thinks it can wait a few days.

When they do finally send ships out, the men find nothing but rubble, dust and desiccated corpses. At first, they credit Cesar with even more bloodthirsty thoroughness than he admits to, but when he sees scans of the area, he can only scratch his head and say there is no way his little ship did all that damage.

It looks like someone scorched the Moon Base down to the bedrock.

The only explanation they ever get is a short message playing repeatedly on the Moon Base's outgoing message beacon. The antenna is the only thing left functional.

The message shows a single person, a tall Asian woman staring into the camera. Trevor replays the message about a million times and can never glean any information about the kind of ship she has or where she came from or where she went.

She only says, "Goodbye, my Captain. I hope you found what you were looking for."

And she smiles. It's a pure and sweet expression and it makes her look like a young girl with her whole life ahead of her. No one ever sees her again.

Larry is the only person not appreciative. His favorite topic of conversation for far too many weeks is how women should mind their own business and give a man a chance to use all the weapons he's got stockpiled for just such an occasion.

"What about us?" Cesar finally blurts out on the longest walk of his life. "You and me? Where are we going? Not right now, but relationship-wise. Like as a couple? As a family."

Penelope starts messing with her hair. "So, I understand why you left. You felt you had to go to protect Ithaca and your family. I get that. But why didn't you come back?" she asks in a very small voice. "I need to understand that first."

Even though Cesar has been expecting this question for the past decade, it still knocks him flat.

"Well, you told me not to come back," he mutters, his voice cracking a bit. "You hated the War. You loathe violence. You didn't want me back even before I obliterated Mexico. I figured after that, you were definitely never going to forgive me. Truth be told, I didn't think I deserved to be forgiven." Cesar rubs his eyes.

Penelope arches an eyebrow. "Really? You didn't just decide it was too much work to be married and raise a kid? You didn't just blow us off to prance around the spheres having drunken adventures with scantily clad women?"

"No," laughs Cesar. He knows he should be a little offended that she would think this of him, but he isn't up to it right now. "No, I'm just dumb, I guess. Kept thinking if I made a big pile of money or did something heroic that didn't kill anyone, you'd forgive me. Never managed to keep a big pile of money if I made it, though."

Penelope giggles, "That was pretty dumb. Next time, just come home."

"I don't plan to leave ever again, so it won't come up," he promises, kissing her fiercely. She is flushed and dazed when he's done. Cesar feels he ought to take advantage of that.

"So can I stay? Here with you? Can we try again?"

Penelope studies the ranch house in the distance and replies slowly, "Well, you could do that. It's one option. But you've also got that shiny ship. You could leave and go anywhere. And I've got the ranch. It's going to need so much work after the last couple of weeks."

"I don't want to go," Cesar says stubbornly.

"But I do," Penelope finally admits. "I don't want to stay."

Cesar must have stuck out his lower lip because suddenly Penelope says, "Oh, wow, that's the same expression Trevor gets every time he throws a temper tantrum. So that's where he got it."

Cesar asks, "What do you mean you don't want to stay? You can't stand being around me so much that if I'm here, you are leaving?"

She shakes her head and sighs one of those deep, important sad sighs. "I've been here for fifteen years. I'm tired of it. I want to see the spheres. I know you came back because you are tired of adventure and want to settle down, but I've been settled all this time. Now I want to act up a bit, see the sights, you know?"

She gestures up and around, probably meaning the colonies around them. "Maybe even go back down to Earth and have a close up look at that big crater my husband made."

That makes him crack a smile.

Holding his hands in hers, she says in a rush, "I do want to be with you. I want to try being your wife again. We'll probably be horrible at it and fight all the time and eventually give up, but I'd like to try. Except I really want to go and you really want to stay. Maybe if I promise to come back as soon as the wanderlust empties out of me?"

Cesar laughs, but Penelope just arches an eyebrow like she can't tell if it was a happy laugh or a bitter laugh.

"Lady," he says, gently wrapping his large beefy hands around her small white ones. "You seem to be under the impression that there is some way you can get rid of me. It just isn't so. Home is wherever I'm with you. If you want to go, then I'm going to follow you."

Penelope lets out her breath.

"Oh good," she half gasps. "I was hoping you would say that."

Caesar pulls Penelope into his arms and she melts against him. He crushes his lips against hers.

"Don't leave me again," she whispers, smiling as a few tears course down her cheeks.

Cesar fleetingly thinks that it must be more exhausting to be a girl than a guy, but he never allows insightful thoughts to interfere with the moment, so he passionately kisses his wife.

"You are divine," he whispers raggedly when they break apart.

A delicious smile curls across Penelope's lips. She whispers back, "You are mine."

They might have stood together like that for hours, but Trevor comes limping up to interrupt them. When he sees his parents blatantly making out in full view of the whole world, Trevor stumbles to an abrupt stop and starts studying his feet, but he doesn't leave.

"Hey, uh, guys? Mom and Dad?" he coughs loudly. "Sorry to interrupt, but it looks like maybe Nausicaa didn't so much ask her parents about coming back to Ithaca with me."

Cesar and Penelope break apart and stare at him.

"What?"

"Yeah," Trevor says, looking apologetic and scratching his shoulder. "I guess she more like just left without telling them, you know?"

"Oh," says Cesar.

"Oh dear," says Penelope.

"Yeah," admits Trevor, shuffling from one foot to the other. "And I guess her parents are totally freaking out now on account of the raiders here and all the fighting. Lazar House just had that Sectarian riot, you know? So they want her home now. I was thinking maybe the easiest thing would be if I could go and drop her off in Dad's ship?"

"Oh, I don't think so," snaps Cesar in his best dad voice.

"No wait," Penelope says, putting a hand on his arm. She looks into his eyes for a minute and then winks. "Maybe we can all go and drop Nausicaa off?"

Cesar smiles so wide he thinks his face might crack. "I hear Lazar House has great curry."

"I've always wanted to try curry," Penelope replies, grinning back at him.

"Cool," Trevor cries, limping off to tell Ness.

"We'll ride off into the sunset," Cesar tells his wife, twining his hands in hers. "I'll show you the worlds. Together, we can do anything."

"We can spin the sky."

THE END

ACKNOWLEDGEMENTS

I would like to thank the following:

> My husband and chief technical adviser for agreeing with me when I thought the book needed more explosions

> Elle Van Hensbergen for a really fantastic critique

> Ross Lockhart at Night Shade Books for being so darn good at his job

> Laura's wooden leg

ABOUT THE AUTHOR

Katy Stauber has degrees in Biochemistry and Mathematics from Texas A&M University. She currently lives with her husband and two sons in Austin, TX. Her first novel, *Revolution World*, was published in 2011 by Night Shade Books. *Spin the Sky* is her second novel.